THE PRIESTS' CODE

B.B.Bathis

THE PRIESTS' CODE

B. B. BALTHIS

Matador
9 Priory Business Park,
Wistow Road, Kibworth Beauchamp,
Leicestershire. LE8 0RX
Tel: 0116 279 2299
Email: books@troubador.co.uk
Web: www.troubador.co.uk/matador
Twitter: @matadorbooks

ISBN 978 1788039 239

British Library Cataloguing in Publication Data.
A catalogue record for this book is available from the British Library.

Printed and bound in Great Britain by 4edge Limited
Typeset in 11pt Aldine by Troubador Publishing Ltd, Leicester, UK

Matador is an imprint of Troubador Publishing Ltd

To bring the dead to life
Is no great magic.
Few are wholly dead:
Blow on a dead man's embers
And a live flame will start.

(Robert Graves)

PROLOGUE

Vengeance is mine; I will repay.
(Romans 12:19)

2013

Matti Jonsson stood at the window, looking out into the black night. It was snowing again and even that looked black as it came down, in large, soft clumps. He could only just make out the lights from his nearest neighbours, a few hundred metres away.

His main base was a London flat but, like many Icelanders, he had a small log cabin perched on a mountainside, a few hours' drive from Reykjavik. If something was bothering him, as it was now, then this was where he came.

His work as a renowned archaeologist meant that he travelled widely, but the past few months had been spent in England, working for the British Museum. It had been a particularly long and complex assignment, and one that had left him with considerable unease.

He walked over to the wood burner, threw in a few logs, and firmly closed its door. He then sat at his desk, picked up a file, and began to flick through a report he had written last week. He had been asked to visit an old church, and at a first glance it had seemed like so many others in the UK and was not likely to *cause too much excitement. Further examination had, however, revealed things that were much less common… in fact, in his considerable career, things he had only ever seen once before.*

He had sent a basic report to the museum, but since then had spoken to a colleague, done more research, and concluded that the church was indeed far more than it had first appeared. He had been left with a feeling of poking a stick into a hornets' nest, and wished he had never set eyes on the place. A final conversation with a trusted, though now retired, professor, confirmed this, and he had been strongly advised to back off, which he fully intended to do.

At that moment, he heard a tapping sound. He went over to the window and peered through it, his face pressed hard against the cold glass, straining to see what might have made the noise. People who had cabins up here looked after each other, and emergencies were not unheard of in the hostile climate. He walked across the room, into the lobby, and opened the front door of the house, pulling on a thick jacket as he went outside. The cold hit him hard, and the great lumps of snow falling from the sky seemed even larger now he was outside. He took the torch from his pocket and shone it in front of him as he peered through the blackness.

'Hello? Hello? Who's there? I can't see you… is there trouble? Please shout and I will come and find you.' He continued to walk around the small, single-storey building and, for a moment, thought he saw a flash of orange at the rear corner of the house. He walked steadily on, his feet sinking into the thickening snow.

Then a voice came from behind him.

'So, Jonsson, we meet again. Charming place you have here. Quite hard to find, but perhaps for you, not hard enough?'

Quickly turning around, Matti didn't recognise him at first. 'Who are you? What do you want?' He reached up and snatched the large fur hat from the man's head. With this gone, he shone the torch right into his face and stared. As he remembered, he stepped back, dropping the hat onto the snow. Gripped with fear, his voice shook as he spoke…

'You? What the hell are you doing here? What do you want with me?'

'I want nothing, Jonsson. But I have something for you… this.'

If he had been able to talk about what happened on that black, freezing night, Matti would have said that he had known what was coming the moment he realised who the man was. When the gun was raised and the shot fired directly into his chest, he had felt strangely peaceful. A sharp bolt of pain… a few flakes of snow on his face… then nothing.

CHAPTER ONE

*There is always a pleasure in unravelling a mystery,
in catching at the gossamer clue
which will lead to certainty.*

(Elizabeth Gaskell)

2015

My name is Father Benoît Balthis, although in England I am mostly known as Father Ben. As a fifty-five-year-old Catholic priest I have lived and worked in many places, but I was born in France and still consider it to be my true home.

My mother was French and my father Lithuanian, and they met in France during the Second World War. My mother was part of the French Resistance in the Languedoc region which was her home, and my father was a refugee, fleeing the Russian armies as they swept through the Baltic states in 1944. He had found himself in this part of France quite by chance, if there is such a thing, but you'll hear more of their story as I continue to write.

I grew up in our ancestral home, which is a part of the ancient Château of Antugnac, a small village in the

Aude region of the Languedoc, and almost hidden in the mountain ranges that were as much my home as the house was.

I was born on the 11th of April 1960, in our home at the request of my mother. My French grandparents lived with us, or I should say, we lived with them, since the house was theirs. My mother had been born quite late in their marriage, and they were elderly when I arrived, my grandfather being seventy-three and my grandmother sixty-five. They welcomed my arrival with as much joy and love as I could take, and this I returned to them willingly.

My mother was a small-time dealer in antique furniture, and my father a skilled watch and clock restorer. They were, however, frequently away for weeks, sometimes even months at a time, for which no explanation was ever given. My grandparents looked after me during their absences, and I eventually learned to neither question their disappearance nor talk to anyone else about them. To avoid any tears when I was very young, they took to leaving in the middle of the night, and in the morning I would run around the house looking for them, searching each room, screaming and crying, much to my grandparents' distress.

As I grew older, I became more accustomed to their absence and eventually accepted that this was how our lives were to be. I had my rambling home, my adoring grandparents, and the hills, mountains, and ancient villages to roam from dawn till dusk. I lacked nothing.

Many an evening after supper had been spent by

the huge fireplace, flames leaping over the logs and the resinous scent of wood smoke permeating everything. I would listen, enraptured, to my grandparents, particularly my grandfather, who told stories about the area that he had lived in his whole life, as had his parents before him. My grandmother came from nearby Rennes-le-Château, and I still had a relative living there, just a few kilometres away. A large part of my childhood had been spent in that village, and it was as familiar to me as Antugnac. My closest friend and relative was, and still is, my cousin, Caro, the daughter of my mother's twin. In childhood we were inseparable, and in our advancing years we were still very close.

* * *

Today saw me returning to my old family home. I was taking some time off because of a difficult situation in which I had found myself in England. You'll soon hear of the circumstances that led me to return here in some haste, but for now I was immensely glad to be back in France. An old friend, Arnaud, had come to Carcassonne to pick me up, driving the car that he had recently sold me through his car dealer brother-in-law. I felt too tired to drive it myself and was very happy to allow him to act as chauffeur.

I had thought it best to arrange to have a car straight away, since the village was remote, and I would need to get around immediately. I recognised him at once in the waiting crowd, with his wiry, grey hair, tanned face, and muscular, stocky build. He was a couple of years older than me, but we had grown up in the same village and were immediately at ease with each other. We soon fell into speaking the local dialect, exchanging news, teasing each other, and catching up on the local gossip as though no time had passed at all. I thanked him for his help, and his response to this was a painful punch on the arm.

I sat back in my seat, and before long, we were driving through the familiar lanes of home. Five minutes later, we pulled up outside my house which was placed directly behind the church. Part of the old château, it was thought to be at least eight hundred years old, and the cellars below were almost certainly older than that. A long, simple, three-storey structure; its front dropping down to the river below and the rear showing its last major repair from the wars of religion in the late sixteenth century.

It was typical in style as a house built for the local nobility, although had been split into three dwellings more than a hundred years ago. Now devoid of any turrets or lookout posts, it might easily go unrecognised for what it once was, unless one stands back some fifty metres or so and views it as part of the original defensive circulade, still in existence. Many of these remain in the locality, often Cathar or Templar in origin, some still boasting blocked-up tunnels and arrow slits in their massive stone walls.

At the centre of the – now – three houses, it looked the same as it always had: paint peeling on the shutters, grey rough render, huge blocks of stone around the windows and doors, and an ancient blocked-up archway buried half way into the ground.

Arnaud had the key and his wife had been in to air and dust, and to open the shutters for my return. I was grateful, and told him so.

'No problem at all,' he said quietly. 'Welcome to your home, Benoît.'

I felt emotional to be back, and my eyes glazed over as I placed one hand on the car door.

Seeing this, Arnaud brought me around with another hard punch on the arm, of which, this time, I was glad, since there was nothing like pain to momentarily stop a flow of tears. He helped me with my bags, opened the door, and left, raising his hand as he walked up the steep hill to his own home further up the village, towards the mountains.

I turned from watching him and faced the large, solid front door of the house, slightly ajar and waiting for me to enter. It seemed longer than six months since I had last been here, but as I pushed it open further and looked down into the salon, I was flooded with relief to be back home. The huge room was filled with sunlight and dust motes, lit up by the golden beams that poured in through the open terrace doors and windows. Then the familiar smell hit me: a heady blend of wood smoke, beeswax, lavender, and age from the ancient stones.

The stress of the past week had been immense, and I sat on the first of the worn, stone steps, and leant my head against the cool wall. Closing my eyes for a moment I must have dozed off, because when I opened them again the sun had dropped low in the sky, its beams now less bright on the glowing terracotta floor.

Feeling much calmer, I walked down the steps and gazed around me. The look of the room had changed quite a bit since my parents' and grandparents' time. My grandfather had died in 1980 at ninety-three, and my grandmother just six months later at eighty-five. My parents continued to live here until 2001, when they were both killed in a car accident in Rome. True to form, they hadn't even told me they were going to Italy, and to this day I still had no idea as to why they were there.

* * *

Each time I had come here in the ten years or so after their death, I had cleared out more of the clutter, and kept only my most favourite of the things that had belonged to them. One of these was the large, round, fruitwood table and chairs, polished to a deep treacle tone by my grandmother. I had also kept the huge dresser that stood against the wall, made by my great-great-grandfather, which showed the patina of use by many generations. This held plates and other crockery, and the large drawers the ancient silver cutlery, dented and bent but still beautiful. The shelves were filled with the old glasses and jugs that my family had used for more than a century.

The large, tan leather sofa wasn't theirs; I had bought it in Italy when I had been living there. I rarely bought new things, and certainly not as expensive, but as a priest I spent very little, and my inheritance had been considerable.

Two armchairs sat either side of the fireplace, both worn and old, one leather and the other red velvet, which had been bought cheaply in local second-hand stores. A long Persian rug brought back by my parents after one of their trips still glowed with its faded reds and burnt umber colours, as did the cushions and throws brought back by them from various other places, mostly unknown to me, because they would never say where they were going or where they had been.

The kitchen area was in the far corner and this had changed little in the past century. It comprised a stone sink and drainer with brass taps fixed to the wall, curtains underneath in faded red checked linen, and several scrubbed wooden cupboards providing storage and work surfaces. A large, cream fridge, bought in Italy at the same time as the sofa, stood in the corner, along with an ancient, bottled gas cooker.

There were a few of my favourite paintings on the walls, mostly local scenes, and I supposed that to an outsider, the massive room with its high ceilings and huge beams might look somewhat empty, certainly more so than in my parents' time. However, this was how I liked it. I kicked off my shoes, pulled off my socks, and threw both into the small utility area under the stairs. The glossy terracotta floor was warm under my feet, which was a wonderful sensation after the cold and draughts of my cottage in England.

A long loaf of the local bread lay on the top of one of the kitchen cupboards, and beside it, a bowl of apricots and cherries. I opened the fridge to find it well stocked with basic foods: cheese, ham, butter, eggs, preserves, and water. Mathilde, Arnaud's wife, always did this if she knew I was coming, and my stomach grumbled. I hadn't eaten since the sandwich at the airport, and the large wall clock told me that it was now nearly seven.

On the table was a small vase of flowers, probably picked from my terrace, and the scent of bougainvillea wafted in through the open doors. Underneath the vase was the bill from Mathilde. I noticed that she hadn't charged for the eggs which were probably from her own chickens, and I reminded myself to add a few extra euros when I put the money through her door tomorrow.

I washed my hands and had soon prepared a meal of bread, butter, cheese, and honey. The simple food tasted wonderful, especially when accompanied by a glass of my favourite Valpolicella ripasso. I pushed the empty plate onto the low table in front of me and lay back on the sofa, a second glass of wine now in my hand. Picking up the phone, I dialled Caro's number. She answered straight away and I told her that I was home but too exhausted to talk. I would call her again in the morning when I could string a sentence together.

As I lay there, the silence of the house began to take over and soon I could hear nothing, save for the slow, deep ticking of the clock, the leaves rustling in the breeze outside, and the river far below, winding its way down to the sea. Finally, I allowed myself to think back over the events of the past few weeks that had culminated in my being here now.

CHAPTER TWO

As a priest, I had worked in many places around the world, including Israel, Lithuania, and Italy, as well as various parts of France and the UK. I can speak several languages, including Latin. My parents insisted on it, and what had seemed unnecessary as a child had proved to be a huge advantage in my chosen work. On leaving school, I had studied languages at the Sorbonne before moving on to theology and the priesthood. My most recent post had brought me to Gloucestershire in England, where I was a temporary priest at several small, rural parishes.

I had been doing this for almost two years now, and didn't mind it at all. For one thing, it gave me time to do my translation work of ancient texts and manuscripts, both religious and otherwise, including poetry, which I really enjoyed. I also enjoyed visiting and researching the local churches wherever I was. There were some very old and beautiful ones in these parts, many with Templar links, which I found particularly interesting. I enjoyed the frequent changes in my work life and liked to move around, see new things, and meet new people. My home would always be in Antugnac and so I had no need to establish myself elsewhere, or to root myself in any other place. This fact had given me a certain freedom, which was a definite bonus as far as I was concerned.

* * *

A few weeks ago, at a local church jumble sale, I had come across a pile of old newspapers, music scores, postcards, and letters in a torn brown box. These job lots were often little more than boxes of old rubbish, but on the odd occasion I did find a few things of interest and I enjoyed the anticipation of a possible good find. On that day, I put my hand in my pocket and handed over the five-pound note that was being asked, tucked the box under my arm, and put it in the boot of the car. I had given it little thought until finally, today, I carried it into the small, church-owned cottage that had become my temporary home.

The weather had turned cold, and a sharp wind whistled around the small courtyard garden that belonged to the cottage. Gusts pushed the slanting rain hard against the windows, and one might easily be mistaken for thinking that it was January, not late May. It was almost dark when I put a match to the already-laid wood burner, and the flames were soon roaring away and quickly began to heat the room.

The smell of wood smoke always brought France to mind, and in particular, my grandmother. An image of her sweet face came into my head at the exact same time as the strong and unmistakable aroma of roasting chestnuts. This had happened many times before, but curiously, mostly when I was either very tired, unwell, worried, or in some sort of danger. On the two occasions when my life had been seriously threatened, I had smelt the aroma of roasting chestnuts a few minutes before.

The first time was when a car hit me as I was crossing the road in central London. It had seemed to come out of nowhere and didn't stop. I was lucky to not be killed, and escaped with cracked ribs and a broken leg. The second was in Paris. It was the rush hour and a sharp shove in the back nearly pushed me into the path of an incoming metro train. The platform was so crowded that it was impossible to know where the push had come from, but I was pulled back from a certain death by a strong Parisian man, to whom I was extremely grateful.

I was sure a psychiatrist would find some logical explanation for the chestnut smell; some childhood trigger or similar, but I preferred my own theory on the matter, which was that she felt the need to show her presence as either a support or a warning.

'Still roasting chestnuts, Grandmother?' I asked aloud, in French. There was no answer, of course, and I carried my coffee to the table and started to go through the box.

I pulled out the entire lot, and began to put it in piles: one for rubbish, one for reading later, and one for anything that might be of special interest to me. After an hour, the table and my clothes were covered in dust and my hands were filthy. About a third of the papers were still left. The rubbish pile was the largest and I put these in the log basket to use to light the next fire. The pile of immediate interest to me so far only contained some parish records, letters and cards from unknown persons, and several yellowed newspaper cuttings about the village church. I was nearing the bottom when I came across a small, tatty, leather-bound notebook. I decided to wash my hands before I looked at it, and clean up the dirt and dust on the table. This done, the phone rang and I found myself talking to the relative of a sick parishioner who might not make it through the night. I quickly pulled on my coat and drove off to attend to my priestly duties.

* * *

It was nearly midnight when I got back; cold, wet, and tired. I heated a glass of milk and sprinkled it with freshly grated nutmeg. As I passed the table, I picked up the notebook and climbed the stairs to bed. Propped up on my pillows I opened the book, its musty though not unpleasant odour quickly permeating the air. At first glance, it appeared to be a journal or diary of some age, and each entry had a date at the top left-hand corner of the yellowed page. The words were faint and written in a steeply slanting copperplate script, made more difficult with elaborate swirls here and there, and I sat up further to make it easier to study.

I opened the bedside table drawer to pull out a small magnifying glass, put there just for times like these. I could now read the first entry date quite clearly, and my eyes travelled to the next line.

January 10th 1789

> *C sent word of his arrival home from France. I*
> *am to meet with him tomorrow at C. Much relief*
> *at his return. Danger abounds and there is not*
> *one of us safe, not even in our own beds. I can*
> *only hope that we continue to be spared, and that*
> *the secret can be held in perpetuity.*

I paused here to yawn and look at the clock. It was 1.30am and, although intrigued, I had a lot to do tomorrow. Like most people, I enjoyed a mystery, and it was one of the things that made my translation work so important to me. It was never a simple thing since words rarely translated literally, and the meanings could be so easily misconstrued or even missed altogether. I took the pad of paper that always lay ready by my bedside and began to write:

Who is C?
Where is C?
What secret?

My eyes returned to the book. I couldn't read the next sentence in full because some of the words were faded and smudged. There was also a dark stain of some sort splashed across the page. I could make out some of it though, and I wrote this down on the notepad.

I cannot sleep ... ... fears ... ... devastation that
... come ... ... enemies ... ... our knowledge ...
... free with it.

With some reluctance, I closed the old book and put it on the side table. After tomorrow, I had a few days off, and would be able to study it in much more detail, and when I was less tired. I quickly fell asleep, leaving the wind, rain, and mysterious words of the journal to themselves for the rest of the night.

CHAPTER THREE

It was bright and sunny when I woke the following morning. The rain from last night sparkled in the tiny courtyard at the back of the cottage. Everything looked fresh and clean, and the wallflowers that a previous occupant had planted smelt glorious as the heat of the sun began to evaporate the moisture from their petals. Back in the kitchen, I made my breakfast of poached eggs on toast followed by strong, black coffee. I refused to believe that the butter would eventually induce a heart attack, and anyway, as a priest, I knew that the possibilities of an early death were endless and varied, so I would enjoy it whilst I could.

I looked at the list of visits to make this morning. Afterwards, I had a meeting with the bishop to discuss the diocese, my part in it, and various other church matters, and I was looking forward to this. He was a keen historian and we always found plenty to talk about when work was finished; I had also been invited to stay for dinner. Driving down the street, I waved to several people I knew, but pulled over when I saw the local Anglican vicar, Peter Lacy, come out from the lane that lead to the vicarage and church.

'Fine morning, Ben,' he greeted me, and put his hand in through the car window to shake mine.

'Isn't it just?' I replied. 'I was going to give you a call over the next day or two. I'm really interested in a guided tour of the church, including any local historical knowledge you have. It's a fascinating building, and the relics are so unusual! I've been in quite a few times but would appreciate being accompanied by someone who knows it well. Could you spare the time?'

'There's nothing I'd like more. It is a fascinating building, that's true. I'm no expert, but I'll certainly tell you what I know. When suits?'

We arranged to meet at two the following afternoon, in the churchyard. The weather was supposed to stay fine for the rest of the week, and I looked forward to the tour. Peter was a tall, fair-haired man with piercing blue eyes that seemed to look right through you. They would certainly be intimidating if you got on the wrong side of him, but his handshake was firm and he smelt faintly of fresh juniper and pine.

I found smell to be the most evocative of senses, and was instantly taken back to my time in Italy, particularly Naples, where many of the locals wore a similar cologne, called 'Pino Silvestre.' It was sold in most of the tobacconists and pharmacies, and its forest fragrance, mixed with that of strong tobacco was, for me, one of the essential essences of the area, and reminded me of the wonderful people I had met there. Peter cut a striking figure with his black cassock flying out behind him in the breeze, and I watched for a moment as he strode off down the street.

* * *

16

Over the next four hours I visited the post office, a parish sacristan, and a local nursing home to give communion to two residents. I then made a quick call on a local couple that I had become very fond of. They had just had a baby and I handed over bunches of freesias that I had bought in the local shop. Ian and Gen greeted me warmly and proudly showed me their beautiful baby.

'Do stay for a coffee. We've got cake too and the baby is due a nap.'

'I'd love to, but I've got another visit to make, and then I'm driving up to Oxford. What about next week? I'll give you a ring when I'm about.'

They agreed, and I was soon on my way to a rather beautiful cottage on the outskirts of the town, to visit a man called Adrian Harcourt. The last time I had seen him he had spoken about a particularly nasty divorce, and from what I could make out, his involvement with the Church had increased after a very close brush with death a few years back. He was in his mid-fifties; was witty, sharp, and highly intelligent, and I found him to be good company.

He had sold his national property renovation company for a considerable sum after an accident had left him with a broken back. He had fallen from collapsing scaffolding, and three years on, seemed to have made a good recovery, just occasionally using a walking stick. He came from the area, had an aunt in a nearby village, and provided me with a wealth of local knowledge, as well as an excellent glass of wine from time to time. Overall, he was an interesting character, was well read, belonged to various charitable organisations, and frequently made trips to London to attend to other business affairs which I knew nothing about. One last attribute was that he painted beautiful religious icons, which were much in demand.

As an architect and surveyor, he helped in the diocese as an unofficial advisor in these matters, which was why I had called in that morning. His expertise was invaluable and saved us a considerable amount of money. When I arrived, I found him in his painting studio in the garden, and we sat for a few minutes on a bench in the sun as I handed over papers and letters that needed attention.

'How are things, Padre?' he asked.

'Pretty good,' I answered. 'I'm off to Oxford now to meet the bishop, and then I've got a few days off.'

'Are you going away?'

'No, but I've got a few things planned. I'm having a guided tour of the local church tomorrow, and I'm behind with some translation work. Oh, and I found an old journal in a box of rubbish that I bought at the last jumble sale. I'm hoping it might be from the locality, but the few bits I've read mention France too. Anyway, I'll try to have a good look at it.'

On hearing this, he became much more alert, and shifted his position to face straight at me.

'I wouldn't mind a look at that some time.'

I found myself feeling a little uneasy, and although not entirely sure why, I wished that I hadn't mentioned the journal. I liked Adrian, and from what I knew, he was a decent enough man, but I made no response to his request, pretending that I hadn't heard it. I got up, thanked him for his help, and made my way back to the car.

CHAPTER FOUR

Driving out onto the Bibury Road, I decided to stop at the Organic Farm Shop and Café for a bowl of soup. It would be at least seven hours before dinner, and breakfast already seemed like a very long time ago. I ordered the soup and quickly made my way around the store, filling a basket with my favourite type of food: fresh and local. I paid for my shopping, ate quickly, and was soon back in the car.

It took about an hour to make my way to Oxford, and I arrived outside the bishop's office with ten minutes to spare. Like me, he hated lateness, and I made my way through the formal garden that was at the front of his house. Before I had a chance to knock, he flung open the door.

'Benoît, so glad to see you. Did you have a good journey?'

'Yes, I did, thank you. The traffic wasn't too bad, and I parked easily, so no problems at all.'

'Can I get you tea? Water? Any refreshment at all? Have you eaten lunch?'

I assured him of this and asked for water. He beckoned me into his study and told me to make myself comfortable, which I did, in a lovely leather chair on the far side of his huge desk. He was back in a couple of minutes with tall, ice-filled glasses and a large bottle of water.

'So, how are things?' he asked.

I talked him through the events and happenings in the area that I was covering; the accounts, problems with the buildings, and generally brought him up to date with all that I thought he needed to know.

'I can't tell you how grateful I am for your standing in like this. Few priests these days want to do it. Most of them want their own parish, and that's understandable, I suppose. Are you OK out there in the sticks on your own?'

'I'm fine… I enjoy it.'

'Well, it's yet to be finalised but it looks like there will be a permanent amalgamation of the few small parishes that you've been covering. We would consider you for the job if you would like it? Lord knows, you've moved around so much, perhaps it's time for you to settle?'

I paused for a moment before responding to his question. At times, I had thought about what it would be like to settle down in one place and be a permanent fixture. I'd also wondered if I might be running from something, unable to stay in one place because of some sort of repressed fear or anxiety. If I were to be honest, I did sometimes feel like I was searching for something… maybe the things that were missing from my life as a priest, like a partner, or children, or something unresolved within myself? The bishop interrupted my thoughts.

'Benoît? Are you alright? Is there something you want to talk to me about? You know you can tell me anything; in the strictest confidence, of course.' I looked at his handsome face, seeing concern in his eyes. I wanted to be honest with him, and yet, be honest about what? I barely had the words to describe my odd moments of unease. On the many occasions that we had met over the years, we had got to know each other well. He was aware of my upbringing and the area that I came from; indeed, we had discussed the region in some depth, especially Rennes-le-Château, which had been an area of intense religious and historical debate for many years.

'Thanks for the concern, but I'm fine, Bishop, really I am. I suppose like all priests I find myself having a mini crisis of faith at odd times, you know, when things happen that are beyond my understanding. That was especially strong when my parents died.'

'Yes. I know that was a particularly difficult time for you. I always felt that we didn't support you enough back then.' He was silent for a moment, and then spoke again.

'The job that we do isn't an easy one. We wouldn't be human if we didn't have difficulties, or change our thoughts and ideas, would we? If fact, surely it's crucial if we are to be good, decent, and honest priests?'

He continued. 'I've always had a longing for a family; for the intimacy that a life like that would bring. I come from a large, happy family myself and my parents were very close. When I was in my forties, this longing was particularly strong, and I even took a sabbatical

21

to consider my vocation. I came close to leaving the priesthood, you know.'

I hadn't known any of this, although we had spent quite a few evenings over the years, talking long into the night about a whole range of different things. I considered him to be a friend, although his position always placed some small barrier between us, even if was tracing-paper thin.

'Yes, I've had similar longings on a few occasions. I suppose in general, though, my life is a full and happy one. I'm busy a lot of the time with church affairs and, as you know, my translation work means a lot to me. And my interest in history and things and people from the past, their lives, and that sort of thing all keep me sane.'

'Well, do think about the permanent position. I'm confident that you would get it if you wanted it. Likewise, there's always work for you in this trouble-shooter role that you've been in for so long now. As you know, the numbers joining the priesthood diminish each year, and it's becoming increasingly difficult to keep each area covered. We are facing difficult times, I fear.'

He was right, of course. The number of young men wanting to 'join up' was very small, and recent high-profile scandals about sexual abuse within the Church had certainly done some considerable damage. I had often wondered if it might ever be put on the agenda that priests should be allowed to marry and have families, like in other faiths. Several of my colleagues had shifted over to the Anglican church so that they could do just that. I smiled at the thought, and at its improbability.

'Anyway,' he continued. 'I wanted to put it to you myself, straight from the horse's mouth.'

The bishop had another appointment at four, and so we concluded our conversation. We agreed to meet in three hours' time, at a very popular pub hidden in a narrow backstreet, where he had booked a table for dinner. He placed his hand on my shoulder as I left to guide me out.

'God bless you, Benoît; see you later.'

He watched until I was around the corner and out of sight. As an astute and perceptive man, little went unnoticed by him, and my mood had become somewhat subdued after our talk. However, this soon lifted as I walked around the beautiful city. The sun was shining and I began to enjoy myself.

CHAPTER FIVE

I strolled through the covered market and was very tempted by a thick, hand-knitted cardigan in soft brown wool. It would be perfect for the winter, my old one now having so many holes in it that one of my parishioners had taken me to one side and asked me if he could buy me another. He said that he knew priests weren't paid very much, and it distressed him to see me so 'poorly dressed.' As I have said before, I was not a man without funds – quite the opposite – but I felt little need for many clothes and tended to only buy things when I felt I had no choice.

I continued walking around and ended up back at the wool shop again. I bought the cardigan, and as I handed over the money, I thought that at least the parishioner wouldn't have to suffer my offending threadbare garment again. I then went into a delicatessen, still in the covered market, and bought several types of ham: cheese, sour cream, two pots of my favourite olives, capers, pine nuts, fresh pasta and gnocchi, a large bunch of thin asparagus, and bunches of fresh herbs, finally adding two large Sicilian lemons. Their smell was fabulous, and seeing these beauties hanging from the trees in southern Italy never failed to excite me.

I concluded my shopping spree with fresh sardines from the fish counter and walked back out into the street. As a Frenchman, I loved food. It would be impossible to be otherwise given my upbringing, where food and its buying, preparation, and consumption had played such an enormous role in our lives.

I stopped for a coffee, and sat outside in the sun. Watching the people walk by, I was very surprised to see Adrian Harcourt on the other side of the street. I had told him I was on my way to Oxford, and he hadn't said he was also going there. Perhaps he didn't want to be offered a lift, or to feel churlish if he refused, preferring to go under his own steam?

I was no longer in full view, since several people had sat at the table in front of me, but he now appeared to be looking for someone. He paused and gazed anxiously up and down the street. Another man walked up to him, much shorter than Adrian, with thick glasses and a black raincoat, which looked somewhat incongruous on such a warm day. They spoke for a few minutes, again looking up and down the street, and then both moved on in different directions until they were out of sight.

It looked rather odd but, whilst curious, I decided it was none of my business. I got up and walked for some ten minutes to the Bodleian library, putting the shopping in my car at the same time. The bishop had arranged this special visit for me, as I wanted to do some research on the church that I was visiting tomorrow. I knew a little already, like it being mainly Norman but on a site of some antiquity. Cirencester, or Corinium Dobunnorum, as it was known then, was the second-largest walled Roman city in Britain, and many Christian churches were built on Roman and pagan sites. I liked the idea of this, layer upon layer of history, each slice representing moments of time. It fascinated me to think of the people that had lived since then, their beliefs and views, and the constant determination to cover up that which had gone before and to dominate it with a perceived superior knowing.

I sat in the library for more than an hour, with a pile of books that an assistant had helped me find. I made notes as I read, particularly about the general history of the area and the relics found hidden in the church some years ago. One of the books provided me with information on the activities of the Knights Templar and the Order of St John in the area, and their involvement in the construction of local churches. I was greatly interested in these men of immense strength and character. The Languedoc region that I was born in had a considerable historical connection with the Cathars and crusading knights, and many of the hills and mountains near my home had one of their castles or strongholds at its summit.

One of the books, much larger and older than the others, was about ancient abbeys and monastic buildings in Britain. I discovered that there had been two monastic communities near the church I was interested in, as well as a defensive castle. This was all new to me, and I quickly scribbled as many notes as I could, as well as taking several photos with my phone.

It was now nearly half past six. Back out in the busy

streets, I noticed the lengthening rays of sun slant over the ancient buildings and, within minutes, was in the narrow, cobbled lane that led to the pub where I had agreed to meet the bishop for dinner.

CHAPTER SIX

I arrived before him and sat at the table to wait. The building dated back to the fifteenth century, and had dark, heavy beams across its low ceilings. Small pockets of warm light, carefully placed, prevented it from being too gloomy and gave it a cosy and intimate feel. I noticed that it was almost full, even at this hour, and I ordered sparkling water whilst eyeing the selection of wines listed on the menu.

The bishop came through the door a few minutes later. He was dressed entirely in black, a fine cashmere sweater pulled over the purple shirt that he had been wearing earlier, and a plain jacket over that. He was a striking, charismatic man, and several people stared as he walked by, which was a reaction I had seen before.

'So sorry I'm late.' He looked flustered, which was quite unlike my usually calm and collected friend.

'Is everything alright?' I asked.

'Yes, yes, fine, just another problem to deal with.'

'Are you still OK for dinner? I don't mind if you want to cancel.'

'I wouldn't dream of it. I've been looking forward to coming here all week. I do sometimes wonder if it's time I retired though. I'm not as robust as I used to be, and I don't mind admitting it, which is something new. I'm sixty-five, did you know that? My sister has a cottage on the west coast of Ireland that she says she is keeping empty for when I retire. I must say, I'm sorely tempted by the idea, and it has a stunning view of the ocean. A comfortable chair, a bottle of the finest claret, and a large pile of books seems incredibly attractive at times. And it would give some new blood the chance to move up the ladder, of course. You would make a fine bishop, Benoît. I've never really understood why you've never had any ambition in that regard.'

'You look remarkably well for your age, Bishop, and as for my ambition to rise within the Church ranks, quite simply, I have none, you know that.' It was a discussion that we'd had several times before. 'If I retired, or had more time, it would be spent on historical research, or my translations. I'm trying to find the time to work on some manuscripts right now.'

At this point, a waiter arrived to take our order.

'What will you have, Benoît?'

'It all looks fabulous, but I'll have the seafood medley, please.'

'I wondered about that, but I think I'll stick to my usual. Fillet steak, medium rare, please, with all the trimmings and a glass of house red. What would you like to drink?'

'The red sounds great, but I'm driving, so I'll stick to sparkling water, thank you.'

We chatted about various things: Ireland, France, and the shortage of new priests. The evening passed pleasantly; the seafood was excellent and I noticed that the bishop's plate was also empty. I ordered a coffee to keep me alert on the way home, and he ordered the usual vintage port that I knew he was so fond of.

'By the way,' he said. 'I've been meaning to ask you something. How well do you know Adrian Harcourt? I believe he does the accounts, and gives advice on buildings and such like in yours and the surrounding parishes?'

The mention of Adrian startled me, having seen him twice already that day.

'Not that well, I suppose,' I replied, 'but he seems decent enough and helps out with various things. I had dinner with him a few months back. Why do you ask?'

He looked at me and took a sip from his glass before he replied.

'Oh, nothing really. It's just that his name has cropped up a few times and I thought I would ask you. You're usually a good judge of character.'

A good judge of character I may well be, but no more than knowing when I was being kept in the dark about something.

'Well, I can't say much more, really. Actually, I saw him this morning. I called in to drop some paperwork off to him en route to meet you. I then caught sight of him in Oxford this afternoon, which I thought a little odd, since he hadn't said he was coming up, but then, why should he? I'm not his keeper, and he has the right to go to Oxford any time he pleases without a formal declaration. He still has business interests I believe. He used to own a large construction company, specialising in the restoration of ancient buildings, churches, castles, and the like. Then he had a bad accident and sold up for a considerable amount of money, so local gossip says. Paints rather well too. But I get the feeling that there's more to your question than you're telling me?'

'No, no, not at all. Forget it. Just me being nosy. Let's settle up, shall we?'

He paid the bill, refusing all attempts to let me pay it myself. It was now dark and we walked together to my car. I had just opened the door when he put his hand on my shoulder and stared at me for a few moments.

'It's been so nice to see you. I value your friendship greatly. Think about the job, won't you? Let me know, and do take care. God bless.'

I was a little taken aback by this declaration but shook his hand warmly, thanked him for dinner, and drove off. Looking in the rear mirror, I saw, like earlier, that he stood watching until I was out of sight.

The journey back was uneventful and I found myself going over the day, my thoughts focussing on Adrian Harcourt, the bishop's questions, and my own future.

Back home, I put my shopping away, feeling satisfied that I had enough food to last the week, and draped my new cardigan over a dining chair to admire its colour and general new-ness. I would take it into town next week to have leather patches sewn on the elbows, like my old one. I would not, I decided, throw out my old, faithful, worn friend, so deplored by a parishioner. It would do for a while yet, although I resolved to wear it inside only, in a charitable attempt not to distress the man any further.

31

CHAPTER SEVEN

By eight the next morning, I was sat at the dining table; books in piles to each side and coffee and toast on the top of the shelves nearby. I intended to complete the overdue Latin translations today and send them off so that I could relax, knowing they were done. I settled down to work, reminding myself of the church tour arranged for this afternoon.

There were several dozen scans of the parchments found in a small chapel in the centre of Rome. It was usual in this field to be sent scans like this. Many owners of rare and unusual finds didn't trust the internet, and I had strict instructions on completion of the translation, that all copies should be thoroughly burned to fine ash. No one trusted anyone. I imagined that because I was a priest I might be trusted more than some, although this was ridiculous. Priests were just men, after all, and whilst a set of morals was supposed to accompany them, I knew that this was most certainly not always the case.

To begin with, I looked at them repeatedly. I always insisted on colour reproductions, which often revealed otherwise hidden letters. Sometimes I was called upon to handle the actual article itself, since my many years in the field had given me considerable knowledge in dating these things. This time, however, the owner had told me that he had already had them dated in a laboratory to the first century AD, and therefore my opinion on age was not required. Judging by the scans, they looked to be in excellent condition for the year he was suggesting.

I had been told that they were found flat, not rolled, as was so often the case. They had been sandwiched between layers of thick hide and then sealed in several centimetres of a hard, resinous substance before being placed in a small metal crate. They were then buried several feet down under an ancient altar thought to date back to early Roman times. Clearly someone had gone to considerable trouble to conceal and preserve these documents, and I was intrigued. As always, the hair stood up on the back of my neck, revealing my excitement and awe at anything quite so ancient.

I knew that the owner was a collector of antiquities; parchments and ancient manuscripts being his most favoured items. I had transcribed for him over a period of many years, and although we had never met, we had talked on the phone quite a few times. We always spoke in English, but his accent told me that he was Italian by birth. He was always polite and prompt in payment and had never given me any reason to think that he was anything other than a wealthy man who, like many others, enjoyed collecting ancient things.

Even though it was a bright day, I leant my flexible 100-watt lamp over the first of the pages that I had been sent. Initially, I could see several, fairly minor, problems. The text was quite faint in places, although I was used to this. Secondly, there were a few holes in the now-thin parchment, although the placement of these didn't appear to be too crucial.

The third problem was the handwriting itself. Although undoubtedly Latin, the writer had adopted an unusual elongated style, with some of the words joined together and some not.

Using a large piece of paper, I began to copy-write the script that was easy to decipher. This took a good hour, after which I realised that I had entirely forgotten my coffee and toast, which were now stone cold. More coffee made, I opened the windows to let the sun and air in, then sat back down to begin to transcribe the text into English, which was the language that I had been asked for.

This was the most difficult part. Over the years, I had developed a 'three-stage' strategy for this, which involved a quick and rough translation first, using only my general knowledge of the language. The second part saw me go over this again with more thought, and if necessary, using some reference sources. The third stage had me go over it again, reading it aloud and imagining myself as the actual author, who I hopefully, by this time, had some measure of.

As I transcribed I found my heart beginning to race. This parchment differed from the other in that it had two thick lines drawn all around its edge, with what looked like astrological symbols woven between them. This wasn't the usual run-of-the-mill stuff that was still around in fairly substantial quantities. I could barely believe what I was reading and skimmed though the text as fast as I could. I quickly rewrote the initial scribbled translation and tentatively concluded that what I had transcribed appeared to be a letter from the Roman emperor, Tiberius.

I had translated many ancient texts in the past, and much of the two years I had spent in Rome had seen me in the Vatican libraries and vaults doing just that. I was always amazed at how many of these seemingly fragile documents had survived, but at the same time I also tried to check my excitement, reminding myself of how many of them were fraudulent, some executed so superbly as to be almost indistinguishable from the originals, often passing detailed tests and analysis.

Dealing in parchments like this was big business, and I knew that in recent years, the British Library had bought an ancient manuscript copy of the Gospel of St John for the massive sum of nine million pounds!

I stood up and walked out into the courtyard, taking several deep breaths to clear my head before looking at the transcription again. I felt calmer when I went back in and prepared for further objectivity but, as I read it again, it was clear that nothing at all needed to be changed.

MY SUBJECT AND GOVERNOR PILATE

I HAVE RECEIVED YOUR REPORTS ABOUT THE TROUBLESOME JEW NAMED JESHUA AND HAVE GIVEN MUCH CONSIDERATION TO YOUR PLIGHT.

I HAVE CONSULTED WITH ALL WHOM I TRUST AND DELVED INTO MY OWN WORLDS OF KNOWLEDGE AND BELIEVE THAT YOU MUST PROCEED WITH EXTREME CAUTION.

HE IS ONE MAN ONLY BUT APPEARS TO HAVE THE ABILITY TO INSPIRE AND CONVERT OTHERS.

MORE MEN LIKE THIS IN OUR OWN ARMIES MIGHT PROVE FRUITFUL. I AM CONVINCED THAT DANGER IS AROUND US AND PROPHETS BEFORE HAVE SPOKEN OF A MAN LIKE HE.

IT WOULD BE EASY ENOUGH TO KILL HIM AND HIS FOLLOWERS TOO.

WE HAVE ARMIES ENOUGH TO CRUSH ANY REBELLION.

THE DEAD, HOWEVER, OFTEN SPEAK WITH MORE POWER AND MIGHT THAN ALL ARMIES PUT TOGETHER.

I HAVE FORSEEN THIS IN MY DREAMS.

I WOULD WISH TO SPEAK TO HIM MYSELF BUT AM AWAY SOON AND MUST ADVISE YOU ONLY.

THAT ADVICE IS TO SEND HIM AWAY TO ANOTHER PLACE WHERE HE CANNOT COME BACK.

LISTEN TO MY WORDS PILATE AND THE MEANINGS WITHIN THEM AND TAKE HEED.

THE DEAD ARE RARELY SILENT AND WAR IS WON BY MORE THAN MIGHT ALONE.

THIS MOMENT HAS BEEN FORETOLD.

YOUR DIVINE EMPEROR AND MASTER TIBERIUS CLAUDIUS NERO
12 MARCH 33

I went through it for a third time, concluding that the transcription was as accurate as I could make it. The translation had been made much simpler by the fact that there was nothing that involved nuance or humour, or that held any complex or multiple meaning, like poetry might do. The dates on these things were often tricky, though, since the Roman calendar wasn't the same as ours. However, there were several reasonable formulas to use that were readily available on the internet. Once again, there were no complications, since the supposed writer was historically well known, as were his dates and time in power.

If I were to accept the authenticity of the document then without doubt, I had just transcribed one of the most momentous moments in history. I went back outside and sat on the stone steps that ran around one edge of the high courtyard wall. I closed my eyes against the bright sun and began to consider what I should do next.

Only once in my career as a translator had I come even close to an involvement with something like this. That time, I had transcribed a manuscript that included several references made to the preaching of John the Baptist. Badly damaged and with at least half of it missing, it was still an exciting discovery, but after the translation had been sent back to the private owner, I had heard no more about it. In the years that followed I waited for it to hit the historical headlines, but it never did and eventually became a closed chapter of my working life.

At this moment, there was a loud rapping on the front door of the cottage. The room that I was using was at the back, and I was unseen, both here and out in the garden. Not wanting any interruption, I decided to ignore it. If it was important, they would try another method of contacting me. I heard more rapping, and then after a few minutes, a banging of the letter box. Assuming it must have been the postman, I walked to the door, picking up a piece of paper now lying on the floor.

Hello Padre. I was passing by so thought I would pop in and take a look at that journal you found. I assume you are busy, so will give you a call later.

Kind regards, Adrian.

Innocent enough, I supposed, but I still regretted my slip of telling him about the journal that I had found. I returned to the table where I had been working and looked through the second set of scans. The writing was very different from the first. It had a slope to the right and was much smaller and tighter in style. It was also much more faded, and the handwriting made it a little more difficult to decipher. I had, however, worked on parchments far more damaged and complex than these were and, for the first time, I began to wonder why they had been sent to me at all. Surely there were plenty of people in Italy or wherever the owner lived who could have transcribed them without too much trouble?

I quickly worked my way through the words, crossing out and replacing, then rewriting and reading the whole thing until I was satisfied. This one also took the form of a letter. The contents, though, were even more startling; more so than anything I had ever come across in my entire life. Even when working at the Vatican, with all its wonderful treasures and documents to hand, nothing had come even close to what was now in front of me.

My lord and Master Tiberius

I write to advise you as requested of matters regarding the Rabbi Jew of Galilee who has caused so much unrest in recent times here.

I met again with him and we spoke at some length. I can find little with which to accuse him and yet his very presence here continues to cause disruptions amongst the people although none I assure you that cannot be quashed with little force from my men.

I tell you that he is a great puzzle to me. He speaks with a voice so quiet that I strain to hear and yet one is impelled to listen. He says he does no harm and preaches only peace and good to the people. He does not believe himself to be a god nor indeed makes any claim to be a king nor makes any claim to the throne although you know he is of royal descent from the line of David. He says he is a child of god in heaven and that all who believe in this god will too so become and receive their reward.

As he left more than one thousand people including women were waiting for him who hailed him as the son of god and their redeemer. There was much calamity and the soldiers killed two men who would not be silenced.

It would seem his followers are of more trouble than the man himself. I advised him in the strongest terms to return here next week where he will be removed from this place for good.

As instructed, he returned last night with his family. They were escorted to the ship awaiting their arrival and were watched by myself as they departed for Gaul. This is the end of the problem.

I remain your most faithful servant and subject.

Pontius Pilate

I was stunned and needed time to think this through further; both to reconcile myself with what I had just read, and to consider the consequences of any possible public exposure. A glance at the clock showed that I was now only half an hour away from meeting Peter at the church. I had also missed lunch, and opened the fridge to take out some ham and cheese bought in Oxford yesterday. I quickly placed them inside two thick slices of bread and put the whole thing in a paper bag, to take with me and eat as I walked to the church.

I then remembered the documents on the table and, at the same time, the old journal in my bedroom above. I ran upstairs to get it, then picked up the papers that I had been working with this morning, as well as my transcriptions. I looked about me for a safe hiding place. Where would a burglar not look?

Back in the kitchen, I opened the door of the old Rayburn. I had kept it going all winter, but it was now cold and unused in favour of the gas stove. Putting everything in a plastic bag, I pushed it into the oven, closing the door firmly, reassuring myself that this was as safe a place as I could find in such a short time.

CHAPTER EIGHT

It was a beautiful day and I began to relax as I walked down the lane to the church, eating my sandwich.

The bell struck two just as I arrived, but Peter had beaten me to it, and was leaning against the warm, stone wall of the church, his eyes closed. The walls to either side of the main gates were covered in ancient graffiti: initials, dates, and strange symbols, some easy to recognise and others less so. I took a few photos with my phone, particularly of the beautiful, but worn, six-sided flowers in circles, and odd, rune-like scratchings.

As I walked into the church yard the gate clicked and Peter opened his eyes.

'Hello there. Isn't this weather glorious? I almost fell asleep then, standing up like a horse. I probably would have slumped to the ground in a minute or two and broken a hip,' he joked, as we shook hands. 'Where do you want to start?'

'Shall we go inside first?' I answered. 'I've done a bit of reading up, and it really is a fascinating old place. Have you seen the graffiti by the front gate? I love the flower symbol, often used by the Knights Templar, amongst others. Many of the churches around here were heavily influenced by them, but then you probably know that.'

He thought for a few seconds before answering.

'I don't know an awful lot about it, I'm afraid, although a colleague of mine who is the vicar of a couple of the parishes up the road has a church that is well documented for its Templar patronage. I do like the idea though – fine upstanding Christian men fighting for what they believed in.'

'Well, maybe,' I answered, 'although some of their ideas didn't exactly follow traditional Christian doctrine. They were great financiers and held a complex set of beliefs that I don't believe have ever been fully documented. Many thought – in fact, still do – that they were the guardians of secrets and discoveries relating to Christ, and held documents that proved that a bloodline from Jesus existed. I find them fascinating and have been gathering information about them for years. I'd love to put it all together into a book one day.'

'Gosh, Benoît, I had no idea you were so interested. I mean, I've read the usual thriller and conspiracy books like everyone else, and seen the odd movie or two; the boys insist on that.'

I was reminded of his three sons, twins in their late teens and an older one in his twenties now. I had met them once or twice at village fetes and other gatherings. If I remembered correctly, his eldest son was studying medicine, and the younger two must surely be about to leave school, or perhaps they already had? They were all tall and fair like their father, and I could imagine them having their own ideas about things and not holding back in voicing their opinions.

We walked into the stone porch and Peter pushed open the huge, heavy, old door, its surround beautifully carved in an early Norman style. We stood at the back of the church and looked down the main aisle towards the central tower, and then began to walk slowly down to what appeared to be the heart of the building. He mentioned a few details here and there, including the early Norman arches, which were wonderful. The ancient carvings on them intrigued me, as did the Templar-style crosses refixed and set into the old stone walls. There were several large arrangements of lilies and the fragrance mingled beautifully with the undefinable smell of an old church.

* * *

'You're probably more knowledgeable than I am. Tell me what you know, Benoît, and if I can add to it, I will.'

'Well, I know it's an early Norman build. There was an older church here before, and possibly a Roman temple before that, but that's nothing new I suppose. So many old churches were built over the top of pagan sites. These relics are stunning though.'

We both stood in front of the glass box set into the wall, cleverly lit up from behind. In it was displayed a small, carved head of Jesus, accompanied by a single foot showing the wound of the crucifixion. I was transfixed and thought it to be one of the most beautiful things of its type that I had ever seen. The face was so unusual and I couldn't help but be deeply moved.

44

I turned to Peter. 'I read in the guidebook that researchers declare this to be either Spanish, brought over from Santiago de Compostela, perhaps after a pilgrimage, or of northern European or Scandinavian origins. I'm torn between the two, since it looks very southern European to me, with the narrow face and long moustache, but the hair looks Scandinavian. Either way, he looks so peaceful, and like he's having the most blissful sleep ever. It makes the hairs on the back of my neck stand up.'

Once again, he thought for a short while before he answered.

'It does indeed. These bits are just wax copies, as I'm sure you know, but the original was found hidden here in the church, about a hundred years ago, most probably to stop it being trashed by Henry VIII's henchmen. It's assumed that the rest of it just crumbled to dust. Considering it's the best part of a thousand years old, it's amazing any of it survived. So many churches find these things quite by chance when renovating, the people that buried them being long dead. Details of the hiding places were never passed on, or were lost somehow. For instance, I imagine the Black Death would have accounted for a lot of lost information in the Middle Ages.'

I agreed, and we continued walking around the ancient building, Peter pointing out the things that he thought I might be interested in. In the far-right corner of the chancel was a very ornate piscina carved from a single block of stone. It had a castellated top and was wound around with vine leaves. Under this was what looked like a cave or cavern and, most unusually, a man's face looked outwards from it. At first glance, one might have thought that it was a green man; a pagan feature and common in older churches. Closer inspection, however, made me doubt this. It was the face of an ordinary man, and even more curious was the notch indented in his chin. Below the cavern was the water bowl itself. I had never seen a piscina that was quite so strange, or indeed, as beautiful. I asked him about it.

'It dates from the early fourteenth century, but I don't know any more than that, really. There's an older one in the nave. There used to be a priest's room above here, but it's sealed up now.'

As he spoke, my mind drifted back to the cottage, where the parchments and the curious journal lay hidden in the Rayburn oven.

'You've gone quite white, Ben. Are you OK?'

'Yes, sorry, I'm fine, just daydreaming!' We walked back to the main entrance, stopping to look at the beautiful old font. Its lead lining was covered with a mass of graffiti and I took lots of photos, including more of the entrance, which also had ancient symbols scratched into the supporting walls. We both patted the magnificent door and, to my delight, I noticed that it too was covered with areas of graffiti.

Peter spoke. 'I've noticed that before. I even asked the previous incumbent about it, but he knew nothing. It's odd, isn't it? It looks like one should be able to read it straight off, but it's not in any language I can understand. You're the linguist; can't you decipher it?'

I stood back to study it. It looked like a mixture of Latin, Greek, and several other things that I vaguely recognised, but couldn't quite put my finger on.

'Not a clue, but when I get time I'll look at it again.'

We moved outside and walked around the exterior of the church, noting various scratch dials, masons' marks, and a couple of window arches that looked Saxon in style... until we reached the front of the building again. On the right side of the porch was a massive stone sarcophagus, the lid leaning upright on its front.

'What a curious thing. What happened to the person inside it?'

'No one knows,' Peter replied. 'It's been here for some years, though, and is definitely Roman. I think it was found in a much older burial ground near the village, but you'd have to check on that. This pair are a mystery, as well. No one knows who they are or why they're here, but they're believed to be medieval in date. The locals call them "the Lovers" but there's nothing in the church records about them, even though they do go back that far.'

He pointed to the other side of the porch where there was a large raised tomb. A gentleman and his lady were lying on top, oddly covered over with a rug or blanket of some sort from their waists down. I had never seen anything like it and moved closer to take a better look. It was very worn and weathered, as one would expect after many hundreds of years outside.

This type of monument was usually kept inside the church but, even then, I couldn't recall ever having seen effigies like this, covered with a blanket. I did remember a church in London having a large brass on the wall, of a woman with the lower part of her body covered in a blanket, like she was in bed. A local historian that I had asked told me it might mean she had died in childbirth, but I had never seen one anywhere else, despite the many hundreds of churches of differing faiths that I had been into over the years. I was intrigued and decided to do a little research myself, time allowing.

'Thank you so much for taking the time to show me around your lovely church.'

'Think nothing of it. I've enjoyed it immensely and learned a few things too. Do come back with me to the vicarage for a cup of tea... Merry said to ask you, and she's baked a few scones in the hope that you would come.'

I liked Merry, Peter's wife. She was a delightful woman, well versed in her role of support to her country vicar husband, and very attractive as well. Her general demeanour also suited her name to a T, and I could think of nothing better than an hour in her company. To be honest, I wasn't looking forward to going back to the cottage and facing the problem that was waiting for me there.

I accepted the invitation and we strolled around the corner to the large Georgian house that was the vicarage. Peter was a keen gardener and there were roses and other brightly coloured flowers everywhere. I knew there was a much more formal garden at the back, often used to host parish events.

'The garden looks fabulous. It must take a huge amount of work. How do you find the time?'

'It does take quite a bit of time, I suppose, but I love it, and Merry is happy to be my helper. I've even got the twins interested, and Jack has decided to train in architecture and landscape design at university. Josh is going into medicine like his older brother, so come September we shall be rattling around the place on our own. I can't say I'm looking forward to it, but I imagine they'll still be here in the holidays so I must just make do with that, I suppose.'

At this point, his eyes filled with tears, but he was saved any further embarrassment by the arrival of Merry, who surprisingly gave me a big, scented hug. She led us through to the rear terrace, where a very handsome tea had been laid out, including tiny sandwiches with the crusts cut off. There were also beautiful golden scones, which I knew she sold at the local Women's Institute stall in town each week, along with fat, brown eggs from the hens that were kept at the bottom of the vicarage garden.

'So, Ben,' she said, gazing at me in her bright, lively way. 'What do you make of our church? It's quite a beauty, isn't it? People come from miles away to see it, especially the relics of Jesus. How do you take your tea? Do help yourself to everything.'

'The church is really impressive,' I replied. 'And yes, you're right, the relics are exquisite. I could hardly tear myself away from them. That face? I've never seen such a peaceful look in my life, and as a Catholic priest I've seen plenty of crucifixion statues, as you can imagine! And the foot? It's so delicate, and seems to tell a story all of its own.'

We discussed the church and its contents in more detail, as well as the graffiti. Merry told me that she too was very interested in such things, and we talked about our nearest cathedral in Gloucester and the amount of graffiti that was there. I mentioned the tombs and we discussed those too. Interestingly, she told me that an archaeologist had spent some time at the church a few years back, but he hadn't been able to find out very much about them.

'He was an odd man, and I can't say I took to him really. He certainly didn't get a tea like this one,' she laughed. 'I'll dig out the report he wrote if you like.'

Our discussion moved on to non-church-related things. There was no sign of the boys, but some vague thumping music in the background told me that at least one of them was in the house somewhere.

'Thank you both so much for the wonderful tea, and the guided tour. I'll be off now, but I wonder if you would both like to have dinner with me one evening? I need to look at my diary first though.'

Agreeing to call them with a few dates, I walked quickly back to the cottage.

CHAPTER NINE

It was nearly five thirty when I pushed the heavy old key into the door lock. Oddly, it wouldn't turn, and as I tried the handle the door swung open with ease. I knew there had been a few break-ins in the area recently, but I was far more concerned about the translations and notebook than any loss of my few and low-value belongings. I stepped warily inside and went straight to the Rayburn oven door. Relieved, I saw that the wrapped package was there, exactly as I had left it.

Nothing seemed out of place, except perhaps the pile of books on the dining table. They looked too tidy and were arranged in a straight, neat way that I would never have done. My laptop was still there too, which would surely have been something that an average thief would have taken. The thought of a stranger reading personal things was an unpleasant one, and I had taken the precaution of having three sets of passwords that needed to be entered, as well as encryption, some time ago.

I was, however, convinced that someone had been in, though there would be little point in calling the police since nothing had been stolen. I remembered the note from Adrian Harcourt earlier. Was he so desperate to see the journal that he would break in? And if he was, why? I didn't even know what it was about yet, so how could he have such a strong desire to look at it, unless he knew more than he had said?

I resolved to find out more about him if I could, remembering the bishop's questions. Clearly, I was missing something but would need to tread carefully and not be too obvious with my enquiries. I locked the door again, this time from the inside, and pulled across the two big bolts top and bottom. No one would get through that lot in a hurry, and the back was unreachable because of the high courtyard wall and the other gardens that were behind it.

I picked up the phone and dialled the number for Mick, a retiree, who did odd jobs for all the churches around here. I knew him well as he attended one of my services, and after two rings he answered.

'Mick, it's Father Ben. I hope I'm not disturbing you. I was wondering if you could fit me an extra lock on my front door?'

'No problem at all, Father. I've done quite a few over the past two weeks. Better safe than sorry. I've got to come over your way tomorrow morning, so I could do your lock at about ten if that's OK?'

'That's fine… thank you, Mick. I'll see you tomorrow then.'

Putting the papers and journal back on the dining table, I went out into the courtyard. The shrubs that I had planted in pots last year were wilting, and mindful of the magnificent vicarage garden, I picked up the can that stood by the outside tap and quickly watered them, as well as the small flower borders left by a previous inhabitant of the cottage. This done, my thoughts strayed to dinner.

* * *

Opening the fridge, I took out the sardines bought in Oxford yesterday, intending to fry them and make a strong tomato sauce, with capers, red wine, and garlic. Ten minutes later, it smelt fabulous, and I spooned it over the top of the browned fish. It was a dish that my grandfather used to cook, and accompanied by several thick slices of bread, and a large glass of red wine, it was delicious. Putting the dishes into the sink to deal with later, I went through to the sitting room and sat at the table, which was now almost always used as my desk.

My problems returned to me, although with good food in my stomach and a glass of wine to hand, I felt slightly less anxious. Firstly, I had to deal with the translation. At that point, the phone rang and I recognised Adrian's number straight away.

'Hello, Adrian, sorry I missed you when you called over earlier. What can I do for you?'

'Well, Padre, I thought I might be able to help you, actually. I've got a bit of spare time on my hands and wondered if you needed any help with that journal you found. I love things like that and am knowledgeable about the area, as you know. Perhaps it's something we could do together?'

The one thing that was becoming very clear was the desire to get his hands on the journal. What I didn't know, was why? As for his having time on his hands, this was clearly a lie. He was always very busy and had far more to do each day than he could get through. He had told me several times that he was busier in his retirement than he ever had been when he was working.

'I've got a lot on right now. How about I give you a shout when I have a moment, and we can talk things through? I appreciate your offer of help, but really, it's just an old journal, and of no importance, I'm sure.' This wasn't entirely true, since I thought that perhaps it was indeed of importance, and clearly, he thought so too.

'Father, I don't think you understand. From what you've told me there may be a lot of trouble that comes with the journal. Believe me, I know about these things. You may be in danger. I wouldn't want anything to happen to you.'

Now, I may be a priest and an academic of sorts, but a fool I am not. I recognised a threat like any other man and felt annoyed to be bullied in this way. My hackles rose and I wanted to put an end to this conversation, and the persistence of the man that I was now beginning to dislike.

'Adrian, I appreciate your offer of assistance, really I do, but I must say, I am beginning to feel somewhat harassed, which isn't going down too well. I'm not an idiot, and clearly you have some agenda going on here. Either tell me what it is, or leave me in peace. And one more thing; if it was you who broke into my house today, be warned. Any more pranks like that and I shall get the police involved – you can bank on it.'

There was silence for a moment on the other end of the phone.

'I'm so very sorry to have upset you. That wasn't my intention I can assure you, but truly, you don't understand. Please call me if you need help. I'm not your enemy, believe me.'

At this point he hung up, but before I could ponder on our conversation the phone rang again. This time, after a few clicks, I found myself talking to the man who had given me the translation work. Had I done it, he wanted to know? I told him I had. He had a man in the area tomorrow who would call by at exactly eight in the morning to pick it up, and please could I have it ready.

'Listen,' I started to say. 'This isn't like the other work I've done for you. Do you have any idea of what you gave me?'

Surprisingly, he answered in Italian, showing it to be his native tongue, just as I had thought.

'Yes, of course I know. I'm not entirely stupid.'

I continued the conversation in Italian. I had become fluent whilst living there, although now had little chance to speak it.

'I never thought you were, but really, I'm unsure why you even sent me the parchments. I mean, they're not that difficult to translate, and Rome has several excellent Latin academics who could have done it for you. If they're not forgeries, I'm sure you know that they're of immense importance, and priceless. But that's not what concerns me. It's the impact that they might have if they get into the wrong hands. To be honest, I wish I'd never seen them.'

He replied, again in Italian. 'They're not forgeries, Benoît, there can be no question of that. I've known of their existence for some years, but getting hold of them took time. You're right though, I shouldn't have involved you, but I desperately needed an opinion other than my own. Yours was the only one I knew I could trust. I'm so sorry, forgive me. I know I needn't tell you this, but please destroy every copy you have immediately. You'll be paid extra for your trouble. I must go now, but your safety will be considered in the coming months.'

He hung up, and I sat for a moment with the phone in my hand. Not only did I have the hassle with the journal, but I now had this to contend with too. I doubted that I had heard the last of the matter, but at this moment, didn't feel unduly worried. I had no idea how he was going to take account of my safety, although clearly he thought I might be in some danger. If he was right, then who or what from, exactly? If I knew this, then I would be better placed to protect myself. Anyway, surely, they would go after the Italian and the originals, not me and a few photocopies that were useless and proof of nothing?

* * *

Going totally against my normal practice, I set aside two scans of the original parchments and made two of the transcriptions that I had done. I repeated this, making copies with my scanner. Putting the others in an envelope, I sealed it ready for collection the following day, then put the rest of the copies in the grate and set them alight with a match. It soon caught, and I watched whilst it burned to the finest ash. I then put a firelighter and some newspaper in, and set this alight too, which should take care of any tiny pieces.

Once again, I watched as it burned down and then re-laid the fire ready for the next cold evening. Taking my own two copies of the parchments and translations, I put one set in an envelope and sealed it in heavy plastic, kept for sending parcels abroad. Popping it into the grate of the Rayburn, I placed several small logs on top, so that, if opened, the package would be entirely invisible.

Folding the second set as flat as I could, I tucked them into the layers of the thick, lined curtains that hung from the sitting room window. The hem had been coming down for a while and I hadn't got around to having them mended. As I did this, I was reminded of one of the stories that my grandfather used to tell me, about when the Nazis had invaded France. All the locals had stitched their cash and anything else of value, including paintings, into their curtain linings and soft furnishings, and much had been kept hidden in this way.

My house in France had a large safe dating to the First World War, but with the house being so frequently empty, the nearby bank held the few things I had of any value. It made sense to do the same here, and I decided to put the documents in a safety deposit box in town, moved here from London, where it was previously held.

A solicitor had strict instructions to send everything to my cousin, Caro, in France, should anything happen to me. She is like a sister, and my will leaves everything to her. Likewise, she, as an unmarried woman of fifty-five, has left her entire estate to me. Thinking of her now, I picked up the phone again and dialled her number. I was about to hang up when she finally answered.

'Oh, it's you, Benoît,' she said, sounding breathless. 'Odd you should ring – I was thinking about you earlier, and thought I might make a trip over to see you soon. I was in the garden. Everything's growing like mad and it's really hot, so I was watering.' She paused for a moment to catch her breath. 'Are you OK?'

'To be honest,' I replied, 'I'm not sure. I might be in a bit of bother, but I can't talk about it right now. Tell me more about the garden and what you've been up to.'

'Now I'm worried. You know you can tell me anything. Look, I won't press you now, but I will ask you again.'

'Thank you.'

We chatted about various things including our last remaining relative, Aunt Hortense, and Caro ended the call by saying she would phone me tomorrow with some flight dates. As a retired history professor, she lived alone in a beautiful old house on the edge of the hilltop village of Rennes-le-Château, a few kilometres from my home at Antugnac. Her spectacular views were of the mountains and valleys, with castles and other villages in full view, and I wholeheartedly wished I was there right now, well away from here and my current problems.

CHAPTER TEN

It was now nearly ten and I was exhausted. Within half an hour I was in bed, the journal open on my lap, and pen and paper by my side. I re-read the first few lines and copied them down before continuing to read the elaborate script.

January 11th 1789

> *Met with C today. He is much fatigued and quite thin with it. His wife is engaged in trying to fatten him up like a goose, which is causing much mirth in the household. After dinner we retreated to the library and spoke of matters which must be heard by us alone. He assured me that nothing has been moved in Rome and there is no need for concern. Work was done in secret and movements between A and R were completed. He assured me that records have been kept safe amidst the turmoil in France, and all is now invisible and we should rest in the knowledge that nothing should come to light until the enlightened seek it.*

None of this was too difficult to read, although a small tear across the bottom of the page slowed me down for a moment.

January 12th 1789

No rest last night in thought of meeting C. I am not convinced of the enlightenment of the human race ever, and this sets me low in myself. Feel unwell, and have taken to my bed where I write this. Appetite is lost and the maid worn out and ill-humoured with trailing up and down the stairs with morsels sent from the kitchen to tempt me.

There were no more entries until the 17th of February and I assumed that this was because of the illness he had spoken about.

Am finally well enough to go downstairs much to everyone's relief including my own. The slightest thing makes me tired, even writing this. C visited me today. He has heard from Abbé B at R and is told all is well, and quiet as it should be. This being the case, why am I so filled with unease?

At this point, I jumped out of bed and went downstairs. I had decided to write the script out as it had been written, in journal format, and wanted to get a new notebook for it. I loved good stationery and had bought a dozen soft, leather-bound ones in Venice whilst on holiday a few years ago. There were some beautiful stationery shops in the narrow lanes, and they were surprisingly cheap. As a man who, apart from food, hates shopping, when I see something I like I buy it in bulk, and am frequently glad that I do. I chose a dark red one from the cupboard that I stored them in. Going back upstairs, I glanced at the clock, which told me it was now half past midnight. I decided to transcribe the few bits that I had read, and then, once again, try to sleep.

Back in bed, I did just that. It made the whole thing so much easier to follow and suited my translator's methodical mind. I then put both books back in the drawer and the sheets of used paper on the side for burning tomorrow.

CHAPTER ELEVEN

Within minutes of waking up the following morning, there was a sharp rapping on the door, and I dashed downstairs to find the usual black leathered, helmeted courier waiting to collect the envelope. He spoke the two words that I had been told to expect before handing anything over, and within seconds, was back on his bike and roaring down the lane. Mick arrived as I was eating toast and I made him a coffee and talked to him as he worked.

'Done nothing but replace locks recently... there's no punishment you see, Father Ben. Seems to me that unless you murder someone you can get away with anything. My cousin's house got broken into last month. Smashed the window and everything whilst she was out at a friend's. To be fair, there wasn't much to steal, even the telly's ten years old. The police took six hours to come out, though, and she was left really shaken. It takes a while to get over that sort of thing, doesn't it?'

I agreed that it did, and remembered my own shock and anger yesterday at finding someone had been into the house.

'This new lock should do the trick. Trouble with these old houses is that there's no end of people that have had the key over the years. You end up with half the county that could get in if they chose to.'

He was probably right, and promising to visit them soon, I handed over a box of chocolates for his wife, who I knew had been unwell. A few minutes later, I was driving to the bank and considering my unorthodox actions further. Should I have destroyed everything? I always had before, so why not this time? What right did I have to keep these and break the trust of the man who had given them to me? But on the other hand, what right did he have to expose me to them? He knew I was a priest. I might have been most affronted or damaged even by what I had read. In truth, though, whilst I could well do without any hassle, my faith seemed irrelevant to the whole episode.

Deciding to be a priest had made me neither blind nor stupid, and I had come to terms with the various possibilities that surrounded Jesus and his life a long time ago. Living so close to Rennes-le-Château, its considerable history alleging to connect it to an alternative version of Christianity was impossible to entirely ignore. Whatever the truth might be, nothing took away the inexplicable spirit of Jesus the man, and I felt no need to rip apart my faith by using science or discovery. I knew that many priests might find this shocking, but that was their problem to wrestle with, not mine. Anyway, this was a discussion that I rarely had with anyone. My years as a priest had repeatedly shown me what purpose faith had in the lives of human beings and, for the most part, I was content with that.

My musing came to a stop as I arrived in town, and my attention was taken with finding a parking space. That done, I took the package, tucked it into the large pocket on the inside of my jacket, and walked straight to the bank some two hundred yards further down the road. I was told that the bank manager was busy, but his assistant agreed to see me and within thirty minutes the papers were in the box and locked away. I was glad to escape the stuffy, stale atmosphere and get back out into the street.

* * *

It was market day and there were various stalls lined up selling their wares. I didn't need anything, already having stocked up on food in Oxford, but as usual, I was lured by the smell of fresh bread, and ended up buying a large caraway loaf which was a favourite of mine. I then went to buy a coffee to take with me and whilst queuing, I noticed that a small, tanned man had come into the café behind me. I wondered if he would be disappointed with the espresso in the UK. Living abroad so much had sharpened my ability to spot another foreigner, and he looked decidedly foreign to me, probably southern European.

I had become like the locals when I was living in Italy, and had nipped into cafés for a quick shot at various times throughout the day. Remembering my conversation with the Italian last night, it crossed my mind that he might be following me. Within minutes, I was on the road back to the cottage and he was promptly forgotten.

Stopping off at the church in the village, I took more photos, especially of the inscriptions cut deep into the ancient wood of the main door. I couldn't resist going in to see the relics, and once again was mesmerised by the beauty and calm carved into the face of Jesus. I wondered for a moment about its maker. Surely, he must have experienced such peace himself to replicate it in his wooden carving? Or was that faith too? Had he imagined what utter, blissful peace would look like, and then gone on to create it, with this in his mind? Either way, I was in awe of any craftsman that could do such exquisite work.

I took more photos of the tombs outside, both the blanket-covered, medieval one and the open Roman tomb, which looked even more bizarre this morning. Why would anyone open it up like this, put it right by the church door, and leave it there, with the lid propped up on its side? It most blatantly spoke out 'I'm not here anymore. I've gone somewhere else!' But where? Still puzzled, I quickly drove the rest of the journey home. No one had broken in this time, which was a great relief, but I still pushed both bolts home, which felt even more reassuring. Making tea and a sandwich, I went to sit outside. The sun had gone in and although it was still warm, a stiff breeze had come up, and I quickly finished my lunch and went back inside.

CHAPTER TWELVE

I intended to read as much of the journal as I could today, since I only had another two days off and had a lot in my diary for the following week. I went upstairs to collect the new and old journals, and sat at the dining table. The sitting room now seemed quite dark, and I switched on the bright reading lamp that I often used for my translation work.

February 25th 1789

Am feeling much better in myself and have been outside a few times. Walked to church and back again, but needed to rest in afternoon to gain strength. C sent word of a visit next week. Again, I am uneasy. Household much engaged today in brewing and baking. I spent evening in study by warm fire and read new book which I had ordered some months ago in London. It is one on ancient history of the Crusades and the Knights of Jerusalem and a rarity indeed. C has offered to borrow it which I may or may not agree to.

I smiled at this and was reminded of another journal, which I always kept by my bed, that of Parson Woodforde, who wrote in similar times. The humility and character of the man always warmed me and he was a person who, if it were possible, I would love to have met. The journal continued with mostly domestic affairs until an entry in 1791, which caught my attention.

September 1ˢᵗ 1791

C called to tell me B has decided that because of the troubles in France he is to give up his duty at R and go on pilgrimage to Spain, and has no intention of return. I am unsure if this is good or bad although we are in no position to stop him as he is an elderly man and can surely end his days as he wishes. Once again, C assures me that all is well, and the secret will be kept. He brought with him a letter from his wife, and a basket of vegetables from his garden which I received thankfully.

The diary was only written in occasionally over the next couple of years, with little of much interest historically, and no more mention of the secret that he and 'C' shared. Near the end of the notebook, however, one entry made me alert again.

15th April 1794

Clare tells me that he has been told that B did
never go to Spain at all, and has died near the
coast in France. Why did he lie? Did Clare know
all the time? I have no power over any of this, and
my failing health means I shall surely join B in
another place soon. I tell Clare that I have had a
dream of my end, and that he must do all he can to
ensure our secret is kept, both in France and here.
He looked at me in that strange way of his and held
my hands so tightly that I thought they might be
broke. I will play my part, says he, and there is no
more I can do. We are but mortal, and our role as
protector and keepers of the future of mankind will
soon be given over. I am old too, he said, and after
we have gone who is to know what will happen then?
This is the most I have ever heard him say on the
subject, and I viewed him in a different light today.

1st September 1794

My heart near broke when I heard today that
Clare fell off his horse last night and was drowned
in the river. How can this be? He was more sure of
himself on a horse than any man I ever knew. I do
not believe that this can have been an accident, and
I now know that my warnings to him were real,
and not the ramblings of an old and decrepit man.

Throughout the pages of the journal, the writing had become weaker, and the last few entries showed a much shakier hand. His lapse into using full names, instead of initials, gave me reason to think that he was becoming increasingly frail in both mind and body. I was deeply moved by his story, even though I didn't fully understand it, and felt enormous empathy for both men that I had read about and come to know. I was reminded once again of the frailty of all living things and how easily life was snuffed out. I turned the page and found more writing in another, and entirely different, hand.

> *My beloved brother Richard Harcourt died this day 10ᵗʰ September 1794. He was the best of men and I am bereft. He died with his journal closed and held tightly in his hand. His family will keep it for posterity, sealed and closed, as private as was the man himself.*
>
> *Isabel Harcourt.*

Clare and Harcourt. It was now late afternoon, and I had been sitting here for the best part of three hours. I had rewritten the whole journal into the notebook, and it was only as I was nearing the end that I had been presented with these names. Of course, I knew another Harcourt… Adrian… and Clare, another name not entirely unknown to me in my studies of the Knights Templar. I jumped up and grabbed my jacket. I needed to get back to the bank and deposit the original journal. I could then give myself time to think about what to do next.

Picking up both books, I put them in the inside pocket of my jacket. Then I stopped for a moment and thought... what if I was mugged en route? I decided to scan the most important pages, save them, print them, and take photos with my phone, which I had ensured was virtually impossible to get into if I lost it. I suspected that Caro would accuse me of 'Ben's OCD.' She had always used this phrase when we were young, in response to my needing to know where everything and everyone was.

In later life, she put it down to the frequent and unexplained disappearances of my parents, but right now, I didn't care what it was called. It felt appropriate to have the most important papers kept together in a wad. This took me about eight minutes in total, and I almost ran out of the house, although not so quickly that I didn't lock up properly. I was in the bank thirty minutes later, and the same young man brought out my box and looked away whilst I deposited the journal. To give him his due, he said nothing, and business was soon concluded.

I felt a huge sense of relief at knowing the original journal was safe, and patted my jacket to make sure the new one was still there. As I left, I noticed the same small, tanned man seen in the café earlier that day, standing to one side of the large doors. In a flash, I recognised him as the man that Adrian Harcourt had spoken to in Oxford before going their separate ways. I was being followed, that was for sure, but by whom?

The Italian had said on the phone that he would attend to my safety, which didn't bother me too much, since I was certain that I had been followed for much of my time in Italy. I had become used to a shadowy figure watching me from around every corner, and had even tipped my sun hat to him once or twice. The people I had spoken to about it had told me not to worry, and in the end, I assumed that it was something to do with the work I was engaged in. But how could that be anything to do with Adrian? Why had they met, albeit briefly, in the Oxford street?

Back in the car, I drove along back lanes to the village. Pulling up outside the cottage, I noticed a red car parked on the road opposite, with someone sitting in it.

'Now what!' I said aloud. I was hoping for a quiet evening, with perhaps a little Templar research thrown in for good measure.

I got out, ignoring the car in the hope that it would prove to be nothing to do with me. I began to unlock the front door, now a lengthy process because of the added lock, when I heard my name being called by a very familiar voice.

CHAPTER THIRTEEN

❦

'Benoît... Benoît... hang on a minute. You ran up the path like the hounds of hell were after you!'

'Caro! It's you. I can't believe it. What are you doing here? We only spoke on the phone last night.'

I let us both in before giving her a huge hug. I had no idea what the villagers would make of a priest having a woman to stay, but I would surely be made out to be a gigolo of sorts, which I was quite happy about. I could almost see the curtains twitching as I closed the door behind us.

'I can't believe it!' I said again. 'Caro, you're here! What a surprise!'

'Well, I felt so worried about you last night after we spoke that I jumped on the first plane this morning and came over. I flew into Birmingham, which wasn't too bad, and it only took me just over an hour and a half to drive to your cottage from there.'

It was now nearly six, and I decided to open a bottle of my favourite vintage prosecco, always kept in the fridge for times of celebration, just like this. Putting it in the freezer for a few minutes, a necessity in my eyes, I hugged her again, putting her bags on the stairs to take up later. She could sleep in my room tonight and I would use the sofa bed in the sitting room. I took the bottle out of the freezer, gently popped the cork, and poured us a glass each.

'Trust you, Ben,' she said. 'This is delicious!'

'It's my favourite. Have you eaten? Would you like to go out to eat? There are a few reasonable restaurants in the town, or we could always go up to Oxford if you want to?'

'I'd rather stay here, if you don't mind. It's been a long day, and if I know you there will be a fridge stuffed full of food, so cook me something.'

'I was going to have pasta piselli. Will that do?'

'Absolutely,' she replied. 'I love it.'

Pasta piselli was an Italian dish made with tagliatelle, ham, peas, and cream, and was a favourite of mine. We moved through into the kitchen, Caro sitting at the table whilst I began to get out pans and things from the fridge.

'So, are you going to tell me what's going on? You said you might be in a bit of bother, which if I know you is probably an understatement.'

I thought for a moment. I wanted to share everything with Caro, who apart from the bishop, perhaps, was the only person I felt I could totally trust. I was, however, concerned about the implications and risks that any external involvement might bring. Whilst I might not be overly anxious about my own demise, I would never forgive myself if she was harmed in any way. 'Later. Let's eat first. I'm starving!'

As I cooked, we chatted about what she had been doing over the past few weeks, and some people that we both knew.

73

'Come and stir this lot around,' I said. We often cooked together in France and assumed our usual positions with ease. Within ten minutes it was ready, and we sat down to eat, like the true gluttons that we were, and in typical Mediterranean style, by lowering our heads to the bowls and shovelling it in with a fork. It wasn't the cleanest type of food, and soon there were splashes on the table as well as us, but we carried on until both bowls were empty. Quantities of bread mopped up the last of the sauce and I leant back, rubbed my full stomach, and groaned.

'I think I might just explode – I warn you, it could be messy!'

We both laughed, and I was reminded of how much we used to laugh as children, often ending up helpless, weak, and sometimes collapsed on the floor, much to the exasperation of both of our sets of parents. We didn't end up on the floor of my kitchen this time, but I was glad she was here, and told her so.

'Come on, let's go through and sit down properly. We can do the dishes in the morning.'

Picking up our glasses, we went into the sitting room and I lit the fire. Remembering the few bits of paper torn from the pad last night, I went to fetch them and threw them in. The other notebook was still in my jacket, which was hanging on the hook behind the door. She looked at me keenly, all traces of humour gone.

'So, come on… spit it out.'

'Oh, I don't know. I don't want to involve you or

put you at risk in any way. It'll probably all just go away anyway, and then I'll have worried you for nothing.'

Caro fiddled with her glass, and went quiet for a moment.

'Look, Ben, you mean more to me than anyone. We grew up together, our parents are dead, and our only other relative is Aunt Hortense. She's so frail now, and when she dies it's just us. If you're in trouble and there might be a way in which I could help, even if it's just by giving you support, then I want to do it. I remember when you were in Italy and that man followed you around all the time. And when you nearly got pushed in front of a train? And I never was convinced that it was an accident when you were run over in London. It wasn't, and we both know it. What I'm saying is that I'm prepared to take the risk, so come on… confess the whole ghastly lot. It'll make a change for you to be on the other side of the box, so to speak.'

'OK, but you must understand that what I'm about to tell you must stay only with you. I know I should assume that as a given, and that I can trust you, but I needed to say it anyway – it's really important. I have reason to believe that I have become unwittingly mixed up in something of great importance, and as expected, a few shady characters seem to be crawling out of the woodwork. As for being followed, I'm sure I am being, right now. He's a small Italian-looking man in a black coat.'

I told her the whole story, from finding the old journal in the box of papers, the translations from the

Italian, Adrian Harcourt, the bishop, and my various trips to the bank. I also mentioned Peter the vicar, his lovely wife, and the village church and its treasures, but our lighter mood had now completely vanished, as had any effect of the alcohol that we had drunk.

* * *

I got up to make coffee and pour us some Calvados over large lumps of ice, which was Caro's favourite. The smell of apples was wonderful, and the cold, fiery liquor was perfect with the strong shots of black coffee. She looked at me, her face pale with concern and fear.

'I knew it would be something to do with one of your blasted manuscript translations. All that secrecy and cloak and dagger stuff, deliveries, collections in the middle of the night, as well as the assumption that you'll say nothing to anyone… ever. That implies a threat without one even being stated. It's downright dangerous! Can't you stick to the poetry, Benoît?'

'I'm sorry, but no, I can't. I love doing it, and I don't want to stop, not even the cloak and dagger stuff – it's all part of it. It makes me feel alive somehow, and as for the danger, I rarely think about it. I can't explain it any more than that, except to say that I shouldn't have told you.'

'I'm glad you did, and I do understand the feeling alive bit. Discoveries are always invigorating and exciting, I get that, but I don't want anything to happen to you. You don't seem to care, and I put that down to your upbringing and being constantly abandoned by your parents, but I do. I don't know what I'd do if anything happened to you.'

'Maybe you're right about the not caring bit. Don't get me wrong though, I don't want to die any time soon.'

She sighed and then spoke again.

'Let's start from the beginning. The parchments from the Italian… don't you have any idea who he is? Can I see a copy? I might be an atheist, but I am a history professor, and not entirely inexperienced in such things.'

I got up to draw back the curtains, rifling around in the linings to find the papers that I had placed there yesterday. Had it only been then? It seemed like an age ago.

'What the hell are you doing? Perhaps there's more of the French peasant in you than I thought… hiding things in the curtains indeed. You'll be pulling up the floorboards next.'

'Actually, that's not such a bad idea.'

I handed over the transcripts, watching as she slowly read them, carefully taking in every word.

'I'm stunned. If these are for real, can you imagine what might happen if they were let loose? Bloody hell, what was the Italian man thinking? Is he from the Vatican, do you think? It seems most likely to me, although surely they would have pulled you into Rome if they needed your help with something as important as this? That's the preferred scenario as far as I can see. If he's Mafia or similar, we might as well order your coffin now. I don't know why I'm joking; this is serious! What are you going to do?'

'What can I do? The way I see it, there are so many

people who might be involved. Contacting any one of them might make things worse and expose me to even more trouble. I've no idea who the Italian is, and I'm not certain that the Vatican is more benevolent than the Mafia, to be honest. They've silenced enough people throughout history, you know that. The journal's an added complication. It's a real coincidence that I found it when I did and as I said, Adrian Harcourt is very keen to get his hands on it. And did I tell you that the cottage was broken into? They didn't steal anything, but I'm sure it was the journal they were looking for.'

I got up again and went to get the copy book that was still in my jacket pocket. I handed it over to Caro, put another couple of logs on the fire, and slowly sipped my drink.

'There's no such thing as coincidence, Ben. I prefer the term synchronicity. It's more accurate, but it's quite bizarre that you found the journal while you were doing the translations. Double trouble. This first bit, where there are a few words missing, what's that about?'

'Ah, I've worked that out now, but haven't had a moment to write it in. It had some dirt on it, but a bit of my special cleaning fluid did the trick.'

I took the book from her and, picking up a pencil, completed the text.

'It reads like this.'

I cannot sleep for my fears of the devastation that would come if our enemies were to gain our knowledge and make free with it.

By now, it was almost one in the morning, and we were both stifling yawns. We decided to turn in and Caro took her bags, and went upstairs to the bedroom. I tidied up, carefully putting the documents back in the curtain linings. In bed, I flicked through the notebook once again. Written at the time of the revolution, the visits to France would have been dangerous to say the least. And the secret it spoke about? Was that just in France or here too? Apart from it being about a relative, why was Adrian so desperate to get hold of it? At this moment, I had no idea, but suspected that one way or another, I was going to find out.

CHAPTER FOURTEEN

'Morning, Ben – you were up early. You've washed up too, and with coffee and toast at the ready. I'm honoured.'

'And very lucky! What would you like to do today?'

'I'd like to see the church that you told me about yesterday, and the relics. I might not believe in God but I still find the whole thing fascinating. These old churches are some of the most ancient and important buildings that we have, in France and here, although you wouldn't think so, given the way they're allowed to fall into disrepair. Romans populated this area, didn't they? Are there any museums nearby?'

We agreed to go to the church first and then into town to the library and museum, time allowing. We were soon in the car and driving the short distance to the village church, but not before I had tucked the copy journal carefully inside my jacket pocket and fastened the button firmly. Caro watched as I did this, but said nothing, and we soon arrived at the church gates and got out of the car. Agreeing to do the outside first, anti-clockwise from the porch, we immediately came across the massive empty Roman sarcophagus.

'What a strange thing to do, just leaving it open and

empty like that. I wonder what happened to its occupant? What do you know about it?'

'Apparently, very little is known about it, except that it was brought into the churchyard from a much earlier burial ground in the village.'

She walked around it again, examining it carefully, and taking several dozen photographs with her phone.

'Don't look now but I think we're being watched. There's a car on the other side of the railings? Let's just carry on.'

We continued to walk around the church, pointing out items of interest to each other. There were several ancient tabletop tombs and we stopped by the largest one to read the worn, lichen-covered inscription.

William de Clare
Died 31ˢᵗ August 1791
No more to ride this once bold knight
His life he lost but not his fight.

'Do you think that might be your Clare from the notebook?' Caro asked me. 'We don't really know where the journal was written… and Harcourt? Does his family come from the area too?'

'Well, the name's right, and the year, so it's quite possible that it is him. And I do know that Adrian's family have lived in these parts for a long time, because he told me. It's something that he seems to be very proud of. I'd assumed that the journal was local because everything else in the box was, but it doesn't necessarily follow, I suppose.'

* * *

Walking around the back of the church, we eventually arrived at the other side of the porch, now unseen by the car occupant. We studied the ancient tomb of the couple, laid together with what looked like a blanket covering their lower bodies.

'The vicar said that a few parishioners call this one "The Lovers," but no one seems to know much about it, and there isn't anything in the church records either, which is odd, since they go back further than the tomb does. It's medieval though, early fourteenth century, I believe. This type of thing is usually inside a church, not out in the graveyard.

I told her more about the possible meaning of being under a blanket in burial terms, but that this made little sense with the man by her side.

'I've never seen anything even remotely similar, and like you, I've visited hundreds of churches all over the world… what a bizarre thing.'

We walked into the church porch, and she immediately noticed the unusual inscriptions and graffiti written on the massive old door and more photographs were taken.

'What do you make of them, Caro?'

'You're the linguist, but I can see EL written several times, which was one of the Hebrew names for God, of course. I find the number eleven much more interesting though. It's been engraved in multiple places on the door, and is symbolic in many ways if taken to be the number two as well. We can talk about it when we get back.'

Inside, we studied the beautiful font and noticed more pairs of number ones, some surrounded by a square. There was also a considerable amount of beautifully engraved 'tree of life' designs inside the lead liner. They were graffiti, of course, but it was hard to call them that when they were so well executed. The crossover between paganism and Christianity fascinated me, as did things like numerology, even more so when all jumbled together in this way.

Continuing to wander around, we eventually reached the relic copies of Jesus in the lit-up glass cabinet. Caro stared in awe, which I could quite understand. Once again, she took more photos, including some of the unusual vine-covered piscina, with a man's head looking out from an empty cave, and the castellated tower on top.

'Again, I've never seen anything like it. What's that notch on his chin? I can't quite work it out, and have you noticed how many *Hel Eyes of Fire* there are scratched into the stone everywhere?'

'You mean the squares divided into four triangles? Yes, I did notice them. I assume you mean *Hel* the Norse Goddess? As for the notch, it baffled me too.'

'Yes, the goddess of the underworld and the dead. This symbol, *The Eye of Fire*, is supposed to mean that she could see the truth and nothing could be hidden from her. I've seen it elsewhere, but never so many in one place. Of course, there are constant belief crossovers here, as in any old church: Roman, ancient Briton, Saxon, Viking, Norman, and so on. Symbols used to be so important in expressing views or ideas. For many people, it was the only tool they had. We take language, literacy, and freedom of speech so much for granted now, don't we?'

I agreed, and finishing our tour, we headed back to the car; the man who had been watching us now nowhere to be seen. We drove into town, parking in the market place.

CHAPTER FIFTEEN

'Do you mind if I go off and do a bit of clothes shopping first? You know how hard it is to buy anything decent near home in France, and I doubt if you want to traipse around clothes stores with me.'

'I don't mind at all. I'll go to the library and wait for you there.'

The librarian helped me to find what I needed, and I was soon ensconced in a quiet corner, the books open in front of me. The families that I was most interested in were the Harcourts and the de Clares. It didn't take long to find the Harcourts. They appeared to have lived in the region for some time, and their connections to the Knights Templar came up several times within a few minutes of reading. The origins of the family seem to have been either from Normandy or Scandinavia, and their involvement with royalty was well documented, as well as their titles of lord, sir, and earl. Both origins seemed plausible.

The most recent manor attributed to them was in a village a few miles away from where I lived, although if it was the building I thought, it had been converted into apartments some time ago. That village had its own church too, which might explain why I had found no

Harcourts in the graveyard where de Clare was. Looking in Debretts Peerage, I checked any titles still given to the family. Adrian, the only Harcourt I knew, was indeed afforded the title of 'honourable' and it came as no surprise that he currently lived about a mile from his ancient ancestral home.

How odd it all was. If he had reason to believe that a book belonging to his family was missing, then why not just say so? Maybe it was to do with the 'secret' written about? If knowing about the 'secret' put me in danger, as he had alluded, then did it put him in danger too?

* * *

I moved on to the de Clares. This proved to be a little more difficult. There were plenty of de Clares throughout history, and the Templar links were well documented, but I couldn't clearly identify any in the locality. William de Clare was buried in the churchyard near my cottage, so there was a definite link with the area. I thought for a moment and then picked up another, slightly later, book. My eye ran down the page, until at last I found what I was looking for. William Saint Clair, also referred to as St Clare, and even later, as Sinclair. I should have known that this name had changed considerably throughout the last thousand years, as indeed had the Harcourts. The ancestral pile of the Clares was still partly in existence in the village, but was now a spa and conference centre owned by an American chain.

At this moment, Caro came through the library

doors, laden down with multicoloured bags. I gave the books back to the librarian and helped her with the shopping, which was soon stowed away in the boot of the car.

'That was great fun. I won't need to go clothes hunting for several years. You're so lucky to live near civilisation.'

She paused for a moment and then spoke again.

'Actually, I wouldn't change where I live for anything. It's so deeply a part of me that I don't think I would survive very long without it.'

'You probably would. You'd just adapt, but I know what you mean. My home is in France, not here. Just knowing that means I cope very well with my many temporary abodes. When I feel too disconnected, I just pop back for a few weeks, and then I'm fit to go off on my travels again. What would you like for dinner tonight? Or would you prefer to eat out?'

'I was just thinking about that. Do you know what I would really like more than anything? Chicken cacciatore, like grandmother used to make on the open fire. I dream about it, I swear. Can you make it?'

'Of course, I can make it, although on a gas stove, not a huge open fireplace that can sit six people in it.'

It was a robust Italian dish, made with tomatoes, onions, mushrooms, olives, herbs, and red wine, and we walked to the butchers at the other end of the High Street to buy the chicken.

'Stay there, Benoît – I'll be back in a minute'.

She dashed off across the street. I chatted briefly to

the butcher as he packed up the meat, and then waited for her outside. She appeared some ten minutes later, holding another shopping bag.

'Don't look now, but Black Coat is still following… how very odd. How do you cope with it?'

I shrugged. 'Just ignore him. As you know, it went on for several years when I was in Italy, and I barely gave it a thought in the end. I'm worried about you, though. You shouldn't be involved at all.'

Now nearly half past one, we once again put the shopping in the car and walked back over the road to a café above an antique shop. Ordering a sandwich and coffee apiece, we sat by the window, watching the people in the street below. I told Caro about my research from the library, agreeing to talk more once back at the cottage. The visit to the museum would have to wait.

* * *

It was gone four by the time we were back, and the car emptied. After locking the door and putting the kettle on, Caro presented me with a large, cardboard box, tied up with a blue satin ribbon. I didn't think that anything had been wrapped like that since the fifties, but was surprised and very pleased with the soft, camel-coloured cashmere dressing gown inside.

'Thank you so much. It's beautiful and will be perfect for the winters here.'

'Well,' she explained, 'I saw your old threadbare one on the back of the bathroom door. I remember your mother buying it for your twenty-first birthday. By all means, keep it for sentimental reasons, but really, Benoît, you're a wealthy man. You don't need to go around looking like a tramp.'

I resented the tramp allusion, and the accusation that I 'go around' in my dressing gown, since no one sees it but me. However, I was grateful, and thanked her again. I knew that I needed a new one, and had even turned the corner of a page in a catalogue, but that was it. As for my being wealthy, truthfully it was something I rarely thought about. Caro had been left large sums of money and property by her parents too, but, like me, this fact was concealed from others. Money often changed people and usually not for the better. However, it was good to know that I would never starve, and could support myself well if I needed to.

She proceeded to show me the clothes and other things that she had bought for herself, before taking them upstairs to squash into her suitcase. We had barely sat down with a strong cup of Lapsang, when there was a loud knocking at the door. I dragged myself from the chair, and when I opened it, peeking through the gap left by the security chain, was very surprised to see the bishop standing there.

CHAPTER SIXTEEN

✎

'My dear Benoît,' he greeted me. 'I'm so sorry to disturb you when you are having time off, but I wanted to have a word.'

'It isn't a problem at all – do come in. It's rather humble I'm afraid.'

Despite our friendship, and me knowing full well that his name was August Dillon, I had always called him 'Bishop.' Neither of us minded this and so it had stuck. He had never been to the cottage as I had always driven to Oxford to meet him. I led him into the tiny sitting room and introduced him to Caro.

'Bishop, meet Caro, my cousin. We grew up together. She's popped over from France for a few days. Caro, this is Bishop August.'

'Ben, if you had ever seen the house that I grew up in, you would hardly apologise for your delightful cottage. There were eight of us in a one roomed shack on a hillside. Humble wasn't the word for it, I can assure you, and Caro, my dear, do please call me August. My parents lacked imagination when it came to names, and we were all called after the month we were born in. One of my brothers was called September, but we soon shortened that to Seb! I've come on a fool's mission, I fear, but it was worth it just to meet you.'

'It's an amazing name! Ben often speaks about you… it's wonderful to meet you at a last.'

'Do sit down, Bishop. Would you like tea? We were drinking Lapsang, but I know it's not everyone's favourite.'

'I love it, so yes please. Now, let me tell you why I'm here.'

'Let me guess. You've received word that I am entertaining women, am a gigolo, and need to be defrocked and thrown out of the Roman Catholic Church. Is that somewhere close? As you can see, there are no women here, only Caro.'

'Spot on. Ludicrous of course, and I did remember that you had a cousin you were close to, but I was driving through on my way to Gloucester, so thought I would pop in.'

'Watch it, Benoît. I might not be a woman in your eyes, just the tomboy you roamed the mountains with, but I am one, nonetheless, and I'm not too old to give you a good thump either.'

The bishop roared at this and I left them to it whilst I went to make more tea. He had never mentioned his living in poverty when he was a child. Obviously, I knew he was Irish, and that he had several sisters and brothers, but that was about it. Of course, he didn't know everything about my childhood either. However, I was intrigued, and intended to ask him about it again in the future if the opportunity arose.

We chatted about various things for a while, he and Caro becoming engrossed in a discussion about Ireland in the Middle Ages, and I sat back and listened. It was now six-thirty, and I wondered if the bishop would like to eat with us. I asked him.

'But, Benoît, I wouldn't want to be a nuisance. You probably don't have enough food anyway, and I fear that I've ruined your evening already.'

'Bishop, there's enough for half a dozen people so no worries on that score. We'd love to have you.'

He seemed delighted, and made a quick call to his driver, advising him of a later pick-up time. Caro went into the kitchen coming out with two bottles of wine.

'A surprise,' she said. The bishop and I looked at the labels; Lacryma Christi, one red, and one white.

'Where did you get that?' we both said at the same time. 'It's so hard to get hold of over here.'

The bishop had also spent many years in Italy, several of them in Naples, and was as keen on good and unusual wine as I was. Lacryma Christi was made from grapes grown on the slopes of Vesuvius, and the name quite literally translated to 'Tears of Christ.'

'I know,' she answered. 'I couldn't believe it when I saw it. He only had a few cases, and I knew you would want them, so I bought the lot. He said to give him a ring, and he'll deliver them when it suits.'

'What a surprise! Thank you so much. We'll talk about money later.'

I knew I would have a battle on my hands to be allowed to pay, and went to fetch the best crystal glasses, of which there were now only four. I had moved so much, and each time I did, another one seemed to get broken. Opening the red bottle, I left it to breathe for a few minutes, and put the white one in the fridge. The bishop carefully poured the rich, blood-coloured wine.

'Cin cin, salute.'

'Now, if you'll excuse me, I'm going to start dinner.'

'Carry on, Benoît,' said Caro, raising her glass. 'I always wanted a private chef!'

As I pottered about in the kitchen, I could hear them both talking animatedly. They certainly seemed to have hit it off, and I was happy enough to be cooking on my own, without any distractions. I had decided to do rosemary potatoes and green beans as an accompaniment, and began to prepare them, as well as laying the kitchen table. The one in the living room had books and papers on it, and anyway, it was easier to eat in here.

'Need a hand, Ben?' Caro shouted from the sitting room, with the glibness of one who had no intention of helping at all. I went through to chat to them for a while, although they were now deep in discussion about the vandalism perpetrated by the Victorians towards ancient churches.

Back in the kitchen, I finished things off, and then called to them.

'Come on then you two… it's ready.'

'Benoît, this is stupendous. I rarely eat proper food like this, and it's such a treat, I can't tell you. Thank you so much for asking me.'

I was reminded that the life of a priest could be a

93

solitary one, even if you were a bishop, and resolved to ask him over to eat in the future, perhaps inviting Peter and Merry at the same time.

'I nearly forgot,' said the bishop. 'Have you heard from Adrian Harcourt?'

'A few days ago… why?' Not more intrusion from Adrian. Really, I had gone from seeing or hearing from the man once a month, to almost every day.

'Well, it appears he's gone missing. He was supposed to attend a meeting about the renovation of the local churches here, and didn't turn up. One of the wardens phoned his housekeeper, and she went over to see if he was OK. I believe he injured his back some time ago falling off some scaffolding? Anyway, he wasn't in the house, although his car was there. He doesn't have any very close neighbours, and his aunt who lives nearby said she hadn't seen him for days. I'm sure he'll turn up. Probably some business thing or other, but do let me know if you hear from him, won't you? And I forgot to say that there was a man in a white car outside your house when I came in. Gave me a look like he was chewing lemons – a phrase of my grandmother's. When I used the bathroom an hour ago, I opened the window and he was still there. Did you see him?'

I got up to look outside. I did, of course, know who it was likely to be, but how could I tell the bishop that I was being followed by an Italian who might be the Mafia, because I had good reason to believe that Jesus wasn't crucified after all, had a family, and was exiled instead? The poor man would probably pass out in shock.

'There isn't anyone there now. Probably someone who was lost or something.'

As I made coffee, Caro disappeared and came back with a large box of handmade chocolates that she had bought whilst I was in the butchers. She offered one to the bishop.

'It's a good job I don't come here on a regular basis. I wouldn't fit in the confessional and there would be plenty to confess to, the main thing being gluttony.'

We all laughed. I had noticed as the evening had worn on that the bishop's soft Irish accent had become much more pronounced. It suited him, and added to the general attractiveness of the man.

There was a soft rapping at the door.

'Ah, that will be Declan, my driver. I can't thank you enough for having me tonight. The food was excellent, and I've enjoyed myself so much. Caro, the next time you're here you must come to Oxford, and I'll take you both out. Let me know if you hear from Adrian, Benoît?'

He kissed Caro on both cheeks, and I walked with him to the door.

'God bless, and do take care, won't you? Call if you need anything – anything at all.'

'Of course, and you're very welcome to drop in, any time… we've really enjoyed your company. Have a safe trip.' Once again, he seemed to be concerned for my safety and well-being. It was very odd, and left me feeling uneasy.

* * *

I closed the door, and we both went into the kitchen to clear up, maintaining our usual childhood places, with me washing and Caro wiping.

'What a charming man. I'd no idea you had such wonderful friends. And that lovely Irish accent? If he wasn't a priest, I might find myself interested. The world is so short of decent men, you know.'

I pondered on this statement for a moment. It was sad that she had never found a partner to share her life with and have a family. My own desire for this had been fleeting, and was never really part of my 'grand plan,' not that I'd ever really had one of those either.

'What did you make of Harcourt going missing? He'll probably turn up, but what if he doesn't? What do you think has happened to him?'

'No idea, but I hope that he'll stay away for the foreseeable future.'

'What do you know about him?'

'The bishop asked me that too. Not a lot really… he had a successful renovation company, not cottages, but castles and cathedrals, and he broke a few vertebrae after some scaffold collapsed. He sold up, is a rich man, does lots of charitable work including helping the Church, and I'm told he still has some business interests.

'Oh, and one more thing, he paints beautiful Icons. I nearly ordered one, thinking it would be a few hundred quid, but he wanted three thousand pounds! I'd rather buy an old one if I was going to hand over that much. He's divorced, with no children that he's ever mentioned. I nearly forgot – I saw him speak briefly with Black Coat when I was sitting outside a café in Oxford. They then went off in different directions. It was only later though, that I realised that the same Black Coat was following me.'

She thought for a moment. 'The whole thing sounds very odd, and I certainly wouldn't trust the man like you all seem to have done. Still, I'm glad that he's disappeared and not you. I mean, we don't know what pies he has fingers in, and he sounds dodgy to me, but you're the one who read the parchments and has the journal. Of course, you also have Black Coat, which may have kept any trouble at bay. Maybe he hasn't disappeared at all, and is just having a break somewhere. Perhaps we're making too many assumptions.'

Later, in bed, I thought about the bishop. He seemed to have enjoyed the evening and Caro had certainly taken to him, but I was still left with a residue of unease. He had never come to the house before, and even if complaints had been made about my cohabiting with a woman, surely he could have just rung? On the rare occasions when my mother used to talk about her time with my father in the Resistance during the Second World War, she often spoke of instinct.

'L'instinct est tout Benoît,' she would say. 'Instinct is everything, and you would do well to remember this in your life.'

She would look very serious as she said it, and shake her finger at me to emphasise her words. If she was right, then what was my instinct telling me? That the bishop was 'dodgy,' as Caro might have put it? And, if he was, why?

CHAPTER SEVENTEEN

By eight the following morning I was showered and dressed. Luckily, I only needed four or five hours sleep a night, which had caused my parents considerable angst when I was young. When Caro came down twenty minutes later, we drank coffee and talked.

'Do you want to go anywhere today? I'm happy to take you wherever you like.'

'Not really, Benoît. Let's stay here and go through some of the photos I took of the village church and look at Harcourt's diary again.'

I asked her to go and get my copy of the journal from my jacket hanging up in the small lobby by the front door, whilst I switched on my laptop ready to upload the photos.

'Ben,' she called. 'It's not there. Did you say your jacket? The black one? All the pockets are empty.'

I got up and went through to the lobby to check for myself. I put my hand into the inside pocket, which was where it had been last night. She was right – it was empty.

'It was definitely there when we got back from town yesterday, because I remember feeling for it when I took my jacket off and hung it up.'

'It's gone, hasn't it? There were only the two of us here yesterday, and then the bishop in the evening.'

'Exactly.'

'You don't really think he took it? How could he have known about it at all? You only told Adrian, and I thought the bishop didn't know him very well? I suppose it's also possible that someone knew that the journal was in that box, but believed it to be junk and of little value. Maybe they bragged or joked about selling it, or maybe just told someone that they had given it, and other things, to the sale?'

'They're all possible, I suppose.' I remembered my unease the previous evening regarding the bishop's visit and comments when he left. I was also worried for Caro's safety, especially now the copy journal had been stolen, and told her so. Today was Friday, and my last full day off. Tomorrow I had a few visits to make and a meeting to attend. On Sunday, I had an early mass to take for a priest who was away. Caro's flight back to France was in the afternoon and I had to make sure she was safe until then.

Rummaging around in the curtains, I pulled out the scans hidden in the hem, and then heard her muttering.

'Benoît, le paysan.'

'It's a good job I am a peasant, isn't it? At least I still have these copies and the ones in the bank vault.'

Having uploaded the photographs onto both laptops, we made more coffee and sat down at the table to look at them. If this was William de Clare's local church, and he was from a line of Templar knights still actively involved

99

in keeping secrets, as the journal suggested, then there may well be clues in the church about what the secret was. The Templar connections to many of the churches in this region were well documented, and they were renowned for their squirrelling away of gold, relics, treasures, and documents, as well as the holding of secrets.

Putting the photos in groups, firstly, we looked at the tomb of William de Clare. The inscription was an interesting one and seemed to confirm his status as a 'knight' of sorts, with a 'battle' on his hands. Making notes, we moved on to the Roman tomb with the lid off, brought at some time in its history into the churchyard. Where was the occupant? Had he been stolen or moved for some reason? It was a massive structure and would most certainly have held someone of considerable status or wealth.

'Ben, do you remember when I said that I had noticed something, but the man in the car was watching us? Well, if you look here you can see a small Templar-style cross. It's clear enough, but in a dip in the stone, so you don't see it unless you are at a certain angle. There are several of them. Obviously, they wouldn't have been on the tomb when it was first made, but it's possible that the Templars may have had something to do with the moving of it or its occupant. And one more thing, on the inside near the top you can just make out 'HIC SITUS EST.' That's very common in Roman tombs. It simply means 'He lies here.' The name of the person is usually above it, but it looks like that's been chiselled off.'

* * *

Moving into the church, I took quite a few photos of the *Hel Eye of Fire* symbols, the square with the four triangles inside. The goddess of the underworld and overseer of the dead, meaning that nothing can be hidden and that truth will always be seen – to those that are looking for it, anyway.

'In numerology, the square is **22**: the master builder, and representative of immense and unlimited power; great ascendancy, a bridge between humanity and the divine, and symbolically, of the cross. I've often wondered if the origins of **22** as a master builder came from ancient Egypt.'

'How so?'

'Well, they were often referred to as the race of master builders, and used numbers amongst many other things to understand the world around them. Anyway, back to *Hel*…

'It's all very neat and tidy, since $2 + 2 = 4$, the four sides of a square, and four triangles inside it, four symbolising truth. In runic symbolism, commonly used by the Norse tribes, the **22**nd rune, Ing or Ingwaz, is representative of the square, as well as the Holy Grail, which is particularly interesting when in a church. It all sounds like a rather clever puzzle. The triangles inside the square also symbolise the trinity or, in more humanistic terms, a man, a woman, and their offspring – a child.'

CHAPTER EIGHTEEN

I moved a bit closer to study the photos carefully.

'The graffiti on the door is really interesting too – look at this. At first, I thought it was LH, but when I looked at it carefully, I decided it was LII. Roman numerals. Fifty-two in English. I wracked my brains and came up with a couple of things. Firstly, in numerology, the number seven, which is what they add up to, is symbolic of the seeker of truth, spiritual awakening, the occult, and alchemy. But then I thought of the Bible, and Psalm 52. I might not believe in God but I was taught at the same school as you, and know it well enough. Devilish tongues, deceit, and evil, if I remember correctly.'

'When did you do all of this?'

'Last night. I couldn't sleep for an hour or two.

'And there's "Then their eyes were opened" Luke 24:31. That's a number one in numerological terms. And *Ilan*, also on the door, which is Hebrew for *tree of life* or oak tree. In many beliefs systems, the tree of life symbolises immortality, truth, fertility, mother earth with the roots, and father sun with its branches and leaves... very pagan.

'It's the same with the pairs of ones, on the door and in the font. In many faiths and beliefs, it represents duality: man and woman, yin and yang, light and dark, truth and lies, good and bad, not forgetting the Cathars, with their dualistic faith. There are various quotes, biblical and others, saying something like "A man and woman though two in number are made one in marriage." It's a good fit to the symbolism, especially in a church. There are quite a few mentions in the Gospel of Thomas too, about one becoming two, and two becoming one.'

'That's true, and some of it looks so deliberate, doesn't it? Like this one on the door? Tho II. That could be Thomas verse two?'

Let one who seeks not stop seeking until one finds
When one finds one will be troubled
When one is troubled one will marvel
And will reign over all.

It sounded somewhat appropriate to our situation. To keep searching for the truth was such a human trait, and the Gospel of Thomas was a favourite of mine. It never failed to intrigue, inspire, and give me hope, and a copy of it lay permanently on my bedside table.

We looked at more photos of the font, covered entirely in graffiti, some clearly just initials, and others much more curious, with beautifully etched vines and trees of life, done with considerable skill. There were many more pairs of ones, some set inside a square.

'The whole thing is intriguing, and needs a lot more research. I keep wondering about who might be responsible for the graffiti? Initials, dates, and things like masons' marks are very common – most churches have them – but these are much more unusual. It certainly wouldn't have been just the local peasants having a go when the priest wasn't looking.'

She moved along a few pictures, showing the many carved stone crosses.

'There are Templar crosses everywhere. Even though they may not be in their original setting, they can't be ignored. I've never seen so many in one church. It's just occurred to me, but depending on the reference source, the Templar knights were originally founded in 1118, its first order consisting of eleven men? Plenty of ones there, and a numerological 11 if you add them up.'

'You're right. And the relics of Jesus… they're very early. It wouldn't surprise me if they were even slightly earlier than the date stated, and someone certainly went to a lot of trouble to bring the whole thing here in the first place. There's something like it in the Auvergne. I took a group of students there once, but it's nowhere near as good as this one.'

* * *

'The green man piscina… it's covered in leaves and vines, but he doesn't look like any green man I've ever seen before. In fact, I'm sure it isn't a green man at all. It's a man's head looking out of a cave with a two-tiered tower on top of it, covered with vines. We're back to fertility: life blood and blood lines. Jesus supposedly said, "I am the vine."'

'I definitely agree about him not being a green man, but what do you make of the indent on his chin? Perhaps there was something attached there at one time, like a beard? Or perhaps whoever the head represents had a cleft chin? It's really baffling me.'

I watched her as she pondered for a moment. She started to pull at her bottom lip with her thumb and forefinger, just as she had done when she was perturbed as a child. She had been told off for it constantly, but it had never stopped her.

'That's it; I've got it!' she shouted, giving herself a somewhat vicious slap on the head in a typically Italian gesture. I had seen it hundreds of times when I had lived there, but she had been particularly brutal, and I momentarily wondered if she had injured herself.

'What the hell... Caro, are you alright?'

'What an idiot... it's so obvious. It's a carved keyhole. I knew I should know what it was. It seemed so familiar, but was just out of context – and it's not on the chin at all, but in the mouth. The keyhole is in the sealed open mouth, completely blocking it. Look Benoît, look!' She was almost shouting by this time, and was very excited.

'There is a secret, I'm sure of that now, although I've no idea who the man actually was. He could be an incumbent, a monk or abbot, a local lord or crusading knight, or even someone who was several of those. He's saying, "my mouth is sealed." Or perhaps more than that: "you will need to find the key to the secret." And there's a cave under a two-tiered castle or tower. And, under that, water. The water from the piscina translating to a pool of water or cistern of some sort. But where? If we stick to Harcourt's diary, it could be here, I suppose, or possibly France, which was where he said de Clare was. We need to look at it again.' She had become quite agitated, and began to pace around the small room.

'Lastly, we mustn't forget the medieval tomb of the couple with their bodies covered by a blanket. It's important, since most couples don't have a statue carved of themselves lying in bed and then put it in a public place. The symbolism is so blatant it almost shouts it out.'

'I think I can do this part,' I replied. 'The cover being turned down is a revelation; a literal uncovering. It shows a certain intimacy, or joining, with both lying there like that. They might shout "Our eyes are uncovered; we can see! Can you?"'

'I agree, and I can't help thinking of the secret that Harcourt wrote about. There's one more thing. There's a sealed-up room in the tower. I read about it. But why? There must be a reason for it being sealed.'

'Peter told me about it too. We could ask him.'

'Maybe, but let's keep it to ourselves for now. I think that the less people we involve the better. And one more thing – I'm starving. What's for lunch?'

'I'll make some sandwiches.'

Caro followed me through to the kitchen. 'What I find so fascinating is the thought of a story being told in so many ways, over different time periods and using different symbolic and belief references. It's like the church has been used as some sort of 3D book, and why not, I suppose? It was already being used to record other important details, like births, deaths, and marriages.'

CHAPTER NINETEEN

'So where do we go from here, Ben? I'm almost more excited by the notebook and church than the parchments. I'm still wondering about any possible connections between the two, although I can't see how that could be.'

I had been fairly quiet so far, taking in everything she had said. She was a smart woman, as well as a vastly experienced historian. It would be foolish not to listen to an opinion like hers.

'OK, let's sum things up. Firstly, there are the parchments which speak for themselves. The Italian assured me they weren't fakes, and I think I believe him. I imagine there would be plenty of people who would want to get their hands on them if they could, and there's no way that he's the only person who knows of their existence. That puts him in danger and, by proxy, me, because I've seen them.

'Then there's the journal found quite by chance in a box of junk from a jumble sale. Enter Adrian Harcourt. He wants to get his hands on it, but apart from giving me a warning of danger, he won't say why. The cottage was broken into, probably by him, but nothing stolen. There's Black Coat following me, but I'm assuming the Italian has something to do with that. I don't understand why Black Coat spoke briefly with Adrian in Oxford, though. The copy journal has now gone missing, most likely stolen by the bishop, who I thought was my friend. The parchments might be of interest to him, but how could he have known about the journal? And, finally, the local church seems to be holding some mysterious secret from the past, possibly linked to the journal, which alludes to connections with France during its last civil war.'

'Your summing up almost covers it, apart from the parchments. I'm getting that déjà vu feeling, cousin of mine! I think we've been here before, haven't we? I know we've been skating around the issue for years, but perhaps it would be best if we just faced it?'

I looked at the clock. It was nearly three in the afternoon, and I felt exhausted. I decided to make a strong cup of tea first and take a breather for a few minutes. I reached to open the kitchen window, which was at the front of the cottage. The white car was parked up on the verge outside with Black Coat in it, and he appeared to be working on a small laptop perched on the steering wheel. It was overcast and windy, and I allowed the fresh, clean air to blow into the kitchen, inhaling deeply.

I carried the tea and a plate of Italian biscotti back through to the living room. I knew exactly what she was referring to, and reflected for a moment as she flicked through the copies of the parchments and the journal, and studied the photographs again.

* * *

My parents' and grandparents' house, now my own, was part of the ancient Château of Antugnac; now almost unrecognisable as a château, but of great importance in its heyday. There were huge vaulted cellars underneath, believed to be much older than the building now standing, which itself dated back to the thirteenth century. The cellars had small passages running between them that would come to sudden dead ends, blocked up many years ago, for reasons that were now unknown.

An ancient church stood behind the house, with remains of earlier buildings beneath its stone floor. I supposed that it was quite likely that there would have been a passage or two going up and into the church; in fact, there appeared to be several that headed in that direction. There was even one that sloped downwards towards the river, also blocked off by rough-hewn pieces of stone. As was usual when one was used to something, and indeed when it was fairly commonplace, my family took little notice of the remarkable cellars, which would make most historians of today very excited indeed.

We stored our wine down there in terracotta racks against the wall of the first cellar. Often a large ham would hang from a hook in the ceiling, and strings of onions occasionally, but our terrace was too small to grow anything, and my grandparents were too elderly to bother with the plot of land they owned on the edge of the village. My parents weren't remotely interested in gardening, so we bought most of our fresh food from neighbours or the local markets. My grandfather kept his boxes of tools in the first cellar, as well as a large pile of dry wood for the fire, and some ancient chairs that used to be on the terrace outside. The cellar next to this had bits of junk in it, things that might 'come in handy' sometime, and other bits of rubbish that would never come in handy but were kept there anyway.

There was no electric light in the cellar, but an oil lamp hung on a hook in the wall, and several stumps of candles were usually placed about with boxes of matches nearby. It wasn't particularly damp but smelt ancient and dusty, and was a magnet to two very inquisitive children with active imaginations, namely Caro and myself. On very hot summer days, which in that region could reach 40°C, it was a haven of coolness and endless amusement. We would set up the deckchairs, play cards and other games, drink cold squash, and sometimes tell each other ghost stories, which usually meant we would be back upstairs very quickly. No one minded, and if we had been missing for a while this would be the first port of call to find us.

* * *

We were thirteen when it happened. The day was blisteringly hot, the sky almost bleached white by the sun, and we went downstairs with our usual iced drinks and games. We were both restless and roamed around the cellars adding to our map drawn on the wall of the different rooms and blocked passages, giving each one a name. I then went to fetch two of my grandfather's chisels, and we slowly began to scrape out the soft, sandy mortar between the blocks of stone at one of the passage ends; the one that was at the highest point and facing in the direction of the church. We had been doing this for some months now, after reading a few of the 'Famous Five' books brought back, once again, from my parents' travels.

The passage was low, five feet high at most, and as we worked we chatted about what might be on the other side. I favoured skeletons, Caro treasure, and we planned our futures in this way for hours. Finally, we reached the point where several of the stones were loose, and we eased them out with a small crowbar. Lighting a few more candles, we crawled through the dust and dirt, emerging into another cellar room, much smaller than those beneath the actual house, but with a vaulted ceiling and what looked like a small stone altar at one end. A few half-rotten sacks lay on the hard floor, but it wasn't until we held the candles closer to the walls to look for a door that we saw the paintings and etchings. They were everywhere.

Caro spoke first, her voice almost a whisper. 'Who do you think has been down here doing this? It must have been a long time ago, because the room was closed off.'

'No idea, but it must have taken ages. Perhaps they were prisoners? I'm sure this passage leads to the church, so they could have been monks, I suppose.'

We held our candles up to the walls to look more closely. On the left wall were several scenes of boats on a choppy sea with five people in them: two men, two women, and a child – all with halos. We were both at a Catholic school and knew full well that we were seeing religious scenes. We had also seen enough locally by way of statues, paintings, and churches, to guess that many of the pictures were of Jesus and Mary. This was not surprising to us as children. We lived in a religious, mostly Catholic country, and with Rennes-le-Château nearby, and its many mysteries, we were used to it.

Directly in front of us were several images of a woman in red robes and it was obvious to us that this was Mary Magdalene, holding a golden jar and with the usual halo. There was another of a boat scene with two men in it sailing out to sea – two women and child standing on the shore.

The front wall showed two men set against a green hill scene, a tall tower at its top. Both had staffs supporting them as they walked. Near that was a painting of what looked like a side view into a narrow cave or tomb. A man lay in it, still with a halo and his eyes wide open. There were various mountain and hill scenes, some looking very local, some much too lush to be from the south of France. One hill scene showed a village at its top, easily recognisable as Rennes-le-Château, a bright sun overhead and many more variants of suns between the larger paintings. The initials C.D. were written in each corner.

The walls to the right and left showed numerous depictions of two knights on horseback, one with a long brown box, lit up with beams of light. The same box was shown again in a boat sailing on another choppy sea, between two strips of land. Several more were of Jesus and Mary together, looking regal and serene, with crowns and halos; the ever-present jar making Mary easy to identify.

All the walls had Templar-style crosses and bees, randomly placed. Finally, around the edges of each wall were symbols of alchemy, astronomy and Roman numerals: ones, twos, fours, and keys; lots of keys, keyholes, and padlocks, painted in black and gold. The blocked entrance was quite clear from inside the room, and at its top was a triangle wound around with vines. In the centre was a crown, a large letter S transposed over it, and written below *Amor Vincit Omnia*: Love Conquers All.

To us, it was like the inside of an ornately painted church, of which there were many in the region. Whilst it was an exciting find, it wasn't the skeletons or treasure that we had been hoping for.

CHAPTER TWENTY

Caro's voice brought me back from my reverie.

'Do you remember when your mother came in? She was like someone possessed.'

'How could I forget?'

It had happened a few weeks after our initial discovery. We had decided to copy the paintings and were in the decorated cell, candles lit, happily drawing and chatting. We heard our names being called, scrabbled to our feet, and were just crawling out of the hole we had made in the wall when my mother marched around the corner. She was furious, dragged us to our feet, and slapped us both very hard, so hard, in fact, that I fell back down onto the dusty floor. She then pushed us in front of her, through the passages and other cellar rooms and back up the stairs to the salon.

'She was so angry.'

Back upstairs, my grandparents tried to calm her down, but she would have none of it. She made us swear to tell no one about the painted room and said that we would go to hell if we did. It was such an odd threat, since neither she nor my father were churchgoers, so surely didn't believe in hell.

'I've never been as terrified as I was on that day, not

ever, in the whole of my fifty-five years. She sent you home, do you remember? They disappeared for several months after that, and for the first time, I was glad they were gone. I even hoped that they would never come back.'

Within a few days, the cellar entrance had been blocked up, and we never went down there again. I didn't even know what had happened to our painting books. It hadn't stopped us talking about it though, and we had spent many weeks going over what we had seen, and trying to make sense of it. Now that the house was mine, I could, of course, open the cellars up again but so far, anyway, I hadn't felt inclined to do so. As an adult, I knew full well what I had seen, and so did Caro.

'It still really upsets you, doesn't it? It does me too, but not so much. Your mother's reaction was so odd and out of character. She was usually such a controlled woman. It feels like that whole unhappy episode has come back to haunt us. Or maybe we should look at it another way. Not to haunt us, but for us to accept and make peace with after all these years?'

'I don't know… maybe.'

'I've been doing a lot of research back home for a book I'm putting together. I suppose I'm rehashing most of the stuff we'd discovered before we went off to university, although I have come across a few new things. Do you remember that summer, Ben?'

'I remember it very well.' We had spent our last summer trawling around the hills and villages, putting together an enormous amount of information about the

115

history of the area going back thousands of years. We had researched in considerable detail the various myths, legends, and facts regarding treasure buried in the region by the Romans, Visigoths, Carolingians, Franks, Cathars, Templars, and everyone else in between. We had compiled a huge dossier on the local churches, the priests that worked in them, and the always-present, subliminal messages about Jesus and Mary Magdalene. They refused to be silenced entirely, and the often unspoken beliefs of many people in the area that they had both been here bubbled under the surface constantly, like all unspoken things did.

We knew the area very well, better than almost anyone except for a few elderly men who had lived here all their lives, and age was beginning to shut down their memories and voices. We knew all the villages, mountains, and hills, with their caves and grottos, and we knew each stream and river. We had spent our entire lives until then roaming around, often leaving the house at dawn and not returning until dusk.

'Your language skills were brilliant, even back then. Do you remember the notebooks we made, full of alchemical, Teutonic, kabbalah, Celtic, and other symbols, and their meanings? I've still got them all, you know.'

'That was the year that you decided, categorically, that you didn't believe in God, and voiced it quite clearly to the priest, which didn't go down very well. His face went so red that I thought he was going to have a stroke.'

She laughed. 'I remember! It was always harder for

you, wasn't it? I saw things in a very black and white way back then. Either something was true or it wasn't. In my early days as a historian, it was something I had to battle with constantly, since the word "truth" is an oxymoron in history to say the least. Even as a young boy you engaged with things differently... made meanings differently. Your love of, and I might say, obsession, with Jesus as a person, was always there.

'I wondered at one time if you were gay, and your fear of expressing this and the reaction it might have had at home turned you towards him as a way of expressing that desire. Gosh, Ben, I'm talking a lot. Sorry. I think I'm worried about you, that's all. This could all turn very nasty. It seems like it already has, through no fault of your own. And yet the whole thing is intriguing and fascinating, and anyway I'm involved now, so we're in it together.'

* * *

She reached over for the copied transcripts and pulled out the ones from the journal. I knew what she was going to say and told her so.

'I think I know what you're going to say Caro – it's the French connection, and of course I've seen it. The dates in the journal, the French Revolution, Abbé B at R, and movements between A and R.'

She nodded her head and let me carry on.

'Abbé Bigou, Rennes-le-Château – Antugnac and Rennes-le-Château. It's the same old thing, isn't it?'

117

Abbé Bigou was the priest at Rennes-le-Château in the latter part of the eighteenth century, and was frequently cited as being central to the Rennes-le-Château mysteries involving treasure, Jesus and Mary, and the Holy Grail.

'We seem to be as deeply entrenched in it now, as we were when we were children, although I'm still baffled as to how all of this this could land up in our laps again. Is that synchronicity? Or do things keep coming back to a person until they're resolved, like Jung said about dreams? Maybe I shouldn't question it so much. Suppression is pointless, since things usually break through in the end, I know that.'

'I'll second it too!'

'Do you remember that time in Paris, when I was walking past a phone booth on the street and it rang? I picked it up, which I wouldn't normally do, and it was you calling to tell me that grandfather was very ill? You had dialled the number of my landlady. I don't know how that happened, but it did... strange things do happen. There is an explanation, I'm sure, but we simply don't understand what it is yet...' I stood up.

'Come on you mad academic. Let's go out and get some dinner. And if we're kidnapped, we must just hope that we have eaten first. We are French, after all!'

Putting on our coats, I opened the door to find the wine delivery man standing there, his finger poised to press the bell. All three of us jumped, then laughed, and I quickly brought the boxes into the house. As expected, Caro had refused any money for it. She said that since we had left everything to each other in our wills, she had, in effect, spent my own money. There was some logic to this, and so I let it go.

I picked up the papers and my laptop, and put them in my leather shoulder bag. Men in France carried these all the time, but it still hadn't quite caught on here in Britain. I slung it across my body, where I intended to keep it for the rest of the evening. If anyone broke in, they would find nothing of value, except perhaps my four remaining wine glasses, and I assumed that they would neither be looking for, nor wanting, these. There was no sign of Black Coat outside and we quickly got into the car and drove off.

* * *

'So, Benoît, where are you taking me?'

'Well, there's supposed to be a really good Indian restaurant in Stroud, which is about forty minutes from here. It's been recommended several times, and I would like to try it. I'm just in the right mood for a spicy curry. Would you like to do that or find somewhere nearer?'

'Ben, I'd love it. I often make a curry at home, but it's never as good as the real thing and it would be nice to see some of the countryside. I hardly know this area at all, but from what I've seen so far, I really like it. I must say, I miss the mountains though, even after just a few days… they're magical. No place like home, eh?'

She was right of course. The mountains of home were magical and majestic, the history of the area seeming to constantly echo around them. They had been

119

witness to so much over the last few thousand years, some of it brutal in the extreme, like the elimination of the Cathars and Templars, who had held such a strong presence in the region. I had heard hundreds of visitors over the years talk about the 'atmosphere,' but it was so difficult to explain. The lure towards one's homeland was a strange phenomenon, but existed nonetheless.

I pointed out places to her as we drove along the tree-lined roads. The fields and hedges were lush and green and bursting with life. One field was full of rabbits, and Caro spotted a deer in the distance. As we sped across the hilltops and an area of common land with stunning views of the valleys below, I began to feel better than at any point that day, and determined to make the evening a happy one.

The inside of the restaurant was arranged in booths, like railway carriages, which made a cosy and intimate area for each set of diners. We ordered our food after taking advice from a friendly waiter called Babu, and sat back to relax with our drinks, chatting about our surroundings as well as one of our usual topics… food, which when it arrived, sizzling and fragrant, was fabulous. It had been a good idea to get out, and we began our drive home, almost dark now, in good spirits.

'I think we've got a tail.'

'It's like being in a movie… I can't believe this is happening. Thinking about it logically, who or what are you in danger from? What are you being protected against? If he is a protector, that is. Black Coat might be on the wrong side for all we know.'

'Well, there's the Italian with the parchments,

whoever he is, Vatican, Mafia, or some other organisation, or maybe he is just a private collector. He might want to kill me now I've seen the documents, but then he said he would protect me. He could have been lying, of course, but I don't think so. I've no reason to say that, but I don't think he is out to get rid of me, not right now, anyway.

'Then there's the journal. Adrian Harcourt is definitely involved, and I don't trust him at all. There's the bishop, although that still feels like an awful thing to say. I'm pretty sure that he took the journal from my pocket, though. Maybe they are both in it together, but if they were, why would the bishop have asked me what I thought of him when I was in Oxford? Surely if they were in it together he would know more about him than I do! And I saw Adrian and Black Coat together, which is a bit confusing. The problem is that I have no idea who knows about the journal, or who knew about it before I bought it. They might have now heard of its existence and want to get their hands on it… and who else might know about the parchments? What would getting rid of me achieve?

'The parchments allude to Jesus being sent away, not crucified, which is a massive thing because Christianity was founded on that story. It doesn't bother me in the slightest, as you know, but it might bother a lot of people if it could be proved. I could almost see the whole world order change because of a revelation like that.'

'I suppose you're right. Stable rational people would be able to see their way through it, but there are plenty of people in the world who are neither of those things.'

She paused for a moment, then continued. 'And have you noticed how many people have tried to minimalize and discredit the stuff at Rennes-le-Château lately? I'm sure some of it is rubbish, but most certainly not all. I suppose there could be any number of people who would rather keep a lid on everything, or perhaps there's money, greed, and blackmail involved? In fact, I'd bet on it!'

At this point we arrived home. Our 'tail' had sped past us and we went into the cottage, and locked and bolted the door securely behind us. My bag was still over my shoulder, and I took it off to empty it of the papers and laptop. We were both tired, and Caro soon went upstairs to bed. Once again, I lay on the couch mulling things over, until I finally fell asleep at around one in the morning.

CHAPTER TWENTY-ONE

I had several visits to do the following morning, and insisted that Caro lock and bolt the door after me, and open it to no-one. She was an independent woman and wasn't used to being told what to do, but she didn't argue, and as I left her I heard the bolts on the door being drawn across. As I started to drive down the road, Peter came around the corner, and I stopped the car and opened the window.

'Morning, Ben, I was going to call you. How are things?'

'Fine, thanks. I've got my cousin staying at the moment.'

'Yes, I'd heard… the village grapevine is very effective. We were wondering if you would both like to have a drink with us tonight, say seven-thirty?'

'I'd love to, and I'm sure she would too, so I shall say yes for both of us. Thank you.'

'Great, I'll see you later then. Off anywhere nice?'

I assured him that my outing was strictly one of routine church affairs, and drove off, a whiff of his aftershave lingering in the car for good measure. I did two visits, one after another, and then drove towards the hospital in town to visit a parishioner who had recently

123

had hip surgery. I stopped quickly at a fruit shop and bought a large bag of grapes and a coffee for myself from the café next door. I phoned Caro from my mobile to check she was OK.

'Hi, Ben, yes, all fine here. Peter called by a few minutes ago. I didn't let him in the house, so don't be cross. He said we were going there later and to call if I needed anything whilst you were out. What a nice man, and he smelt gorgeous too. I'm really looking forward to meeting his wife. Can you buy a bunch of flowers whilst you're out to take with us?'

'OK, but make sure the door is locked, and don't let anyone in, not even the vicar!' I went back into the shop and bought a large bunch of rather unusual roses, which resembled raspberry ripple ice cream, placing them carefully on the back seat of the car. On an impulse, I darted over the road to a very upmarket jeweller and went inside. As a single man, I didn't spend much time in jewellery shops, but my eye was caught immediately by a silver pendant of small descending circles with clear stones in their centres. The top circle was of rose gold, which finished off the whole piece beautifully. It was absolutely Caro, and I bought it straight away. I was very grateful for her company and support over the past few days, and hoped that she would like this small token of thanks, bought with her own money if her analogy was correct.

Ten minutes later, I was at the local hospital. Bill had lived in the area his whole life, as had his ancestors for many generations. He was a lively and interesting bachelor in his early sixties, and I always enjoyed talking to him. He loved history, and had been head of a local grammar school for nearly thirty years until he recently retired. Greeting me warmly, he told me that he hoped to be back home by the end of the week, and asked me to tell him the village news.

'Well, Bill, there's not a lot to tell really.' Not that I can tell you about anyway, I thought. 'I've had a few days off, and spent some time with my cousin. The vicar gave me a guided tour of the parish church, which was fascinating. Have you been in there?'

'Oh, yes, Padre, lots of times. It's a rum place, what with the tombs and Templars and secrets. It's always had a bit of a reputation locally. My mother wouldn't let me go anywhere near it as a child, but I did of course, I just didn't tell her.'

'What do you mean Bill, what sort of reputation?'

'Oh, that it was only just this side of pagan until a few hundred years ago, that there were bodies buried secretly in the night, tombs moved, buried treasure, black magic, alchemy, that sort of thing.'

'Gosh, Bill, I had no idea. What do you think – was any of that true?'

'Well, in history, things like that often have some basis of truth and then the rest is made up, like Chinese whispers. It's an odd place, though, with the weird tombs, graffiti, relics, and the strange piscina. There was an earlier church, and probably something Roman before that. I just find the whole thing fascinating; even talking about it makes me want to go and visit it again.

I will do as soon as I'm up and about. Perhaps we could have a good mooch around together, although I might not be too steady on my feet for a few days.'

I assured him that I would like nothing more. At this point the lunch trolley came around, and I made my farewells and left. It was almost two when I got back to the cottage. Caro had done some tidying up, washing, and ironing, and had also done more research on the village and its surrounding area.

'The phone rang earlier, but when I picked it up it went dead. I did check the number in case it was a shocked parishioner not expecting to hear a woman's voice, but it was number withheld. Sorry.'

I supposed that it was most likely a church-related call and dismissed it from my mind. If it was important, they would call back. I put the flowers in water, and then went back into the sitting room and handed her the present. Opening it carefully, she seemed genuinely thrilled by the necklace, and put it on straight away.

'I love it, thank you so much. It's just the sort of thing I would have chosen for myself.'

'I'm so glad. It's part of a range, so at least I know what to buy you for Christmas and birthdays! I've got a meeting in the next village at six, which won't take any longer than an hour, and then we can walk to the vicarage.'

I had bought a loaf from the village shop and we made sandwiches for a late lunch. I told her what Bill had said about the church.

'That's interesting. Most of these things usually

have some basis of truth, and the alchemy is particularly fascinating. It was a huge part of people's lives centuries ago, although it wasn't always about turning things into gold, well, not in the literal sense anyway. Most of it was about healing sickness, and using herbs and concoctions that brought about chemical reactions, things like that. That was the saddest thing about the witchcraft era, when so many healers and herbalists, usually women, were murdered, and all that knowledge lost. Even things like love, and cooking, and any type of simple transformative process was considered to be alchemy.

'It's one of the things that's always fascinated me about my work. You simply can't apply modern principles and ideas to times past. People thought differently, and their lives were based on ways and knowledge that is lost to us now. It's sad, but it's that obsession with the past that keeps historians going, and all people connected somehow. I've been writing about it in my latest book that I was telling you about. The desire for connection being part of the human condition. After everything that's happened here over the past few days, I feel really fired up to get writing. When are you coming home again, Ben? I want to show you a few things that I've discovered locally.'

'Probably not for a couple of months, but I certainly intend taking a month off around then.' We chatted for a while, and as I got up to go to the meeting I warned her again to lock the door and not let anyone in, no matter who they were. I waited outside until I heard her draw the bolts across, and then set off.

The meeting was quickly dealt with, apart from one awkward moment when I was asked about Adrian Harcourt and his disappearance. I said, quite honestly, that I knew no more about it than they did, but that he had probably gone somewhere on business and forgot to tell anyone.

'Funny things going on around here at the moment, Father. Strangers snooping around for one thing, and there was another break-in last night in the village. It's not good, and the police haven't caught anyone. It's a strange world we're living in, isn't it?'

I agreed – it most certainly was, but for this evening anyway, even if it was a strange one, I drove back to the cottage to pick up Caro. I got my Frenchman's handbag out again, put my laptop and the papers in it, and slung it across my shoulder. Luckily the laptop was a small one, since I would be keeping the bag on for the rest of the evening. I didn't want to take any chances. It was a lovely warm evening, and we enjoyed the walk to the vicarage.

CHAPTER TWENTY-TWO

'What a beautiful garden. It's so different from the Languedoc... most of this wouldn't survive in the heat.'

'The back's super too. I'm sure Peter will show you around... he's very proud of it.'

The door opened, and we were warmly welcomed.

I handed over the flowers and a bottle of my Lacryma Christi, and we sat on the rear terrace with our drinks and dishes of delicious nibbles which Merry had made. We were both hungry since we hadn't yet had any dinner.

'Please – eat the lot. There's plenty more where that came from. I love cooking, you see, it's like an art form for me. Putting the ingredients together and creating something special – it's like alchemy.'

I was a little startled by her use of the word alchemy. It was the third time I had heard it that day, and I told them about my visit to Bill, and what he had said about the church in times past.

'Yes, I've heard similar things too. I can assure you that we haven't taken to grave robbing or witchcraft yet, or turning water to wine, or two pence pieces, which are placed in plenty in the collection bowl on Sunday, into gold. It might be a good thing if I could, though. The ongoing maintenance costs a fortune, and there's never enough money.'

Merry jumped in at this point.

'Oh, Benoît, I almost forgot. I dug out the report that the archaeologist did on the church some years ago, and copied it for you.'

She handed over a sheaf of papers. I might have been mistaken, but I thought I saw a momentary flash of irritation and disapproval on Peter's face as she did so. Caro looked at me questioningly. She had seen it too. He got up.

'Caro, would you like a tour of the garden? I'm creating some new flower beds for the open gardens scheme in a few weeks, which might add a few pounds to the church fabric fund.'

'I'd love to. I like gardening, and have a large plot at home, but I must admit it's becoming a bit of a chore these days.'

We wandered around the beautiful garden, listening to his plans for more trees and shrubs. Back in the house some thirty minutes later, he showed us around the ground floor.

'It's so nice to see original features. So many are stripped out and lost for ever.'

'I know, and it's nice to show them off. We don't get that many people coming in, at least not those that are interested in the house. The cellars underneath are older than the house, and there's a blocked-up passage or two, probably leading to the church. I've always wondered why so many passageways end up being sealed. I would love to be able to nip up to the church in the dry, especially in mid-winter. So many crypts are blocked up too. It makes me think of secrets and hidden things, or else why would they do it? But what secrets, and what hidden things? The mind boggles! Perhaps we should try and open them up? What do you think, both of you?'

Caro picked up this question to answer.

'Sounds like a great idea. I suppose they might have collapsed by now, though. Most old houses in France have cellars beneath them, although they're usually for the storage of food and wine. You know how it is… food and drink first, and everything else after!'

We all laughed at this, and I caught Caro's eye, to thank her with a wink. A quick look at my watch told me that it was nearly nine-thirty. We thanked our hosts for a lovely evening, and Merry kindly handed us a parcel of the remainder of the snacks she had made for us. They both waved as we walked down the lane, and we agreed that it had been a pleasant evening.

'But, Ben, did you see the look of annoyance on Peter's face as Merry handed over the report to you? What on earth was that about?'

'I did notice, yes. It was like he disapproved somehow. Maybe we imagined it? Anyway, I'm starving. Let's go straight into the kitchen and get something to eat. I've got some gnocchi that I bought a few days ago. They only take a few minutes to cook, and I can quickly make up a sauce with other things in the fridge. Does that suit you?'

'Need you ask? I love it.' She poured us a glass of

131

wine apiece and started to set the table. I quickly made up a sauce from various bits and pieces that were in the fridge, including asparagus, ham, cream, and lots of pungent, grated parmesan. Piling the lot into two plates, I poured swirls of truffle oil over the top and we sat down to eat.

'Ben, I have eaten in some of the best restaurants in Paris, and never had anything as wonderful as this. It's fantastic!'

'Thank you. I just love cooking, so it's no hardship. Adding a bit of this and that to create something unique, well… to me, it's like art – if that not too much of a cliché?'

We lapsed into silence as we ate our late dinner, and when we had finished, I took out the remainder of the chocolates to accompany the coffee.

'I'm glad I'm going home tomorrow, but I'll certainly miss the food – and you too, of course.'

'I'm going to the airport with you in the hire car, and then I'll get a train back to Oxford and a cab from there.' She argued with me but I was determined.

'On your own, you would be a really easy target for any lunatic that might be out there. I'll relax once I know you're on the plane and out of the country.' She conceded, and we started to clean up the kitchen quietly, lost in our own thoughts.

We were both tired and not long afterwards, Caro went up to bed. I had to take Mass the following morning, and I spent a while thinking about a sermon that would be both helpful and interesting to the congregation. I decided to speak about family and forgiveness. Since our discussion about the painted cellar in France, and my mother's reaction, it had brought home to me how I had never forgiven her for what she had done that day, and our relationship had suffered as a consequence.

After the sudden death of both my parents some years ago, I had felt a huge loss, not only for them as parents, but for who they really were. I had known so little about them, and then in a flash it was too late – they were gone, and I was full of regret. They did love me, I knew that, but they seemed to be involved in another world to such a degree that normal family life became impossible. I made my notes for the sermon and settled down to sleep, a little easier in mind than I had been for a few days.

CHAPTER TWENTY-THREE

'Don't open the door to anyone, do you understand? I mean not anyone at all, even if you think you know them. Pull all the bolts across too.'

'I will, and stop worrying… It'll be fine. I'll pack, and tidy up a bit, and you won't be gone for long.'

Again, I waited until I heard the bolts being drawn across before walking down the path to the car. Black Coat was parked under a tree, and I thought he would follow me, but he didn't. I drove for a minute or two and then pulled over to call Caro.

'Black Coat was outside when I left, but he didn't follow me. I don't like you being there on your own with him outside. The door is bolted, isn't it? Don't open it for anyone, do you understand? Call 999 if you need to. I'll be back in about an hour and a half.'

I hurried on to the church and was greeted by a few parishioners who had arrived early. I was feeling particularly anxious, but gave what I hoped was a decent sermon. I intended to keep the topic in mind for myself, and I hoped my congregation would too. They certainly shook my hand warmly and I left as quickly as I could, anxious to get back to the cottage and make sure Caro was safe. Black Coat was nowhere to be seen, and she quickly let me in.

'All quiet here, so you can stop worrying. I'm all packed up and ready to go, and have scanned and copied the papers that Merry gave to us last night. I'll read them on the plane. I've packed up your manbag too. I thought it would save time, and the peasant's curtains are empty. Your laptop's in there too, and there are sandwiches made for the journey.'

'You have been busy. We had better get going I suppose. Thanks for tidying up – the place looks spotless.'

We put the bags in the car and I carefully locked up the cottage. There was nothing to steal, but I could do without any hassle when I got back. Within half an hour we were on the motorway and heading towards Birmingham airport. The traffic was quite heavy, but moving smoothly, so any delay seemed unlikely. Caro began to talk about the parchments and journal.

'What do you think will happen, Ben?'

'Hopefully nothing. Best case scenario is that it all quietens down and I get back to normal. Adrian will probably turn up, and the bishop will stop telling me to look after myself. I might carry on investigating the village church, but quietly though!'

'Well, I'm very involved in writing my book. I'd really like you to see it. There are a few new things I've discovered, and I'm going to research the connections between France and here too.'

'Be careful. Do it quietly, and don't tell anyone for the moment. I hope to be over for the whole of August, so we can go through it then, and keep your eyes peeled for anything suspicious. Lock up the house properly every time you go out, things like that. And use your parents' old safe in the cellar. I know it's a hassle, but a lot less so than if anything gets stolen. And phone me if there's a problem; in fact, phone me the second you get in.'

We dropped off the hire car, and I walked into departures with her. They were already loading the bags, and I stayed until she was about to go through passport control. She hugged me tightly.

'I'm going to miss you. I'm so sorry to have you mixed up with this. I deeply regret it... I should have kept it all to myself.'

'I'll miss you, Ben. And don't worry, I'll see you in a couple of months, and will call you later as soon as I'm back home. You be careful too.'

* * *

I waved until she was out of sight and waited for the next train to Oxford, eventually arriving back at the cottage almost three hours later. I had become used to Caro being there, and it felt odd to be going in alone. As I walked up the path my heart sank when I saw that the front door was wide open.

I paused for a moment: what if someone was still inside? I didn't want to get clobbered on the head or worse. Should I call the police right now? I quickly decided that if I stayed outside I would probably be safe, but just in case I picked up the cast iron doorstop and held it firm. My bag was across my body, so I had both hands free.

Still outside, I began to shout. 'Hello? Hello? I've called the police, so come out.'

I heard a shuffling inside and I raised the iron cat that was the doorstop. It would give someone a nasty dent in an ear shape if I hit them with it, and a good job too! At least it would make for easy identification if they managed to get away. Then suddenly someone was in front of me. It was Peter, the vicar.

'Good God, man. I thought you were going to bludgeon me,' he said. 'You've been broken into. The place is a mess, I'm afraid, and I've called the police. I stopped by to put a card through the door from Merry to thank you both for the flowers yesterday, and I found it like this. I'm so sorry. I gather you've taken Caro back to the airport?'

I lowered the iron cat and put it back on the path, my hands shaking. A siren could be heard and was getting louder by the second; the police were clearly on their way.

'What the hell is going on? One more second and I would have hit you on the head with a lump of iron.'

Two flashing cars screeched to a halt, and suddenly the pathway seemed full of policemen and women, two of each to be exact. Peter explained what had happened and I told them where I'd been. He then excused himself as he had an evensong to attend, but said he would call me when it was over.

'I used your phone to call the police and leave a message for Merry to tell her I would be late, as I didn't have my mobile on me. I hope that was OK. I'll speak to you later. You can stay with us if needs be.' He nodded to the nearest officer. 'You know where you can find me if you want a statement,' and with that he dashed off down the street.

CHAPTER TWENTY-FOUR

The officers and I walked into the cottage. To say that it was a mess was an understatement. It had been completely turned over in every sense of the word. Drawers and cupboards had been emptied, the curtains were in shreds, and my beautiful old glasses were smashed to pieces on the floor. The Rayburn doors were open, as was the wood burner. There were bits of ash on the carpet, but as I looked more closely I saw that the ash from burning logs over the past week was gone. I knew exactly why that was, but the police had started to ask me questions and I concentrated on that. The forensics team arrived and started to dust handles and other items for fingerprints.

'I doubt that we'll get anything though,' one of them said. 'It looks like a professional job to me, not the usual petty thieving that we've so much of.'

They carried on looking around whilst a statement was taken. Nothing appeared to be missing; there was nothing of any value to take, and I told them this.

'It's very odd,' continued the forensics man as he brushed his powder everywhere. 'Most of the burglaries around here have involved electrical equipment, laptops, and jewellery. Straight in and out jobs... nothing like this. Will you be OK? Is there someone you can call for help?'

I assured him of this, and within an hour and a half, they were all gone. My hands still shook as I closed the door and bolted it. The locks weren't damaged at all, so as the police said, it had been the work of experts. The phone rang, and I walked through the debris to pick it up. It was Caro, telling me she had arrived home safely.

'I'm home. Everything's fine here. All OK your end?'

I explained what had happened.

'Oh no, oh, Ben, how awful. It isn't going to go away; I didn't think it would. Come home – just come home.'

'I'd love to but I can't just leave. I need to clear up and there's work to consider. I'll be fine. I was invited to sleep at the vicarage, but I might as well just stay here. The door's bolted, and unless they use sledgehammers no one can get in, so stop worrying. I'm going to have a good think this evening, and I'll call you tomorrow.'

Ending the call, I picked up the phone again to ring the vicarage and tell them that I was going to stay put, and clear up. Using last number redial showed the emergency services number, and the number before that was mine, calling home that morning when I was out. Perhaps I had misheard Peter when he said he had called Merry? I looked the number up and left a message, assuring them that I was shaken, but fine, and would stay here for the night.

I went upstairs and started to create some order,

putting things back into drawers, straightening the mattress and fresh bedding that Caro had put on, and hanging the clothes back in the wardrobe.

Downstairs took longer with books to put back on shelves, but I was thankful that I had so few belongings over here. The curtains were ruined, and I took them down and put them in the dustbin outside. A few things in the kitchen were broken, but mostly it was OK, and I put everything back in the cupboards and wiped the surfaces down. The bathroom hadn't been touched. I pulled out the vacuum and pushed it around to clean up the debris and bits of ash. I assumed that the burglars, for want of a better word, had thought they might be able to decipher bit of words from what was left in the grate, but I was positive that this would be impossible. The fire had been used several times, and there would be nothing at all left that would be legible.

It was now nearly nine, and I was exhausted when the phone rang. It was Merry asking if I was OK, and was I sure I didn't want to spend the night with them? Or could she come around to help me? Or bring me a meal? I assured her I was fine, and that the place was pretty much back to normal.

* * *

Almost immediately it rang again. I thought it would probably be Caro or a local person checking up on me. When I picked up the receiver and said hello, there was no one there for a few seconds… then I heard a man's

141

voice. Speaking in Italian, I recognised him straight away as the owner of the parchments that had been given to me to transcribe. He spoke quickly, over some considerable noise in the background.

'Listen to me, Benoît, and do not speak. I am sorry to tell you that I can no longer ensure your safety. Everything has changed and you are most definitely in danger. I will do my best but you need to go into hiding. I am at even greater risk and am fleeing as we speak. Trust no one. Do you hear me? Trust no one. I am unsure when I can call you again. I thought I could contain things but several organisations are now looking for the parchments and seem to know about the existence of the journal. I have made it known that you are innocent and no longer have any involvement, and that your sister is not involved at all, but these are ruthless people, Benoît. I'm so sorry to have involved you. It was wrong of me. I'm so sorry.'

His voice was drowned out by what sounded like an engine, and then the line went dead. So, that was that. I felt strangely calm; it had been inevitable really, I knew that. The second break-in and the removal of the ashes from the wood burner had confirmed that I had become involved in something very serious indeed. I needed to act and get away, but where to? France? Surely it wouldn't be too difficult for them to trace me to my house in Antugnac if they really wanted to. If they, whoever 'they' were, really wanted to find me, they could probably do so just about anywhere. The main advantage of going to France was that if I really ended up having to go into hiding, it would be the right place to do so. For a start, my house was built like a fortress, with walls over a metre thick. Breaking in would be almost impossible.

Secondly, Caro and I knew the hills and mountains so well. They had been a major part of our younger lives, and there were caves, tunnels and hiding places that we knew about where no one would ever find us. That was a distinct advantage. Odd that the Italian had called her my sister. He had obviously been informed that she was staying with me. We did look very alike, though, and I could see how that mistake might have been made.

Then it struck me. He had mentioned the journal. How in the hell did he know about it? There was no way he could have been spying on my every move, and anyway, me buying it in the first place had been a random event that no one could have predicted. Was my phone being tapped?

I thought for a moment. If someone was that desperate to listen to my conversations, then my mobile would be tapped too. Deciding to use it anyway, I called Arnaud. He was an old friend of mine from Antugnac, and would do as I asked without bothering me with too many questions. He answered within two rings, and I explained that I would be coming back to France tomorrow or the next day and would need a car of my own. His brother-in-law was a car dealer, and I knew that Arnaud helped him out from time to time.

'No problem, Benoît. We've just taken in a very tidy Peugeot 107 in part exchange. It's seven years old, has low mileage and a full service history. What do you think? Will it do?'

'Perfect. I used to have one a few years back, and it's a great little car.' A few minutes later, and we had struck a deal.

I have known Arnaud for my entire life, and we slipped back into our old and familiar friendship immediately.

'I'll come and pick you up – just let me know the times.'

'That would be great if you're sure you don't mind? I'll call you as soon as I've booked the flight and have the exact arrival time. Thank you so much.'

'It's nothing. No problem at all,' came the reply. He then teased me by saying he had made a very good deal by selling me the car, and the airport pick-up had already been added onto the price.

It was a huge relief to have sorted this out, and to have a car waiting for me was a real bonus since the region of France where I live is quite remote, and getting around locally is impossible without a car. Ten minutes later, he agreed to pick me up at Carcassonne the following afternoon. It was a relief to not have to bother Caro, or worry her any more than I already had.

By the time I had cleared up a few more things, had my suitcases out ready for packing tomorrow, and had climbed, exhausted, into bed it was past midnight. I intended to get up early to pack up the things I needed to take with me, as well as generally sorting out my absence with the diocese. I would need to call the bishop too, or at least his office, and find a way of getting to the airport. East Midlands was further than Birmingham, where I had taken Caro to, but flew to Carcassonne, which was much nearer to my home in France. A cab to Oxford, a train, and then another cab seemed easiest.

When I got to France, I could email or phone anyone else who needed to know that I would be away for a while, and sort things out as best as I could. My mind was buzzing with all that I had to do, but I fell asleep almost immediately, to be woken by the alarm at what seemed like a very short time later.

CHAPTER TWENTY-FIVE

I jumped out of bed, and began to pack a case with whatever I might need for the next few weeks. I was glad I had so few belongings in England, and anyway, I had plenty of clothes in France. I did, however, have some of my most used reference books here and intended to take them with me. The cottage was already furnished when I moved in, and apart from my own kitchen equipment, bedding, towels, and a few ornaments, there was little left of my own. My beautiful antique glasses were now gone, so if someone took everything that remained it wouldn't be too upsetting. Anyway, I told myself, I would be back as soon as things had settled.

At nine I called the bishop's private phone, which was answered by his secretary. She told me that she was taking his messages because he had been called away for a few days on family business. I explained that I too had family problems and needed to go back to France straight away, probably for a few weeks. She was clearly very annoyed.

'Well, that leaves me in a right pickle, Father Ben, if you don't mind me saying. It's bad enough with the bishop heading off like that without having to try to find a replacement for you. As you know, you're already a replacement for someone else, and I have no idea where I'll find extra cover. If you don't all watch it, I'll go off too, and then what would you do?'

I apologised to her as sincerely as I could, and said that I would be in touch as soon as I knew more.

'I'll let the bishop know when he comes back, although I've no idea when that will be. Will you be picking up your emails?'

'Oh yes, of course.'

She apologised for her sharpness although this wasn't necessary, since as far as I was concerned, and given the circumstances, it was well justified!

* * *

The next thing on my list was getting to the airport. At that moment, the doorbell rang, and in response to my shouting out to ask the caller to identify themselves, Merry's voice came back to me and I let her in.

'Ben, I thought I should pop over to see how you were? What an awful thing to have happened. Did they steal very much? Peter said the place was quite a mess, but I must say, it all looks very ship shape now. What luck that he happened to be strolling by and raised the alarm. I was out for most of yesterday and didn't get back till late, or I would have come straight up to help you.'

'It was quite a shock, that's for sure, and the house was a dreadful mess, but it all went back into place quite quickly. There really wasn't anything here to steal, since I had my laptop with me. The TV's ancient, and the radio isn't digital, so the burglars must have been very disappointed indeed! The only things of any value were a few old wine glasses and they smashed those, so they clearly knew nothing about antiques!' Silently, I wondered if they had been smashed out of anger and frustration at not finding the documents or journal, and thought this quite likely.

I took her through into the sitting room where my suitcases were standing, packed and ready to go. I explained that I was taking a couple of weeks' leave and was going home to France, but would be back soon.

'I expect you'll need a break after this. It's such an invasion of one's privacy, isn't it? I was broken into once when I was a student, and it took me months to get over it. How are you getting to the airport? Do you have a lift arranged?'

I explained that I would get a cab to the station in Oxford, and that the train from there should get me to the airport in plenty of time.

'Ben, do let me give you a lift. I've nothing on at all today. Peter's away for a couple of days and the boys have gone to stay with friends, so it really wouldn't be any trouble. Do let me help.'

I didn't want to put her out at all, and said so, but she insisted, so I finally, and thankfully, relented and agreed to the lift, after insisting on paying for petrol. Vicars are not well paid, and with three boys soon to be at university they must be hard pressed for cash.

'I'll be back at eleven on the dot. Is that OK?'

'Perfect. Thank you.'

'Oh, I nearly forgot. I've got a card here for you and Caro to thank you for the flowers and wine. I enjoyed meeting her so much, and the flowers were lovely. I've put them in the front window and several people have commented on them. The friend that I went to see yesterday has just started up a greetings card company, and so I bought a few from her whilst I was there. This is the nicest one, I thought. I hope you like it.'

I thanked her and closed the door... then I remembered what Peter had said last night. He said he had called round to drop a card off from Merry. But she had just said she wasn't back till late, and had only bought the card whilst she was at her friend's house yesterday. Perhaps he had written one himself and brought it round because he was lonely?

Or perhaps he had wanted to talk about something? I remembered when he had spoken about the boys leaving home and had become tearful. I also remembered the look of annoyance he had given his wife when she offered to show us the archaeological report on the church. He was beginning to sound, to use Caro's word, as 'dodgy' as the bishop. Nothing made sense right now, and I felt considerable relief at the thought of leaving it all behind, no matter what problems might be waiting for me in France.

* * *

I was waiting outside when Merry pulled up. The cottage had been left clean and tidy, with food from the fridge thrown out, water and electricity switched off and the door locked. I had my laptop and papers safely in my manbag across my shoulder and two suitcases, which I stowed in the boot of the car. I insisted that she pull into the nearest petrol station, where I filled her up her car and bought her a bottle of wine from the chiller cabinet. It felt good to be getting away, and the further the distance grew between us and the village, the more relaxed I felt.

'Did you get a chance to look at those papers I gave you about the church research done by the archaeologist?' she asked.

'Not yet, but they're in my bag to look at on the plane.'

'That's a good idea. As I said, he was a strange man – nervous, and not very friendly, but the report is quite interesting. The lord of the manor in the very early days of the church was instrumental in the setting up of the Knights Templar. Not many text books tell you that, but it's true. I suppose it's likely that he or one of his relatives brought back the relics, and goodness knows what else. I often wonder what other secrets are held in the place, walled up and silent.

'I did a degree in the history of art at Oxford, you know. I wanted to do a master's, but then I met Peter, and the rest, as they say, is history, albeit of a different kind. Sorry about the unintended pun! Now, of course, I cook. It doesn't sound great, does it? It feels like such a waste of an education, and I've been considering doing a master's now, especially with the boys all off to university.'

I knew nothing of her academic past, but was glad

that she had decided to pick up the reins again and do something for herself.

'That sounds like a great idea, and you're still near to Oxford, which should give you plenty of scope.'

We spoke about Caro's work, and the books she had published. It seemed like no time at all had passed when we pulled up outside the airport terminal. I got my cases out from the boot.

'Thank you so much for the lift; it was a real help. I should be back in a week or two, but I'll send you both an email.'

I waved as she drove off. The check-in desk was open and I soon moved into the departure lounge and bought a much-needed sandwich, water, and coffee, and sat down to wait for my flight. The past week had been very intense and I wondered what would happen next. Nothing, I hoped, but I needed to be prepared for the worst.

I couldn't think of anything that would make my house in France more secure. Unless an intruder was a skilled climber, there was no way of entering from the front, since there was a thirty-foot drop down from my small terrace to the river. Without doubt, this had been deliberate when the house was built, to prevent easy access for any marauders. The river also ran around at least half of the current buildings in the circulade, although these days it was usually shallow unless there had been heavy rain.

Both sides were blocked off with my neighbours' properties, and the only accessible point of entry was the rear door, which was made of solid oak and was hundreds of years old. There were two very sturdy locks and a cast iron outer door, which was common to the area. It would take a huge effort to get through, and I thought that this was unlikely given the amount of noise it would make. My neighbours were elderly, and in most of the time, and without doubt would hear any major commotion and call the police.

CHAPTER TWENTY-SIX

Once up in the air, I took out the archaeologist's report that Merry had given me. The author started by giving a description of the exterior of the church building, which he described as very early Norman, possibly in part late Saxon. He described several layers of building, which he believed meant that the present church stood over an earlier one, and he described many of the features that we had seen for ourselves, including what he described as Norse/Viking symbolism throughout. There were several pages about the Knights Templar, and their involvement with the building, and he waxed lyrical about the relics and the piscina, which he described as the 'most bizarre and odd' he had ever seen. He continued by saying;

> It is quite clear that there is a purpose to the unusual design of the piscina, and further research is required to determine what that purpose is. Undoubtedly the person who placed it there had a message to leave, and I have some thoughts about what that message was. However, I intend to consult further with colleagues who have specialities in this field.
>
> Likewise, the graffiti and symbolism around the

church appears to be purposeful and significant, much of it based on the idea that the building is holding a secret of much importance. Some are aware of the secret and appear to embrace it, and others do not embrace it at all.

A room in the tower was sealed many years ago, but a veteran of the First World War set a tiny stone staircase into the wall to allow access to the room again.

I stopped reading for a moment. Peter had most definitely told me that the room was sealed up. How very odd. Why would he lie like that? I read on.

What is most curious is the huge ornate Norman doorway leading from this room to nowhere. It is blocked up now, and if one were to unblock it one would fall right down to the ground at the front of the chancel. There are also a host of other strange carvings in there, which would be most unusual for a room destined to be seen only by a priest.

I strongly suspect that, at one time, the door must have led on to further rooms. I shall consult with a colleague and will hopefully bring him with me on my next visit. Records may tell us more, and the vicar has agreed to make available any old records that he has at my next visit, which may give further explanation. My expectation is, however, that the records will not go back far enough to explain this anomaly.

There are two tombs in the graveyard that are most unusual; one, in fact, is unique as far as I am aware. The first one is a huge Roman structure, thought to have come from a nearby earlier burial ground, and supposedly found quite by chance.

The second is most rare indeed, and shows a man and woman of medieval style atop a tomb, their lower parts swathed by a blanket or covering of sorts. To find something like this outside is rare enough, but the blanket covering is extraordinary and urgently needs further investigation. 'Conservation' work apparently revealed early medieval pottery and mortar, giving the tomb a similar date to the piscina. Altogether, the church is complex, intriguing, and of great importance historically. I will revisit the building as soon as possible with specialists.

Just as I finished reading this page, the seatbelt light came on and the plane began its descent. I put the report away, deciding to read it again when back home and less tired. I had no idea what the next few weeks would bring, and knew that I was most certainly in danger, but how much? Enough to be killed for what I knew? Surely not, but then Caro was convinced that the hit and run, and the attempt to push me under a train, were not accidents. I didn't think they were either, especially the thump on the back in Paris, but if they were attempted murder, why? And by whom? Would they hurt her too?

I had no time to continue this train of thought, and it wasn't long before I walked through passport control and saw Arnaud scanning the people passing by, looking for his old friend Benoît. Finally, he saw me and shouted my name, before embracing me in a firm, garlic-scented hug.

CHAPTER TWENTY-SEVEN

I woke up to find myself still lying on the sofa. I had been here for the entire night, and from my position still flat on my back, it didn't look like I had moved at all. The sun was slanting in through the window and terrace doors, which had been left open the whole night. Even at this early hour it was warm, and I slowly got up to make myself a coffee. I decided to do it properly and began to grind the beans with an old wooden grinder that had belonged to my grandmother.

A few minutes later, and I was outside on the terrace, sitting on an old bench set against the front wall of the house, sipping the sweet, aromatic brew. The air was fresh and clean and I could barely contain my joy at being home. I closed my eyes against the morning sun, and for the first time in what seemed like weeks, I prayed.

I knew that I was, perhaps, not your average priest, and that my beliefs differed from many, but prayer had always baffled me, and had been one of the most difficult things for me to grasp. It had always seemed to me that 'prayer' was, in general, a long list of requests and favours asked for, and as such was totally anathema to me. Who would want to listen to that, or feel inclined, in any way, to answer?

Trying to pray without asking for anything was a discipline that took an immense amount of thought. Giving thanks was always a good start and not just to a God but to anyone who had had an impact on the day, either positive or negative. It was a massive subject of debate amongst the theology students that I had once taught, and one that I found endlessly stimulating.

* * *

I could have stayed outside for the whole morning, but I had a lot to do. Climbing the tall, twisting stairs, I unpacked and took a much-needed shower. Feeling a lot better for it, I was soon back downstairs, and lifted the phone to call Caro. It was early, but I was sure she would be up.

'Morning Benoît. I can't tell you how glad I am to have you home. Are you coming up later, or have you got other plans for today?'

'I've got quite a few things to do this morning. I need to pay Arnaud and Mathilde what I owe them, and then I must go shopping.' This meant a trip to the nearest small town, and probably the supermarket, since there were no markets until Sunday, nearly a week away.

'I've got a few emails to write and appointments to cancel, but I can come up after that, say around one, if that suits you?'

'The prodigal cousin has returned!'

'Yes, and I shall expect a good meal waiting for me. Three courses, and the best wine in the house. In fact,

157

I'm so glad to be home, that I wouldn't care if you gave me a bowl of cabbage soup. I'm even looking forward to the shopping and putting petrol in the car!'

'It's good about the cabbage soup, since that's what you'll be having. I might stretch to some stewed apples for pudding if you're lucky.' We both laughed.

Was it possible that it was less than forty-eight hours since I had seen her? It felt like weeks had passed. Then I remembered the words of the Italian and his warnings. I was supposed to be in hiding. I had to bear this in mind, and began to think about the preparations that should be made, ready for any eventuality that might possibly lie in the days ahead.

* * *

I switched on my laptop to deal with any emails and cancel all appointments made for the next two weeks. I wrote a cheque to pay Arnaud for the car and the insurance he had arranged, and put it in my wallet. I stowed my documents and laptop in the safe, noting the hunter's rifle in the corner that had once belonged to my grandfather. As a countryman, or 'peasant' as Caro might say, I still held a licence and was trained in the use of the rifle, although I hadn't shot anything living since I was a boy.

I did enjoy clay pigeon shooting though, and had done this several times over the past year at a local range just outside Cirencester. I fully intended to clean it, making sure it was ready for use in extreme circumstances. There was plenty of ammunition stacked in boxes, and I would check this too, and make sure it was still fit to use. I took some of the euros from the pile stacked in an old cigar tin, and once again I thought about 'Benoît le paysan.' No peasant worth his salt would be without a stack of money hidden somewhere, and I always topped this up each time I came to France. I felt another huge rush of joy in being back here, and whatever the future held, I knew that right now, this was where I was meant to be.

With everything locked up, I jumped into the car and drove up the narrow road towards the mountains. Arnaud's house was just a few hundred yards on the right, and I pulled up outside. His front door was open, and business attended to, I accepted the offer of a coffee. Within half an hour I was heading in the opposite direction, stopping at the nearest garage for petrol, including filling a metal can and checking the spare tyre. Some of the roads here in the mountains were strewn with small pieces of grit and rock, which sliced through a tyre with ease, and I needed to be prepared.

After the bank and boulangerie, where I bought a beautiful pear tarte tatin to take to Caro's as well as bread, I was soon in the small supermarket on the other side of town. I had almost nothing in the house, and with a siege mentality, stocked up on everything I might need over the next few weeks.

'Are the Nazis about to occupy France again?' asked the checkout operator. 'Please give me an early warning, and I'll stock up too,' she laughed. I laughed with her, but wondered what the response would be if I told her that the Mafia were after me and that I might have to hide in the mountains for a while. Whilst packing the bags, I pondered on how unpalatable the truth was and how often we avoided it.

CHAPTER TWENTY-EIGHT

Back at the house, I sorted out several boxes of items to put back in the boot, including water, biscuits, and other non-perishables, a couple of thick old blankets, candles, matches, torch, sturdy boots, and my ancient rucksack. It felt like a fantasy thriller movie, and hiding out in a cave for a few days sounded so ludicrous and surreal that I couldn't believe it would ever happen. Putting everything else away, I stacked the cash in the safe. I would see to the gun when I came back from Caro's.

I arrived at her house just before one and she rushed out to greet me. The sky was bright blue, and the Pyrenees were in clear view, as was Bugarach mountain, renowned for its supposed alien activity. There were several fortresses nearby, built on the tops of steep, mountain peaks, and I had great admiration for the people of those times and their staggering strength and ingenuity.

It had been recorded that there was once a huge city of some thirty thousand people on the site of Rennes-le-Château and the slopes below, then known as 'Rhedae.' The Romans, Visigoths, Franks, Cathars, Knights Templar, and many others before and after had settled in the region, and in Rennes-le-Château, because of its hilltop position and being able to see for miles in every direction. It certainly made a great lookout post, and the atmosphere was still highly charged, although tinged, I often thought, with great loss and sadness.

It was a small village now, but the tourist trade was brisk because of its history, tales of buried treasure, and the infamous priest, Bérenger Saunière, who had lived here more than a hundred years ago. His apparent discoveries of parchments in the church about Jesus and Mary Magdalene residing in the region and having a child, had made him a wealthy man for a time. Even now, it still fuelled a fierce ongoing debate, as well as another on treasure being buried in the locality.

* * *

Caro's house dated to the early seventeenth century and had been in her father's family for generations. Since her parents died she had modernised it throughout, but had kept many original features and almost all the charm of the old building. She had a large garden, and owned some of the fields and steep rocky slopes that ran down towards the valley.

Her father had been quite a few years older than her mother and they had made an unusual couple. He was an archaeologist; an odd but amiable man who had spent a lot of his time away on digs and explorations. He made up for this by sending Caro long letters and bringing her presents of scientific instruments, fossils, artefacts, and books on the most diverse of subjects. I once remembered him bringing her an ancient human skull. She must have been about seven at the time and it had sat in her room for years, gathering dust. He would often walk around the village with us both, pointing out various things of historical importance, and it was from him that we both imbibed our love of history and all ancient things.

When I thought about her mother, my aunt, I realised how like my own mother she was. They were non-identical twins, but had the same mannerisms, tone of voice, and urgency of speech. She was certainly around a lot more and cared for her family greatly, sometimes possessively, but you never felt like you really knew her. They were both so different from my grandparents, and I had frequently wondered what had gone so wrong that they had turned out like they did.

CHAPTER TWENTY-NINE

'Benoît... Benoît... you're miles away. What were you thinking?'

Caro was staring at me closely and gently shaking my arm.

'Oh, I was thinking about our mothers and how odd they were. It suddenly struck me; how could they have been brought up by our grandparents and yet have been so different? There's something else too – you must have wondered it yourself. How did they both accumulate so much money? I'm not sure how much you have, but there are so many noughts on my bank statements that I often can't make out what the actual sum really is. It's beginning to bother me. It's probably all this trouble with the parchments and journal, and being broken into and threatened, but it's important, nonetheless.'

'I've been thinking about it a bit too, and where it should all go when we're gone. We've been ignoring it for too long. And, like you, the number of noughts is staggering. I was haggling at a flea market the other week over a pile of old plates, and I suddenly thought how insane it was to haggle over a few euros like that. I gave the woman twice the amount she was asking for in the end. She must have thought I was mad.'

'She was right there, ma chérie; you're as nutty as a British fruit cake. And, talking of cakes, I bought you this.' I handed over the tarte tatin.

'Ah, I see. Either you don't trust my cooking, or you've brought a gift that you have every intention of consuming yourself. Very clever, Benoît... very clever indeed. And from old moneybags himself, so laden down with cash that he can barely walk. Ha!' She thumped me on the arm and started laughing.

I wondered why people had started to thump me. I had noticed several bruises when I was in the shower this morning from Arnaud's double assault yesterday, and now Caro was also at it.

'Do I look like some sort of victim? Arnaud thumped me twice yesterday, and now you. I'm covered in bruises. As soon as this "situation" is over, I'm taking up bodybuilding!'

We both laughed at this and probably the hilarious, but unlikely, image of me becoming muscle-bound enough to scare people away.

'Come on you weakling – let's go inside and eat.'

She had roasted a chicken stuffed with lemon and herbs, and had made a large salad, grown in her own garden. A crystal bowl gleamed with bright tomatoes, slices of mozzarella, and large basil leaves, all drizzled with olive oil and salt crystals, which glittered across the top. Tiny baby potatoes with garlic butter were taken from the oven, and sat on the table steaming gently. As I sat down she pulled a hot, fragrant loaf from the old bread oven inset into the rear of the huge fireplace.

'I had to light the fire to make this, and it's so hot today. Consider yourself very lucky.'

'Are you sure you can afford the fuel? Would you like me to pay for my share?'

She raised her arm to thump me again, and I quickly picked up a spoon and started to fill my plate. I was glad that the atmosphere had been lightened, and we chatted as we ate, eventually taking our coffee outside to the terrace with its glorious mountain views.

* * *

'So, Ben, what's happening? Tell me everything.'

I told her again about the break-in, the ash being removed from the grate, the shredded curtains, about Peter being there, the phone call from the Italian, and the potential danger we might be in. We discussed this for a while, our voices becoming quieter; all joviality now gone.

'There have been theories about Jesus, and his not being crucified, for hundreds of years, especially in the past sixty years or so with freedom of speech, and so much media coverage available… but there has never been any tangible evidence. And, as you know, so much rubbish has been put out over the years, which gives the Vatican, and everyone else who has a vested interest in trashing the evidence, ammunition to do so. I'm convinced that a lot of the false clues and dossiers are more than just a few pranksters having fun. They're deliberately put out to confuse, and stop people from seeing what's right in front of their eyes. There are powerful people out there, Caro, not just in the church and other vast financial organisations, which include the Vatican, but politicians too.'

I paused for a moment to collect my thoughts.

'Actually, there's more to it than that. People like you and I could cope with an honest base to construct our beliefs upon: to consolidate historical fact and truth with some form of internal knowing and faith. But there are a lot of crazy people in the world, who might thrive on the chaos that could be caused if the whole basis of Christianity was disproved. The word to focus on here is *proved*.

'Anyone with an interest in the subject already knows that Christianity and its basic construction in the format that we know it was compiled by the Romans, namely Constantine, before, during, and after the Council of Nicaea in AD 325, including the construction of the Bible. It took a while to pull the thing together, of course, and there were several other splinter groups to contend with, but overall, he succeeded. As you know, he even condemned and excommunicated Arius, accusing him of heresy for his assertions that Jesus was an ordinary man and not a divine being.'

I poured myself more coffee and sat back in my chair.

'I know my own beliefs might vary somewhat from other priests, but I also know that there are plenty of us who hold views that vary considerably from traditional doctrine.'

'I don't doubt that, Ben... not at all. In fact, I'm

167

relieved to hear you say it. For myself, there's no doubt at all that Constantine's efforts were nothing more than a political manoeuvre to consolidate, control, and ultimately create a massively powerful weapon, which he then presented to the people as a religion and an appeasement – both at the same time.

'I view it as an incredibly clever construction of psychological warfare, like nothing ever seen or heard of before or since. A mass compilation of oral traditions, desires, and fantasies, as well as a web of huge complexity: intrigue, truths, half-truths, fables, and downright lies, whilst still leaving all control to Rome. And whenever any part of the Bible proved tricky or contentious, they just removed or changed that bit. Very smart indeed, so much so, that its power is still being exerted today. They may be gone as an occupying army, but they're still in occupation – quite literally, if we think of the Vatican. And we view the threat of nuclear warfare as the ultimate control threat?'

'Put like that, you're right… it is rather impressive. Whilst nuclear warfare threatens to wipe out cities and hundreds of thousands of people at a time, religion controls with the promise of ultimate salvation. Suffer now, and you'll get your reward in heaven. But look at how many wars are going on right now, supposedly based on religious and racial intolerance? Even after the horrors of the Holocaust, nothing has changed.'

* * *

168

Caro stood up. 'Personally, I'd like to see organised religion disappear entirely. I'm sorry if that offends you, Ben.' She gave a big sigh. 'Anyway, I suppose humans would just find other reasons to kill each other... they always have. How very sad it all is. I could weep right now.'

It was hot, and I shifted my chair further into the shade.

'It doesn't offend me, but as a priest I know that having a faith can be a huge source of comfort to a person in difficult times. It helps people to make sense of the complex world they live in. Throughout history, and well before Jesus's time, we were at it. Worshipping the sun, the stars, the moon, mother earth, constructing huge buildings of stone and attaching meaning to them, idols, Isis and a whole host of other gods and deities. Even devil worship, although the definition of the Devil is a massive area of debate as far as I can see. I can think of quite a few despots in the past century alone who would more than qualify for that badge. We've even gone in for sacrificing people to appease the gods, which no doubt made some sense at the time. Of course, politics and power play a huge part, often using the Church as a controlling body, like with Henry VIII and the dissolution of the monasteries. It's not just religion per se. I feel like I'm lecturing you; you're the historian, you know all of this. I'm just running it through in my own mind really.'

'Carry on, Ben... it's all very well turning out a load of academic books, but feeling it is what makes it really

169

stick. I think that about all history. If you don't feel it, it's almost impossible to make any attempt at a decent interpretation. Without passion, it's just a dead thing slipping through one's hands like sand.

'But where does it leave us? There are plenty of people out there who would kill for what we know, or, indeed, to suppress it – I don't doubt that. And the Italian? He has the original parchments. Will he have to hide himself and them for the rest of his life? Where does it leave you as a Catholic priest? Is it enough to believe in Jesus as a man, even if he was a very special and inspiring one at that?'

'You just don't understand... you never did, did you?'

She looked hurt at this, and I apologised.

'I have tried, really I have. But you're right, I don't understand.'

'I've known a lot of priests, Catholic and otherwise, who speak of a calling. Some talk about visions, or voices, and a whole lot of other things that they have interpreted as an indication from God that they've been singled out for a special purpose. I haven't had that, and used to feel very uncomfortable about it too. But it's a feeling, Caro... a feeling. You spoke about that just now in relation to understanding history. Well, my feeling comes when I think about Jesus.

'It started when I was a young boy. I can even remember the first time that it happened. We must have been about eight, and we were with your father, Charles. He was giving us one of his guided tours of the church here at Rennes-le-Château, and his interpretations of what Saunière's revamped interior symbolised. He began talking about Jesus and I felt warm all over. That's the simplest and most accurate way of describing it. And the more I learned about the man, the more I warmed to him, in every sense of the word. As for him being a human being, and not some form of deity or God... that made not the slightest bit of difference, quite the opposite, in fact. It affirmed and added to how I felt. The other day you said you thought I might be gay? I even asked myself that, but I'm not, I can assure you of that.'

'Thank you, Benoît. Thank you for explaining it to me. I don't feel like you do, but I do understand it a little better now. I recognise the danger that we're in too; I even feel uncomfortable out here, in full view for any sniper to have a go at.'

'Let's go back inside and discuss tactics.'

We got up and went into the now cool interior of the house. With tall glasses of iced lemon tea, we sat with the windows and doors open to allow the breeze, and any murderer, I reminded her, in.

'The thing is, Benoît, I don't want to be silenced by fear. That's what has always been done, and I won't be a part of it. I'm an academic and a historian, not a puppet to be controlled by a bunch of morons flexing their muscles. We've got masses of research that we've done in the past on the subject, and a whole lot more that I've done recently. The parchments that were sent to you add to what we already know, and the journal adds to it again. I want to explore it further, and I've had some ideas that

171

I'd like to run by you. I'm writing a serious book, not some rubbish to send people off on a wild goose chase around the mountains looking for hidden Templar treasure. And whilst I don't want to make a point of antagonising dangerous people, or creating chaos, I must be allowed to speak. You do see that, don't you?'

'Of course I do, but you might need to wait for a while. And you don't have any right to use the Italian's parchments without his permission, you know that.'

CHAPTER THIRTY

Caro had promised to go and see Hortense, her father's sister, that afternoon. It was a hot day, and there would be quite a few tourists milling about in the village. This was good for us, since it was unlikely that we would be the focus of an attack in those circumstances.

Hortense lived in a small cottage not far from the church. She was very elderly, but still managed to live alone with a little help from Caro, her neighbours, and a home help who came in every day. She always had her finger on the pulse regarding village affairs, missed nothing, and had a memory as sharp as a knife. Wanting to take some food for her, as well as a basket of vegetables from the garden, we decided to take the car, and drove up the steep hill to the car park. The view was magnificent from here, reaching as far as the Pyrenees, and we stood for a moment to take it in before walking into the centre of the village.

A few steps later and the church of Saint Mary Magdalene was in front of us. There were quite a few tourists milling about, and I stood back to let some walk by. We had been here many hundreds of times, but never tired of seeing the beautiful little church, which wore its age as proudly as anything that was well over a thousand years old should. It would be impossible to say exactly how old the place was, but I was quite sure that parts of it dated to at least twelve hundred years ago. Given the amount of times that invaders had sacked the area, this was quite an achievement.

Without doubt, another church had stood in its place before, and quite possibly a Roman site of worship before that. It was known that in the early ninth century Guillaume de Gellone and his sons had built a castle on the land to the side of the church, and Caro's father had found many artefacts relating to that time, and earlier, which he loved to show to us.

Subsequent Gellone generations had gone on to become Templars, and it was true that the now tiny village was steeped in history like a sponge in water. If it could only be squeezed as easily to extract everything that it held, then one would surely have a spellbinding story to tell. The passage of time was so tangible here, more than anywhere else in the world that I had been, and most people, tourists and locals alike, were quiet as they walked around, as if in reverence to those that had gone before.

Caro led the way and we walked inside. The last group of tourists was just leaving, and for the moment, we were alone.

'The place is still amazing, isn't it? It has the same effect every time I come in. Even though we thought we had combed every inch of it, I've still found a few new things of interest that link to both the parchments and the journal. And I keep thinking about the painted room

174

under your house. We left it out of our research before, but I do think we should add it to what we know, even if its location is kept secret. What do you feel about that, Benoît? It's your house, after all, and we haven't set eyes on the room for more than forty years.'

'Well, my house is never going to be turned into a theme park. And before you get on your high horse I know that's not what you were suggesting. You're right, though; we could look at it again and use it for research, and I promise to think about it. But this won't be like any other history book you've written, will it? There's already so much information out there, granted a lot of it deliberately false smokescreens. I'm just not sure how it can be done without turning it into another treasure hunt. I don't want my name on anything either. Luckily you have a different surname to me; de Morny and Balthis are about as different as you can get! Oh, and you seem to have forgotten something. We've been warned by several people that we're in danger, and I think we need to pay some attention to that, don't you?'

'Yes, of course, you're right. I'm sorry. Shall we have a quick look round and then go on to see Hortense?'

* * *

Back outside, the entrance to the graveyard of the village was padlocked, but Saunière himself had now been moved into his garden and buried in unconsecrated ground, which I found to be the oddest thing. It seemed unlikely that someone was going to dig him up overnight,

175

but if that was a real concern then why not just make the original burial site more secure?

'I never understood why they reburied him. He left instructions that he was never to be moved, and yet they did just that. Maybe there were reasons that weren't apparent, but now he's under five tons of concrete and away from Marie Dénarnaud, his long-term housekeeper, companion, and friend. How very sad.'

I nodded. 'Isn't it just? I've wondered about the motives of those who made the decision. Did they think that they would find something in his tomb? If they genuinely thought it would put a stop to some of the myths surrounding him, then the opposite has happened, with another mass of conjecture and questions as to the real purpose of the exhumation. I was told that a court case had followed, and that the prayer book that he had carried with him everywhere had now gone missing.'

Whatever the truth, the whole thing was appalling. It seemed that controversy and misunderstanding had followed Saunière since his arrival at Rennes-le-Château in 1885. I found the man himself to be of much more interest than any buried treasure myths. He had what an old friend of mine, now dead, would call a 'chaotic aura,' and the title certainly seemed to fit.

'So little has been written about his personality and who he really was. I've been trying to find out more about him for the book, basic things, to try to define his character, but it isn't easy.'

'Grandfather spoke about him sometimes. I'll have a think, and jot down a few bits for you, if that would help?'

Caro walked over to the Tour Magdala, a lookout tower dedicated to Mary Magdalene on the corner of Saunière's domaine, which was once used as a library. I sat on a wall to wait for her, and was soon lost in thought. Coming here had strongly reminded me of the immense speed at which we were pulled though life, seemingly with little control of its outcome. It felt like some sort of externally controlled game, and I thought of Macbeth and one of the most poignant things ever written:

To-morrow, and to-morrow, and to-morrow,
Creeps in this petty pace from day to day,
To the last syllable of recorded time;
And all our yesterdays have lighted fools
The way to dusty death. Out, out, brief candle!
Life's but a walking shadow, a poor player,
That struts and frets his hour upon the stage,
And then is heard no more. It is a tale
Told by an idiot, full of sound and fury,
Signifying nothing.

CHAPTER THIRTY-ONE

~≈~

The wind had picked up, and clouds began to scud across the sky, illuminating everything with sun one minute and casting it into shade the next. I thought how very fitting this was to my mood. Caro startled me when she put her hand on my shoulder.

'Gosh, you really jumped then. Are you OK?'

'Just tired, probably. And coming up here, well, it all makes everything seem so futile, doesn't it? Oh, don't take any notice; a strong coffee will sort me out. Let's go and see Hortense. I'm sure she'll talk some sense into me; she usually does.'

We walked back out of the garden and past the church. On the corner was a tiny cottage. It had a strange sundial painted on it, using various astrological and alchemical symbols, as well as Roman numerals, all painted in black. It had been there for as long as I could remember, and I took a quick photo, to study later. It was much quieter now, and we made our way down the narrow lane opposite that led to Hortense's cottage.

It was on the end of a long row, and looked badly in need of a lick of paint. I knew that Caro had offered to have it done, but Hortense had refused, saying that she could do what she liked with it after she was dead but she didn't want the trouble of workmen about the place at her age. The sun shone on its gabled front which, combined with the honey-coloured render, made it look like it was glowing. I lifted the knocker to announce our arrival, although I knew that she rarely locked the door in the daytime. We heard a shout from inside, 'entrez,' and I turned the iron handle and leant against the heavy door to push it open.

* * *

Hortense was standing in the kitchen making coffee. She looked like she had shrunk since I was last here, and when I hugged her, I could clearly feel her protruding bones. Caro continued with making the coffee and putting away the food we had brought, whilst I sat with Hortense in front of a roaring fire. She clearly felt the cold and given her current state of emaciation I could see how she might be chilled, especially if she wasn't moving about very much. Her mind, though, was as sharp as ever. She always insisted on speaking English since I had been living there, and we were soon being given the latest news.

'Ah, yes, I was told you were here, Benoît. A bit of a rush, wasn't it? I heard you were in trouble. Hopefully there isn't some woman involved?'

I was startled by this, but she didn't wait for a reply and continued.

'There are some funny things going on around here, Benoît, more than the usual hippies and treasure seekers. I don't miss much, and I've seen them: men in

179

dark glasses, snooping about the place. I know their sort and I don't like it one bit. What are they looking for? Blanchefort's gold?'

At this, she started to laugh, at first quietly, and then so much that she held her sides. We started to laugh with her, although I must say mine was held back somewhat by concern for her frailty, in the face of so much body-shaking humour.

'Oh, oh, it makes my stomach hurt,' she said, her amusement now reduced to stifled giggling. 'You two used to laugh a lot when you were children, do you remember? You used to fall on the floor and roll around till you were weak with it. Strange children.'

At this point she reached down by the side of her chair, and pulled out a small bottle of Chabot Armagnac. Despite our protests, she poured a measure into each coffee cup and we had no choice but to accept our coffee being laced. It did taste fabulous, and I asked to see the bottle. Looking at the label, I recognised the contents as a rare twenty-year-old vintage. It must have cost her quite a bit of money – perhaps a hundred pounds or so. Was she rich too or had Caro bought it? I would ask her later.

'Of course, I wasn't born until about six years after Saunière died, but even before then there was talk and gossip, the same as there is now, really, only without so much hysteria. I knew Marie Dénarnaud, though. She was a reserved woman; didn't have a lot to say, and kept to herself. She led a very lonely life after he had died.' She paused for a moment, all the laughter now gone, and looked at us both in turn with great seriousness.

'I grew up with the treasure myths, you see, we all did around here, and it's not surprising, is it? So many people have come and gone over the centuries and so many battles fought. They all left their mark in one way or another, n'est-ce pas? That's what people want to do, leave something to be remembered by so that their lives weren't lived for nought. Pah! In the end, we are nothing but dust blown about in the wind, and others try to snatch that dust as it blows them by.'

At this she raised her hand and made a snatch in the air to affirm what she had just said. She shifted in her chair, and spoke again.

'I almost feel like selling the tourists nets to try to catch their dreams in, or someone else's dreams, which is just as unlikely. Benoît, you know what I mean, don't you? I can see in your face that you've been thinking such things too.'

Once again, Hortense had hit the nail on the head. She had always been like this, and I supposed that some people might call her psychic. I should be used to it by now, but she still managed to startle me with her astuteness.

'It's true, Hortense, I do feel that way, especially over the past few days. I've been thinking a lot about my parents and how little I knew them. They were so odd, and when I think of them now it's like they have a veil over them, so I can see even less. I want to grab it and pull it off, but truly I don't know how.'

'Very true, Benoît, very true… they were as cloaked as our Curé Saunière. My two children, I don't think I am going to last much longer, and there is something I must tell you.'

At this declaration both Caro and I exclaimed, shocked at her sudden announcement.

'No, surely not, you'll live for years yet!'

'Why, we'll look after you ourselves, won't we, Benoît? Come home with us now.'

She raised her hand to silence us.

'No, it is done, and now you must listen. These are not bad things that I'm about to say. They are good things. And you, Benoît, as a priest, you will come to terms with what I must tell you. You're not like any priest I have ever known anyway.'

Unsure if this was an insult or a compliment, I stayed silent and let her continue.

'You have both grown up together in these mountains like brother and sister, and as you have said, Benoît, there is much that you do not know. I have written it all down for you, and when I am gone you will know it. But, for now, you will know this. You are brother and sister. Caro, my dear, your mother couldn't conceive at all, and it made both her and your papa so very sad. And then, out of the blue, Benoît, your mother is pregnant. She had made no plans to have a baby, you see, given how things were, but it happened nonetheless. And then she found out it was twins. They decided between them, the sisters, that they would have one each, and that is how it was. They paid to have the birth certificate changed, et voila! You were cousins. And now you are returned to how you should be. It's a miracle!'

'Actually, Hortense, I already knew. I found a letter about it, written to papa from all those years ago. It was after he had died and I was clearing out his things. Thank you for telling us, though. It was the right thing to do, and if I hadn't already known I would have liked to know. Benoît? Are you OK?'

They were both looking at me, trying to gauge my reaction. Hortense was smiling broadly, as though she had just given me a huge gift, but Caro seemed more hesitant, perhaps reluctant to smile in case I was angry that, once again, I had been kept in the dark. As a child, I had always wished that she had been my sister, and that she didn't have to keep going back home to her parents. Then the words of the Italian came into my head. Your sister... he had known. But how? I could think about that later, but at this moment, I had no intention of upsetting either of them. My wish had come true, even if it was rather late. That was enough. I got up and kissed them both, picked up the bottle, and poured an extra shot into their glasses.

Now it was my turn to start laughing.

'No wonder we look so alike. I never did understand why you had blonde hair when neither of your parents did. How very odd. I must admit though, I am shocked, but not in a bad way. I expect it will take a bit of time to sink in.'

* * *

Hortense spoke again. 'Caro, could you open the cupboard under the stairs and pass me the carved wooden box? It's heavy, so be careful.'

Caro did as she was told, and put the old chest on the table beside Hortense. It was about eighteen inches wide, twelve deep, and was beautifully carved all over. I had never seen it before and wondered where it had come from. Hortense leaned forward and took off a chain that was around her neck. On it were two small keys, one silver and one gold, as well as a circular pendant of gold, which was much bigger. She had worn these for as long as I could remember. Unlocking the box, she pulled out a bag of thick, linen cloth with a drawstring top.

'You were one, then you were two, and now you are one again, so this is for you both. They belong to Charles and I, but Christiane wouldn't have theirs in the house, so I kept them here.'

Caro took the bag and loosened the strings. I could hear the chink of metal and when she pulled her hand out, it was full of golden discs, exactly like the one on Hortense's chain. They were of the brightest yellow, totally untarnished, and I could tell from where I was sitting that they were almost certainly solid gold and likely to be of some considerable age. In today's market, they would be worth a fortune. She seemed stunned, her eyes transfixed on Hortense as she spoke.

'They're the same as the one on your chain. But Hortense, where did you get them from? I've never seen anything like them before.'

'It's all explained to you in my will, and there are documents there about other things too. It will all become clear when you have them, but I'm too old to become involved in it anymore. It took its toll on us all, and keeping secrets is never an easy thing. I believe that there are some things that should be known to everyone, and to be controlled by lies has never sat easily with me. It wasn't how I wanted to live my life, but telling the truth is not always simple, children; I have learned this. It never was, but even less so in these dangerous times. I see that very clearly, and hopefully you will too. I know and trust that you will do whatever you feel is right, but sometimes one must look at life in a much broader sense. Everything is connected, and nothing can be changed in isolation. If you remember nothing else, please remember this.' She paused for a moment.

'For all that your childhoods were strange in some respects, you come from good stock, and nothing can alter that. Blood is thicker than water… is that how you say it? Those that have gone before speak out through you, and that's how it should be. It will keep you strong, but I'm glad that I won't be alive to witness what happens from here on. It has already started, has it not, but later than I thought? I have watched them in the village, and they too have been watching me. You are in danger, but I think you know that.'

'You have to come and live with us, Hortense. We'll look after you and make sure that you're safe.'

She raised her hand to silence me.

'No. That isn't needed. I do not wish it, and the disturbance would be too great for me. There is one more thing I must give you. Caro, your father loved it, and thought it the most beautiful thing, but your mother took against it, like the discs. She thought it would bring bad luck but I don't believe in rubbish like that. Luck is an issue of attitude alone. I have loved to have it in my house and have had a very happy and fortunate life. I am ninety-two, so have nothing to complain about.'

She opened the box again and pulled out a beautiful casket, made from a dark red, shiny material. It looked like cinnabar, a type of stone mined in various places around the world, which had a high mercury content. The Romans and others had used it for that alone, although in the Far East it had historically been used for carved ornaments and jewellery. I had seen a few ancient Church vessels made from it in the past, although these days it was hardly seen at all.

Hortense's casket was inlaid with golden vines running all around the box, and was exquisite. She used the small gold key on her chain and then opened the lid to reveal a stunning golden cube, perhaps eight centimetres square, with engravings on each side. Caro got up to look at it, and then handed it to me. It gleamed like it was lit from within, and we all stared at it, totally mesmerised.

'It's so beautiful. Where did he find it?'

'Soon, you shall have all of this information to do with as you will. For now, though, I'm tired, and Angeline will be here shortly.'

She handed the chain with its keys and gold disc to Caro and silenced her attempts to question this by another raise of her hand. She spoke again, using her

186

native French this time, and in a loud, clear voice, as much, it seemed, to herself as to Caro and myself.

'Ma part est terminée. C'est fait!' Then in English: 'My part is finished. It is done!'

She looked exhausted, and I felt concerned. I wrote my telephone numbers on the pad by her phone, and intended to call Angeline, her home help, later on. I knew that she slept with Hortense each night now, which made me feel a little easier, but not entirely so.

Everything was put back in the chest and wrapped in an old table cloth. We kissed and hugged Hortense, both Caro and I fighting to hold back the tears, and promised to call her in the morning, telling her to call us anytime. The wrapped wooden box was very heavy and awkward to hold, and I struggled with it as we walked back to the car. It was now well past six, and we were just about to drive off when I saw a car pull into the almost empty car park. Caro recognised Angeline as the driver. She jumped out and I followed her.

CHAPTER THIRTY-TWO

'Angeline, we're so worried about Hortense… she seems so thin and frail. Benoît has to work, but I'd happily have her live with me, although she refused, of course.'

'You're wasting your time, she won't leave that cottage. I've even offered to live with her full-time, but she won't have it. Don't worry, I'll look after her, and if I'm at all worried I promise to call. The doctor sees her regularly, and she's happy enough. What more can anyone do?'

She was right, and we thanked her, checked that she was being properly paid, and although not happy, acknowledged that short of forcing Hortense into the car and taking her with us we could do no more. Back in the car, we began the short drive to Caro's house.

'Are you alright, Ben? About us being brother and sister? It must have come as quite a shock.'

'I'm surprisingly OK. Nothing's changed really, has it? It's just the secret thing again. Another one to add to the list of many. Why didn't you tell me when you found out?'

'I agonised over it for ages. I was quite upset myself for a while. I was the one that they gave away don't forget. I would have told you eventually, but the main reason I decided against it, was because I was worried about you becoming even more angry with your parents.

I didn't want you to have any more turmoil than you already did. Was I wrong? I'm so sorry if I was.'

'It doesn't matter. I'm glad I know now. What other secrets are going to come out of the woodwork, I wonder? Nothing would surprise me anymore. I mean, we've got a boot full of gold at this very moment. What other revelations does Hortense have for us? I don't know whether to be excited or scared.'

'I know what you mean. I think I'm excited and scared.'

'Anyway, let's collect your bags. You're coming back with me. Your house is quite isolated and it's not safe.'

I braced myself for an argument, which I was determined to win, but it didn't happen. Back at her house, whilst she packed a case, I gave her garden a good watering and filled two large baskets to the brim with various fruit and vegetables. With everything loaded into the car, the windows checked, and the alarm switched on, we began the winding descent down the mountain side. I had seen a car in the lay-by opposite the drive when we had come in, but this wasn't that unusual because of the many tourists that came up and down the road. However, the same car now appeared to be behind us.

'I think we're being followed. I saw them parked in the lay-by when I pulled into your drive earlier. Hang on tight… I'm going to try to lose them. There's a narrow track a few hundred yards from here, which cuts around the side of the mountain and ends up on the main road below Antugnac.'

She gripped the handrail above the door and put her

189

other hand on the dashboard of the car. Within seconds, I took a sharp left and with dust flying we sped down the rough, gritty track.

'Hang on,' I said again. 'Once we're on the main road we'll be fine, and so far there's no one behind us.'

We passed a few farmhouses and a small cluster of cottages, the dust now hovering behind us in a thick cloud. They would think that we were lunatics to drive by at such speed, but I hardly cared, and we were soon at the junction of the main road at the bottom of the hill.

'Wow, I enjoyed that. I knew that short course in rally driving would come in handy one day. I won it at the church raffle. Did I tell you, Caro? Caro? Are you OK? You look a bit green.'

'I'm wonderful… just wonderful. Can we go home now please?'

Five minutes later we pulled up outside my house, turning the car around so that, if necessary, we could drive straight out. There was no one to be seen and we quickly unloaded everything in silence and let ourselves in. I locked the outer metal door from the inside, which I didn't normally do, and then the internal one too.

There were no accessible windows at this side of the house and I thanked the foresight of builders in times past for securing the back of the house in this way. The walls were well over a metre thick, and without dynamite, getting in uninvited would be very difficult indeed. If someone was determined enough, the locks of the door could probably be smashed, but it would make a considerable amount of noise, which would at least give us some warning.

CHAPTER THIRTY-THREE

Caro took her suitcase upstairs. The house had changed a lot since my parents and grandparents had lived here. There were four rooms on the first floor then, with just one bathroom, and it didn't really work for me. I had all the internal walls taken down and two large bedrooms made, each with a bathroom of its own, as well as a spacious study for me. The top floor was one room, and was so vast in width and height that I had no idea what to do with it. Apart from a new bathroom installed into one corner, it hadn't changed at all.

On the stripped floor was one of my parents' huge Persian rugs, and a large bed, wardrobe, drawers, and dressing table that had belonged to my grandparents. On one wall were a few paintings done by Aunt Hortense when she was younger. She was a talented artist and had gained quite a reputation in the region at one time. They were mostly of the mountains and villages nearby and were beautifully executed and very atmospheric. The size of the room still dwarfed the pieces of furniture, though, and I hardly ever went up there since the rest of the house provided more than enough space for me and my belongings.

I opened the shutters and windows at the front of the

house, as well as the doors that led to the small terrace. The sun was out again, and it was still warm, even though it was nearly seven in the evening. I put the chest from Hortense on the table, opened the safe, and took out my laptop and the rifle and ammunition to check over and clean. I had no intention of dying myself, but my main concern was for Caro… my sister. How odd that sounded.

I remembered again what the Italian had said on the phone before I left England. 'Your sister.' Somehow, he knew too. What else did he know about me and my family? I also wondered about the men who followed us earlier. It certainly wasn't Black Coat. There were two of them, both with the obligatory gangster dark glasses, and they drove as close to my bumper as they could, which was an obvious sign of aggression.

And what of Hortense? She said she had seen men around the village, and they had seen her. What did she mean? Was she also at risk? Surely they wouldn't hurt an elderly lady. I trusted her judgement, though, and picked up the phone to call her house. Angeline answered and responded to my questions carefully, trying to reassure me that all was well.

'Please don't worry, Father Benoît. Hortense is fine. We've just eaten dinner: the lovely chicken you brought and the potatoes, and Hortense had a large slice of the tart. She's just settling down now to watch her favourite TV show.'

I thanked her and rang off. Caro came down at this point and I told her about the conversation and what the Italian had said about her being my sister.

'That is odd. If he had taken the trouble to find out that I was there, he must surely have known who I was, which at that time was your cousin. I get the feeling that he knows an awful lot more about you than he has let on, and I keep thinking about our parents. My birth parents, I mean, Celestine and Henrikas. They were away so much. Don't you have any idea of where they went, Ben?'

'No, not at all. The only thing I could think of that made any sense was that they worked for the government, or were spies or something. Otherwise, why wouldn't they say? Every time I asked I was told to not ask questions that couldn't be answered, and in the end, I just stopped asking altogether. As you know, when they died they were in Rome. They were in their seventies, so should have retired by then, surely. I never found out why they were there. There was no trace of any flights being booked, and their bodies were returned to France. All I got was a phone call to tell me that they had been killed in a car accident, and that they would be back in France at a certain time.

'That's really odd.'

'I tried to call the municipal offices and various other places in Rome over several months, but no one knew anything about it, and so I finally gave up. The other oddity was the huge bouquets of lilies all over the church. I had no idea who put them there, and still don't. Do you remember them? They wouldn't have looked out of place in a cathedral, never mind Esperaza. And why Esperaza? Why not here at Antugnac? It had been written into their will so there were no doubts about what they wanted. Their whole life was one big secret. I did know about them being in the Resistance; she used to tell me the odd story about that, but my father, or, should I say, our father, rarely did.'

'Do you remember the stories he used to tell us about Lithuania though, Ben? Forests and fairies and goblins and bold knights. And he used to sing such beautiful and sad songs. He was such a handsome man too; it's where you got your looks from. I think I look more like mother, but she was attractive enough, and I'm not complaining. I'm hungry! Make me some supper if I have to live in this fortress of yours.'

I did as I was told and rustled up a tomato salad with olives, tiny cubes of strong cheese, finely chopped onion, anchovies, fresh basil, olive oil, balsamic vinegar, salt, pepper, and brown sugar. I tore some chunks of bread from a large loaf and put the lot on the table. She had discovered my favourite wine, and we ate and drank in silence, both lost in our own thoughts. Mine were about our parents, and I suspected that hers were too. We were both tired, and after clearing up we put the chest and its contents back in the safe to look at again tomorrow, and went up to bed.

* * *

I was back downstairs by seven the following morning and made a large pot of coffee. I drank the first cup on the terrace in the early morning sun and then went back inside to switch on my laptop and read my emails.

There was one from the bishop's secretary to say she hoped all was well, and that the bishop had called to say he wouldn't be back for a while. She had found cover for the next few weeks, so not to worry. Bill had written to say he was coming out of hospital today, and was looking forward to a visit any time I could manage it. He said he had some information that might interest me about the church. I replied, saying I was away for a while, but could he tell me what the information was by email. The next one was from Merry. Again, she hoped all was well, that the boys were away with friends, and that Peter was also away, although she didn't say where. She had been trying to find more information on why the archaeologist that had written the report about the church had not come back as he had said he would.

> Benoît, I was shocked to read that he had been found dead at his house not long after he had written the report. He died under suspicious circumstances, and I've searched everywhere online, but can't find out any more than that. I'm concerned about Peter too. He's been behaving very strangely lately. I'm sorry, I shouldn't be bothering you with that. I've begun to research possible master's courses and am beginning to feel really excited about it, as well as motivated, which I haven't felt for a long time. I've been by your cottage a few times, and it all looks OK.

I replied, telling her about the weather and Hortense, as well as encouraging her about her future studies. What she had said about the archaeologist was intriguing, as well as the bit about Peter. I asked her, subtly, I hoped, about what concerned her. There were a few other emails that were easily dealt with, and I put the machine to one side in case any replies came in.

Whilst Caro was still asleep, I cleaned my gun, which didn't take long since it hadn't been used since last cleaned nearly a year ago. Putting it back in the safe, I took out Hortense's carved chest.

It was a lovely thing; I wished I'd asked where she'd got it from, and would certainly do so next time we spoke. I took out the bag of discs and emptied them onto the table. There were one hundred and twelve in total, and all the same size, about four centimetres in diameter but with differing designs. Each had a horse with two riders on one side, which I recognised straight away as a well-known symbol of the Knights Templar. The impressions were clear and crisp, showing no signs of wear at all, and the detail was quite astonishing. I started to sort them into piles.

At this point, Caro came down, and I made breakfast while she looked at the discs.

'These are sensational… look at the colour. They quite literally gleam, don't they?'

'They do; there's no need for electricity with these around. They must be of the purest gold possible. I've sorted them into groups, and there are four different impressions in all.'

Putting the breakfast on the table, I sat down beside her. She picked up a disc from the first pile.

'These are obviously Templar in origin. It would be impossible to mistake the two men on horseback, wouldn't it?'

I agreed. 'And look at the scene on the back.'

CHAPTER THIRTY-FOUR

The image on the rear of the first disc was of an open boat sailing on the sea. Five people were inside it, all with halos: two men, two women, and a child. One of the women held a jar, and the man by her side had his hands raised up in front of him, palms forward, making them look large and out of proportion to the rest of his body.

'Before you say it, yes, I know. We've seen the image before, and not a million miles away either.' My hand shook as I placed the disc back down on the table, and an image of that terrible day, some forty-two years before, flashed through my mind.

'Exactly. In the painted room, right underneath our feet. The past is most definitely coming back to haunt us, whether we like it or not. It's not exactly difficult to decipher... Jesus and Mary, their child, and I would say Joseph of Arimathea and his sister, Martha. Did you ever see the Magdalene frescos in Assisi by Giotto di Bondone?'

'Yes, they're amazing, but you mean the Magdalene boat scene arriving in Marseilles? The resemblance between the two is striking, I agree. Look it up on your laptop.'

'I was already doing it. Here it is.' She turned it round so that we could both see it. I had seen it in situ several times, and like the one in the cellar, it showed a boat on a choppy sea, with the same five people inside, arriving at a port during the night.

'It's so atmospheric, and I love the dark colours that he's used, particularly of the sky and sea.'

'I always thought it odd that he did the boat scene in such a public place, since it hardly fits with the religious doctrine of the time. Perhaps he was a secret supporter of the Templars? It's dated to 1320, so it wasn't that long after they were condemned.'

'You may well be right, or perhaps he had a patron who was? We'll probably never know.'

* * *

The second image was of a jar, and on its front was a symbol that I recognised straight away. It was an alchemical glyph called 'Squaring the Circle.' It comprised a circle within a square, within a triangle, within a circle. As well as being a symbol for alchemy in general, it also had many esoteric, mathematical, and geometrical meanings, its origins dating back thousands of years with links to many cultures.

'Squaring the circle. One of the greatest conundrums of all time and so apt on the front of Magdalene's jar like that. And look what's written around the side of it, Ben: *Beata Maria de Rhedez*. It's the church at Rennes-le-Château... I can't believe it.

I've got goosebumps all over. Pour me some more coffee... I need it.'

She continued to talk as she examined the disc. 'Symbolically, the circle represents infinity, femininity, and the spiritual realm. As you know, in alchemical terms the union of a woman and a man was believed to be a merging of physical and spiritual elements, often represented by a triangle, symbolising the union of mind, body, and soul, or male and female and the result of their union: a child. The square or cube represents solidity, stability, truth, the physical realm, and a numerological **22**: the master builder and the most powerful of all numbers. In runic symbolism, the **22**nd rune is representative of the square, as well as that of the Holy Grail.'

Twenty-two and four were numbers that had come up time and time again in our research of Rennes-le-Château and the surrounding area. I thought for a moment of the many square symbols in Peter's church. Variations of this symbol were often found in old churches, and were still used today in various forms by the Freemasons.

Interestingly, carved on one of the massive, ancient stones surrounding a rear window of my house were the numbers three and four, and according to my grandparents they had always been there. We had studied alchemy in some depth when we were younger, initially because of the many symbols we had found in Rennes-le-Château. It fascinated us both, and Caro's father, Charles, was always enthusiastic and encouraging. I

200

supposed that these days, we might be called nerds or geeks, but neither of us cared about that, not then, nor now. I had gone on to research symbolism in some detail whilst I was at university studying theology, as had Caro during her many years as a historian, and it was a subject that we still found fascinating.

* * *

I picked up a disc from the third pile and studied it carefully. The impression was of a classic standing figure of Jesus with halo, also with enlarged feet and hands, palms forward, one hand with the first and second fingers raised. I had seen stone carvings like this before, of Saxon and early Norman date, the hands strangely large, but in this instance, it was clear that there was a point being made.

'Look at the hands held out in front like that, palms forward with no crucifixion wounds. That's quite a statement. And the huge raised heart? It wouldn't look out of place on a Valentine's card. The detailing is quite perfect, and clearly they've never been used as currency. Let me see the last one.'

* * *

I passed her the fourth golden disc, this time impressed with a Fleur-de-Lys surrounded by a triangle, with a vine twisted all around it. Written around the edges was a Latin inscription, 'Amor Vincit Omnia.' Love Conquers

All. I had seen this one before, also in the cellar room below. It was painted on the wall above the opening and was an almost exact replica.

'It's so beautiful, and like the painting down in the cellar. It reminds me of Rosslyn Chapel in Scotland. Do you remember when we went there? What an extraordinary place, but I was thinking of the earl's poem: "Love, truth and life in triple union stand." The three sides of the triangle, but based on human reality rather than the traditional holy trinity. Rosslyn has love quotes everywhere. If these are Templar in date, and I've seen nothing that might make me think otherwise, can you imagine what they must be worth? And Hortense just had them in a cupboard. Where did they come from? She said she would tell us everything in her will, so let's hope we find out one day. Anyway, you know what she's like. It would be pointless to push her any further now.'

She was right. If Hortense had made up her mind about something, then no amount of persuasion would change it. Her frailty also bothered me, and I had no intention of inducing a stroke or heart attack through bullying.

'Whenever I see triangles in symbol form I always think of Lithuania. In Vilnius, the capital, they're everywhere, especially with the eye inside. It's like being spied on, the ancient version of a security camera. Of course, the Teutonic knights were all over the Baltics. Lithuania and Poland were very powerful rulers in their time, and the crossover of knights during the crusades was well known. I can't stop thinking about our father, though. What role did he play in all of this, and why do we know so little about him?'

'I was thinking about him last night too. I've known he was my father for some time, and I suppose I saw him about as much as you did, but he feels so distant, even more so than our mother. We need to find out more.'

'When this is over, I'm thinking of going back to Lithuania to do some digging around. There must be something or why so secretive? But then I think I might not like what I find, which is always a possibility.'

We fell silent for a moment, hearing nothing but the familiar ticking of the clock. What a con time was. When you were young, you were tricked into thinking that you had plenty of it, whereas in reality, there was almost none. A few breaths, and you were finished. We were fifty-five, and had barely known our parents at all. How could that have happened? I thought about the painted room downstairs. Clearly our parents and grandparents knew of the room, but why were they so adamant that we never see it? Was our mother's fury that day based on fear, and a desire to protect us from an involvement with something that might, potentially, be dangerous? It certainly hadn't felt like that at the time.

CHAPTER THIRTY-FIVE

Caro began to run the discs through her fingers, making a solid chinking sound as they fell.

'I don't think these are coins in the traditional sense. The Templars moved about an awful lot and often used passwords or objects for rites of passage or entry, sometimes to deposit or access money or other things that they needed, like a horse or a boat. I'm pretty sure that this is what they are, but it doesn't look like they've ever been used. Maybe they didn't have time to circulate them, and hid them somewhere. And by the way, if you go to Lithuania, then I'm coming too.'

'Understood. I've been thinking about the painted room in the cellar. Someone, a Templar, one assumes, spent quite some time down there. Do you think he was in hiding?'

'I would say that's very likely,' she replied. 'They were horribly persecuted in the end, although many of them did survive in various places around the world. When the king's men arrived at La Rochelle, the port where the Templar ships were anchored, they were all gone. Every single one. Apparently, quite a few joined up with the Hospitaller and Teutonic Knights. They didn't just cease to exist, although there certainly seems to have been considerable propaganda spread around that they were entirely annihilated.'

'I have a feeling that we shall find out where the discs originally came from, and maybe more about our parents, when we get the papers that Hortense has put with her will. Meanwhile, we must keep on trying to work it out for ourselves, and I've had a few ideas.

'I've done a lot of research on this house over the years, but it's been difficult to be exact about dates. I know it was given over as a seminary or abbey of some kind for several hundred years. I also know that the de Nègre, d'Able's and de Couderc families all intermarried, and were the lords of the manor here in Antugnac and owned the original château that is now, in part, this house. The Coudercs, in particular, had established and well-known Templar connections in the region.

'As you know, the château dates back, in part at least, to the thirteenth century, with some fairly major rebuilding in the early seventeenth century after the wars of religion. I think the cellars below are almost certainly original to the earliest building. It seems quite plausible that a Templar knight or knights would be allowed to hide out here in troubled times, by either the lords or the abbot. I'm almost sure that there would have been a passageway up to the church, and one down to the river, if the directions of the blocked passageways are anything to go by. Imagine being shut down there for days on end, with the marauding king's men baying for your blood. I should think a spot of painting would be very therapeutic. Seriously, if you thought you were about to die and have all your records destroyed, then leaving messages and documents of a different kind would seem like a very urgent and important thing to do.'

'You're right. We know that the church here had Templar involvement. The stained-glass window has Templar symbolism, although it doesn't date to that period, and many of the saints' statues are the same as the church at Rennes-le-Château, but I've come across something much more important than that. I haven't had time to tell you about it yet. I'll go and get my papers. Can you give Hortense a quick ring? I'm worried about her.'

She ran up the stairs, and I called Hortense's number.

'Ah, hello, Benoît. Are you checking up on me? I'm fine, and I've just been polishing up my pistol. Charles got it for me years ago, and I like to be prepared. There's trouble afoot, which I know is why you're back here, but please don't worry about me. Look after yourselves, and stay in that castle of yours. Angeline will be back this evening.'

'Please, Hortense, let me come and fetch you, and bring you here. And I'm not sure you should have a gun. Have you got a licence? Do you know how to handle it?'

'My dear boy, I was active in the Resistance against the Nazis for the whole of the war, and I'm not sorry to say that I shot quite a few of the bastards, although nowhere near enough for my liking. And I won't come there. This is my home, and this is where I'm staying.'

I knew I wouldn't be able to convince her otherwise, and rang off, promising to call later. I was worried about the gun though. I was sure that she had been a great shot all those years ago, but she was ninety-two! I told Caro about my conversation when she came back down.

'Oh, she's always had guns. I've got one too. Charles always had guns and taught me how to shoot, and I came out with you and grandfather many times. I did a fair bit of training a few years back when you were abroad, and I've kept up my licence. I still think of my real father as Charles, you know, and I always will. He was a good man, and I've no regrets at all about growing up in that household rather than here. Let's call Hortense again later when Angeline's there.'

She put a pile of papers on the table.

'I knew you'd done some shooting, but had no idea you still kept a gun. Mine's in the safe if you need it, cleaned and ready to go. You know the code. Well, you're still able to surprise me, you and Hortense. I like a nice quiet, simple life!'

'You could have fooled me. There isn't much about your life that's simple and never has been. Quite the opposite, in fact. Perhaps you're more like our parents than you think, addicted to danger and intrigue.'

'Do you really think so? Until recently, I never even considered it, but maybe you're right.'

'There's no maybe about it! Anyway, let's not go there now… let's go through this. I'll start with the Rennes-le-Château stuff first. There's loads of it, but I'll stick to the most important bits. Get comfortable, Ben. This could take quite a bit of time.'

CHAPTER THIRTY-SIX

'I think we're in agreement about a lot of the hype that's around. Dossiers, maps, faked documents, treasure trails, and implied codes so complex that no one can decipher them. That's because there is no code to decipher. People have been set up, I'm convinced of it. Smokescreens and mirrors to send them on an array of random wild goose chases and deflect from what is right in front of their eyes. I think there are several organisations involved in doing this, either separately or jointly. The Church and worldwide governments are at the top of the list, but I suspect that's just the tip of the iceberg. I do see that there may be concerns about world order if the basis of Christianity were disproved, but essentially I believe that money, power, and control are the main driving forces in trying to maintain the status quo.'

'Agreed, but many people might not want to believe it, even with hard evidence, you do realise that? And even if there was evidence that shattered everything that so many people base their lives on, would you want that responsibility? I'm not sure.'

'People can construct whatever reality they want, Ben; they always have. What I simply cannot accept is a pack of lies being fed to millions of people across the world. It's wrong, and nothing so far has convinced me otherwise.' She passed me a sheaf of papers, and twisted her long, curly blond hair into a knot on the top of her head.

* * *

'Right. I'm going to start with Dame Marie de Nègre. Could you get me some water, please?' She waited until I had sat back down.

'She and her gravestone are central to the story that Saunière left to be deciphered. She was the last of the nobility to live in Rennes-le-Château, outliving her husband by some twenty-eight years. There were no surviving male heirs, although she had several daughters that she didn't get on with. Abbé Antione Bigou was the priest at the time of her death in 1781, and it was he who had her gravestone made and placed in the churchyard. The inscription is bizarre to say the least, and you and I have looked at it numerous times and not made any sense of it.

'I was beginning to think it was all another con. An assumption was made that her tomb was below it, and why wouldn't anyone think that? No tomb for her has ever been found, though, and she certainly wasn't placed in the crypt with the rest of her husband's family, since it had been sealed by then. There was probably a headstone as well, and my theory is that the upright cross on Saunière's original grave may well be hers. The inverted

N on the INRI would fit in with that, quite literally symbolising a turnaround of the truth. The "supposed" Priory of Sion documents that were leaked about the inscription on another stone were nothing but fakes. It wouldn't surprise me if money had changed hands at that point, and the documents were put out solely as a diversion. Eventually, the men involved admitted it was rubbish. They're all dead now, anyway.' She took a long drink of the water, ice cubes chinking against the sides of the glass.

'I totally believe that she told Bigou about various secrets that had been held within her family over the centuries. I think he did his best and hid parchments and various other things for her. Quite rightly, he felt the need to leave information and messages for those who would follow him, or it might all be lost forever. Hence the bizarre tombstone.'

'I agree with you so far, but it's important to remember that Marie's nobility wasn't just from her marriage. As I said earlier, her family were lords of the manor here in Antugnac and other surrounding areas for centuries. It's known that the Cathars lived and worked here, and when Simon de Montfort and his army arrived to take over, the people of Antugnac refused to be ruled by him and senior officials became involved.'

'OK, noted. A few years on, and there were troubled times ahead with the French Revolution. Bigou decided to go into hiding, as so many clergy did at that time, possibly to Spain. It's likely that Bigou left further information hidden in the church around the time that he left, and it would certainly make sense if he did. Enter the journal, and de Clare and William Harcourt.

'If we run with the belief that the journal is a record of events at that time, then they too were concerned about what might happen to the documents and secrets. It's possible that the old tombstone was replaced with the coded one then, but I'm fairly sure that even if it was, Bigou left information of his own. Either way, whoever wrote it was no Pythagoras, but given the fact that no one yet has worked it out, they did quite well. Of course, I say no one has deciphered it yet. I have. In the end, it was easy.'

She paused, and drank more water. It was mid-morning, and the sun streamed in through the open doors and windows, with the promise of a very hot day. I went to speak, but she raised her hand in a gesture not dissimilar to that of Hortense.

'Hear me out, and I'll show you how it works… it's all about the oddities in the script, each one being part of the clue. I started at the top and then made the word from the random letters, like an anagram.' She handed me a piece of paper with the inscription of Marie de Nègre's gravestone on it.

CT GIT NOBLe   M
ARIE DE NEGRᴱ
DARLES DAME
DHAUPOUL Dᴱ
BLANCHEFORT
AGEE DE SOIX
ANTE SEₚT ANS
DECEDEE LE
XVII JANVIER
MDCOLXXXI
REQUIES   CATIN
PACE

The letter T is missing from the name HAUTPOUL	**T**
The capital E after NEGRE is smaller than the rest.	**E**
The M from Marie is standing out on its own	**M**
The letter P from SEPT is below the word and small	**P**
The letter L is from NOBLE because the letter e is in lower case. So you go back to the letter before	**L**
The I in CATIN is in the wrong place. It should read REQUIESCAT IN PACE	**I**
The E from DE is smaller than the rest	**E**
The R in DARLES is wrong. It should be B	**R**
The S from the REQUIES is wrong. It should be REQUIESCAT	**S**

'TEMPLIERS… Templars. It was that easy, and the more I looked, the more I found. Bigou and any helpers he had, perhaps Harcourt and de Clare, were smarter than I first thought. In the general text, I can also find Marie Magdalene, Jesus, Joseph of Arimathea, and, get this one, "Jesus n'a pas mourir sur la croix." Jesus didn't die on the cross. That's particularly interesting considering what he wrote in the church records just before he fled. "Jesus de galilee n'est point icy," Jesus of Galilee is not here, over and over again.

'Now, if he was telling someone that Jesus wasn't there, he wouldn't write 'Jesus de Galilee.' As a priest, he, and everyone else locally knew full well who Jesus was. I suspect that what he did was copy something that was told to him, or that had been written by someone else from a long time ago; I'm sure of it. I'm not sure about the spelling of *ici* with a 'y,' but maybe they used both then? Either way, wherever he got it from, it shocked him enough to feel the need to write it down. Anyway, that phrase is written on Marie's tombstone as well, using an I, not a Y. And "Antugnac" is written backwards, using letters from the bottom two lines, and the top two lines. 2+2 = **22**, which is a common denominator in Rennes-le-Château.'

* * *

'And there's more again, Ben. The word Croux and Croix is written all over the tombstone text if you look for it. Even more importantly, Chappelle de Croix.'

'OK, I get all of that. Clever old Bigou, and clever you too. All that from a few words on a gravestone. But that last bit, Croux and Chappelle de Croix? What's that about?' Caro got up and began to walk around the room.

'The area of Croux is just up the road, and part of Antugnac. The Rue des Templiers is in Croux. The little church, Chappelle de Croix? It's in the Rue de Templiers, in Croux. The word Croux isn't French… its most likely origin is Occitan. The Templars used Occitan, of course, as well as various other languages. And the Occitan cross is now used to represent a Templar cross. There's an ancient Templar-style cross on the top of the chapel that has a more recent date on it now, but that was added later. The original building is now a ruin, but is believed to have Templar connections.'

'I do know that a few years ago, a major archaeological dig discovered it to have a *Mikveh,* a pool for Jewish ritual bathing, dating back to at least the third century, which confirms without doubt that a Jewish community was there at that time. Croux was certainly known to have been a very important place over the past few hundred years. In the nineteenth century, it raised its head as a place of historical interest and then died back down again, especially after the arrival of Saunière.'

Caro nodded. 'That's right, and I've wondered if Marie was buried there, somewhere near the Mikveh, or in the little chapel or its grounds. I believe bodies were found there when they undertook the dig and don't doubt that someone else had thoughts about her being up there too. I think Antugnac church was stripped around the same time. It certainly sounds like someone was looking for something. Moving on, the de Fleurys also married into the Hautpoul/Blanchefort family, but I'll come back to that.'

'When we can let's go to Croux and have a look… I haven't been up there for years. I'm beginning to see how Harcourt and de Clare might fit in now. The journal on its own is historically very interesting, but the problems lie with the parchments coming along at the same time.'

'You're right, Ben. It was bad luck, but on the other hand, maybe not. Last night, I kept thinking about what Hortense said about luck being a question of attitude. Maybe we need to change our mindset?'

CHAPTER THIRTY-SEVEN

'The parchments, and I'm making the assumption that they're not forgeries, the painted room, the journal, our old research, and my new discoveries; they all confirm what I already believe about Mary and Jesus being here in France, and Jesus not dying on the cross. It's a story that's been around for hundreds of years, anyway. I've still got a fair bit to tell you, but the very fact that so much interest has been stirred up by the parchments and journal, adds weight to the theory.'

'I think so too.'

'You asked me about responsibility? I've thought about what Harcourt said in the journal about the enlightened seeking the truth when they are ready for it? Surely that can only happen over time, since some will become enlightened and want truth, before others. After talking with Hortense yesterday, I concluded that all we can do is take the opportunity to work the story through, and try to understand why we're in this position. Maybe if we're clear about what we know, then we can find a way out the other side? One thing's for sure: we can't hide in here for the rest of our lives. Of course, we've also got the Templar discs and the cube. I need to see it; can you get it out of the safe, please? I'm sorry, I'm lecturing you again. Old habits die hard, eh?'

'Well, you certainly know how to talk, that's for sure.'

She leant forward to thump me but I was too quick for her and leapt out of the way. I went to the safe, took out the cinnabar box, and handed it to her.

'I'm hungry. Will salad, bread, and cheese do, Caro? I'll cook later.' I went into the kitchen and opened the fridge.

'That's fine, thanks. I worked out another thing from Marie's gravestone too. It's the incorrect date, where a C meaning 100 has been missed and a 0 put in its place? Obviously, it now totals 1681. There's been so much conjecture and wild, fantastical theories, but once again it's simple. 1681 was when the Assembly of the French Clergy took place. It went on until 1682, and in essence it removed any powers from Rome to have a say in how the Church was taxed. It put a greater burden on the Church to cough up money, and even forced them to give free gifts to the crown, not only from land and tithes, but from what each church owned.

'It's obvious that at that time the churches would hide away anything of great value, claiming that they had none, or replacing gold items, for instance, with a cheaper metal. The nobility in each region, who mostly supported their churches greatly – they certainly did in Rennes-le-Château – would have helped with this. I think that what Bigou was trying to say with the date was that the church treasure hidden from that time, and I use the word "treasure" in the broadest sense, was buried with Marie or under the tombstone.'

218

'Whilst you're eating, Caro, and therefore silent, I'll take the opportunity to add to what you've said about the 1681 date. I don't have notes, but I remember it well enough. You might learn something you don't know!'

She smiled apologetically, and I raised my hand like she had done.

'There's been so much conjecture about the date. We know that Saunière reused the Carolingian pillar that he pulled out from under the old altar during the renovations of the church. He inscribed it with the word "Mission" and the date of 1891. Upside down, it does of course, read 1681, but 1891 was significant enough, although I suppose it could have had a double meaning.

'1891 also saw Pope Leo XIII declare a feast of the apparition of "Our Lady of Lourdes" and, indeed, Saunière put a statue of her on top of the pillar in his domaine that year. Lots of the local children received Holy Communion, and he had Ferrafiat, who was a diocesan missionary, speak at the event. Did you know that Ferrafiat was a descendant of St Vincent de Paul and he was a missionary too?'

'No, I didn't.'

'Of course, Saunière had his own mission along with various other clergy as an anti-republican, and had got into hot water because of it before. We also know that he had ideas about having some sort of priests' retirement home at Rennes-le-Château. He did literally turn the whole pillar upside down, of course, which inverted the old cross on it. He was knowledgeable enough to know what an inverted cross would symbolise, so my guess would be that he was, quite literally, turning the crucifixion of Jesus "on its head." He was saying that it didn't happen. It's also quite likely that he came across small relics in its cavity, or found something buried underneath.'

She nodded, her mouth full, and I carried on talking.

'And 1891 was also the year that Saunière worked at Antugnac Church. That may well be significant. And there's evidence to say that he found a golden chalice, which he gave to his close friend, Eugene Grassaud, priest of Amelie les Bains. It wouldn't surprise me if he found it hidden beneath Marie's gravestone, and it's highly likely that there were more valuable items underneath it or others, kept hidden from the greedy hands of Louis XIV since 1681 or maybe before then. It's well known that she was penniless towards the end of her life, so it certainly wasn't personal valuables that were found.'

* * *

Another 1681 came to mind. I had come across it in Coustaussa, once a Cathar village, still with its beautiful but wrecked fortress, and directly across the valley from Rennes-le-Château.

'Inset into one of the cottage walls near the old graveyard in Coustaussa is a strange piece of carved stone that looks like the top of an ornate doorway. Written on it is **1 B C 681.** 1681 again, although I haven't worked out the **B C** yet. Upside down it's 1891, of course. I haven't been able to find out where the stone was found, although it looks like the top of a doorway, or possibly a gravestone. Having the **1** at either end is interesting too, because one of its many numerological meanings is that of an entrance or portal to another realm, which may well include another realm of knowledge.'

Caro pushed her almost empty plate to one side. 'Have you been inside the church?'

'Not for years. I tried, but it's locked up now.'

'I got in a few months ago and, like Antugnac, it's been stripped back to the stone, which looks so odd in this region. Thank goodness they haven't managed to do that to Rennes-le-Château. The water stoup has been all but destroyed, and there's a picture of Pope Leo XIII in the room at the back of the church amongst bits of furniture and other rotting debris. He comes into my research again later.'

* * *

Abbé Antoine Gélis had been the priest at Coustaussa during Saunière's time, and they were close friends. One night, at the point of his retirement and leaving the village for good, Gélis was viciously hacked to death. His house had been ransacked for papers, but gold and other valuables were left behind. 'Viva Angelina' had been written on a cigarette paper and left in his house. Like everything else connected to Rennes-le-Château, there was much conjecture as to this meaning.

'Did you ever work out the meaning of the *Viva*

Angelina on the cigarette paper found in Gélis's house after he had been murdered?' I asked.

'Of course. I hate to say it again, but it was simple. The meaning of the name Angelina is *Messenger of God*. Several strangers had been seen in the village that day, and although they were arrested, oddly they were let go, on their claims that they were travelling bar singers. Ha! Much more likely they were church agents, and definitely messengers of God, or should I say the Church, intent on silencing him and taking any important documents that he held before he left the village. No doubt the police force involved was told, in no uncertain terms, to let them go... I'd bet on it.'

'I'm impressed. Mind you, you've got nothing to do all day long so a bit of research here and there is no hardship, is it?' At this point, she picked up a crust of bread from the table and threw it at me. It missed, but only just and we both laughed.

The poor man's tombstone had added further conjecture. 'I went to the graveyard twice in one afternoon, the second time with a compass. Instead of the usual Christian eastern alignment, Gélis's tombstone faces almost directly to the west, and the rest of the gravestones face south-south-east, towards Rennes-le-Château. When I got home, I checked on a map and he faces directly towards Antugnac and Croux. How odd it that?'

'Very, and even more odd is that you didn't say!' She looked at me, sighed, and shook her head slightly from side to side. 'It's like you don't trust me.'

'That's not true. I suppose I just don't feel the need to share everything, or I forget and move on to something else?'

'I don't believe that you forget anything, Ben, I really don't.' She sighed again. 'Anyway, I suppose that because it's so rocky up there the other graves could have been placed for ease of burial, or maybe they continued to use a historic alignment used in Cathar times? But that doesn't account for the way he faces, which must be deliberate. At the very least I would say it was to state a direct contradiction to normal Christian practices. In recent years, the terraced house that was the presbytery and his home was pulled apart, literally stone by stone, in a blatant search by the Church for more information that he might have hidden. How desperate is that? I wonder if they found anything? It's been rebuilt now and is let out as a gîte.'

CHAPTER THIRTY-EIGHT

Caro had opened the cinnabar box, and the cube gleamed at us. The gold was the same colour as the discs; an intensely rich and buttery yellow. With the sun streaming in from the open doors and window, it reflected flashes of light which bounced and danced on the walls, seemingly with a life of their own.

The cube resembled a large dice, but instead of dots it had an image impressed on each side. The images were the same as on the discs, but larger. The craftsmanship was superb, and with the extra size, the images were even clearer. There was, of course, one more impression, on the sixth side. It was of a key and stood out clearly in relief. It looked a bit like the old key to my door in England, and I supposed that little had changed in basic key design between the Middle Ages and the seventeenth century, which was when the cottage dated to.

She looked up at me. 'What an awesome thing. It reminds me of some gold bars that were brought up from a sixteenth-century Spanish galleon a few years back. There were coins too, not dissimilar to ours, and a few even had Templar-style crosses. It's the perfect symmetry that makes it so astounding, although I suppose that's the whole point. Perfect symmetry, perfect balance, and multiple facets making a whole. The cube has always been a symbol of truth because of each side being the same size. Should we be keeping it here, Ben? It must be of immense value.'

'Probably not, although even if anyone found the safe they would need dynamite to open it. The whole lot should go to the bank vault, though. Let's go down now. It's broad daylight, and mid-afternoon, so there should be plenty of people around. I already have a safety deposit box, so I can put it in there. Take photos, and let's keep a set of discs each.'

She did just that whilst I quickly tidied up and locked the safe. When we went out to the car there was no one in sight, and we jumped in and drove the couple of kilometres to Esperaza. I managed to get a parking space right in front of the bank, and we were soon inside. Caro and I were well known here. The manager was the same age as us and we had gone to school together. His family and ours had known each other for several generations, and that counted for a lot in a rural community like this. We were soon in his office, and my safety deposit box was brought out. He politely looked away as I placed the bag of discs and the cinnabar box with the golden cube inside. I told him that we were depositing coins, and an ornament in a box, and he noted this down. Within minutes everything was back in the vault and we thanked him.

'Not a problem at all,' he replied. 'There have been quite a few burglaries in the area over the past couple of months. Even the church here in Esperaza has to stay locked because of vandals.' He saw us to the door. 'Take care – nice to see you both,' and then went quickly back inside.

'Right, now hold my arm. I'm serious. I think we're both at risk of being kidnapped and we need to make that as difficult as possible. Let's go straight to the bakery, and then the mini-mart to get a few bits. Look, the fish man has a stall. I forgot it was Wednesday. Let's get some prawns and I'll make a risotto tonight.'

Prawns bought, we quickly crossed the square to the bakery. As usual, there was a long queue, but eventually we bought two large loaves and some pastries, which would last for a few days, and headed towards the small supermarket. A man that had been behind us in the bakery queue, was now following us to the supermarket. He might have been going there too, of course, but I held Caro's arm close to mine and we kept walking.

'Steady on, Ben, you've almost stopped the flow of blood.'

'Never mind that, I think we're being followed. Keep walking.'

We reached the supermarket, quickly buying the things we needed, including a kilo of my favourite white peaches. The man didn't come into the shop and within minutes we were back outside. I didn't see him until he made a grab at Caro's arm from behind one of the stone pillars to the side of the shop. He had obviously been waiting for us, but she held on and we almost ran into the café next door. There were quite a few people inside, including some that we knew, but once again the man didn't come in. Ordering two large coffees, we sat down near the window.

* * *

'Phew… that was close… he actually grabbed my arm! What was he going to do, drag me through the square? Isn't that a bit obvious and rather stupid, since I would have yelled my head off? I'm feeling really scared now. What a nightmare this is all becoming.'

'I know. These guys are serious, and my bet is that if he had managed to get you apart from me, a car would have come screaming up alongside and you would have been in it within seconds. I've seen it happen quite a few times in Rome and Naples, and whilst a few people turn their heads, most just carry on for fear of becoming involved. They're used to it there, of course, which we aren't here, but you can bet that the car would have been gone in a flash and would probably have had false plates on it.'

Our coffee arrived, and we chatted to the bar owner for a while until he went back to serve another customer.

'A family I once knew in Naples had been held up at gunpoint three times by the Mafia-style Camorra, and robbed of everything they had because they wouldn't pay protection money. They were lucky not to get killed. The police did nothing, of course; I suppose there was little they could do, given the influence and power these gangs often hold. Let's stay in here for a while and hope that he gets bored and goes away.'

We drank our coffee and relaxed a little, Caro changing the subject to that of Esperaza church.

'It's such a shame they have to lock the church now. It's so beautiful, and a real tourist attraction. Did you know that someone smashed one of the altars? What on earth is that about? If you don't like churches, that's fine, keep out. I can't help feeling it's something to do with Abbé Rivière, the priest in Saunière's time who built the odd statue of Jesus in a grotto with his eyes open. Perhaps people are angry at being conned for all these years, or it could be the opposite, I suppose. They see the statue as heresy of some type and are angry at that. But then why smash the altar, which would be a type of heresy in itself. In Couiza church someone even put excrement on the altar. How sick is that? Sorry to be chattering away. I'm nervous. Actually, that's an understatement!'

'Don't worry. It's my fault. I should have kept you well out of it.'

She shrugged her shoulders.

'You're so cool about everything, Benoît. I'm beginning to feel like I don't know you at all!'

This time it was my turn to shrug my shoulders and change the subject.

'I think your first idea about the smashed altar was probably the most accurate.'

Rivière, the priest here in Esperaza at the same time as Saunière was at Rennes-le-Château, had the strange grotto built after Saunière had died. It was said that when he went to give him the last rites, he had come rushing out of the room looking deeply shocked, having not done so. Saunière didn't get the last rites until after he had died, which seemed rather pointless, and a short while later, the statue was made on Rivière's orders and put in Esperaza church. I got up.

'Right, have we got everything we need for the next few days? We don't want to have to come here again anytime soon – it's too risky. Hang on tight and we'll literally run to the car. It's only on the other side of the square, and I'll make sure the doors are open using the remote. But I'm warning you – I'll be driving fast, so brace yourself!'

CHAPTER THIRTY-NINE

The man who had followed us was nowhere to be seen, and we got to the car safely and sped off. Not speaking at all, we were back at the house within ten minutes and I made tea whilst Caro put the shopping away. It was now almost five, and I got my laptop out to check for emails. Both Merry and Bill had replied.

Bill's email said that he was finally at home and was sitting on a chair in his front room, which although uncomfortable, was wonderful. It was what he wrote next that caught my interest.

> I wanted to tell you something that I had forgotten about the church. It's just a small thing, but those are often the most telling. When we were children, if we'd been cheeky and answered back or used inappropriate language of some sort, my grandfather used to tell us that if it didn't stop we'd find our mouths locked up like the man in Temple's corner. He was referring to the man's head in the piscina in the right-hand chancel corner. I'm sure you've seen it. I've never given it much thought since then, but it's the Temple thing that's interesting, because I think he meant Templar. No one talks about it around

here anymore which is odd, since the lords of the manor were heavily involved in the setting up of the Knights Templar. You'd think they'd be proud of the connection, but the whole thing seems to have been silenced. Plenty of other churches around here are very open about their Templar origins, but even in history at school it was never mentioned. It's almost like it's been deliberately quashed.

When you add it to the other things I told you, about it being viewed as pagan, and bodies being moved in the night, alchemy, witchcraft, and the like, well, I would say something was being covered up. There's a rumour that one of the bells is silver. I haven't managed to find out why, but there's no doubt at all that there has been Templar involvement in the building anyway. The only other strange thing I can think of is the sealed room. Have you ever been in it? Well, it has some interesting and ancient features that most certainly wouldn't have been put in a priest's quarters, which was what most of these rooms were for. There are old carvings and pillars, but the oddest thing about it is the huge ornate Norman door that is now blocked off. Why would anyone build such an ornate door on the inside of a priest's room? It doesn't make sense at all. Obviously, the church was a lot smaller in its earlier years. My view is that this door opened into a room that extended right across the church and was probably used for meetings or God knows what. It's the only thing that makes any sense. There's a tiny staircase in the wall now, as you probably know, but that was made in more recent times, just after the First World War I believe.

I hope this is of use to you in your research. It's so important that these stories are passed on, or they end up being lost for ever, which is a great shame. Let me know if I can be of any further assistance whilst you are away. I can get about a bit now, and can do anything on the computer if that would help at all. I heard your cottage had been totally trashed during a burglary. What an awful thing to happen. No wonder you felt the need to take a break.

He signed off with best wishes, and I was reminded of the report that the archaeologist had written, saying very much the same thing. And yet Peter had said that the priest's room was sealed. I would definitely have gone up there if I'd been given the option. How come I hadn't even seen the door since there must be one? I showed Caro the email and asked her what she thought, since she had read the guidebook too.

'It's mentioned in the guidebook but it's a bit confusing, because it talks of a lost chamber and shows photos, but doesn't say anything about a staircase. The email from Bill clarifies it, and I think his theory is probably correct too. Peter probably simply forgot to show you. Perhaps he's got claustrophobia and didn't want to go up the stairs. If they're in the wall, they'll be tiny. I must admit, though, it does sound like some sort of conspiracy. It's interesting what he said about the piscina and the bell, and he's right about the importance of writing the stories down. So much history has been lost for ever because of not doing that.'

I went on to read Merry's email.

Glad all is going OK out there in France. Peter is still away, and I don't know where he is. I thought he was at some Church do, but when I rang their office to find out what time it finished, they said it had already, yesterday to be precise. He texted me earlier to say he was going to see an old school friend for a day or two en route home, and would call me later, so I'm footloose and fancy free. I'm quite enjoying the freedom. I think he's having some sort of empty nest crisis. I always thought it was women who got that.

I'm not worried about the boys going at all. They'll be here for years yet in the holidays. The church warden said someone made an attempt to break into the church last night. No real damage done, and anyway there's nothing to steal. As you know, the relics are reproductions made of wax, and there's never anything in the church money box. A few buttons and a sweet wrapper is fairly normal. Let's hope they don't come back. I've taken to locking up like someone with OCD since your burglary. I even wedged a chair under the back door last night. Love to you both.

Caro read it too. 'I thought he looked unhappy when we were round there. Very jolly and everything, but when

233

he thought no one was looking his face dropped and he seemed to be worried about something. Let's hope they get it sorted. We've got quite enough on our plates without taking on a depressed vicar.'

At this moment, the phone rang. At first, all I could hear was a jumble of voices and what sounded like sobbing.

CHAPTER FORTY

'Hello? Who is this? Hello?' Finally, I heard a female voice...

'Father Benoît, it's Angeline. Something terrible has happened and Hortense is dead. The house is a mess... please come! I've called the police and they've just arrived.' Then a man's voice came onto the phone.

'Is that Father Benoît?'

'Yes, this is he,' I answered.

'Father Benoît, this is Chief Inspector Fabrice Niort. I am sorry to say that there has been an incident with your aunt, Hortense de Morny. We were called by her helper, Angeline. I must tell you, sir, that your aunt is dead. Please could you come to her home, and we can talk further. We need to ask you some questions.'

Caro had come close to the phone when it was clear there was something wrong.

'What is it, Ben, what is it? Is it Hortense? Tell me please... what is it?'

'It's the police. Angeline found Aunt Hortense dead and they want us to go up there. We should have forced her to come here. We should have dragged her if needs be.'

'Don't be ridiculous. We could hardly drag an elderly

woman screaming her head off down the street. I refuse to take blame for that and so should you. But what an awful shock. She knew something was going to happen, didn't she? Let's get up there quickly. Is everything locked away here?'

We put anything of value back into the safe, checked all the locks and within minutes were driving up the steep hill to Rennes-le-Château. Parking as near to the house as we could, we walked through the open door. There were several officers inside, and Angeline was stood in one corner, crying. She threw herself on Caro, who had also begun to cry.

* * *

Hortense was sitting in her favourite armchair. I had expected a horrific scene, but this wasn't the case. She looked serene, and appeared to have a smile on her face. In her hand was a small pistol.

'I'm so sorry to have to call you in circumstances like this. Forensics will be here soon, so please don't touch anything. The doctor is on his way to give us an initial examination and hopefully tell us how your aunt died. She fired the gun, you know. Were you aware that she had a gun in the house?'

'The whole family certainly had guns in the past, inspector, but I've never seen her with one.'

'There are a few drops of blood on the floor over there, and some outside, so I imagine she hit her target. The area is being looked at now and samples taken.

Clearly there was some attempt to burgle; drawers have been emptied out, but I noticed a jewellery box upstairs with a few rings and necklaces in it, which doesn't appear to have been touched. Perhaps you can tell us if you think anything is missing? Did she keep any other valuables or cash in the house that you know of?'

Before I had a chance to answer a car drew up outside, and several men got out with black bags. They introduced themselves as the forensics team, and without another word started to get out their apparatus and take samples and photos. Within minutes the doctor also walked through the door. He was from Couiza, a few kilometres from Antugnac, and we knew him well.

'Benoît, Caro, I'm so sorry. Hortense was a great lady and so full of spirit. I shall miss her a lot.' He looked towards the inspector. 'May I make a quick examination?'

'Please do. We're interested to know if there are any obvious signs of injury or restraint.'

Whilst he did this, Angeline gave her statement to the inspector, and encouraged by us, she left. I felt very sorry for the poor woman, who was obviously deeply shocked. As a priest, I met with death frequently, and therefore coped with it better, but my hands were shaking and I tucked them into my pockets and took some deep breaths. We carefully walked around to see if we could identify if anything had been moved or was gone. Neither of us had any idea if Hortense had kept money in the house, but it was obvious that this wasn't the work of a petty burglar. The jewellery box was in full view, and its contents intact.

We quickly looked around the ground floor and

went back into the sitting room, where the doctor had just finished.

'Looks like her heart gave out. She'd had problems for years. I checked her over last week and to be honest, I'm amazed she's lasted this long. I see a lot of dead people, as I'm sure you do, Benoît, but she looks happy, doesn't she? I wouldn't recommend an autopsy. It would be pointless, since there are no signs of physical injury at all. It will be up to the coroner in the end though. Shall I call the undertakers?'

He looked at Caro, myself, and the inspector. We all nodded, and thanked him, and he stepped outside with his mobile in his hand to make the call.

'Didn't any of her neighbours hear anything? You would have thought a gunshot would make a fair bit of noise.'

'It would appear not. The cottage on the back is a holiday home, but it's empty this week. The one across the lane is lived in, but they were out at work, I believe. That type of pistol has a built-in silencer; it's very unusual. I can't think where she would have got it from. It's a very specialised thing, and not something you would expect an elderly lady to have.'

Caro now spoke up. 'Hortense was no ordinary lady, inspector. She was very active in the Resistance during the Second World War. I don't know much about it, but I think she held a fairly senior position around here. Sometimes people don't let go of times like that, do they? People hang on to the parts of their lives that were the most emotive or important. I've seen it happen quite often.'

The inspector was silent for a while whilst he took this in. 'Yes, I've seen this too. Did you see anything unusual in the house? There's no sign of a break-in, so either the door was unlocked or she invited them in.'

'Nothing unusual at all, and she often left the door unlocked during the day. We told her not to, but Hortense always did her own thing, inspector. Still, with the blood you would be able to identify the intruders, wouldn't you? And someone else may have seen something?'

'As you know, Father Benoît, it's mostly tourists here these days, and we have no way of tracing them. But we've sent an alert out to all the hospitals for several hundred miles around in case someone turns up with a gunshot wound, and we'll make further enquiries of course, you can count on that. I have your address and phone number, and yours too, Professor de Morny. Please rest assured I shall do all I can to find out who the intruder was. I'm very glad that your aunt wasn't injured in any way though. That would have made it so much worse for you. Here's my number in case you need to reach me – any time at all. I'll be in touch. Ah, the undertaker is here. We'll take the gun for now. May I call you if I need access to the property after today?'

We assured him that he could, and went outside to let the undertaker do his work. Half an hour later he had gone, taking Hortense with him. The police stayed for another hour, and it was dark when they finally left and we closed the door after them. Caro turned to look at me.

* * *

'Oh, Benoît... Benoît... Hortense has gone. What are we going to do now?'

She started to cry, and I put my arms around her and we wept together. Hortense had played a considerable and important role in our lives. As was the case with our parents, there were parts of her life that we knew nothing about. I trusted that that this was soon to change, and that the shadows from the past would begin to lift and reveal some truths about the people we had grown up with, but barely knew. I knew that Hortense would continue to influence our lives, even though she was no longer here but, in this moment, we felt nothing but the intense loss of our last living relative.

We were bereft.

CHAPTER FORTY-ONE

It was almost ten in the evening when we got back to Antugnac, and the village was silent as we let ourselves into the house. I poured us both a Calvados over ice, and its fiery, apple-scented warmth was soothing after such a traumatic day. We were exhausted, and Caro lay down on the sofa whilst I made toast.

'She knew something was going to happen, but how? Thank goodness she gave us the discs and cube when she did or they may have been gone for ever. I'd give anything to have her back, but the one consolation was the look on her face. I'll never forget it. She shot one of the intruders and I think that gave her enormous satisfaction. It does to me as well. She was an amazing woman. I wish we knew more about her and her life.'

'She was amazing, it's true. Maybe we'll learn more when we get the documents that she told us about. I hope so. It's like all the family around us have held secrets and kept us apart from them, and yet we've become involved anyway, which was inevitable, really. I think they thought they were protecting us, but it didn't work. Their secrets refused to be silent, and now the opposite of what they thought they were doing has happened. It's like a genetic encoding. Even though nothing is said, it gets passed down the line anyway. What a waste; all that time lost, and for what?'

'I can only assume that what they were doing meant a lot to them. Or perhaps they knew how dangerous it all was, whatever "it" is. Maybe if it wasn't for your involvement with the parchments and the journal, we would still be out of it. Except for Hortense, of course. She intended to tell all and involve us, no matter what. We just have to hope that her decision to do so was the right one, but it will be up to us to decide what to do with it. We might even wish we didn't know! But there's more to it. What about the Italian knowing we were brother and sister, and the failed attempts to kill you?' She pulled a tissue from her pocket and wiped at the few tears that were creeping down her cheeks.

* * *

I poured us both more of the Calvados. 'But where do we go from here? I keep thinking about who to ask for help, but there's no one. One of the first people I would call under normal circumstances would be the bishop, but given that he stole the copy journal I certainly don't feel inclined to do that, and we've got no family left. When I was in England, I did think that I might make more of an effort to forge stronger friendships. I thought I might do that with Peter, but I'm not so sure now. I'm not convinced that he's entirely stable, and I've got more than enough problems already.'

'What do you mean "not entirely stable?" He seems

like a nice enough chap, just a tad depressed.'

'Yes, I thought that, but I keep thinking about when we were there the other evening, and he gave Merry that weird look when she mentioned the report from the archaeologist. He wasn't pleased, I could see that, and you mentioned it too. And he said that you couldn't get into the old priest's room in the church, when you quite obviously can. And he was in my cottage straight after it was broken into. Or that's what he said, anyway. He said he had a card for us from Merry, but he didn't give me any card, and when I next saw her she gave me a card she said she had just bought, so that was another lie. I might be wrong, but there's something amiss there.

'I even thought of telling Inspector Niort everything, then the cat would be totally out of its straightjacket, and we would have no control of the outcome at all. Perhaps that shouldn't matter, but somehow it does, for now, anyway. I thought Adrian Harcourt was a decent bloke, but he was desperate to get his hands on the journal, and I'm sure it was him that broke into the cottage the first time. And I saw him talking to Black Coat. That's really confusing and anyway, no one's seen him for days.'

I sipped my drink, and looked at Caro.

'Do you know what…? I think the only person I would ask for help at the moment is the Italian. I've no reason to trust him really, but at least he called to tell me I was in trouble, which considering it's all his fault isn't such a great thing, I suppose. And Black Coat works for him, I'm sure. We could certainly do with a bodyguard right now.'

243

'And we've lost Hortense, which is a real blow,' Caro
added.

* * *

Everything was silent for a moment apart from the ever-
present ticking of the clock and the chinking of the ice
in our glasses.

'I keep thinking about her and wondering what she
would advise us to do. She knew we were in trouble, but
didn't seem all that concerned. I think we need to sit it
out. Anytime soon, someone will show us their hand.
They'll have to. I mean, if we needed to, we could stay
here for weeks. The freezer's full, there's loads of dried
food, and I'm sure Arnaud would bring us something if
we asked him. He's very discreet. Somehow, though, I
don't think the men that are after us will be that patient.
If we must, we can take to the mountains. We know them
better than anyone. Yesterday, Hortense said something
that really struck me; "everything is connected." I think
she was telling us something. It will all play itself out;
things always do in the end, one way or another.'

I hoped she was right. It was now almost one in the
morning and I didn't feel tired at all.

'I feel numb. Perhaps it's the shock combined with
the alcohol. I don't want to go to bed though. Do go up
if you want to, Ben, but I'll stay down here for a while
yet. Could you get my papers and things out of the safe
please?'

I did as she asked, also picking up the few gold discs

to look at again. It felt quite chilly so I made up a fire, which was soon crackling away. Arnaud had brought me a load of apple logs from a tree that he had cut down in his garden, and the aromatic smell began to permeate the room which, along with our Calvados, was very comforting. It reminded me of times past, and I sat gazing at the flames whilst Caro flicked through her papers.

We would have to think about Hortense's funeral, but we needed to see her will first in case she had any special requests. I would refuse an autopsy if possible, since it was quite clear from what the doctor said that she had died of heart failure. Maybe this might still constitute manslaughter, though? I was unsure. Anyway, I would call the solicitor in the morning and let him know that Hortense had died, and no doubt he would take it from there.

CHAPTER FORTY-TWO

'I've been looking at the inscription on Marie de Nègre's tombstone again. Considering how few letters there are, it makes an impressive amount of pertinent words, with none of them having to reuse any of the letters. I take back all I said about Bigou not being Pythagoras. I've been trying to make links with Harcourt's journal. Harcourt's there, de Clare, Cirencester, and the name of your village, piscina, secret, Sangreal, Sainte-Andrè, that's the church here, and even "Assemblée du Clergé de France." I know that basic sets of letters can make up lots of words, and usually I'd be the first person to question it, but as a tombstone inscription with an obvious attempt to give a message, I'm inclined to think that it's deliberate.'

I got up to throw a few more logs on the fire. 'I think so too.'

'And there's something else. You know the grotto that Saunière built himself in front of the church? It held a statue of Mary Magdalene? She's gone now, vandalised, I think, but the numbers and letters underneath on the ledge have never been decoded. Until now, of course. It was so easy. Bérenger clearly had an interest in runes and the whole area is riddled with both runic and numerological symbols. Once you know that, you can decode just about everything. The Templars used them, as did many other people, of course. I got into his head, and thought about him as a person, not some gold digger who had no thoughts but finding a hoard. I think he was intelligent, and inquisitive. He liked to acquire new knowledge, and his priest friends were all intelligent men. Anyway, back to the ledge. Like I said, you just need the two codes.

XXSLX

'I read somewhere that the first letter is a K, but it isn't. It's definitely an **X** squeezed in a bit tightly, because of what looks to be a modern repair. The **X** in runic terms is Gebo. It's rune number **7**. A fortuitous number in many belief systems. Anyway, in runic terms, its basic meaning is a union of two humans in a relationship, a sexual marriage, a sacred or mystical union, balance, harmony, peace, gifts, love, partnership, and perceiving the divine.

'But there are two **X**s side by side. In gnostic teachings of runes, two crosses together usually standing upright is the rune Ing or Ingwaz. Believed to be the rune of the Holy Grail itself, it's also symbolic of the seed of life, DNA, the god and goddess, unity, partnerships, fertility, and the continuation of the generation. It's also the **22nd** rune, which is another **22** linked to Rennes-le-Château.

'So, we have the symbol for the Holy Grail, and then **S** and **L**. Hmmm… What word begins with **S** and ends in **L**?'

'Even I can get that, Caro. San Graél obviously… or sang raél. Holy grail… or holy blood.'

247

'Exactly. Then there's the last cross. Using numerology as well, an **X** in Latin is ten. Times that by three and you have thirty, which makes a numerological **3**. **3** symbolises the trinity and the physical union of a man and woman and their offspring. It all makes absolute sense. The two crosses on one side for Jesus and Mary, then sang raél, then another cross for their child.

XXSLX

'Saunière's use of numerology and runic symbolism shouldn't be that surprising, since it's held considerable importance throughout history. It was particularly fashionable and undergoing a revival during the time that he was at Rennes-le-Château, and he used it as best he could.'

* * *

'**22** is particularly interesting when relating it to Jesus as a master builder, not in the bricks and mortar sense, but of humanity. The carpenter bit is rubbish anyway, just an error in translation. He was of royal descent, though, and a Rabbi, and was hardly likely to have been messing about chopping up bits of wood or stone. I think quite a lot of the Bible was written in a metaphorical or allegorical sense, but so much is lost because of poor translation, perhaps deliberately so. I've also wondered if parts of it are a type of codex, not unlike the mysteries at Rennes-le-Château. They just need to be understood correctly and then deciphered. And, like a lot of the hype about Rennes-le-Château, some of it is pure fantasy, put in to deliberately confuse and deflect from the truth.'

Caro nodded her head. 'That's also my view. There's more though. Saunière's date of birth is a numerological **22**. And Mary Magdalene's feast day is the **22**nd. There are lots of other **22**s at Rennes, including steps and crenulations. In the Coptic calendar, St Antoine the hermit's feast day is the **22**nd. And we mustn't forget the **22** letters above the church door, *Terribilis est locus iste*. That's part of several phrases taken from the bible, Genesis 28:17: "how dreadful is this place," meaning full of dread and fear and awe, not terrible in the sense that we know it. The other part is Mathew 21:13. "My house shall be called the house of prayer but you have made it a den of thieves." Very appropriate.

'One of the things that most people don't notice at Rennes-le-Château is the keystone above the door. It's the coat of arms for Pope Leo XIII. Notice the keys? A Templar symbol, and remember the head in your village church with his mouth sealed and locked? And there's more to it. Pope Leo XIII died on a numerological **22**. Even more significant than that is the vision that he had and is officially recorded and documented. It happened in 1884, the year before Saunière came to Rennes-le-Château. He had just held Mass in his private chapel and was leaving when he stopped still and went into a trance for about ten minutes. When he came around, he said he had heard voices which he believed to be of God and Satan engaged in a conversation. It goes like this:

Satan.	I can destroy your Church.
God.	You can? Then go ahead and do so.
Satan.	To do so I need more time and more power.
God.	How much time, how much power?
Satan.	75–100 years and a greater power to those who will give themselves over to my service.
God.	You have the time, you have the power. Do with them what you will.

'I hardly believed it when I read it, but it's true. It could have been written for Saunière, couldn't it? I know I keep using the word, but the synchronicity is startling. Saunière probably didn't have the power to reveal all at that time. Not like there is now, with much more freedom of speech and media cover, although I still think the powers that are out there would have a damn good go at stopping it. How very appropriate to put the arms above the door, along with those phrases. He did everything he could to pass the message on, and I admire him hugely for it.'

'I've come across it, but not in this context. How very odd.'

'I know, and going back to symbolism, remember that **22** adds up to four. The fourth rune is Ansuz. This rune is all about the transmission of language through signs and symbols, the voice of the universe, the ancestors, linguistics, word power, divine communication, creative wisdom, and open paths of communication.'

CHAPTER FORTY-THREE

'It's well known that the saint statues in the church form an M for Magdalene if you draw a line between them, and taking the initial of each makes graal, or grail in English. That's if you use Luke from the four evangelists. We worked that out a long time ago, as did lots of others, but the reason he chose the saints that he did is very revealing.

St Germaine
St Roch
St Anthony the Hermit
St Anthony of Padua
St Luke

'I'll go through them in turn, but leave Germaine till last. You'll see why in a minute.

'OK. Roch. Patron saint of a few things, but for Saunière it was that of all those who had been falsely accused. Saunière was accused of becoming involved in politics, attempting to influence his parishioners, grave robbing, and various other things over the years. I'm not sure when the statue of Roch went in, but probably before the accusation about his finances. I also think he's using Roch to point to Marie de Nègre: Roc Nègre? The *black* mountain opposite Blanchefort supposedly full of gold mines? Roch did a lot of work with victims of the *Black* Death, and shows off his own plague pustule. Apparently Roch was born with a red cross on his chest, like a Templar emblem, confirming Saunière's desire to include the Templars in his narrative.'

* * *

'I can do Anthony the Hermit, father of all monks, tempted in the desert with gold and silver. Saunière may have seen himself as being tempted by pay-offs and gold that he found. I don't doubt that he used the situation to his best advantage, but I think it was much more complex than many assume, and he was as vulnerable to criticism as the rest of us. One of the most famous images of Anthony is on a Coptic icon, where he is standing in a brown monk's habit, with a hood, holding a walking stick, and a scroll.'

* * *

Caro nodded, and shuffled her papers. 'Anthony of Padua, patron saint of lost things. Bérenger found many lost things, we're very sure about that.'

* * *

'The message of Luke is more subtle. He was the patron saint of historians and artists, which is how

Saunière thought of himself, but more interesting is chapter 19:10 in the Gospel of Saint Luke, which is very appropriate for both Saunière and Jesus.'

For the son of man is come to seek,
And to save that which was lost.

CHAPTER FORTY-FOUR

'Excellent, Caro. He must have had great fun putting it all together, but what about Germaine? We always thought it was simply the flowers, and the connection with the local Fleury family, who married into the Hautpoul/Blanchefort clan.'

'Yes, but I've discovered something much more important than that. If you remember, there's another so-called Fleury memorial, *The Sermon on the Mount*, at the back of the church. It has flowers scattered all over it, like Germaine's skirt? The story goes that Germaine was treated badly by her stepmother, who accused her of the theft of food. Germaine opened her skirts and thousands of flowers fell out, not from the area at all. The Fleurys were long gone by Saunière's time, though, and I really couldn't see why they deserved two memorial/statues, so I kept on looking.

'The ancient family of de Fleury certainly had Templar connections, and links to the Voisins, part of the Hautpoul family, which may have brought information down the family line. Marie de Nègre was estranged from her daughter, who married Paul François Vincent de Fleury in 1767, and they were all crippled with debt in the end.

'There is another Fleury that he may well have been

254

aware of – François Richard Fleury, a painter, born in 1777, a numerological **22**, who died in 1852. He was a favourite of Josephine de Beauharnais, Napoleon's Josephine. One of his most famous paintings was called *The Hermitage of Vaucouleurs*, which showed Joan of Arc going to a hermit to ask for advice. He also painted Jacques de Molay, the last of **22** Templar Grand Masters. It's possible that he was some relation of the Fleurys of Rennes-le-Château. He was an interesting character because of his involvement in the Scottish Rite Masonic Lodge of Isis. In 1815, he was given the *Knight, Legion of Honour* award. Joan comes back into the story a bit later, as does Molay, but there's more, Benoît, so pay attention, please!'

'I'd be too scared not to. Is this how you treated your students?'

'Only if they were very lucky! Now listen. I felt that I was missing something, so I kept on searching, a bit like Saunière, I suppose. One of the most famous de Fleurys in history was Hugo de Sancta Maria de Fleury, a Benedictine monk. There were a whole host of other names for him, including Huges de Sainte Marie, Hugues de Santa Maria and Hugo De S Maria Floriacensis Monachus.'

'Yes, I know. I've heard of him, of course.'

'I should think so, you being a priest and translator. Anyway, he was called Hugo or Hughes of Santa Maria after the village church that his father owned along with the actual village, sometime in the mid-eleventh century. No one knows who his father was, though, or anything about him at all, which is odd. It's almost like it's been written out of the history books, and perhaps it was. But it's likely that he was noble by birth, and possibly illegitimate.

'Let's take a side-step for a minute to Campagne-sur-Aude, just down the road. The name is on Marie's tombstone too, of course. It's a renowned Templar town and church. Do you remember the statue of a very much alive, Jesus, being brought down from the cross by a monk?'

'How could I forget it, although for some reason it's less well known than some of the other connections, like Esperaza and the Jesus statue in a grotto, with his eyes wide open. The church at Le Bezu, a Cathar and then Templar stronghold, has a crucified Jesus statue with his eyes wide open and staring too. It's most odd. Are you thinking that the one in Campagne-sur-Aude depicts Hugo de Fleury removing Jesus from the false story that he was crucified?'

'Yes, possibly. If you weren't allowed to speak out, then these were the kind of things that you could do, to tell the story. Antoine Beaux, the priest of Campagne-sur-Aude, was a friend of Saunière's, and don't forget *Templiers* in Marie de Nègre's tombstone, made up from the incorrect letters? Hugo de Fleury was a scholar and translator from Fleury abbey at St-Benoît-sur-Loire. Note the Benoît. Synchronicity playing its part again! And that name is also in her tombstone inscription.'

'I know he wrote enormously important books about the lineage of Frankish kings, the history of royalty and the church. He had access to the most ancient and important documents that were around. Charlemagne had supported the abbey in his time, and many of the abbots were of royal lineage themselves; Merovingians, Carolingians, and goodness knows what else. Even Cardinal Richelieu du Plessis.'

'That was a lot later, but he had Templar connections, albeit from some time before. Theobaldus who was believed to be a Merovingian from the early 600s, was most likely the founder of the abbey, and by the mid-ninth century it had what was believed to be the best and most comprehensive library in the west. It's quite possible that Hugo found some old documents, or already had them because he came from this area, which ended up in the hands of the Cathars and Templars, or someone else linked to Rennes-le-Château. It was much bigger and more important back then, and was frequently fought over and sold.

'Quite a few Bérengers owned it, mostly from Spain in the eleventh century onwards, and Saunière's mother was a Hugues. They were a well-known local family, and there were known Templars with both of those names. It's just an oddity to note, but I've often wondered if his family knew more than they let on. This is going to sound ludicrous coming from me, but I'm beginning to think Saunière was meant to find what he did.'

'What do you mean? Like destiny or something?'

'I suppose so, but I can barely put it into words. I get a shiver down my spine just thinking about it.'

'If there is such a thing, then it's happening to us too. Who knows?'

'Who knows indeed. Did I tell you that Bérenger's birthday is a numerological **22**? Did you know yours was, Benoît? And mine, of course, now I'm your long-lost sister. Oddly – and I came across this quite by chance whilst browsing on the internet – the name Henrikas is thought to represent a numerological **22**. Oh, and Bérenger died on the **22**nd. Marie Dénarnaud died on a numerological **22** as well, and Saint Germaine died when she was **22**. Bérenger came to Rennes-le-Château in 1885, which is a **22**. Another friend of his was Henri Boudet. He wrote a rather odd book called *The True Celtic Language*. Anyway, he died on a numerological **22**, some say in suspicious circumstances after a visit from two men earlier that day.'

'It's bizarre in the extreme, but surely if you were to believe that this was something more than just coincidence, then you would also have to make room for other unknowns, like God?'

Caro looked at me for a moment, her eyebrows raised.

'No, Ben. I can't agree with that statement. We know there are things that we don't yet understand, and hopefully, at some point in time, we will. But that doesn't mean that there is a single superior deity or God controlling everything that we do, and I'm certainly not about to get on my knees in front of a giant number twenty-two and beg for mercy, or pledge eternal worship and love. How very provoking you are sometimes.'

'Nothing wrong with that. A bit of challenging never hurt anyone, and certainly not you.'

She smiled. 'True enough. Anyway, there's something else that I've been thinking about, to do with Germaine and the Fleury monument, but I want to show you it at the church, along with the new discoveries I've made in the Stations of the Cross.'

CHAPTER FORTY-FIVE

I got up to get some water, and when I sat back down Caro had fallen asleep, her notes slipped down onto the floor. I crept upstairs to get a blanket and carefully tucked it around her. She didn't stir, and I put everything in the safe, checked the fire, and went up to my own bed, just as dawn was about to break.

It was nearly eleven when I finally woke up, a strong smell of coffee wafting up the stairs. I pulled on my dressing gown and went down to find her making scrambled eggs and toast.

'I thought we ate so little yesterday that I would do a decent breakfast. How are you feeling this morning?'

'Not too bad. I must have slept for about six hours. You passed out on the sofa so I thought it best to leave you there. Thanks for the eggs – I'm really hungry.'

'Good! I called the solicitor and left a message. Oh, I nearly forgot, the phone rang earlier, but they hung up. It was an unknown number.'

'I wonder who it was?' I suddenly felt anxious. 'I've got an awful feeling that something's going to happen.' When the phone rang again, I looked at Caro before reaching for it. It did cross my mind not to answer it at all, but it might be the Italian offering help, which right now, would be very welcome!

'Hello, is that Ben? It's Bishop August. I've tracked you down at last.'

'Hello, Bishop. Yes, you've tracked me down. How are you? Your secretary said you were away. I hope everything's OK?'

'Yes, yes, no problems. Just a family thing to sort out. I heard you had a family problem too?'

'That's right… my aunt has died, I'm afraid.'

'Yes, I'd heard – I'm so sorry. There must be a lot to sort out. Of course, you have your cousin to help. How is she? Such a delightful woman.'

'Well, we're both upset obviously, and there's a lot to do. I won't be back until after the funeral, and I don't have a date for that yet. I'm sorry to let you down.'

'No problem, Benoît. We'll sort things out this end. Such a fascinating area that you live in there in France. Rennes-le-Château. I've never been, but would love to see it all. You must know quite a lot about the mysterious priest Saunière and his discoveries, growing up in the area?'

'Yes, I suppose I do, but there are so many red herrings, deliberately misleading treasure trails, propaganda, and downright lies written about it. Anything worth having is probably already in the Vatican vaults. I'm sure that you'd find far more there than you would here.' The thought of the bishop trying to get access to the most secret files in the Vatican was an amusing one, and I laughed. 'Oh, by the way, did Adrian Harcourt ever turn up? I remember you telling me that he had gone missing.'

'I'm not sure, Ben; I haven't heard. If I do, I'll let you know.'

We agreed to keep in touch, and ended the conversation.

'What do you make of that? I put the call on loudspeaker so you could hear it. Sounds like he's going to be poking around sooner or later, if he isn't here already. He was definitely fishing! I used to think he was a friend, but since he stole the copy journal everything has changed. You wouldn't do that to a friend, so clearly, he isn't one at all. Maybe it's a case of "keep your friends close and your enemies closer still." Perhaps that's how he sees me?'

Caro thought for a moment.

'And there's something else. How did he know Hortense had died? You haven't spoken to him, and neither have I. No one knows but us, although I suppose it might get into the press eventually, if her involvement in the Resistance gets out. It wouldn't surprise me if he's a lot closer than England. We had better keep our eyes open. As for Harcourt, he's up to no good too from what you've told me. I can't see what part Peter the vicar might play in it all, but he's an oddball. Merry's far too good for him. I wonder what's happened to the Italian? I'd like to give him a good slap for involving you in the first place, no matter who he is.'

At this point, the phone rang again. It was the solicitor who was dealing with Hortense's affairs, and we made an appointment to go to his offices in town the following morning, and go through her will.

'We need to go up to Hortense's cottage and have another look around. She may well have left other things for us, hidden away somewhere. In fact, I'd bet on it. I think the house has been left jointly to us both, Benoît. I read it in a letter that she had written to Charles. What shall we do with it?'

'Let's keep it for now. Property up there rarely comes available and there's no rush. I'm not keen on letting it out either. I know most people are respectful and interested, but all the churches around here have been vandalised, and as you know, a lot of damage has been done at Rennes-le-Château over the years.'

'Even the Nazis took to dynamiting the place during the Second World War... morons. Seriously, do people really think there are pits full of gold lying around? The church warden at Esperaza told me that when he turned his back for a few minutes, he found a couple of men digging up the floor behind the altar. Even if there are tombs there, and all old churches buried the most important people inside, they're hardly likely to be a couple of inches down, are they?'

'If we're going up there, I suppose when it's full of tourists would be best, but I'm not sure we should leave the house at all.'

'I know, but I'm desperate to get out, and we really should check Hortense's cottage. Talking about vandalism, did I tell you that the Jesus of Antugnac statue that Saunière erected facing Rennes-le-Château has had its hands chopped off? Do you remember they used to be gold, with Maltese crosses in the palms and

263

hearts in the centre with the letter M on them? Why would anyone do that?'

'Of course I remember it, but it was with hands last time I saw it.'

'Let's drive up that way and look.'

'OK, but don't blame me if we end up in another chase, or worse. The car is packed for an emergency though. How do you fancy a night or two in a viper-infested cave? It might end up with that, the way things are going. I'm just going to have a quick shower.'

* * *

Whilst I was upstairs, I went to the top of the house to look out of the front and rear windows. I couldn't see anything that looked remotely suspicious. Fifteen minutes later, and we were driving up the steep lane that led to the statue. There was no one to be seen, and I pulled over, leaving the engine running.

I stared at the statue in dismay. The whole thing had been whitewashed, head to foot, and a few metres in front of it was the fence of a large new bungalow. As Caro had said, some sick person had smashed the golden hands off, leaving his arms in stumps.

'I've just noticed something else. I always thought that he faced directly towards Rennes-le-Château, but he doesn't. Look, Ben, he's staring right at Antugnac church. Rennes-le-Château is slightly to one side.'

'So it is. Odd we never noticed that before. Someone's had a go at the cross too.'

There was a large, stone cross behind the statue. It had the initials B.D. on it and a date of 1838. INRI was carved at the top, but with the N inverted. It had always been like that, but not now.

'Someone's chiselled out the inverted N and put one in the right way around. Look at it. What the hell is going on?'

'Inverting it in the first place is deliberately and literally turning the truth around. INRI is Jesus the Nazarene King of the Jews. It says he wasn't – the Nazarene King of the Jews, that is. The cross on Saunière's old grave was the same.'

'I get that, but why change it? Who is so desperate to obliterate history? It makes me really angry.'

'I know, but don't get upset. There's nothing you can do to stop it. There's a bit more to it than just turning the truth around, anyway. It's the runes again. The inverted shape is like the sun rune Sowilo, the exposure of fate and truth. Also, if you use N as the fourteenth number of the alphabet, the fourteenth rune is Perthro. It's the rune of chance and coincidence, lost meanings, unwanted and disturbing knowledge, and using it in the most appropriate way.'

'The past week has been disturbing, that's for sure!'

'Even more so when you consider that in biblical terms, the fourteenth number signifies the genealogy of Jesus. In numerological terms, it's the karmic number of progressive change, trials, danger, and chaos, which can be turned into great financial gain. I've no idea who put the cross there in the first place, though, or when, or even what B.D. stands for, although I've tried to find out.'

Back in the car, we drove towards Rennes-le-Château, checking on Caro's house first. Once parked, we almost ran to Hortense's cottage and quickly locked and bolted the door behind us.

'It's awful having to sneak around like this, but it's happening just like I said. The bishop has shown his first card, and the others will follow. It's so strange being here without Hortense to boss us around; I miss her so much. Let's go upstairs first. Can you go into the loft, Ben? I don't think there's much in there but we should check it, and I'll check the cupboards in the bedrooms.'

* * *

I pulled down the ladder and climbed up into the loft. It had been boarded out a long time ago, and we used to play up here sometimes when we were children. A single bulb hung down in the centre, dimly lighting the space. When we were young it had been full of boxes of old clothes, ornaments, and other objects in various stages of decrepitude.

She must have had it cleared out, because it was now almost empty. I picked up the small metal trunk, which I knew contained photographs and postcards. I shouted to Caro and passed it down to her, along with an old leather suitcase, which I hadn't seen before. None of the boards looked like they had been lifted, and anyway,

I was sure that Hortense would have either told us or given us anything of great value, like she had with the discs and the cube.

I switched off the light and went back down the ladder.

'There's nothing else up there – clean as a whistle.'

'I've got the jewellery box. There isn't a lot. As you know, she wore the disc and keys all the time. The place is spotless. Angeline looked after Hortense and the house so well. We should buy her a gift, although I suppose that Hortense may have left her something in her will.'

Carrying everything down, we went into the kitchen to make some coffee. It was simple and uncluttered. Charles had made the cupboards from local wood many years before, and they had aged beautifully. He had also made a long matching sideboard, which was in the sitting room. There were false backs on two of the drawers, which had always fascinated us as children, and I remembered that Caro had something similar in her own house. There was nothing other than a few old bills in the first drawer, but in the second, was a small battered box. Inside was an ornate, gold pocket watch and Hortense's old wristwatch, which I hadn't seen her wear for years. We tucked them, and the jewellery box, into the leather suitcase, empty apart from a few sealed brown envelopes, deciding to look at it all properly when we got home.

We then checked the cupboard under the stairs, where Hortense had kept the cube and discs. Most poignant were a few pairs of shoes, and Caro stopped for a moment to wipe away more tears. A large stone jar held several umbrellas and her collection of walking sticks. Some of them were very beautiful, with silver embossed tops of various styles. We were familiar with all of them apart from one. It had a heavy golden handle in the shape of a large bee, with bees engraved into the dark, polished wood below it. Every few inches a golden bee had been inlaid into the shaft of the stick.

'Look at this. Have you ever seen it before?'

'No, never. It's stunning! I wonder where she got it from?'

At this moment, there was a heavy banging on the door. We looked at each other and I shook my head at Caro, and put my finger to my lips. We waited... there was more banging and then a voice.

CHAPTER FORTY-SIX

'Father Benoît? Professor de Morny? It's Inspector Niort. I would like to speak with you.'

I opened the door. 'Sorry about that, inspector, we weren't expecting any callers. Do come in. Can I get you a coffee? We were just having one whilst we tidied the house. Have you got any information for us?'

'I will have a coffee, thank you. I was going to call at your house, but saw your car and assumed you would be here. Sorry to disturb you, but I was hoping you'd be able to help me. To answer your question first, I've no more information regarding the intruder that your aunt shot. None of the hospitals know anything, and I seem to have come to a dead end. I can see little point in an autopsy, but I'm waiting to hear from the coroner, so you may need to wait for a day or two before the body can be released.

'No one locally heard or saw anything, except for one resident a few doors down who said that she had seen a black car here on and off over the past few weeks. The village is so small; I could understand that a local might notice something like that, but like I said before, it's mostly tourists now. Your aunt was a very interesting lady, though, and had many connections, certainly when she was younger, anyway. Were you aware that she worked for the French Secret Service?'

Caro and I glanced at each other before she answered. 'No, inspector, we didn't know that, but I guessed that she must have had some sort of important job. She was frequently in Paris when we were younger, and always seemed to have her finger on the pulse where politics was concerned.'

'She worked for them for many years, until well into her seventies. She may have made some enemies in that time, in fact it's quite likely, or she may have come across some information that other people want. And the name de Morny; what do you know about it?'

'Nothing at all. Neither my father nor my aunt ever wanted to talk about it, and there are no relatives left that I know of. As I'm sure you know, mine and Benoît's parents are dead, and our grandparents died a long time ago, so the trail has run dry, I'm afraid.'

'I see. Just one more thing, was she involved in the Rennes-le-Château mysteries at all?'

I thought about the cube and discs but more than that, what came to mind was her laughing when she had mentioned Blanchefort's gold the evening before she died.

'I honestly have no idea, inspector, but I doubt it. She certainly thought that the constant treasure hunting was ludicrous, and said so many times, but you know how it is when you live here. I think she found it a nuisance more than anything else. I wish there was more we could tell you. We're desperate to know who was here that evening and what they wanted with her.'

'Thank you anyway and thanks for the coffee. I'm sorry to have taken up more of your time. Do contact me if you hear of anything.'

He got up and walked towards the door, then stopped and turned around.

'I nearly forgot, there was one more thing. Have you heard of anyone called Adrian Harcourt?'

I was shocked at the mention of Harcourt's name. What the hell was going on?

'Forgive my surprise, inspector. He wasn't someone I expected you to ask me about. Yes, I know him. He lives in England quite close to where I've been working, and he helps the church from time to time in an advisory capacity. He used to have a property restoration company, but he's retired now. I don't know much more than that apart from the fact that he paints icons. Why do you ask? Has something happened to him?'

'Not that I know of. I just came across his name whilst researching your aunt's affairs from the past, and only made a connection because he lived so near to where you live in England. Is he the sort to be involved in anything criminal do you think? What sort of man is he?'

I thought for a moment. I needed to be very careful here. Part of me wanted to blurt the whole thing out, and ask for protection, but my instinct told me to keep quiet.

'Inspector, as for him being involved in anything criminal, I really have no idea. He has always seemed like a decent enough man. I saw him a week or two ago to drop off some papers. In what way was he connected to my aunt?'

'I'm sorry, I can't give you that information right now. Please be assured that I shall do all I can to find out what happened on the evening your aunt died. If you are at all concerned or remember anything that might help, do please give me a call. You have my number.'

I let him out, closed the door and locked it again.

'What do you make of that? The plot thickens. Just who is Harcourt, and how can he possibly have anything to do with Hortense? One thing's for sure, he's on the wrong side of the law as far as I'm concerned. You were right about things unfolding in time; in fact, it feels like it's about to explode! We should be getting back. You hold the suitcase and the sticks, and I'll carry the trunk. Don't deviate, go straight to the car, and lock your door as soon as you get in. OK, let's go.'

We noticed Niort chatting to some tourists at the front of the church as we drove by.

'Perhaps he's doing more investigating on our behalf?'

'Or perhaps he's interested in the "mystery," as he called it, himself. Nothing would surprise me. The man makes me feel uneasy, Caro. I'm not sure why, but I don't trust him, or perhaps I'm just being paranoid.'

'He knew an awful lot more than he was telling us, that's for sure, but so do we, I suppose. We're playing a game. Each knows that the other is holding something back, and I'm wondering who's going to break first.'

* * *

The drive home was thankfully uneventful, but on trying to open the outer door to the house I could see some slight buckling of the metal around the lock. The key still worked and we were soon inside, the phone ringing almost immediately. It was my neighbour, saying that he had seen someone tampering with the door, but he had shouted at them and they had run off. I thanked him and we chatted for a minute or two about recent burglaries in the area and then rang off.

'Even if they had managed to break through both doors, which is highly unlikely, they'd never have got into the safe. I don't think they'll be back, especially now they know my neighbours are always in. How about risotto for supper? We need to use the fish from the market or we'll have to throw it out.'

'Sounds good. I'm going to have a look through the trunk whilst you do that. Hortense may well have put something new in there. I've never seen the suitcase before; we can do that later. Can you open the safe? I want to see if I can find out anything about the watch. It's really unusual.'

I unlocked it, and went back into the kitchen to make an early dinner, enjoying the welcome, if short, relief from current problems. It was soon ready, with a final drizzle of olive oil, chopped parsley, and parmesan sprinkled on top, and I put it on the table with some of the bread that we had bought yesterday.

CHAPTER FORTY-SEVEN

'It's ready. Come and eat.'

'That smells fabulous… thank you so much. I like cooking, but I'm nowhere near as proficient as you. Do you remember grandmother's risotto that she did over the fire? She was a great cook, which must be where you get it from.'

I poured two glasses of the white wine that was in the fridge, and we began to eat.

'I remember it well. I've been thinking about them all quite a lot lately. I've still got grandmother's chestnut pan, and quite a few of her other pots and dishes. I love using them'.

'You were always her favourite, Ben; I knew that, and didn't mind. I had fabulous parents and always thought I was very lucky. Have you given any more thought to opening up the cellar again?'

'Yes, I've thought about it, but I'm not sure what we would gain. I remember what was painted on the walls quite well enough, and I don't really fancy opening up the tunnels. We've got quite enough going on as it is. Why? Do you think we should?'

'Yes, I do. I remember it too, but that was a long time ago, and there may well be things down there that would help with our current situation. How is the cellar entrance sealed?'

'Blocks, I think. We'd need a sledgehammer.'

'I've got one in the shed. Look, you don't have to decide now. I've been going through the photographs in the trunk. There are loads of us as children. I suppose we spent a fair bit of time with Hortense; she was such a lovely lady.'

I cleared away the plates, put a bowl of fruit on the table, and picked up some of the photos. There were quite a few of both our parents, and many of Rennes-le-Château taken over a period of about eighty years. She had loved the village, and of course, so did we. Like all things, we took it for granted because it was so familiar, but the photographs, especially the older black and white ones, made it look very different: more sinister, somehow, and not familiar at all.

'This pocket watch; it's exceptional. I can't find anything exactly like it, but there's one online that's similar, with the eagle on it. It was Napoleon Bonaparte's, but I imagine there would be quite a few copies around. There's a bee on the inside of ours, a bit like the walking stick, and the hallmarks look right for that period. Bees were used as Napoleonic symbols. Did you know that he went to great lengths to investigate the Merovingian kings, who also used them? Josephine's family was supposed to be of Merovingian descent, and I think he hoped that he was too. Do put the sticks in the safe, won't you, Ben? They must be quite valuable. Here, have a look.'

275

She pushed the watch across the table towards me and I picked it up. It was a beautiful thing, and clearly of superb quality and considerable value. As for the possibility of it belonging to Napoleon, who knew?

'When things calm down, shall we take it to an expert? I'd love to know more about it.'

I agreed. 'So would I. Let's do that. Did you look in the leather suitcase?'

'No, not yet. I'll do it now.'

* * *

I got up, opened the small case, and took out the brown envelopes. There were six in total, and I put them on the table. Caro picked up the first one, which was stuffed full of more photographs. Some were of people I had never seen before, and there were quite a few of Hortense, at what looked like very formal social functions, with glittering dresses and glamorous surroundings. There was even one of her standing next to Charles de Gaulle, with a group of other dignitaries, and they gave us a glimpse of a life that she had led that we knew nothing about. She looked vibrant and happy, although I found it hard to link the woman in the photographs to the Hortense that I had known. It was like she had been two entirely different people, which I supposed she was.

* * *

The second envelope was also full of photos. 'I think you need to see these, Caro. This is something different altogether.' They were very familiar indeed, and I passed them over to her.

'I thought we were due to come across something soon. It's your village church in England. Look, photos of the graveyard, the old tombs, the couple under a blanket, the Roman tomb, and the de Clare tomb. And there are lots of the interior too. Have you seen these of the piscina with the locked mouth head, and the relics and graffiti? What do you make of it, Ben? I've got goosebumps all over... this is so weird.'

'Honestly, I'm not sure how many more shocks I can take. Clearly, she's been there, and probably not as a holiday, either. Hortense's photographs make it look even more bizarre. And more secrets! She never said she had been there, and yet she quite obviously wanted us to know. It's so frustrating to be kept in the dark like this. Never mind frustrating; I feel downright angry. What were they all playing at, messing with our lives in this way? If they were here now, I would have a real go at them. How dare they?' Caro's eyes filled with tears and she looked away.

'I'm sorry, I didn't mean to upset you, but I'd like to give them a piece of my mind, really I would.'

'I know, I feel the same, but Hortense has just died, and I hardly know how to react to anything. We have no relatives at all now, Benoît, not that we know of, anyway. It's just you and me. I feel so alone. I know that's ridiculous, but it's true. Try to not be angry. There must be a reason for some of it, at least.

'The photos from England simply reinforce the connections between your village church, here, and the diary, and I'm sure that the movements they talk about are documents. It makes sense to link what we already know, what they knew, and the discoveries of Bérenger Saunière.'

'I loved Hortense too, but there are more lies and secrets, and she was part of it.' I took a deep breath and picked up the photos again.

'It's the link with England that's thrown a spanner into the works, although why wouldn't there be links? Many of the Templars came from England, and we know that the area where I've been working was riddled with various knights dashing about all over the place in the Crusades. We also know that one of the lords of the manor founded the Knights Templar with Hugues de Payens in 1118. Some of them may well have fled back home when trouble hit to try to hide, or pass on information, and I don't doubt that they would have sorted out whatever they felt they needed to, by whatever means they had.

'We know they had contacts everywhere, and were surprisingly mobile, despite the lack of transport as we know it today. Money speaks, both then and now, and they certainly had plenty of it. One of the things that I find curious is the fact that although so many people have been holding secrets for so long they still feel the need to leave a trail, to leave clues for anyone who is interested enough to find them. Do you remember when de Clare said in the journal that the clues would be deciphered

278

or found when people were enlightened enough to find them? Do you think people are enlightened enough now, Caro?'

'Hardly. There are wars everywhere, many of them in the name of religion. For myself, I believe in truth. People could create a faith based on truth and honesty, not on a pack of lies created to control the masses. I honestly have never understood why anyone would prefer that, and I never will. There's a quote by Mark Twain that describes my thoughts on the matter quite accurately. I know you like his writing, don't you? You certainly did when you were younger. He said, "Religion was invented when the first conman met the first fool." Forgive me if that sounds disrespectful to your beliefs.'

'I have come across it, yes, and I do still love his writing. And don't worry about the disrespect. As I've told you before, I came to terms with the limitations of religion a very long time ago, and even though I've been giving it a lot more thought lately my feelings haven't changed. Is there anything else of interest in the envelopes?'

* * *

Caro tipped out the contents of another envelope. This time there were no photographs. Instead, there were several articles and documents relating to the Beauharnais family: Josephine and Hortense; Josephine known for her marriage to Napoleon I. I knew very little about the subject apart from history lessons at school.

'What do you make of this? Perhaps Hortense was interested in the Bonapartes and their wives. I find that hard to believe, though, since she never seemed to have any interest in that sort of thing at all.'

We spread it all out on the table. There were various articles and historical information, including quite a few about Hortense de Beauharnais. Caro picked up one article and studied it.

'Well, what do you know? It looks like my father, Charles, and Aunt Hortense may have been related to Hortense Beauharnais. Look, she's underlined it here. Hortense Beauharnais was the daughter of Josephine de Beauharnais before she married Napoleon. It looks like she had an illegitimate child whilst she was married to Bonaparte's brother by a Charles Joseph Duc de Morny. I always wondered where the name came from; it's so unusual. I never knew my grandparents on their side since they were both dead, and there were no cousins as it was just the two of them and Hortense never married. Of course, the Beauharnais/de Morny family are no blood relatives of ours, but it's still fascinating.'

'It certainly is. According to this, Hortense Beauharnais died in 1837, which doesn't seem that long ago, really. She's buried next to her mother in Paris, in Rueil-Malmaison. I've been there. It's the church of Saint Peter and Saint Paul, and the whole area is supposed to be jinxed with bad luck. They may be no relations of ours, but Hortense and Charles may well have some distant cousins. I wonder if they ever knew any of them, although I don't suppose we'll ever know

now. Another secret kept from us! I'm beginning to feel angry again. Our whole lives were based on one lie after another. We may not have been treated cruelly, but we were certainly treated unfairly.'

'I know what you mean. I'm dreading the will reading tomorrow. Who knows what will turn up then? We'll probably find out that we're long-lost relatives of Jack the Ripper... or worse!'

We both laughed at this absurdity. Our situation was certainly becoming more ridiculous by the minute. Caro made some tea, and I opened the doors to the terrace. It had been a bright, sunny day, and even now as dusk was falling, the terracotta tiles were still warm under my bare feet. I walked out to the end of the terrace and stood on the low wall that looked over the river. How clever the medieval builders had been. Despite its many incarnations, the house was as protected now as it had been then, and for this, I was very grateful indeed.

* * *

The next two envelopes contained letters that Hortense had received from Charles when he had been on his archaeological travels. They were fascinating, and we set them to one side to read later.

The final one contained a few black and white photographs of both sets of our parents from the forties. Each one was carefully dated on the back, to the years of the Second World War. They all looked so young, barely more than children, and it was almost impossible to imagine the lives that we knew they were leading at that time. There was a close-up of my mother and father, their eyes shining with what looked like happiness. I had never seen them like this, and once again, felt tinged with the anger and hurt from times past, and slipped the photo into my pocket. I knew that Caro had seen me doing this, and she looked at me, concern showing in her bright blue eyes. For once, I felt unable to meet her direct gaze, and looked the other way.

I went to bed early, exhausted by the lack of sleep from the previous night and the turmoil of my emotions, leaving her in the large shadowy room, still busy on her laptop.

CHAPTER FORTY-EIGHT

Before leaving the following morning, I looked out of the top-floor windows on both sides of the house again. Everything appeared normal and we drove quickly into town. Parking right outside the solicitor's office, we hurried in and sat, waiting for any further revelations from Hortense's will.

Monsieur Couderc welcomed us warmly and took us into his office.

'I'm so sorry about your aunt. She was a phenomenal woman and I had huge respect for her, as did everyone who knew her. I once asked her to marry me, you know. The age difference meant nothing to me, but she refused, and I never met another woman who came anywhere close to taking her place.'

He cleared his throat. 'Please, take a seat, and I'll go through things with you.'

Sifting through the piles of papers on his desk, he eventually pulled out a thick brown folder.

'Here we are, everything's in order. To begin, she left these for you.'

He handed over two brown envelopes, and I caught Caro's eye. We both smiled as we thought of our conversation from the night before.

'Now,' he continued, 'she left very specific instructions. For Angeline, her home help, she left five thousand euros. She has left fifty thousand euros to assist specifically with the ongoing renovations of the church at Rennes-le-Château. She asks that you both oversee this, as she was concerned that the money would disappear into general church coffers, not just for Rennes-le-Château. Secondly, she left a small sum of money to oversee the maintenance of the tomb of Bérenger Saunière, and to ensure that flowers are regularly placed there. The rest of her estate is left to the both of you, equally. Are either of you aware of your aunt's financial affairs?'

'No, not really. We know she worked for most of her life, and didn't have any children so we assumed she wasn't short of money, but that's all,' Caro replied.

'Well, you may be surprised to know that she had accumulated considerable wealth.'

We looked at each other again. Monsieur Couderc pushed a statement across the desk for us to read. He was right – it was considerable. More noughts than we could easily count... again.

'If you leave your bank account numbers with me I will see that the sum is split in equal parts when the due legal process has been completed. It might be a good idea to open another account for the deposit of the other monies. I shall contact Angeline myself.'

We agreed to do this and both wrote down our bank details. 'I'll open another one, and let you have the number as soon as I've done it. I'm sure the church money will be very gratefully received, and we'll both be very happy to oversee it. To be honest, we're both a bit staggered about the amount she left us. Do you have any idea where it all came from?'

'No, not at all. Just like your parents, she was a very private person and didn't give much away, about herself or her life.'

'That was certainly true.'

'I've decided to retire in a couple of months. I'm well into my seventies and have had enough. I want to get some decent fishing in before I'm called, but if you need anything I have an excellent replacement lined up, so no need to worry.'

We shook his hand and wished him well.

'Thank you so much for your help, and for looking after Hortense's affairs so well.'

'Not a problem. I had a very soft spot for her, as you now know, and I shall miss her.'

'So will we… we already do.'

When we reached the door, I held onto Caro's arm. We needed to get bread, and that entailed another dash across the square. This was achieved without any problems and we were soon back in the car, the two large loaves nestling in tissue paper on the back seat and giving off a wonderful aroma.

'That was all a bit easy. I expected black cars and shady looking men, but there's nothing. Perhaps they've all given up and gone home, whoever *they* actually are.'

I had been thinking the same thing, although I didn't think for one minute that 'they' had gone home. Their absence only made me more anxious, not less.

'Benoît, can we pop up to the church at Rennes-le-Château? I need a couple of photos to add to my book, and I wanted to run through the details in the Stations of the Cross with you. If I must be incarcerated in your house, I might as well get on with my work. We can get straight back and open the dreaded envelopes that tell us we're the children of a mass murderer.'

I thought for a moment. The Stations of the Cross were a fourteen-step Catholic devotion, commemorating Jesus's supposed last day before he was crucified. Usually in paintings or 2D relief form, they ran around the walls of the church to assist with reflection and prayer. The Stations in Rennes-le-Château were very ornate and had been overpainted and added to by Saunière as part of the trail of clues he left for others to find. Oddly, they ran backwards, or anti-clockwise, which generally represented an opposite, or reversal, or symbolic rewind.

'I don't know… it's not safe.'

'Oh, come on, Ben. There should be plenty of people about, and the restaurants will be open. We can park close by and it shouldn't take long.' I gave in, and headed in the right direction.

'Wasn't that sad about Couderc and Hortense? I nearly burst into tears there and then.'

'I know, I wonder what their relationship was, and why she refused him; her job, perhaps? Or maybe she just didn't feel the same as he did?'

She pulled a tissue from her bag, and mopped her wet face before continuing.

'What a waste, all these secrets. I'm going to make sure I write a fat autobiography before I die.'

'You do that, Caro. I can't promise to do the same, so if there's anything you want to know, ask now!'

CHAPTER FORTY-NINE

We were soon in the car park at Rennes-le-Château. There were a few people milling about and the outdoor restaurants looked full, the murmur of voices carrying across to the path by the church. We walked in, the interior dim for such a bright day. An American couple walked out, talking quietly as they went and leaving the church momentarily empty.

'Hang on a minute. I just want a few snaps of my old friend, Asmodeus. The others didn't come out very well.'

'Asmodeus' was a large and somewhat startling devil statue, crouching by the entrance to the church, with a water stoup shaped like a large clam on his back. There were two salamanders above it, as well as the four archangels, in various poses of the Catholic ritual of crossing oneself. One of the angels had a finger pointing down towards the water stoup, and an inscription:

PAR CE SIGNE TU LE VAINCRAS
translating to
BY THIS SIGN YOU WILL CONQUER HIM/IT

There were also the initials B.S. As with the rest of the church interior, it was brightly and ornately painted, and like everything else to do with Saunière, caused much interest and conjecture.

On the back wall of the church was an enormous and ornate relief, showing Jesus on a mount with adoring people around him and flowers everywhere. Known as the Fleury Monument, it was made with Saunière's specific instructions, which he then added to. Caro came over to stand beside me and we both looked up at it.

'I know we studied this years ago, but there are a few new bits of information that I've found.'

The whole thing was split into two parts, summer and winter: flowers and leaves on one side; bare twigs on the other. It was a pictorial metaphor for before and after Saunière's discoveries, everything symbolically turning to winter when truth revealed itself to him.

At the bottom-right of the winter side was a well-painted, ornate pilaster top, representing the one that he had removed from under the pulpit. It was here that he had supposedly found Bigou's letter, and if you looked carefully, you could even see a roll of paper coming up through it. It was difficult to dispute, and the pilaster with its cavity still existed, having been bought by a villager some time ago.

'The pilaster top is obvious, but the plank of wood at its side was harder to work out. I just kept staring at it until it came to me. It's a piece of the cross that Jesus was supposed to have been crucified on. It never happened and so it's being shown broken, alongside the truth, which was written on the parchment found in the pillar. If you look just behind that, you can see the top of the Carolingian altar pedestal and the square cavity in it. Undoubtedly it would have held a relic, most likely of a saint.'

She was right. Once pointed out, it was easy to see. Saunière had pulled out the old Carolingian pillar from under the altar as part of his renovations, and it now stood in the museum to the side of the church.

'And there's also a small gravestone; Marie de Nègre's, I assume. We're familiar with the little priest figure at the back representing Saunière, but it wasn't until I magnified it that I saw the parchments in both hands. He's saying that he still has them; they're hidden somewhere. There's no way he would have handed them over without having either kept the originals or taken copies. His little self-portrait looks so sad and lonely on the winter side with his discoveries. It must have had a huge impact on him. He did train to be a priest, after all, so must have had deep religious beliefs at one time.'

I stood back a little further. 'What do you make of the sack of gold at the bottom of the hill?'

'I don't think it is gold; it's a sack of rocks. If they were gold, he would have painted them bright gold, like he's done elsewhere. I think it's a metaphor saying that, although he gained financially and literally found gold, he lost his faith and so discards the sack, along with his belief in God.'

'You may well be right. Isn't it odd; we spent so much time studying it, and yet we didn't see what we see now. Once pointed out, it's clear, although I suppose all paintings are like that: the more you look, the more you see?'

At this moment, a few people wandered in, and we stood quietly in front of the large statue of John the Baptist pouring water on Jesus crouching down in front of him, in a strangely submissive pose.

CHAPTER FIFTY

⁓

'We need to be out of here as soon as possible, Caro.'

'I know. Can I just quickly run through each one of the Stations that Saunière altered? Then we can go.'

'OK, but speed it up.'

'Right. Saunière uses the Stations to give a narrative of his discoveries using, as before, the codes of numerology and runic symbolism, as well as local and historical references.'

* * *

'In Station **1**, Pilate's assistant reads from a parchment, which replicates the discovery of Bigou's letter. We noted that before, but he then gives several references to his discovery of Marie de Nègre's tombstone and what was underneath. If you look at the hem of the floor covering, you can clearly see an R, in black, which I believe refers to Roc, or Roque, and Rennes-le-Château. A bit further along, he's painted in a small black mountain, under the black stone slab, with a black child standing on it. This is a reference to Nègre, which I assume is derived from the Latin *nigrum*, meaning black.

'Roque-Nègre, or Black Mountain, is opposite the old

Templar watchtower of Blanchefort, and the mountain was historically mined for gold and silver. In mythology, the Golden Griffin was the guardian of treasure, a symbol of the divine, and of Jesus. Its feathers brushed across the eyes restored sight to the blind, which is a direct message from Saunière, telling people to open their eyes to the truth. Pilate wears a veil to represent veiled truth, and washes his hands in a silver bowl. The theme of silver bowls, discs, and dishes is prevalent throughout the stations. Silver is a symbolic representation of the moon, and links with water to provide protection for travellers on the sea. It also represents childbirth, divine marriage, the feminine, fertility, illumination, writing hidden meanings, and inner knowledge. The bowl also links up Asmodeus, and the piscina on his back, but I'll come back to that.'

* * *

We moved across to Station **2**. I could hear voices from outside, but so far no one had come in.

'Some of that's entirely new to me, but I'm feeling really edgy.'

'There are too many people about for anyone to make a move on us, surely. I'll be as quick as I can, but I want you to see the details as I talk. Station **2** is much simpler, but so interesting, and everyone else seems to have missed the most obvious clue. The silver Migdal tower in the background brings Mary Magdalene into the story, *migdal* being the Hebrew word for tower. The modern town of Migdal is built over the traditional site

293

of Magdala, where some say she came from. If you look just above the crucifix, you can clearly see a painted silver pilaster top, just like the one in the Fleury relief, and where he found Bigou's letter. Jesus is also pointing down to a black rock on the ground, and a man bends down and picks up a flat black slab, reiterating Saunière's finds under Marie de Nègre's tombstone.'

At this point, a couple with two small children walked in, and she lowered her voice. The children proceeded to climb on the pews, one falling onto the tiled floor. The church was filled with loud shrieks and, thankfully, they soon left.

'What a dreadful noise…! I can't believe we didn't spot the pilaster top before.'

'I know. Very odd.'

* * *

'Moving on, Station **3** is much more complex. If you look to the bottom of the cross, you can see an etched triangle. It's been painted over recently, but it's still there. As you know, it symbolises a union of mind, body, and soul, or male, female, and offspring, as well as sacred or royal bloodlines. The number **3** is symbolic of the ascended master, a great teacher, prophet, or healer, now in the spiritual realm, and the third rune, Thurisaz, represents a rising of consciousness from the unknown to known.'

'It's startling. How can it be coincidence? It all fits like a jigsaw and I'm absolutely convinced that it's all deliberate on Saunière's part. No question at all.'

'I challenged myself repeatedly when I first realised that Saunière was using the numerology and runic symbols as codes. I'd be the first to argue a weak theory, but I don't question it anymore. Now, look at the golden horn, shaped like an arc. This is wordplay; a homophone, referring to the nearby Cathar abbey/château/stronghold of Arques. It belonged to the Abbey of Lagrasse until the Albigensian crusades. They were an ancient community of Benedictine monks, who were highly competitive in the acquisition and creation of books, documents, and manuscripts.

'In 1231, Arques was taken by the crusader, Simon de Montfort, who gave it, and Rhedae, including Rennes-le-Château, to his lieutenant, Pierre de Voisins. It was taken from him by Oliver de Termes, who then sold it back to Voisins a few years later. The Voisins, d'Hautpoul, Blanchefort, de Nègre, and Fleury families all intermarried over the next few hundred years and were the Lords of Rhedae right through to Abbé Bigou's time in the late eighteenth century.

'In the background, the château looks remarkably like the one here in the village. One of the towers, known locally as the alchemy tower, is round and surrounded with myths and legends. Records refer to a woman in the region at the beginning of the first century, called Mary the Jewess, who was an alchemist. Mary the Ebionite, the term for the early Jewish Christian movement in the first few centuries, is also recorded, and it seems likely that both Marys, and Mary Magdalene, were the same person.

'I also think there's a Joan of Arc clue here. She always

carried a banner bearing the names of Jesus and Mary. Many believe that Joan had Templar lineage and that the stories of her being a peasant are untrue. She certainly had connections in high places, and even visited Fleury Abbey after taking part in a nearby battle. There's a statue of Joan in Antugnac church, where Saunière was stand-in priest for a year in 1890/91. I think that the golden arc might also refer to the Ark of the Covenant. They're all spelt differently but have similar pronunciation. I want to talk to you about Brenac church, but we can do that at home.'

'I wondered if you'd bring that up. It's the Ark painting, isn't it?'

'Yes… and something else too.'

A party of tourists came in, and we sat down until they had gone.

* * *

'Station **4.** The white sail, symbolising the journey by boat of Jesus and his entourage to France, and possibly of Joan's banner. It's worth noting the number of four-sided towers, both plain and silvered in the stations. Apart from the Migdal reference, we already know that **4** represents truth, fate, illumination, knowledge, wisdom, and the energy of the four Archangels. $2+2 = 4$. The gnostic interpretation of the **22**nd rune, Ingwaz, is of the Holy Grail. There are also four silver discs or bowls on the sail, with the silver and numerological symbolism. A couple of points worth mentioning are that Joseph of Arimathea was a dealer in metals, including tin and silver, and that Saunière may well have been building his own Magdala tower by this time.'

* * *

'Stations **5**, **6**, and **7** have no additions, so let's move on to **8**.'

'The most obvious clue is the St Andrew's tartan wrapped around the child.'

'Correct. Do you remember how much trouble we had in finding a book on Scottish tartan? There were no computers back then.'

'I do remember.' It was in the mid-seventies. We didn't want to tell anyone why we wanted it, and eventually, Charles sourced one from a friend.

'Good old Charles.'

'I know. Oh Ben… I miss him so much. I miss them all.' She wiped a few tears from her face and gave a big sigh.

'The fortified church in Antugnac is dedicated to Saint Andrew, patron saint of Scotland, and we know the manor was once owned by the de Nègre family. Of course, because of your house we know about the tunnels, the painted room, and its use by the church some years ago. On the Andrews coat of Arms is *victrix fortuna sapienta*, "wisdom is the conqueror of fortune," which also seems very appropriate. Perhaps Saunière was a member of François Fleury's Scottish Masons? There are eight letters in Antugnac. There's nothing of note on **9** apart from the fact that some moronic vandals have lopped off Jesus's head, so let's go to **10**.'

'I think you're right about the Masons. Look, Caro, we've been in here for twenty minutes. Another ten and were leaving.'

'OK, boss.'

'That's a laugh; since when?'

'Very funny.'

* * *

'OK, Station **10** is all about the three dice being thrown by the Roman soldier. The same morons have lopped off his arm. It makes me sick! Anyway, they show a **3**, **4**, and **5**, totalling **12**, which totals **3**. We've covered numbers **3** and **4** already, but **5** represents sexuality, and the fifth rune, Raidho, represents the journey in narrative form, which seems rather appropriate. The twelfth rune is Jera, representing the human passage of time from birth to death and waiting for the correct time to act. Adding the numbers from the station and dice together, $10 + 12 = 22$. Again!

* * *

'Station **12** shows Magdalene holding a prayer book that looks very like the one that Saunière carried with him everywhere. As you know, when he was exhumed and moved, his prayer book was taken from him.' She paused, and looked at me. 'Ben, I can't help thinking that someone's reached this point before us, but there's nothing published

298

about it anywhere, which is even worse. The whole area is slowly being stripped clean. It's all so sad, but only makes me more determined to write my book.'

'You're right, and for the first time, I'm beginning to understand how important it is that you do, but it worries me as well.'

'Don't worry… it'll be fine. I've nearly finished…'

* * *

'The only thing of note in Station **13** is that the tower in the background looks just like the one Saunière built, but Station **14** is a little more interesting, since Jesus's hand seems to disappear into a long scroll. Earlier photos show this area as a poorly constructed hand over lumpy folds of fabric. Maybe it was vandalised and this is the repair, or this is how it was before being covered over? I'd need some much earlier pictures to know for sure.'

* * *

'Finally, I wanted to show you the interlocking fingers on the Magdalene relief under the altar that there has been so much conjecture about. You just need to use runic symbolism again. The interlocking fingers form a double cross, one on top of each other, imitating the **22**nd rune, Ing or Ingwaz, and symbolic, as before, of the Holy Grail. If you look carefully, just behind her shoulder on the hillside, what initially looks like castle ruins are the letters J and M: Jesus and Mary.'

CHAPTER FIFTY-ONE

I walked towards the altar to take a closer look. Saunière may have been dead for nearly a hundred years, but his presence lingered on. Good for him, I thought... I doubted that I would be so lucky. I jumped as something stirred in the shadow behind the pulpit.

'Gosh, you made me jump then,' I said, thinking it was a tourist, or even a child that had been hiding. 'Good Lord, Peter, what the hell are you doing here? You really scared me. That's the second time you've done that.'

Peter looked at me, his face pale and almost expressionless. He was dressed in black from head to foot and had large, dark circles under his eyes, as though he hadn't slept for days. He also looked unkempt, and even from my position a few metres away, he smelt stale; quite unlike the forest fresh fragrance that he usually left in his wake. His blue eyes continued to stare at me, and in that moment, I felt afraid. There was a type of insanity that could be seen in a certain look of the eye, and I had witnessed it several times when I was the chaplain at Wormwood Scrubs, some years ago. I had, over time, come to associate it with a psychopath, and a shiver went down my spine. He didn't blink, or move, and then I heard Caro call out.

'Peter, is that you? What on earth are you doing out here? You're the last person I expected to see. Is Merry here too? How nice to see you.'

At that moment, he pulled his hands from the grubby raincoat. I held mine out to shake his, but shaking hands had clearly not been his intention. He raised his right arm, now holding a black pistol, and pointed it at me, then her, and then me again.

'CARO, GET DOWN! GET DOWN NOW!' I shouted. 'Peter, get a grip of yourself, man; you're not well. Let me help you.'

'I don't need any help from the likes of you, Father Benoît. Interfering and meddling in things that are nothing to do with you. Damn Catholics are all the same, thinking they're better than everyone else. Well, not this time, you've gone too far. Think you've discovered the secrets of my church, do you? Well, let me tell you this. They've been held for hundreds of years, and we're not going to let scum like you or anyone else ruin everything.'

'Peter, stop this nonsense. I don't know what you're talking about.'

'It's "grand master" to you. Get down on your knees and show some respect before I finish you off. It's very fitting that you and your stupid sister should die here. Saunière nearly wrecked everything, and you two are the only people who have come anywhere close to what he uncovered. There's plenty of room in his old tomb, I believe. Perhaps you can go in there with his whore, Marie. In fact, I'll see to it myself.'

He aimed his gun over to the side of the building

301

and fired a shot. Even though it was silenced, the noise still echoed around the church and Caro screamed.

'STAY DOWN, CARO,' I shouted.

'Peter, you're out of your mind. What would Merry say if she saw you like this?'

'I couldn't give a damn. I saw whose side she was on when she gave you that church report. She can go to hell for all I care.'

He raised the gun, and Caro screamed again.

'BENOÎT.'

At that moment, another shot was fired, and a small wound on Peter's forehead began to seep blood as he collapsed onto the black and white tiles, almost in slow motion. I quickly looked round, but seeing no one, I grabbed Caro, pulling her up from the floor where she had been hiding behind a pew. We ran to the car as fast as we could, Caro losing a shoe in the process. I almost threw her in, and within seconds we were speeding down the small road that curved around the hillside. Caro was sobbing and I was shaking all over. This was the first time I'd had a gun pointed directly at me, and it was terrifying.

'When we get back, keep your head down, and stay there until I've unlocked the house door. Do you hear me? Stay right down until I shout.'

'You're shouting now. It's nearer to my house. Should we go there?'

'Not safe enough. Too many ground-floor windows. Do as I say.'

There didn't appear to be anyone following us, and

302

we took the normal route, pulling up outside my house some ten minutes later.

Caro did as she was told and disappeared from view. I leapt out and opened the two doors as quickly as I could, dropping the keys at one point. I opened them wide.

'Right, now, Caro. Run! Now! NOW!'

She sped inside and I slammed the house doors shut, locking them as quickly as I could.

CHAPTER FIFTY-TWO

I sat on the old stone staircase that led down to the salon and took some deep breaths; my hands still shaking. Caro was standing at the bottom of the steps and seemed to have returned to her normal, composed self, or perhaps she was in shock.

'You left the bread in the car, Benoît. Can you go out and get it, please?'

'In your dreams. What the hell happened there? The man's insane… insane and dead! I'd better call Niort.' I went down into the salon on shaking legs and picked up the phone. I was told that the police had already been notified and were on their way. Niort would be in touch shortly.

'Poor Merry. Who's going to tell her? Do you think we should?'

'No, I don't. Leave it to the police. We've got enough on our plates already. I hardly recognised Peter… he looked so strange, like he was on drugs or something, and had been sleeping rough. I know I thought he was a bit odd, but he was an attractive man all the same, although definitely not today. What did he mean when he said you could call him "grand master"? Benoît, I was so scared. I thought he was going to kill you. And how come everyone seems to know that we're siblings except us? That's really weird, and who killed him? I was peeping out from between the benches, and whoever it was, they were a very good shot. What are we going to tell the inspector?'

'Nothing. I mean, obviously, we know Peter, we have to tell him that, and the bit about him seeming to have gone mad, but that's it. There are cameras in the church at Rennes-le-Château these days, so they'll probably have it all recorded. I suspect it was the Italian or one of his henchmen that shot him. I mean, who else could it have been? I wish I knew more about him... the Italian, that is. As for grand master, like you I only know it as a Templar name for leader, but maybe some other crackpot organisation uses it? Obviously not from the Vatican though. He clearly hates Catholics, or should I say hated! And he knew about Saunière and didn't think much of him, either. I must say, I'm beginning to rather like the man myself, and how he coped with the position he found himself in. I think we should have a drink of something strong. There's some Armagnac in the dresser... I'll get it.'

There was a loud bang at the door. I went upstairs and looked out of the window from the first floor. Shouting would have been no good, since the door was very thick, and virtually soundproof. It was Niort. En route, I picked up my car keys to get the bread, since any more shootings were unlikely whilst the inspector was standing there. Letting him in, I nipped out to the car. Niort looked at the bread, but made no comment.

'So, more trouble, I see. Are you both OK?'

Caro answered. 'Yes, we're both very shaken obviously, but we're OK. I take it he's dead?'

'Yes, instantly. There are recordings, and we're going through them now. What were you both doing up there?'

She answered again. 'Taking photographs, inspector. I'm writing a book on the history of the area, and I needed a few extra photos. We'd just been into town to see the solicitor.'

'And you know the man?'

'Yes, I do, inspector, although Caro has only met him briefly. His name's Peter Lacy and he's an Anglican vicar, from the village where I've been working in England. I don't know him that well, mostly we just wave or say good morning, that sort of thing, but lately I had tea with him and his wife, and when Caro came to England to see me, they invited us for drinks. He's married, with three grown-up children. That's about all I know, really. Seemed like a nice enough man.'

'You said that about Adrian Harcourt. Can you tell me what happened from the beginning please?'

'Are you saying that you've found out more about him? We're really in the dark here.'

'I'm not at liberty to say any more about Harcourt at the moment, sorry.'

'That's really disappointing, inspector. Anyway, this is what happened. We walked into the church, and Caro started to take her photographs. It was lunchtime and there weren't many people about. We looked around, especially at the Stations of the Cross, for Caro's research. I then walked towards the altar to look at the relief painting under it, and heard a noise. Even with the lights on, it's quite dark in there, so I didn't see anything at first. The next thing I knew, Peter was standing in front of me. I barely recognised him. He looked odd, a bit insane really, and was very grubby and unkempt, quite unlike how he normally is. I told him to put the gun down, that he wasn't well, and that I would help him. He fired a shot to one side, then aimed the gun at me. I heard another shot, and the next thing I knew, he was on the floor. We didn't see anyone else but we were so scared that we ran.'

'I see. What seems clear is that Lacy wanted to kill you, and came here to do so. Have you been followed at all? Or noticed anything else that was unusual? Are you involved in anything else that might put either of you in danger?'

Caro looked at Niort and spoke. 'The only thing I can think of is the connection to my aunt. Do you think that her Secret Service work might have implicated us in some way? I'm a historian as you know, which can make one unpopular at times, but surely not enough to want to kill me.'

'What work were your parents involved in, both of you?'

'Well, my mother was a housewife, and my father was an archaeologist,' said Caro.

'My father used to repair clocks and watches from home, and my mother bought and sold a few antiques. They liked to travel too, and were often away. My grandparents lived with us, so it didn't really matter if they were there or not. I do know that they were all active in the Resistance, and my mother used to talk about it sometimes. I'm sorry it isn't much to go on.'

'Before Lacy was shot did he say anything to you?'

'He said he hated all Catholics, and would bury us with Saunière. When I mentioned his wife, he said she could go to hell for all he cared. Just pleasant chit chat, you know? Look, sorry, inspector, I'm upset, but we've no idea what going on and would really appreciate being told anything that you might know.'

'There isn't any more that I can tell you; I'm conducting every investigation that I can. Meanwhile, if you think of anything else please call me. I suggest you stay inside as much as possible. One of my officers will be coming over in a couple of hours to take a full statement from you both. The coroner has released your aunt's body, so you're free to arrange her funeral whenever you like. Perhaps under the current circumstances, it might be best to delay this for a while. Anyway, let me know what you decide.'

'Thank you. We'll be as careful as we can. Has anyone told Peter's wife yet? What an awful thing for her and the family.'

'That's being dealt with right now. Goodbye, and please get in touch if you think of anything else – anything at all.'

* * *

I let him out, bolting the doors behind him. Meanwhile, Caro had poured us both an Armagnac, and I sipped mine slowly, trying to make sense of what had happened.

'I think that Peter was involved in some sort of born-again Templar group. I've heard of them, of course. And there are the Freemasons, but I don't think they're involved in murdering people. I do remember a colleague of mine in London coming up against one of these organisations when he tried to reveal some important wall paintings in a church that had been whitewashed over. He had archaeological backing and the funds but it got quite nasty and he was threatened. He left in the end. I heard from him a few months ago and he's in the USA now, having a great time. There's definitely something going on in Peter's church, and Hortense's photographs confirm that. Let's go through it all again later. Are you hungry? I'll make a sandwich.'

'Do you know what I would really like? A chicken casserole cooked slowly over the fire. Can we have that? You still have the old iron pot, don't you?'

'I do. It's a warm day, though… can you cope with the fire too?'

'Of course.' In seconds, she was on her knees, putting paper and sticks in the grate. I made a couple of cheese sandwiches and coffee, and then started to fill the old iron pot that I usually only used in the winter. The chicken in the fridge needed eating, so it wasn't such a bad idea. I chopped it into eight pieces and put in onions, carrots, potatoes, white wine, water, salt, pepper, and some fresh herbs from the terrace. The stand had been placed over the newly lit fire and I put the pot on the top. It would take a few hours to cook, maybe three, but that was fine. We had other things to do, including going through the contents of the brown envelopes from Couderc and the arrival of Niort's officers.

Poor Merry and the boys. I wondered how they were coping, especially when they found out that Peter was at the point of killing me. I decided that I wouldn't contact her for a few days; she might not want to speak to me, and she had my email address if she wanted to make contact.

I opened the door to the terrace, and took my sandwich outside. The warmth was blissful and Caro came out to join me. One could quite see why people had worshipped the sun, and it was one of the things that I missed so much when I was living in England.

'Shall we go through those envelopes, Benoît? Maybe we'll get some answers there. I'll get them.'

I went back inside. The two envelopes were addressed to us both, and we tipped them out onto the table. The first contained three smaller white envelopes, each with a date on, and we put these in order. In the second were two thicker packets, which we decided to look at last. I picked up the first of the dated envelopes, opened it, and read it out aloud.

CHAPTER FIFTY-THREE

January 2015

My dear Benoît and Caro

If you are reading this, then I am no longer with you. I had hoped I would live for ever, but alas, this was not so. Over the last few years, I have been collecting together the things that I think you need to know that have been kept from you. Please believe me when I say that I have never agreed with this, but it was what your parents wanted, and I have had no choice in the matter.

Hopefully, you will already know that you are not cousins but brother and sister, since it is my intention to tell you myself. You were both very much loved, but I think you know this. Your birth parents, Celestine and Henrikas, didn't intend to have children. Christiane, your birth mother's twin, and Charles were unable to have children. Between them, they decided to have one each, and this is what they did. I thought it would be wise to tell you, but they thought there would be upset about which one was given up and why, and so they decided against it. I can tell you that there was no favouritism at all. They were adamant that they would never want to be accused of this, and quite literally drew

311

straws to decide who would have which one of you. It was their intention that you would grow up together and be a part of each other's lives, and in this, at least, they were successful.

I know that my brother Charles and Christiane loved you both as their own, and I believe that this too was a success. I have also loved you as if you were my blood family, and as far as I am concerned you are. I intend to leave my entire estate to you both to do with as you wish, with a few bequests.

I now want to tell you a little more about your birth parents. As you know they met during the war when they were very young. They were both in the French Resistance, as indeed was I. They were hard times. We witnessed things that no person should ever have to see, and it coloured the rest of our lives and altered the paths that we chose.

In their battle against the Nazis towards the end of the war, your parents were helped on many occasions by an emissary from the Vatican. I never met him, and your parents refused to talk about him, but it's my belief that his name was Angelo Roncalli who, I'm sure you know, went on to became Pope John XXIII. They continued to work for the Vatican for many years, perhaps because of this connection. Your mother was deeply affected by the murder and slaughter that had become part of our everyday lives. She was only sixteen when she became involved in the Resistance. She came to fervently believe that people needed a firm and decent structure to live their lives by. Interestingly, she didn't believe in God, none of us did, but she had seen what evil there was in the world and sought to control it. This was absurd, and it's my belief that she was not entirely sane after the war ended.

I certainly didn't believe in her cause nor the work she undertook, but she set out on that path, and Henrikas went along with her. He had already witnessed mass slaughter with the Nazis in Lithuania, and knew that worse was to come with Stalin. He and some of his friends managed to escape and ended up in France. That I am aware of, all his family were killed. Peace was also of utmost importance to Henrikas, although I'm not sure that he entirely agreed with some of the missions that they were sent on, which often involved suppression of the truth regarding Christianity. Given where we live and the evidence that was all around us, particularly for educated people, I always found it ludicrous and, if I am entirely honest, my relationship with them was often a difficult one. Christiane played no part in any of it and contented herself in staying at home to look after her family.

They were in their seventies when they were summoned to Rome to look for some parchments that the Vatican had heard of. They were of great importance, and several other organisations of considerable power were also searching for them. They were thought to disprove the very foundations of Christianity, and so you can understand why the mission was so dangerous. Henrikas told Charles that they had been trying for some years to remove themselves from this type of work, *and they had been doing less and less, that was true. He also told Charles that they no longer had any faith in suppression and wanted to live out their retirement in peace. Anyway, one way or another they ended up in Rome, and that was the last time we saw them alive. As you know, they were killed in a car crash. Or murdered, I should say. I have no doubt about that. It's my belief that they were brought to Rome solely to be removed and silenced for good. They were too old to be of much use anymore and knew far too much.*

I am sorry to spring so many surprises on you at once, but I need to tell you the full story. I worked for the Secret Service here in France. They were the best years of my life, although not always easy. As you know, I never married, and that has always been a great regret. I did, however, have you, and that was a blessing. My job also gave me access to certain information. Your parents worked with another Italian agent and had done for many years. They were the best of friends. His name was Franco D'Alessandro, although of course he may have changed his name by now. It was he who sent your parents back to France after they were killed. He seemed to disappear after that, although I believe he is still alive. Anyway, I gave up my job some years ago. He may have the parchments or they may have long ago been reduced to ash, like so many others.

I will write more for you shortly.

Your loving Aunt Hortense

CHAPTER FIFTY-FOUR

'That explains a few things, especially why they kept disappearing, and what she said about Roncalli is interesting too. He was well known for his work in the Second World War and did a huge amount to rescue Jews from the Nazis, amongst other things. He was given the title of Apostolic Nuncio to the recently liberated France on the 22nd December 1944, but I never doubted that his involvement here began way before that. I studied him and his life a few years back, and he was a fascinating man.'

'And interesting dates!' exclaimed Caro.

'There's more of that. It was thought to be highly odd that he chose "John" to be his papal name. There had been 22 Pope Johns before that, the last one more than 600 years before. His reasons included him saying it was a sweet name to him, his father's name was John, that he was baptised in a church dedicated to John the Baptist, that "22 Johns of indisputable legitimacy" had been pope, and that "we have preferred to hide the smallness of our name behind this magnificent succession of Roman Popes."'

'I clearly need to do more research about him. Many believe he had some involvement with the Rennes-le Château mysteries, through requests made by Noel Corbu to the Vatican for education grants for his children. He was the man who bought everything from Marie Dénarnaud, Saunière's sole heir, and she lived with his family until she died. My belief is that he knew of the discoveries well before that, probably through information filtering down the line from Pope Leo XIII. Corbu got the grants, by the way, even though the local bishopric refused the request initially.'

'The number of people who seem to have been involved over the years is huge. Oh, and I'm sure that the Franco she mentioned is the Italian and, of course, the parchments she mentions are the ones he recently sent to me. I must say, I feel a bit stunned by Hortense's revelations. I think she was right in what she said about the war, and it having devastating effects on them all. Hortense and Charles were from a different mould… I can see that now. Our birth parents were very serious people. Do you know, I don't think I ever saw our mother laugh, not once.'

'You're wrong there, Ben, because I saw her laugh twice. Once was at a birthday party of yours when you were running around like a mad thing, and the second time was when we were playing with Bruin, my dog. He was doing tricks and she found that very amusing. But generally, yes, they were very serious, and Christiane was too. She always worried about everything. In hindsight, I think her past had shown her the very worst of humanity and life, and she was scarred by it… they all were. What do we know of hardship and the horrors of war? In comparison, our childhoods and most of our lives have been idyllic. It's all so sad.'

At that point, the doorbell rang, and I ran up the stairs to check who it was. Two officers stood outside, and I shouted down to open the door. They were polite and professional and we recounted the events of the past few hours as best we could. They were particularly interested in who might have shot Peter, and what we saw when we ran outside. We truthfully had no idea, had seen nothing, and told them so. Caro's shoe was returned to her in a clean plastic bag.

We both sat quietly for a few minutes. Caro was the first to move, placed another of the letters on the table in front of her, and started to read.

CHAPTER FIFTY-FIVE

March 2015

My dear Caro and Benoît

I have noticed a few strange things happening around the village and there are people here that do not look like tourists. You may know that the church at Antugnac was ripped apart by 'archaeologists' in recent years. I doubt that archaeology was their purpose, but it is clearly time to tell you more. I know far too much, and this places me in danger. I have no worries about that, but I would not want to die without telling you all that you need to know.

In the 1950s three bodies were found in Saunière's domaine. There has been much speculation about them, most of it complete rubbish, and I want to tell you the truth. The Nazis took over Saunière's Villa Bethany for a while during the war. They were vile, filthy devils, but let me tell you that this does not come anywhere close enough in explaining to you what they were really like. They even took to dynamiting holes all over the place looking for buried gold. Fools. Anyway, one evening, they were very drunk, and demanded at gunpoint that girls from the village were brought in to satisfy their needs. The villagers refused, and one was shot. Several young girls, one of them only fourteen, were eventually brought to them.

I had only just got back from a long mission, but was used to subterfuge, and could see from behind some bushes into the room where they were. I waited until the moment was exactly right, and I shot them through the window, one by one. The fools were so drunk they had no idea what was happening. We threw them into one of their dynamite holes and covered them over. We celebrated that night and even got to drink some of our own wine. I have no regrets whatsoever apart from not having killed an awful lot more of them than I did.

The next thing I wish to tell you about is the money that will, by now, have been given to you by your parents, both sets, and by me now that I am dead. As you will have gathered, the amount that we had between us was considerable. We all worked, of course, including your grandparents in their time, and were very well paid. Indeed, we lived very simple lives, spending little. We never felt the need to spend more, and I suppose there was something of the French peasant in all of us. When you have been through war and starvation, you always keep something back.

However, as you will have seen, there is far more than we could have accumulated, even with extreme frugality, and I want to tell you about this. As an archaeologist, Charles was always very interested in the many rumours that were around regarding treasure in the area. People today have made it into big business, of course, because of the media that you have available, but we were always aware of the possibilities, and this has been the case for many hundreds of years. Given the history of Rennes-le-Château, and its occupation over thousands of years, there were bound to be some hoards stashed away. This is the same everywhere. Just because you do not hear that a hoard has been found does not mean that it hasn't. You must remember, we had been through Nazi occupation and we learned to keep things to ourselves and protect our own.

Of course, you know all about Saunière, our delightful village priest. I was born about six years after he died, but there was plenty of talk amongst the villagers and elsewhere even then, although most remained entirely loyal to him. Your grandparents knew him, of course, and he even spent some time as the priest at Antugnac. He has been in your house, Benoît, many times, and was very interested in history and archaeology, as was his brother Alfred. He was a charming man by all accounts, but full of sadness, which I am told he never entirely shook off.

I will write to you again about this, but for now I want to explain our wealth. The four of us, that is, Charles, myself, and your parents (Christiane refused to have any part in it), used information that Saunière did not have, which we discovered in the cellars of your home. We found well-preserved parchments in the painted cell. I know you both discovered this room when you were children, much to your mother's fury. I must tell you that after her reaction and the walling up of the cellar entirely I didn't speak to your parents for two years. I have never understood her reaction, and never will. You saw the room, and walling it up wouldn't remove the images from your mind. My brother persuaded me for your sakes to engage with them again, which of course I did. Anyway, the parchments were written in Latin and thanked the owners of the château for giving sanctuary to several of the Templar knights during difficult times and allowing them to escape. They left the gold discs buried in the wall in gratitude. There was a considerable number of them.

On the second parchment, they wrote about small pockets of gold buried around the cistern at Blanchefort, one of their watch towers. Interestingly, its location used the dial of a clock combined with a sundial, and gave times on the dial to pinpoint the area around the cistern where the gold was. Most of the monies were long gone of course. They were intelligent men and knew that trouble was coming. Over the centuries their compatriots came back and took what was left, but we found three pockets of buried discs that were of considerable worth. Gold was in very short supply in the years after the war, particularly of that purity, and we sold most of it to a wealthy American for a very large sum of money. I have no idea of its whereabouts now. I kept a few discs for you, as did Charles, and hope that by now you have them. Your parents didn't want to keep any of theirs and sold them all.

Charles found a few smaller stashes of gold in the vicinity, some very ancient indeed, and this added to *your inheritance, as did Charles's buying and selling of antiquities. Celestine and Henrikas also earned large amounts of money on their missions. It is no more intriguing than that. I have hidden the parchments for you. They should be well preserved as Charles did this himself. They haven't been opened since we first found them. I am hoping that you have removed the small leather suitcase from the loft with the photograph trunk. This was the suitcase I used for most of my time in the Secret Service. It has a hidden compartment at the bottom. Look carefully and you will find it. That is where the parchments are. I must go now but will write more soon.*

Your loving Aunt Hortense

CHAPTER FIFTY-SIX

'The fog begins to lift! I thought it would be something like that. Charles was always coming home with odd things. I don't doubt that there are still a few more hoards around, and I suppose that at some time or other they'll be found. I'd like to do something useful with part of my money. I'm not sure what yet, but I'm going to think about it.'

'Good idea. Given how things are right now, if we both died the whole lot would go to the government and I would hate that. And the painted room... even if I never open it again, it needs to be noted somewhere that it exists. It's an important part of history. I felt rather odd hearing what she said about not speaking to Celestine and Henrikas for two years. I don't think there was much love lost there. They were both strong, dominant women, with very different viewpoints. I fear I have some work to do though with regards to our mother. Even now when I think of her I feel anger and resentment. As for Henrikas, he seems to have lived his life in her shadow. Why do you think that was?'

'She appeared to be so much stronger and bolder than him, but things aren't always what they seem.' She gave a huge sigh and wiped away a few tears with the back of her hand.

'I know, I'm feeling pretty low myself. It's been a difficult time and Peter's death has just about finished us off, but I don't think it's over yet. Let's keep going through the letters... at least we'll have accomplished something and I'll make us some tea.'

Caro picked up another of the letters. I was grateful to Hortense for writing to us in this way. I doubted that she was going to tell us 'everything,' but neither of our parents had bothered at all, and in my head, I thanked her and hoped she could hear me.

CHAPTER FIFTY-SEVEN

April 2015

Dear Caro and Benoît

Time is moving on, and I am writing to explain the golden cube, which is now, hopefully, in your possession, along with the golden-topped walking stick and the watch.

Firstly, I need to tell you about the family that Charles and I come from. As you will have gathered, de Morny is an old French name. You may have come across the papers in the suitcase that I left for you. Our great-great-grandfather was also a Charles de Morny. He was the illegitimate son of Hortense de Beauharnais, the daughter of Josephine (who was married to Napoleon I) and Charles Comte de Flahaut. There were several other illegitimacies along the line, but of course, they are not blood relatives of yours. These few objects ended up in the possession of Charles and so now, of course, they belong to you. Charles believed that the stick and the watch may have belonged to Napoleon himself, but quite clearly the cube is of Templar descent and more likely to be of the de Morny line, but at the end of the day, who knows? One reads things about the Beauharnais being of Merovingian descent, but it seems to me that half of France is claiming that these days.

I am sure you will recognise the other photographs. They are of the village church where you have been living in England, Benoît. I visited there many years ago, and always thought it quite odd that you should end up living and working there, but I have seen a synchronicity developing over the past couple of years that is rare, and may not happen again in your lifetime. I know this sounds strange, especially from one who is not given to fanciful imaginings, but none the less it is so.

Rennes-le-Château is a place of unusual events. This has been the case throughout history, and undoubtedly will continue to be so. Bérenger Saunière was involved in a similar event that carried him along on a wave of discoveries that altered the course of his life. He continued with the passing on of the knowledge in the best way he could, and this responsibility has now been given to you both. It's like a giant wave, and there is no way of getting off. One can only ride it, use one's wits, and do the best one can.

The church in your English village, Benoît, is also such a place. That is why it was chosen many hundreds of years ago to hold the secret. It was thought to be for the best at that time. It may no longer be for the best now. I am sorry, I don't want to talk in riddles. You have had enough held back from you throughout your lives, but as I write this I am concerned if someone else should read this letter and the impact that might have.

Saunière found four documents in all. I have seen

copies of two of them through my work, but as cunning as I was, it was impossible to get my hands on the originals. The other two were elsewhere, but I am fully aware of their contents.

There are more documents in your church, Benoît, most likely of all four. I am not entirely sure where, but Saunière knew and if you follow his clues to where they are hidden here I suspect the clues will lead you to the parchments in England too. The letter he found from Bigou told him everything. Some say that Saunière went to your church in England, Benoît, but I cannot confirm that. I am sure you already know where they are here, but, my children, I suspect that they are now gone. I deeply regret not trying to get them when I had the chance, for it was inevitable that the Vatican would take them if they could. Please look anyway. One can always hope that they were stupid enough to be unable to decipher the narrative of truth. A narrative of lies and greed is always preferable, n'est-ce pas? Do not wait, though. The sooner you look, the better. There is something explosive in the atmosphere and it does not bode well. My final letter will tell you everything else I know. You can do with it what you will.

Your loving Aunt Hortense.

CHAPTER FIFTY-EIGHT

'I can't find any more letters, although the deeds to her house are here. Some of the names seem so familiar, it's like I personally know them, and they go back more than three hundred years. And more photographs... look at these of the three of us sitting at her kitchen table. We must have been eight or nine – she looks so young and incredibly attractive. That casserole is beginning to smell marvellous... when will it be ready?'

I got up to check the casserole, gave it a stir, and dropped in a handful of pearl barley.

'About an hour, I reckon. What are we going to do now? If she said she would write again, then I'm sure she has. Perhaps it's in the suitcase with the Templar parchments. To be honest, I'm sure I know what she'll say, and I expect you do too.'

'Yes, I suppose so. I need to tell you about Asmodeus, as well. He's the missing link to much of what Saunière left.'

'I'd thought as much. Even years ago, we saw Asmodeus as a key player.'

'I haven't quite finished writing it all out, but I'll give you a copy as soon as I have. In essence, I've worked out where Bérenger found and re-hid some of the documents. I'm almost positive that I know where they are. Of course, someone else may have worked it out too, and they may well be gone. It's difficult because I shall need some form of permission to access where they are, and the minute I ask for that someone's going to ask me why, and then the whole thing will go to pot. If I tell them why, then undoubtedly they'll get there before me. Like I said, they might be gone already. It wasn't that easy to work out, but surely in one hundred and twenty years someone else has, apart from you, of course. I don't doubt that you've worked it out and have just kept it to yourself.'

She looked at me and waited for me to concede to this point, which I did.

She continued to speak. 'But I'm not sure what to do, and secondly, I don't want to put either of us in any more danger that we already are. In some ways, I wish I'd never found out. And yet to know and not be able to get to it is equally as bad.'

'We need to look, and if they're gone they're gone... we'll deal with it. I've been happy enough to put it all to the back of my mind, but Hortense was right, and we mustn't wait any longer.'

'That's a real surprise coming from you. Just when I think I've worked you out, you change tack! I take it you agree with me that they are in the piscina pedestal here at Antugnac, along with the possibility of them being behind Joan of Arc's flag somewhere?'

'Yes, to all of that. And, yes, that's where I think he re-hid them, although I hadn't made the Joan of Arc connection. I'm sure I can get a key, and it shouldn't take more than a few minutes to look. Let's see what we find when we get in there. Have you thought any more about the funeral?'

'I'll sort it out if you like, Ben. It should be quiet, but people from the village will want to come, and she was very fond of the mayor, so I'm sure he'll be there. Can you give the priest a ring? Do you think we should contact Merry or go to Peter's funeral? Would she even want us to?'

'I'll send her an email from both of us, and express our sadness at what happened and offer help. She may ignore it, but at least we tried. We mustn't forget that we still have a problem. Harcourt's on the loose and so is the bishop. I wish Niort would tell us what he knows about him… at least we would know what we were dealing with, but the bishop confuses me even more. What is he doing getting mixed up with all of this? It could lose him his position, unless he's working on behalf of the Vatican.'

'Somehow I don't think so. Surely they would choose someone much more able: younger, meaner, and leaner.'

'I still can't believe I've misjudged him so badly. As for Peter, I think he got involved with a dangerous group of people, and went off the rails. He certainly wasn't compos mentis when we saw him, was he?'

'If you're going to speak to the priest about getting the key to Antugnac church, you might as well arrange the funeral times. Perhaps we should speak to Niort again and ask him what's going on. The problem is that we've not been honest with him, and I'm sure he knows that.'

'But once we involve him in the journal, the parchments, Saunière's parchments, Mary, Jesus, and all the saints, we've lost the lot! I for one am not willing to let that happen, not yet anyway.'

'I agree. Don't forget I've got a book riding on this, but it's more than that... I don't want to be silenced, which would most likely be the case if Niort got his hands on everything.'

I turned on my laptop. There were quite a few emails for me. Some were basic church things and I dealt with those first. There was one from Bill, asking if I had heard about Peter.

I'm not sure if you know, but Peter Lacy, the vicar, is dead. It's all a bit shady, and no one really knows how or why. He always seemed rather highly strung and anxious to me, but I can't say I knew him that well. The date of the funeral hasn't been arranged yet, and there's a rumour that he wasn't even in England when he died, but I know no more than that. The cleaner at the rectory told me. She had gone up there earlier and found Merry in a bit of a state with the police there. My mother would say that it was the curse of the church! It's more likely to be that he got into a bit of trouble. I had heard he was having an affair, but I try to go deaf when I hear things like that. It must be awful for Merry, who is such a nice woman. I'll let you know if I hear more. I've walked by your cottage a few times (without stick!) and all seems well there. Hope to see you back soon. Bill

I wrote back expressing the appropriate shock at his news and asked him to let me know if he heard any more.

'There's an email from Merry. I'll read it out.'

Benoît and Caro. As you know, Peter was shot dead in France this morning. I am told he was about to shoot the pair of you, but he was killed before he had the chance to do so. How can this be? I am so sorry that you have been put in danger. He hasn't been himself for quite a while now, but I hadn't realised how serious things had become. I'm struggling to imagine him with a gun at all. I feel completely stunned, to be honest, and none of it seems real. I'm sure it will hit me at some point, but right now I'm being very practical and doing all the things that need to be done.

The boys are on their way home, so that will be a help. You may have heard that he was having an affair. I know how gossip gets around the village. I did know, but I doubt if this has anything to do with things. Against my advice, he had joined a modern-day Templar-style organisation, which pledged to uphold Christian principles above all other things. I thought it was ridiculous but he wouldn't listen to me. Anyway, I've told the inspector everything

I know about it, which isn't much, and can do no more.

He had taken to spending hours in the church at night looking for something, but he wouldn't tell me what and always locked the door so that I couldn't get in. What a terrible mess. Once again, I'm so sorry that you've been involved. I think he must have had a major psychological breakdown, but I suppose that now I shall never know. His body is still in France, and I don't know when it will arrive back in England. I understand if you don't want to speak to me given what you've been put through. Love to you both, Merry.

'That poor woman. Send her my love, won't you, Ben.'

I wrote back to her, offering our support with anything she might need, and sending our condolences and love. I didn't say much, as I didn't want to compound an already impossible situation, but I felt deeply sorry for her and for what she and her children had to face in the coming days and weeks.

Caro had gone upstairs and I picked up the phone to dial the number of the local priest. He had heard about Hortense's death, and we agreed on Saturday morning at eleven for the funeral.

'When will you be free to discuss the details? I'm on my way down the hill shortly, because I've got to drop something off in Couiza.'

'Why don't you come after that and stay for supper?

Oh, and by the way, would it be possible to have the key to Antugnac church for half an hour? Caro is writing an academic history of the Razès area, and Antugnac was particularly important because it was one of the few places locally to have a fortified church.'

'No problem, Benoît. I'll bring it with me.' This concluded the conversation, which had been easier than I thought, and Pascal, the priest, had sounded very pleasant. He lived alone in a church cottage and would, no doubt, welcome a bit of company on a summer evening, and it would do us good to talk to someone other than each other for a few hours.

Caro came back down and I explained that we had a guest for supper, and the contents of the conversation. She quickly phoned the undertakers and updated them on the details.

I cleared the table and then wrapped three large potatoes in foil, tucking them into the hot embers of the fire.

The room was filled with the delicious smell of chicken stew, and I realised how hungry I was despite the trauma of the day.

* * *

A few moments later there was a knock at the door, and I quickly let Pascal in. We were soon chatting and he was easy company. He told us that the police had been at the church in Rennes-le-Château that morning and a man had been carried out and taken away in an ambulance.

334

They had taken the recordings from the security camera and had been there for the rest of the day, but were now gone.

'I've no idea what it was about and they were very cagey. Still, I'm glad that the church wasn't closed for days. I'll ring them tomorrow to try to find out more. Here's the key to Antugnac church; I cover four parishes now.'

'It's the same in England. Most priests cover three or four parishes,' I replied.

'I suppose the congregation is shrinking just about everywhere. Antugnac is a strange place, and it's true that it is an unusual building in that it's fortified. The Huguenots tried to destroy it and burn it down in the late 1500s, with all the villagers hiding inside, but they didn't succeed. It's always puzzled me that it's been stripped to the stone on the inside. As you know, most of our churches are very ornate. I'm so sorry about your aunt. She was an amazing lady, even if she didn't believe in God! I had wondered if she would want a church service at all.'

'I know, but if it's OK with you we would still like it there. She loved the church so very much, and hopefully we can arrange things to make us all happy. Come and sit down at the table. Benoît has made a fabulous chicken stew over the fire like our grandmother used to do, so I hope you're hungry.'

'Very. I'm not much of a cook, I'm afraid, so it's a real treat to be offered a home-cooked dinner.'

'Then you must come and eat with me sometimes. I

like cooking, although I'm not up to Benoît's standard. He'll probably be going back to England sometime soon.'

I looked at her as she said this. I had given no thought to my return, and there were still issues with our safety to consider before that happened. We spent a pleasant evening with Pascal and I warmed to him greatly. I hoped they would meet up sometimes. I knew he would never be a partner for her, but at least he was good company, and she seemed to like him.

We arranged a supremely simple service for Hortense, using Jesus instead of God in any prayers, and some simple music that we knew she liked. I doubted that there would be more than a handful of people there since she had outlived almost all her friends and probably her old colleagues too. We waved him off, his little scooter chugging noisily back up the hill.

'What a nice chap. I really do think it's time the Catholic Church allowed priests to marry, and look, Ben, we've got the key to the church.'

'Let's go over in the morning and see what's what. I'm exhausted, and am going straight to bed after we've washed up.'

'Why don't you do that, and leave the washing up to me. I've got some research to do and won't be going up for an hour or two.'

CHAPTER FIFTY-NINE

I was unconscious in minutes, and woke to the sun streaming through the window at eight the following morning. Caro was already downstairs, and I quickly ate some breakfast. She was anxious to get over to the church and then make a few more arrangements for Hortense's funeral the next day.

'I wanted to show you this before our church visit. **Asmodeus**. I'll read it out, but you can follow it through as I read. Or perhaps you would just rather read it yourself? I don't want you to feel like a student. You do already know quite a bit of it.'

'No, I'd rather you read it out – it sinks in more quickly that way. And I don't mind being your student at all. You're the best teacher ever. Did anyone ever tell you that?'

'Are you teasing me, Benoît? Because if you are…'

She made to move towards me, and I raised my hands to declare peace. 'I was being deadly serious. Now hand me what you've written and teach… I'm all ears.'

She handed me several printed sheets of paper, and I sat at the table, placed it in front of me, and sipped my coffee, waiting for her to begin.

'**Asmodeus**, guardian of the gates of hell and of the secret of Solomon's temple. Tricked by King Solomon into giving assistance with the building of his temple, by filling his favourite water hole with wine and then capturing him, although he did eventually escape. The piscina on his back and the water hole is a good 3D analogy. Asmodeus was the king of nine hells, and one of the seven princes of hell, generally thought to represent lust and sexual desire.

'His brother Ihys believed that everyone should have free will and choose their own destiny, whilst Asmodeus believed that the strong should rule the weak and proceeded to kill his brother. There's a parallel here with religion in general, which I believe Saunière is trying to point out after making his discoveries. That is, if the powers that control us all revealed that Jesus was a mortal man, then humanity wouldn't be able to cope with their lives at all. I suspect that it would be much more likely that those in dominant positions would be the ones who wouldn't be able to exist, with their positions stripped from them.

'In the Book of Tobit, or Tobias, a religious novel and part of the canon of the Roman Catholic Church, which represents the sanctity of marriage, Asmodeus falls in love with Sara, the wife of Tobias the son. She ultimately rejects him, but of interest is verse **22** chapter 6, which speaks of the marriage of Tobias the son and Sara. They wait until the third night of their marriage before consummation takes place.

And when the third night is past, thou shalt take the virgin
with the fear of the Lord, moved rather for love of children
than for lust, that in the seed of Abraham thou mayst obtain a
blessing in children.

'Another **22**, and an allegorical narrative used by Saunière, telling us about Jesus being a mortal and created in the same way as the rest of us, his marriage to Mary Magdalene and their offspring, Sara.

'This is reiterated in the writing on the chancel walls and ceiling, where there are dozens of symbols showing the initials M for Mary, J for Jesus, which is inverted to show that the crucifixion didn't happen, and S for Sara through the middle. There's also another one of them in gold on one of the arches, with the symbols of Mary and Jesus to either side: the jar of healing balm and a plain cross. Sara also means princess. No surprises there since both Jesus and Mary came from royal blood lines.'

As she spoke, I remembered that Charles had been the first person to point them out to us when we were children.

'I've noticed how worn many of the wall paintings have become. I hope they don't disappear altogether. Even poor Asmodeus had his head lopped off and stolen a few years back. Listening to you like this, I can't help thinking about Saunière and the planning he must have undertaken. Do you think he worried that people might not understand his clues?'

'It's quite likely, I suppose. And some of the clues are still being argued about. It's like anything: what is clear to one person may not be clear to another, and the bulk of what he did to the church was more than a hundred years ago. Can I have another coffee please?'

I walked over to the kitchen and she followed me, paper in hand.

* * *

'Back to Asmodeus. Firstly, the four archangels standing on his back. That's a numerological four, meaning truth, fate, illumination, knowledge, wisdom, and of course, the sum total of **22**. If you remember the multiple four triangles or *Eyes of Hel* in your church in England, Ben? That might be a deliberate connection between the two churches. There's also the fourth rune, Ansuz, meaning divine communication, ancestral speech, and the use of symbols to understand and transform.

'Each archangel shows part of the Catholic crossing of oneself with blessed water. One points directly down to the piscina below and underneath them is written the phrase:

PAR CE SIGNE TU LE VAINCRAS

'By this sign, you will triumph, take possession of, will overcome it/him. *Him* meaning Asmodeus and the holder of the secret, and the knowledge of the secret itself. People have been trying to crack this code for ever.'

'We spent quite a bit of time on it years ago, although

340

I can't say I've thought about it much since then. Don't tell me, Caro, you've worked it out!'

'Well, yes, I have. I sat up all night with the letters on bits of paper and suddenly, I realised I had done it! I was so excited, I nearly phoned you, but decided to save it for when I saw you next. It's a simple breaking down of an anagram to this.'

R L C
PISCINA
EAU SANG
VERITE

RENNES-LE-CHÂTEAU
PISCINA
WATER BLOOD
TRUTH

'Eureka! You should have phoned; that's some achievement, and after all these years…'

'Thank you. But there's more to it than that. We already know that the phrase is comprised of **22** letters with the symbolism that goes with it. There are two extra letters from the original phrase that this was taken from though. The phrase originated with Constantine, the Roman Emperor, who apparently, whilst in battle, had a vision of these words minus the "le" and with a cross of light. Very handy, and we know he went on to use it at the Council of Nicaea in 325, along with bits of Roman, Egyptian, Greek, and other belief systems, all thrown into the mix to create the new *faith*. Worth noting is that Constantine's birth date, and his death date, are both numerological **22**s. Again.'

* * *

'These **22**s. How can it be? How can it come up over and over like that? Call it what you like, synchronicity or whatever. It's astounding but totally unfathomable.'

'I've got no answer to it. Like Hortense said in her last letter, Rennes-le-Château is a strange place. Maybe someday, someone will be able to explain it properly. I can't help feeling that even all the research I've done is just scratching the surface of what's out there.

'The meaning of the decoded phrase is simple and direct. Saunière is telling us of the whereabouts of the parchments, both found and re-hidden. Under a piscina or water stoop. Which piscina? Antugnac. Why? Because he tells us so in the Stations of the Cross. The plaid cloth around the child in Station **8** is the plaid for the Andrews clan. St Andrew's church is just across the lane here in Antugnac, and is where Saunière worked in 1890–91. Antugnac is written on Marie de Nègre's headstone backwards on the bottom two and top two lines. **22**. It might also be a clue to Saunière's own involvement with the Scottish Rite Masonic order.'

'I'll second that. I have no doubt about his involvement. There is Masonic symbolism in many of the churches around here, and it's well known that the

Scottish Rite were in France from the 1700s onwards.'

'I agree, and the "Le" is interesting in itself, because they're the thirteenth and fourteenth letters. 1314 was the year that Jacques de Molay, the last grand master of the Knights Templar, was burned at the stake by Philip IV of France. As this was happening, he apparently cursed both Philip and Pope Clement V, who were both dead within the year. Philip of France died on a numerological **22**. The order to abolish the Knights Templar altogether was given on the **22**nd March 1312. The royal house of Capet collapsed fourteen years later.

'And there's more. It was on the **22**nd July 1209 that the order was given to start the Albigensian slaughter in Bezier. A **22** and the feast day of Mary Magdalene. And the bishop had drawn up a list of **222** individuals he wanted handed over.'

'And Abbot Amalric's chilling words, "Kill them all, God will know his own."'

'Indeed. But he didn't, did he? God, I mean. No one was spared or saved, not even children.'

'No... no, he didn't... and more **22**s. I'm struggling again. I can understand the deliberate use of the number as a means of explaining something, but not its recurrence over the best part of two thousand years. It suggests some sort of overall plan, or fate, something like that. If Hortense was here I'd ask her.'

Caro shrugged her shoulders. 'I've thought about it a lot, but haven't come up with anything. I've got a friend who's interested in this sort of thing, so I thought I might ask him. Anyway, we already know of Templar

343

involvement at Rennes-le-Château, and in the area, not least because of Marie de Nègre's tombstone, and the code on it that Bigou left. The Templars were accused of worshipping skulls, and a skull is often seen with statues of Mary Magdalene. The statue and the altar relief of her at Rennes-le-Château both have skulls. The skull and crossbones are a well-known Templar symbol; in fact, they used it as the flag flown on their ships. There's also a stone skull and crossbones at the entrance to the cemetery with **22** teeth. That might be a clue in itself, since we know he dug around a fair bit and he may well be leaving another clue to the whereabouts or origins of his finds, or what might still be left there.'

* * *

'Leading on from that is another Templar link, because their full title was *The Poor Fellow Soldiers of Christ and of the Temple of Solomon*. The Templars' true role during their crusades has been much debated over the years, but I am strongly beginning to favour the idea that they were explorers and adventurers. The looting of original treasures of the Temple of Solomon and what was supposedly hidden under it, that is, the Holy Grail and the Ark of the Covenant, along with various other treasures, was their sole aim.'

'That's an interesting conclusion to make, and the right one, I think. Maybe they had reason enough to do it? After all, they wouldn't want anyone else to find it, so the motivation wasn't entirely greed. In the wrong hands, whatever was there may be have been devastating to the world order at the time… the Church would certainly have thought so. And we know that the Templars certainly weren't poor… quite the opposite. One wonders if they really did find the Grail, in whatever form, or the supposed Ark of the Covenant? If the king and pope's demands to hand it over were either refused or their finds denied, then that could be what brought about the massive condemnation of them, and their ultimate slaying or dispersal? I don't doubt, though, that any treasure was long gone and hidden or buried by the time the king's men arrived.'

'I knew you were interested in the Templars, Benoît, but you always keep so much to yourself. You never tell me anything.'

'It's not deliberate… if you'd asked I would have told you.'

'I'm not sure about that, but my belief is that they, along with the Cathars, who I am convinced were part of the story, and ultimately the Church, were involved in a massive conspiracy. Perhaps the biggest in known history, and one that is still in existence today.'

I stood up. 'Why don't we go over to the church now, and we can finish going through this when we get back?'

CHAPTER SIXTY

The lane looked deserted, and we quickly dashed over to the church, which was directly behind the house. Locking the heavy door from inside, I switched on the lights. It was a wholly unattractive place, rather like an old barn, and quite unlike most of the other churches around here. The entire interior had been stripped back to the stone, although in places it was still possible to see where remnants of wall paintings had been, especially on the domed ceiling over the chancel. Whatever had been there, it was a massive loss to the ancient church, and was nothing short of vandalism. One could only assume that it had been removed with great deliberation. Perhaps it showed something that the Church didn't want people to see? I could think of no other reason.

There was, however, a lovely marble altar with golden caryatids across its front, and a pair of fine seventeenth-century statues of Saint Andrew and Saint Peter, with odd, grimacing faces. An ancient but simple baptismal font stood in the aisle at the back, its drain hole filled with rubbish. It had clearly been moved and refixed to the floor, which was made of rough stone. It wasn't difficult to see that most of it had been lifted recently and replaced with pale cement holding down the uneven slabs.

A narrow flight of stairs went up to a mezzanine area where a statue of Joan of Arc stood. A hole came right through the floor from here for the bell ropes, no longer used, but the framework of stone looked very old, and had clearly been reused. The other statues were Germaine, Roch, Theresa, John the Baptist, and Our Lady of Lourdes. Using the A from Arc and the L from Lourdes, there would still be the words GRAAL, like at Rennes-le-Château. I remembered that the statues at the Templar church at Campagne-sur-Aude also spelt this out, as did the statues in Bugarach, along with the chancel being covered in very fancy Rs with an S running through them, and a crown above each one. I mentioned this to Caro.

'Yes, I know. I went to Bugarach a few weeks back. R for Rex, king, from *Rex Deus*, I assume, and S for Sara. If you look carefully, you can also see the M and J, both upside down, at the top and bottom of the R. Did you see the stained-glass window with the boat and tarot style wheel of fortune? Very odd, as is the font covered in hearts.'

'Yes, it is a bit out of place, and the font too.'

Here, the little window of stained glass in one of the alcoves caught my eye, and I had always admired it for its striking simplicity. It showed a red cross, an eight-pointed star, and to either side a fish and eye, which might also be alchemical symbols for the sun and gold. It didn't have any great age, but was beautiful all the same, as were the plainer ones, which looked like they were set back and gave a corridor-like illusion of distance, especially from the outside when it was dark and the church was lit from inside.

* * *

The water stoup or piscina by the door was dusty and empty. We both looked at it with dismay, as it was quite clear that it had recently been moved. The cement on the floor was new and already cracked, and there was pale cement holding the bowl to the side wall, also cracked. The interior of the bowl appeared to have a cement coating, which shouldn't have been necessary with marble, and there was a large X scratched into a slab just in front of it. Clearly there was some reason for this, but short of taking it up, there was little that we could do to investigate it further.

The stone wall behind the piscina and to either side looked like it had been taken out to chest height and had been replaced using pale mortar. On closer examination, the bowl was badly damaged underneath, and had clearly been set upon with a crowbar to try to lever it from its base. It wasn't large, and I should have been able to move the top from its stand, which showed no signs of cement between the two, but it wouldn't budge. We both tried several times to no avail. It was clearly being held together with pins or bolts of some sort, probably coming straight down from the actual bowl, which was why it now had a cement liner to cover up the holes. There was nothing we could do but give up, for now anyway.

'There are several possibilities. Whoever has been

here in the past few years has quite clearly stripped the place. They've taken up the floor and pulled out part of the walls. Obviously, they were looking for something and were very determined to find it. The piscina has definitely been moved, and one imagines that if they had permission to crowbar it, they would have had permission to use more tools to separate the bowl from the stand.

'On the other hand, maybe the damage was done by Saunière, or even Bigou and his English friends all those years ago, and no one has separated the two since then? That's wishful thinking! Maybe someone without permission took a crowbar to it? Oh, Ben, even seeing an empty cavity in the pillar would have been wonderful... I'm sure there is one. What a disappointment, even though I fully expected it. Let's take a look at Joan, because I'm sure he found or hid something there.'

* * *

We walked to the back of the church, and up the narrow staircase to the small mezzanine area and looked closely at the dusty statue.

'She's been got at, Caro. The base has been smashed; she's not standing on it properly, and part of her banner has been damaged. At least it confirms that your theories were correct, which is something. I would say that either the government or the Vatican have been in here. We always knew that would be the most likely scenario, and so did Hortense.'

'You're right of course. And we still have the rest of her papers to go through, which hopefully should tell us what was written on the parchments. I do wonder if anything has been left in Peter's church in England by way of records… it does seem likely. Let's get back; I've got things to do for tomorrow, and perhaps we can go through the papers again and look for the ones we haven't yet seen.'

She took more photos, and we both stopped in front of a statue of John the Baptist. He was also damaged, particularly around the base, where there was a large area showing a white plaster repair. His right arm had also been broken right off and repaired with the same white plaster.

'And they've had a go at John. Look, Caro, two fingers raised instead of one! I think that's the first time I've ever seen that…how very strange!'

We locked the church, and walked around the outside of the building. Built into the wall were several stones with old red paintings on them. One seemed to be of a house or tent, and another had a word written in an ancient script: 'Clovis'… one of the Merovingian kings. We had known these painted stones throughout our lives, but were no clearer about their origins now than we were then. Some parts of history refused explanation, and we had no more than our imaginations by which to understand their purpose or where they had come from.

CHAPTER SIXTY-ONE

Back in the house, Caro made various calls, and an hour later we sat at the table, a bowl of soup in front of each of us.

'To go back to Asmodeus…'

'Carry on, if you don't mind my slurping.'

'No, I don't mind, good job too, considering that eating is your favourite pastime!'

My mouth full of soup, I ignored this dig, and she sorted her papers.

'Right, here we are. If you remember, throughout the Stations of the cross Saunière used silver bowls, silver discs, and other silvered objects. This replicates and links to the clue of the whereabouts of the parchments in the Asmodeus statue.'

'I remember us working that out ages ago, but I never understood the salamanders. Why are they there? Do you know?'

'Yes, I think so. The salamanders above Asmodeus link in with the date 1314 and Jacques de Molay, as well as the painting of him by François de Fleury, and the one of Joan of Arc, who was also burned at the stake. Salamanders generally represent fire and the ability to survive it, as well as sometimes being used symbolically for Jesus and Mary. Saunière was linking them up and expressing the fact that despite death by fire, the truth still survived and lived on.

'Interestingly, Simon de Montfort married into the family of the Counts of Angoulême, who also had a salamander as part of their coat of arms. The Counts of Angoulême had links with Joan of Arc in later years. Montfort comes into the story again, because he was great friends with Almeric, one of the Saint-Amands, also known as Saint-Omer. They went crusading together. It was the Saint-Amands that owned one of the manors in your village in England, Ben. His relative and predecessor, Godfrey de Saint-Amand, or Geoffrey de Saint-Omer, founded the Knights Templar with Hugues de Payens in 1118.

'Their family also had a close friendship with Bernard de Blanquefort, also known as Bertrand de Blanchefort, the sixth grand master of the Knights Templar. That's Blanchefort, or Blanca Fort, near Rennes-le-Château, later owned by the Voisin and d'Hautpoul families. The connections between the Templars and the two places in France and England are considerable, including one Hugh Saint Omer, who died in 1106 holding the title of Prince of Galilee and Tiberias. Godfrey may well have been taking up the reigns of his relative when setting up the Knights Templar, already having been given prior information.'

'That sounds likely. He would certainly have passed on anything of importance, that's for sure.'

'Absolutely, and there's something else I discovered

that might interest you. It's believed that one of the bells in your village church is very valuable and unusual, having a high silver content. There's a story that the Templars at Le Bezu hid a silver bell down a well. It's never been found, of course, but supposedly its ghostly rings can be heard on the anniversary of their arrest by the king of France. Much of their treasure is rumoured to have been stashed at Le Bezu. It was owned by Pierre de Voisin for some time who, as we know, was also lord of Rennes-le-Château, and we mustn't forget the *Templiers* code left on Marie de Nègre's gravestone. Make of it what you will, but I firmly believe that much of the Templar treasure was re-hidden elsewhere, well before their fleeing or arrest, or eventually retrieved by those who escaped, or by their ancestors, quite possibly with some being taken back home.'

'That's fascinating, and certainly possible. We should go up to Le Bezu. I haven't been there for years.'

'Let's do that, Ben. Now, back to Asmodeus.'

* * *

'The circled fingers of Asmodeus's right hand, much argued about as representing various monuments in the region, is where a stick should be. It's as simple as that. The hand on the knee, also much argued about, is a simple historical fact, as Asmodeus is traditionally known as the devil on two sticks who had a limp. The marks on his left wing are not runes or any other language. They're little more than symbolic battle wounds, which he showed off and wore with pride. There are six scratch marks, not the five so often mentioned, but only five are coloured black. The numerological symbolism of five is fire, and six a union. Asmodeus was also the 32nd demon in the Lesser Key of Solomon, a seventeenth-century spell book. 3+2=5.

'As for the B.S. emblem on the front, I suspect it's just the initials of Bérenger Saunière. He had the Asmodeus statue made to his own design, and is quite simply claiming it as such, although it's possible that the B stands for "benitier," a water stoup, and the S for "sous," under. The parchments are under the water stoup or piscina. Take your pick. Maybe, in typical Saunière style, he was saying both. B is the second letter of the alphabet, and S the nineteenth, which is a numerological **3**. Benitier is also the French word for giant clam, which is what Asmodeus is holding up.'

She paused and tidied her papers. 'Our old friend Asmodeus tells quite a tale, doesn't he?'

'Saunière must have spent ages planning it,' I replied. 'I had thought that the Andrews' plaid blanket was conclusive to the Antugnac connection, and had made a guess about the water stoup solely because of the quote above Asmodeus, "by this sign," and the downward finger pointing to the water. A lot of the other information is new to me, though. Did you ever read the booklet written about his year as priest here at Antugnac? It was all taken from his journal; masses of it, even copies of the sermons he preached in the church. He sounds quite manic and over the top, and in my view, he was really scared. It's like he was trying to convince himself of how dedicated and devout he was, and didn't ring true at all. As far as I'm concerned it was just another cover-up.'

'I've got a copy, and that's exactly what I thought. Poor man, his whole life had been turned upside down. I've tried so hard to understand how he might have felt, especially when he had just made a discovery. The nearest I got was a mixture of terror and excitement, but I guess we'll never know for sure.'

CHAPTER SIXTY-TWO

I put Hortense's leather case on the table to try to find the compartment that she wrote about. Caro leaned over and pulled at one of the metal rods that ran along its base, and immediately the bottom flipped up, revealing a compartment, some four or five centimetres deep. Inside was a brown envelope and a stiff flat package, which I assumed were the Templar parchments. Charles had obviously done all he could do preserve them, with various layers of special tissue and card, the edges still showing some of their original wax seal. We both sat down and I began to carefully remove the layers.

As Hortense had said, there were two parchments, both in remarkably good condition. The edges were a little frayed and there were a few shadowy stains across them, but they had survived the years well and were easy enough to read. I found myself holding my breath, as I so often did in the presence of things so old, created by humans to convey messages to those who were to follow. I felt the usual goosebumps as I started to read out the first parchment.

It was written in standard Latin, which I was glad of, because my Occitan, which I knew the Templars also used, was nowhere near as fluent. It was dated to October

1307 and thanked the owners of the château for giving them shelter in the 'most difficult' of times. They used the plural, so I assumed that there were more than one of them. They went on to say that they and their descendants would remain indebted to them in perpetuity, and the small token of their gratitude left behind went no way towards repaying this kindness. At the top and bottom were small Templar emblems of two men on a horse, surrounded by a circle, around which words were written.

AMOR VINCIT OMNIA.

'Love conquers all; What do you think of that? Have you ever seen anything like it? I've got shivers down my spine.'

'Amazing! Like you, I've seen lots of old documents, but to have something connected to your house makes it very special. I hope they escaped and managed to find a place of safety somewhere. Let's look at the other one. It's a map, just like Hortense said. Knowing the area like we do it's rather obvious, as it would have been to our parents. Oh, Benoît, it must have been so exciting for them – I wish I'd been there.'

The map was exactly as Hortense had described. It showed the location of Blanchefort, the Templar watchtower just a few kilometres from here. Drawn over the top of the cistern, which could still be seen to this day, was a circular diagram showing both the dial of a clock and the positions on a compass, one directly on top of the other.

Written down one side were various numbers and letters, presumably to give the positions on the circle of the buried pockets of gold. It was simple enough, and for a moment I tried to imagine our parents, Charles and Hortense, out on the mountainside, probably in the dark, digging for the treasure that had been left for them.

'Me too. What an astonishing experience it must have been.' We were both quiet for a moment, our thoughts, and perhaps part of ourselves, momentarily up on that bleak rocky outcrop, with the past whistling all around us in the wind.

'It's just occurred to me that the piscina in Temple Corner, as Bill called it, in England, could well be some kind of representation of Blanchefort. As a Templar watchtower and stronghold, it was much simpler than a castle or fortress, and may well have been castellated. And we know that there's a large, circular water cistern and caves underneath. Maybe the hidden gold was part of the secret, along with Mary and her Migdal tower? And then there's Jesus – "I am the vine" – with the trailing leaves everywhere. Perhaps the cavern with the head at its entrance also represents Jesus's tomb, empty, and the sealed and locked mouth tells us, albeit silently, of the biggest secret of all: that he never was in the tomb... not in the biblical sense, anyway.'

'I've got goosebumps again. I think you're right, but what really gets to me is the thought of the man who arranged to have it carved. He would have planned it all out and given detailed instructions to the stonemason... and then just hoped. Hoped that it would survive long enough to reveal the truth when the time was right, just like Saunière. What about us? What will we leave behind?'

'A whole heap of money and little else I suspect. Perhaps we should spend it all now? I'll buy you a massive diamond ring. How about that?' She looked at me, tears once again in her eyes.

'I'm serious, Ben.'

'So am I, and at this moment I can't think of a single thing I would leave behind that would be of value and worth to humankind. At least you have your books. As soon as this is over let's have a serious discussion. Meanwhile, think about what would make you happy. That's what I'm going to do.'

She nodded. 'I don't think money can buy that,' she said quietly. 'Do you want to look inside the other envelope? I'm hoping it's another letter from Hortense.'

She opened it, and I recognised the handwriting immediately. It was Hortense's last letter. Wiping fresh tears way with the back of her hand, she started to read.

CHAPTER SIXTY-THREE

May 2015

My dearest children.

I decided to put the last letter in here, thinking it might be safer. As you will have already discovered for yourselves, people who can be trusted are few and far between. Sad, but true. I wanted to tell you all that I know about the letter from Bigou, and the parchments found by Saunière. You will then be able to do what you wish with this information.

The first thing Saunière found was the letter that Abbé Bigou had written before he fled from the French Revolution in the early 1790s. When he pulled out the old wooden pilaster that was under the pulpit, he found a hollow inside it, and a glass vial containing the letter. I saw a copy many years ago and remember its contents well. Firstly, Bigou told the reader about bone fragments of Mary Magdalene in a niche at the top of the old Carolingian altar pillar. They were labelled in Latin, and had been in the church for almost seven hundred years.

They were given as a gift by the Templars (who had been given them by the Cathars) for keeping some of them in hiding during dangerous times. Moving the old altar would have been such a strange thing to do, but now you know why. No one knows what he did with them to this day, although I'm sure he has re-hidden them, and maybe in the future someone else will find them. Maybe they already have? Both the pulpit pilaster and the Carolingian pillar are shown in the Fleury relief on the back wall of the church, which Saunière himself helped to paint.

Secondly, he wrote about the gravestone of Marie de Nègre, the encoded inscription, and of treasures belonging to the church being buried underneath, that had been kept hidden to prevent them being used as revenue by the kings of France. He also spoke of another false tomb in the graveyard containing further relics and gold left by the Templars when they fled. I am unsure if Saunière ever found this in his night-time digging, but I suspect that he did, and used the money for his domaine as well as further renovation of the church. Much nonsense has been written about his selling of Masses. I don't doubt that he did, most priests did at that time, but the revenue was small and did not account for the wealth he once had.

The third thing that Bigou wrote about was that two ancient parchments had been moved from Rennes-le-Château to Antugnac church. One was hidden in the pillar supporting the piscina by the door, and the other was in a hollow in the base of the statue of Joan of Arc. I saw copies of these many years ago, in Paris. Some say that Saunière took these to Paris, but as always, there seems to be little conclusive proof of this. However, I do believe that the Vatican was made aware of some of his findings, and he received a substantial sum to silence him.

To my knowledge no one has ever let it be known that they have the originals, but that does not mean that they are not being held somewhere, most likely in the Vatican. They may of course have been destroyed, either by the government or the Church. I even suspected your parents of their destruction at one time, but am less sure of this now. I once asked Henrikas about it and he denied it. With hindsight, I think he was telling the truth. Both parchments were believed to have originally come from an abbey, which is very likely, of course. As you know, the Cathars, Templars, and other crusaders, were very active in these parts, and so they could well have ended up in Rennes-le-Château by these means.

The first one was a simple and very ancient narrative that told of Jesus and Mary arriving in this area by boat in the early parts of the first century. They had their daughter Sara with them, Joseph of Arimathea, and Martha. After a short while, Jesus left for England with Joseph, and that is where he died. Many hundreds of years later, the Knights Templar took the remains of the body of Mary Magdalene from Rennes-le-Château, where she was hidden, to England and reunited them. The story is well depicted in your cellar, Benoît; I'm sure you both still remember it. The second one was a genealogy of their bloodline over several hundred years.

Lastly, Bigou wrote about the sealed crypt and how

362

to access it through a slab in the floor by the pulpit. He said that there were further secrets down there that had been given to him by Marie de Nègre before she died, that had been kept by her family for many generations. You will know the stone by its name, 'The Knight's Stone,' although it's really a hunting scene. It is known that Saunière found two parchments in the crypt, very well preserved, on which were written communications between the Roman Emperor Tiberius and Pontius Pilate. I have not seen these but I am told that they confirmed that Jesus was not crucified and was, in effect, exiled and brought to France by the Romans themselves. Historically, there is a recorded mention of two Jewish political exiles arriving in the area in the first century so I believe these parchments to be accurate.

Saunière also found more Templar gold and other valuables in the crypt which added to his stash. I doubt that any of this will come as a great surprise to either of you, and as you know, he left a trail behind which was as clear as he could possibly make it, and is easily decipherable to those who have a desire to open their eyes and see the truth. There were many rumours that he also found a map, which would lead him to the ultimate treasure from the Temple of Solomon, the Ark of the Covenant, brought to the region and hidden by the Templars.

Some believe this to be the source of his wealth in the early years, from sponsors expecting a share in any finds. I cannot verify this, but children, the map was once in my possession. I found it amongst other documents in a Nazi camp. As you know, they were obsessed with hidden treasure, although I've no idea where they found the map. The woods were crawling with soldiers, and I hid it in case I was captured. I eventually returned and it remained in my possession for many years.

During a particularly dangerous time in my work, when I suspected that I might be killed, I hid it once more. It may still be there, although this is doubtful. I do not intend telling you where it is and I must strongly warn you both. Please do not search for it. It will bring nothing but misery and destruction to your lives. Evil is rife, not in the Ark itself but in the people who desire to own it. I didn't want to mention it at all, not even the possibility of a map, but there have been enough secrets in your lives. At least now I have had the chance to tell you and to give you my warning. If it ends up in your possession, I must hope that you will trust me enough to heed what I have said.

There is little left to concern me now. My house is yours to do with as you wish, but I must admit I am finding the thought of leaving it to be the hardest thing. Don't forget about the tunnels, and the foundations of the old St John the Baptist church that are underneath. I remember Charles telling you the tale of its destruction by Henri II of Castile in 1362, looking for hidden treasure, perhaps left by his family in earlier times. The church at Arques was also once dedicated to St John the Baptist. Please pass this information on before it is deliberately obliterated from history. St John the Baptist.

This is where my story ends. Do not be sad. It is the

way of things. You must both be extremely cautious and careful with the information that you have. I have heard that you have become involved with some dangerous people. As you will already have gathered, some will go to any lengths to gain power and control over others. Use what you know carefully, wisely, and when the time is right, honestly. That is my advice to you.

If I have any way of contacting you from wherever I am going, I will. Don't worry, I won't do anything to frighten you, but I cannot see any way in which I would leave Rennes-le-Château. Like so many who have gone before me, I have become a part of it, and it, me. I am hoping to be able to join up with Saunière. I have seen him many times on my strolls around the village when no one else is around. In the end, I think he used to wait for me. You may think I am becoming fanciful and a little crazy in my dotage, but I swear that this is true. There is much that we do not understand. I am excited about my next journey. Be happy for me. Be happy for yourselves. I love you both.

Hortense de Morny

CHAPTER SIXTY-FOUR

We sat in silence for a few moments and wiped our tear-stained faces. Caro spoke first.

'I saw him once.'

'Saunière? Really? When?'

'In the church, about six months ago, I suppose. It was quite late and all the tourists had gone. I was taking a few photos and looking around when I heard a shuffling sound by the pulpit. I looked up and there he was. Unmistakably him. Not quite solid, but solid enough. He smiled and then was gone. I didn't want to tell you because I thought you wouldn't believe me, and I didn't want to have to justify myself. I saw him, he saw me, and I wanted to hold on to that. So, I believe Hortense when she said she used to see him. And why wouldn't he want to wait for her? She was the most astounding woman.'

'You're right, she was. I might have never actually seen any ghosts there but the place is full of them; you can feel it. I don't doubt you, nor her, not at all.'

'I'm glad, or I might have had to punch you, and you know how weak and feeble you are. As for any treasure map, I hope we never come across it. I don't want to go searching for treasure, whatever it is, and certainly not now, anyway.'

'Not ever, Caro… and certainly not the Ark. I think we both have enough trouble without courting more, although I'm not surprised by that revelation from Hortense. I still get the feeling that she knew more than she said, and is holding something back. She was right about the deliberate removal of certain parts of history around here. I've seen it happen even in my own lifetime.'

'So have I. I've got a few phone calls to make for tomorrow. Why don't you make us a coffee and a sandwich and then we can decide what we need to do for the rest of the day.'

Then it struck me. I stood up, and steadied myself by holding the table.

'What is it, Ben? Are you OK?'

'I've just had a light-bulb moment! The Magdalene bone relics. Do you remember Station **12**? It shows Mary Magdalene holding a prayer book that looks like an exact replica of the one that Saunière carried everywhere? Were her bones tucked into the book somehow, perhaps in a cut-out? Is that why he always had it with him? Is that why he was exhumed and the book has now gone? Once again, someone's got there before us. The church wasn't always dedicated to Mary Magdalene. Its first mention with that name was in an inventory made by the Knights Hospitaller in 1185, also known as the Knights of St John. They were in the area quite a bit and worked closely with the Templars at times. I've often wondered about their involvement in Rennes-le-Château, especially given their supposed origins as Benedictines.'

* * *

'Of course,' I continued, 'there was another church back then dedicated to John the Baptist. Hortense mentioned it, and her house was built over the top of its foundations. At some point, a dedication to St Peter took place, but that's all rather odd. Why change it from St John to St Peter? Are we missing something here? Is there a link between John the Baptist and Mary Magdalene? Were her relics in the old church and then subsequently brought to the current one, and did Henry of Castile pull the old church apart looking for the relics, not the gold left by his ancestor, Blanche? The Cathars and Templars were well known for revering John the Baptist above Jesus, and the Templars were accused of worshipping a skull, possibly that of John the Baptist. You're usually the one with the theories, but I'm beginning to formulate one.'

'I've been wanting to talk to you about John the Baptist. But tell me about the link between him and Mary. I'm dying to hear more… it's so unusual to see you fired up like this.' She rested her chin in her hands, waiting for me to speak.

'I know, Caro. I'm a lot slower than you. I mull things over, sometimes for years, before I reach any conclusions. Anyway, it isn't a conclusion as such, more like an educated guess or theory. Tell me your bit first, because I've a feeling that the two will sync up.'

'OK,' she replied. 'Like you and Hortense, I've wondered about the John the Baptist church in Rennes-le-Château turning into a St Peter's, and the Baptist one being barely known in Rennes-le-Château history anymore. Arques church used to be a John the Baptist too, but that was changed to St Anne, though no one seems to know why. Couiza is a John the Baptist, and Le Bezu, and lots of others close by. The statue at Rennes-le-Château has always puzzled me, since Jesus looks so submissive; he's almost grovelling at John's feet. Anyway, I visited Brenac again recently.'

Brenac was a small village about twenty minutes from Antugnac. The church was fascinating because of its odd statues and wall paintings, although I hadn't been there for a few years.

She continued. 'I couldn't stop looking at the two side chapels at the back. One has a painting of John baptising Jesus. Again, John looks so much larger and stronger, and Jesus so submissive and weak. God hovers above them, saying "You Are My Son," although it isn't entirely clear which one he's referring to.'

* * *

'The other side chapel is even more odd, and took me a while to work out. There are statues of a man, a woman with a child, another woman, and below them on the floor, what looks like a half-dead Jesus, his blue eyes open just a few millimetres. I'm sure that the man is Joseph and the woman in the middle is his wife, Mary, holding baby Jesus. The woman to her left is obviously Germaine, with the flowers in her skirts, but why put Germaine in that family scene? And why put Jesus down on the floor like that, dead or alive? What was Courtade, the priest there at the time and a friend of Saunière's, trying to say?' She paused for a moment.

'There's another Germaine in the main church, so clearly a point is trying to be made. St Elizabeth, the supposed mother of John the Baptist and aunt or cousin of Mary, Jesus's mother, is also in the nave. Apparently, Elizabeth had John when she was a barren old woman. I'll come back to that in a minute, but as part of my research I've been looking at paintings of Jesus and John as children and grown men, particularly those of the Middle Ages and the hundred or so years after. In so many of them, they look identical, whatever their age, apart from their hairstyles.' She clicked away at her laptop as she spoke, then pushed it across to me.

'Look. The curious thing is that John almost always has his forefinger pointing, either at Jesus or upwards and Jesus always raises two. There has always been speculation about this, but with no conclusions worth noting. Even Da Vinci's *Last Supper* has Thomas raising a finger, which I'll come back to. Going back to Brenac, under the statue of Mary, and above Jesus on the floor, is some writing, "Court Frères" – brief, or fleeting, brothers. It's wordplay again. There's a carved wooden pillar that comes up between the two words, and swivelled out of the way, it reads "Courtade Brothers."

'I was on my way home when it came to me. Germaine had a stepmother – perhaps John the Baptist did too? Perhaps Mary had twins, and gave one to Elizabeth because she couldn't have her own? The baby she is holding is John, not Jesus, and the statue of Jesus on the floor below them firstly takes Jesus down from the cross, and secondly, puts him in second place: John above, Jesus below. The single raised finger from John in all the paintings? He's saying, "I was the first" – the first child to be born of the twins. And Thomas in the *Last Supper* pointing up one finger? The name Thomas in Hebrew means twin. Perhaps he's also reminding everyone of John. Some say that Jesus's two raised fingers are a type of blessing, but my view is that he's being portrayed stating that he was the second twin. At Brenac, there's even a statue of two angels holding one crown at the front of the church.'

'I've seen it,' I replied. 'And in Rennes-le-Château both Joseph and Mary hold a baby each. I thought your theory would lead onto mine. So here goes.'

CHAPTER SIXTY-FIVE

'John was the first twin to be born and was given to be raised by Elizabeth. In the Bible, it says that Mary went to stay with Elizabeth when they were both pregnant, and that Elizabeth had a baby soon after Mary left. If the story has any semblance of truth, I would say that Mary went there to have her babies and left one with Elizabeth. Moving on with the theory, I would say that John, as the first child, married the smart and wealthy Mary Magdalene, and Jesus married Martha, her sister. As was the custom, their marriages would have been arranged when they were children. When John was beheaded, it would have been Jesus's duty under Jewish law to marry his brother's wife if she was childless, which he did. The first offspring they then had under that law must be regarded as the child of the dead brother. It would have been unthinkable at that time that either of them would remain unmarried.'

I paused for a moment to gather my thoughts, then continued. 'There are so many paintings of them all together, Jesus, Martha, and Mary, and many references to their relationship, suggesting rivalry between them. Martha was the homemaker, and Mary much bolder and more overtly sexual in her relationship with Jesus. Everyone forgets that they were traditional Jews. They weren't Christians, since it didn't exist then. Jesus had no children with Martha, and Jesus and Mary had Sara.'

Caro started to click away at the laptop again. 'There are also three cartouche-style paintings in the chancel at Brenac. I've got photos of them.'

I moved my chair to look at the screen.

'Look, Ben... the first shows a pregnant Mary Magdalene holding a grail cup. The second I've assumed to be Martha. She's dressed in green, which is how she is often portrayed, and is pointing her forefinger to symbolise that she was the first wife. The third one shows Mary, Jesus and John's mother, with a heart in her hand. It all makes sense and gives credence to what I said about the greatest conspiracy of all time. Lots of people have known throughout the ages, and left clues as best they could, and I'm convinced that many people know now.'

I nodded, and she continued.

'The Cathars as Gnostics knew, and didn't pretend otherwise. The Templars were also thought to be Gnostics of a type, but were much more covert and tried to keep up a pretence of being traditional Christians. They were certainly suspected of adopting Mandaean/Johannite beliefs, and like the Cathars, gave John the Baptist a higher status than Jesus. And they were accused of worshipping a bearded skull, which many say was John the Baptist's, found at the Temple Mount in Jerusalem, where John was supposed to have been beheaded. That could be why, since medieval times, Mary has always been portrayed with a skull, because John, her first husband, was beheaded. The Bible twists it around to be Martha who returned home as widow, but it wasn't her, it was Mary.'

'Perhaps Roncalli knew about John the Baptist's status, and chose his name because of that?' I replied. 'He certainly made some unusual speeches. One was about "promoting devotion to the most precious blood," which included many references to Jesus being a man. And for the first time ever he publicly condoned Masonic involvement for Catholics. His papal coat of arms even had a Magdala-style tower on it, and the Fleur-de-Lys. The latter is usually associated with the French monarchy, but the Templars are believed to have used it to symbolise a holy bloodline. Joan of Arc used to have it on her banner, and the Freemasons of today still use it…'

'I'm intrigued, Ben… especially about Roncalli. And it's interesting how it's so often been mooted that Jesus was a disciple of John's.'

'That may well have been true, but I feel sure that Jesus would have had his own ideas. Maybe he couldn't come into his own until John the elder was gone? Some even say that it was Mary who funded Jesus's ministry. If that was the case, then she funded John's before that. Have you come across Mathew 11:11? Jesus says, "Among those that are born of women, there has not risen a greater than John the Baptist." Another **22**. At the end of the day, who knows for sure? It feels so odd to be talking in this way. When I studied theology, and did a few years of teaching, there were conversations like this every day, but not since then.'

* * *

I opened the doors to the terrace and the sun streamed in. 'To change the subject completely, I've been thinking a bit more about the Scottish clues that Saunière left. There's Fleury the artist, who was initiated into the Scottish Rite Masonic lodge of Isis, the de Clares hailed from Scotland, and there's a huge amount of speculation about the Templars hiding all their money on Oak Island, Nova Scotia, which is Latin for New Scotland. I've been wondering if Saunière knew anything about that? Another unanswered question, I suppose.'

'The story would be a book in itself. I think I'll stick to this one for now!'

We sat outside to eat dinner, and finalised the details for Hortense's funeral the next morning. It was to be kept as simple as possible. Caro had written a eulogy about her life, which she was going to read herself, and I had chosen to read a poem that I had written myself a few years ago. I was sitting on a bench below the Tour Magdala in Rennes-le-Château, with the mountains and valley spread out in front of me. I had felt deeply moved and had added it to a collection of poems that I had written over the years, with the hope of putting them together into a book one day.

I had also added a couple of short extracts to this, from books given to me by Hortense over the years. One was called 'Smoke and Deception' by Anton Chekhov and the other was called 'Late Fragment' by Raymond Carver. The church was going to be filled with white lilies and red roses, her favourite flowers. I had asked Pascal, the priest, if he could use some church incense, which she adored, and he had agreed. Expecting a few people to come back with us after the service, we had arranged for some food to be delivered in the morning by caterers in the nearby town. We could do no more.

CHAPTER SIXTY-SIX

A few hours later, Caro dozed on the sofa whilst I got out my laptop. There were the usual church-related emails, which I dealt with first. There was one from Merry, saying that she and the boys were supporting each other as best they could and were making arrangements for the funeral, which would hopefully be the following week. She wrote:

I still feel strangely numb. The boys have told me that they had noticed Peter's behaviour becoming increasingly odd over the past few years. One thing I had noticed was that his sermons were becoming much harsher, and far less tolerant to those who strayed from what he considered to be the right way. I've looked through his desk, and there was little in there, but I did find a bundle of old papers and envelopes. I haven't seen them before but the few I looked at were written in Latin. The others are still sealed. I'm no linguist, Benoît, so perhaps you could look at them when you get back? The police turned up this morning and took Peter's computer and went through his desk, so I was glad I got them out first.

They haven't told me anything, though, and I still have no idea why he was in France, nor why he intended to kill you. It all sounds completely insane, and I can still scarcely believe it. Bill came to the house earlier, limping a bit but thrilled to be up and about again. What a nice man he is. He brought flowers and a pie for us that he had made himself. He seems too young to be retired, but then teaching is a hard job these days.

When is your aunt's funeral? How are you both? You are so lucky to have each other. I am an only child, and now my parents are gone, I miss having close family around. Thank goodness for the boys! The friend that I told you about the other day is coming down tomorrow, though. And we're all looking forward to seeing a fresh face. When you think that a couple of weeks ago, everything seemed fine, and now look at it? What has happened? Why? I look forward to hearing from you. Love to Caro.

Merry.

There was another from Bill saying he had been to the vicarage, could he help with anything, and he was keeping an eye on the cottage. The third was much more of a surprise, although I had expected to hear from him at some point. It was from the Italian, or who I now suspected was Franco D'Alessandro, the colleague and friend of my parents.

Benoît, I wish to apologise again for the difficulties that I have caused you. Please believe me when I say that I did not intend to do you harm. If we come through this I would be very grateful if we could meet. There is much for me to tell you. Meanwhile, you must take extreme care. I have been told about your aunt and am very sorry. From what I have learned she was an extraordinary woman, and you must feel your loss greatly. I can tell you that the men that entered her house had every intention of killing her, but she had a weak heart and died before they had the chance. I was also told that she shot one of them. I imagine this would have given her some satisfaction. She knew about the parchments, you see. Whilst they were still buried and the journal lost she was not enough of a threat as an elderly lady for them to bother with her. Bringing them into the open, as well as the finding of the journal started off a chain of events that neither of us could, nor can, stop.

The man you must now fear the most is Harcourt, someone I think you once considered to be a friend. He is no friend of yours, Benoît. He spent many years in the SAS and eventually they dismissed him because of concerns over his mental health. My view is that he is a ruthless psychopath and should be locked up. The times of keeping you in the dark are gone, and you need this information to protect yourself and your sister. Rather like your Asmodeus in Rennes-le-Château, Harcourt believes that the strong must govern the weak, and that control is everything. His ancestors were Templar knights and he considers himself to be above other people.

He belongs to a small group of men who were once part of the Vatican but have now been cut off. The others are as dangerous and insane as he is. As always, the main motivation is money. My view is that most officials in the Vatican believe they would be able to weather a storm such as the one that might break if the documents became public knowledge, without succumbing to murder. After all, they have survived thus far. A glance at history however shows us that there have always been, and always will be, power-crazed lunatics. Sad but true. I will do all I can to continue to provide protection for you, and will be in touch again very soon.

Franco D'Alessandro.

So, he had now shown his hand, although still with caution. There was no email to reply to, presumably because he feared being tracked down by the wrong people. I found it difficult to be angry with him and hoped that we would meet soon. I certainly had a lot of questions to ask him about my parents!

One of the things I was struggling with was that everyone seemed to know far more than me. Were there spies everywhere? Even Aunt Hortense knew everything that was going on. I had expected to hear more from the bishop, but there was nothing. The man that I thought I knew would have sent messages of kindness and offers of support. But then he wasn't who I had thought he was. Everything, it seemed, had changed and I barely knew where my place was in it all.

At this point, Caro woke up, and I showed her the emails. 'It feels like the fog is starting to clear at last. We're beginning to understand who is who and what their part was or is. I thought that would happen in time. I can't wait to see the documents that Merry found, but I'm surprised we haven't heard from the bishop.'

'You're very like Aunt Hortense at times, you know. She may be no blood relative, but that hasn't stopped her transferring part of who she was over to you. It's a way of seeing things, and picking up what people are thinking. I hesitate to use the word psychic, so I'll stick with perceptive! She certainly was, and so are you… you lucky thing.'

'Nurture not nature, Ben? I did spend a lot of time with her. What a nice thing to say… thank you. What are we going to do after tomorrow? We can't stay holed up here for the rest of our lives. An awful thought has just come to me. Do you think that Merry might have come across some of the documents that Hortense thought might be in your village church? And if she has, does that put her in danger? We need to speak to Niort, and perhaps get more information from him.'

'I'll give him a ring. I hope my emails aren't being hacked, because she might be in danger if the wrong person reads them. But is the phone any safer? It probably is. I'll give her a call and tell her to lock them up somewhere – I'll do it now. What are we eating tonight? It's your turn to cook. What about pasta with that puttanesca sauce you did last time I was home? I've got all the ingredients for it, and I love it.'

'No problem. I'll start now.'

I picked up the phone and dialled the number that Inspector Niort had given me. One of his colleagues answered, and said he would leave him a message to call me. I then dialled the number of the vicarage. It rang and rang, and I was about to hang up when a breathless Merry answered after running in from the garden. It was odd talking to her after what had happened with Peter. It would have been perfectly understandable if she felt anger or animosity towards us but this certainly didn't appear to be the case.

'I thought the body would be back by now, but it isn't. I'm still hoping we can have the funeral next week. It's awful having it drag on like this, especially for the boys. Everyone's being very kind, and the freezer is filling nicely with food that's being left on the doorstep.'

'Do let us know if we can do anything to help. Would you like me to try and find out what the delay is?'

'No, don't worry. The police inspector said he would chase it up and call me later.'

'OK. I also wanted to advise you to lock up the documents you found, especially in light of recent events. A burglary on top of everything else would be awful.'

'I'm ahead of you there. Everything is locked in the safe. It weighs a ton, Benoît, so don't worry. Peter kept the church silver in there and the very few valuables that we have. I told you that there was an attempted break-in at the church, didn't I? So many churches have been robbed or vandalised, so I won't take any chances. Any idea when you'll be back? How's Caro? I do hope tomorrow goes OK.'

I answered as best I could, and said that I hoped to be back soon. The situation was becoming more surreal by the moment, and I desperately hoped that Merry wouldn't have any more trouble to cope with than she already had. The sun had disappeared and dark clouds were scudding across the sky, threatening rain for tomorrow. Whilst Caro cooked, I lit a fire which soon filled the room with the wonderful smell of apple wood. She came over, and we both sat on the rug, gazing into the flames. We had sat like this many hundreds of times when we were children, and used to play a game of looking for images in the fire.

'Where have the past fifty years gone? It only seems like five minutes since you and I sat here playing games. Do you think that's how Hortense felt…? Her life gone in a flash?'

'Probably, but she lived it to the full. Did you ever read Tillie Olsen, *Tell Me a Riddle*? She captured it perfectly when she said, "The clock talked loud. I threw it away. It scared me what it talked."'

'What can we do? Try to enjoy every minute? Make the most of everything? That's easier said than done. We get so caught up in the game of life that we don't notice what's happening. Then one night you go to bed aged thirty, and when you wake up twenty years have slipped by. What's that smell? Is it roasting chestnuts? Can you smell it?'

I nodded. 'I always think it's grandmother. I usually smell it when I'm in trouble or upset; I guess it's both of those at the moment.'

'You never said. I've been giving it some thought, and have come to the conclusion that you've always kept things back... even as a young boy. I suppose that's what happens when you grow up in a house full of secrets. Let's eat, before we both start howling.'

The pasta was perfect, but we remained subdued. Caro went to bed early, but I stayed downstairs until the early hours, mulling things over... as deeply entrenched in my 'house full of secrets,' as Caro called it, as I had ever been. Would I ever find a way out?

CHAPTER SIXTY-SEVEN

Caro was up earlier than me and had coffee ready when I came down. The caterers were due any minute, and we aimed to leave for Rennes-le-Château church at around ten. This would give us time to talk to anyone that was there, and make any final arrangements that might be needed. The church would obviously be closed to tourists for a few hours. The doorbell rang. If it was someone who had come to kill us, then so be it… I was sick of it all. Luckily, it was just the caterers and they set about their business with little fuss. Caro had already put out plates, glasses, and cutlery, and there was wine in the fridge and other drinks on the dresser.

The day had turned out bright, but there was a brisk wind and I quickly laid a fire in case we needed it later. Pascal had called to say everything was ready at the church. We were neither of us dressed in black; Hortense would have hated that – and we were soon heading out of the door and getting into the car.

'Are you OK, Benoît? You look a bit pale.'

'I'm fine apart from the obvious. I didn't sleep well. I kept thinking about time, and how little we have. If you had asked me a couple of months ago, I would have said that my life was a happy and full one, but I'm not so sure now… I'm not sure about anything.'

'Let's talk about it more when today is over. Do you think there'll be any murderous lunatics lurking around? I hope not. Surely we'll be left alone for today.'

'I've been thinking about that too. If at any point I shout GET DOWN, then do just that. Drop to the floor. Likewise, if you see something odd, or if it looks like someone is going to pull a gun, then shout out. Hortense wouldn't mind, in fact, so long as we weren't hurt, I'm sure she'd enjoy the drama and excitement. Keep your eyes peeled.'

She agreed, and we took the back route, past the Jesus of Antugnac statue and stone cross.

'Stop, Ben, just for a second – I've seen something.'

I pulled over. 'What is it?'

'Look at the cross. Someone has put the inverted N back in. Two opposing forces… how fantastic that someone noticed, and how curious that someone removed it in the first place! What are they scared of, and how cowardly to remove something just because it threatens what you believe in?'

'It's good to know that someone was brave enough to put it back to how it was. Removing history is no way to carry on. It doesn't work, as we've seen; in fact, it just adds fuel to the fire.'

* * *

We got back into the car, and were soon pulling into the car park by the side of the church at Rennes-le-Château.

There were quite a few cars there, and as we walked to the church entrance, Pascal, the priest, was waiting for us, and I glimpsed several dozen people already sitting inside. The scent of flowers and incense was wafting out, and I felt an enormous pang of loss for Hortense. We slowly walked in to see the huge bunches of white lilies, red roses and candles everywhere. Whether distasteful or not, I took several photos. The coffin was at the front, covered in more flowers, and the Gregorian chants, which she loved, were playing softly, and reverberated beautifully around the church with their glorious sound. How she would have enjoyed seeing her most beloved building like this. Maybe she could? I would hang on to that thought and hope that it was so.

'Let's not be sad, Ben... she would have hated that. And, who knows, maybe she's here, watching everything with Saunière? I like that idea, so let's be glad for her.'

She then gripped my arm, and leant in to whisper in my ear.

'Look over to the right. Unless my eyes are deceiving me, it's August Dillon! What the hell is he doing here? You didn't ask him, did you? What a cheek!'

'I most certainly didn't. What a cheek indeed.'

* * *

At that moment, Pascal indicated that we needed to begin, and stood in front of us, as we walked towards our bench at the front of the church. I could see quite a few people that I knew: the mayor, several of the shopkeepers,

Couderc the lawyer, and almost all the villagers. There was an elderly lady, beautifully dressed, and with a much younger man by her side, and several elderly men, once again impeccably dressed. They certainly put me to shame in my tweed jacket, even if it was a new one. I was, however, wearing a tie that Hortense had once bought me, with tiny bees embroidered onto the dark green silk, and Caro looked very fetching in a floral dress.

Inspector Niort was sitting at the back, and he had slightly raised his hand as we walked by. A few rows to the front of him sat a tanned man in a beautiful dark suit that must have cost him several thousand euros. I would have bet on the fact that he was Italian, and for a second, I wondered if he was Franco D'Alessandro, or one of his men, there to provide protection?

At this thought, and the absurdity of the situation, I gave a slight laugh, and Caro looked at me and smiled. She had seen him too. My mood lightened a little, and I was thankful to the man for this, Franco or not. Arnaud and Mathilde were near the front, and Arnaud held out his hand to hold mine for a moment before we sat down.

CHAPTER SIXTY-EIGHT

Pascal welcomed everyone, and began with a few simple prayers, using the term Jesus instead of any references to God. He then nodded to me, and I got up to read the poem I had written called 'The Sands of Time.'

As the wind blows the sand dunes shift
Each grain a life lived or story told
Everyone a precious gift
A mother, a king, or a warrior bold

The moving sand lies never still
Its voices whisper all the while
With more to settle on the hill
Or spread upon the golden mile

All will come here when they die
The sandy grave will take us all
The hasty hands of time will fly
Obedient, when we hear their call

So think of me when I have gone
Gone to the restless growing hill
No pause for breath I must move on
With shifting sands of time to kill

Caro got up to give her eulogy. She spoke warmly and fluently about Hortense and her life, her involvement in the French Resistance, and working for the French government after that. She spoke about her as an aunt, a friend, a human being, the great sense of humour which she had never lost, and her uncanny ability to know exactly what one was thinking and feeling at any given moment.

By the time she had finished, there were quite a few rustlings for tissues, but I also saw some smiles and heard a couple of laughs, which I was sure was her aim. It was perfect.

Pascal said a few more words, and another beautiful, simple prayer which he must have written himself.

Jesus and Mary, we give our beloved Hortense to you
for eternal safe keeping. We trust in your
message of never-ending love.
Hortense lived her life with this love and with
dignity, kindness, loyalty, and courage.
We are bereft in our loss, but we rejoice in our gain
of having her in our lives for so long.
We live in the hope of meeting with her once again.

I got up to read a story extract and poem that I had chosen. The first one, by Chekhov, was very fitting with my recent thoughts of fleeting time, and I determined to bear it in mind always.

Smoke and Deception

When after supper Tatyana Ivanovna sat quietly down
and took up her knitting, he kept his eyes fixed on her fingers
and chatted away without ceasing.
'Make all the haste you can to live, my friends…' he said.
'God forbid that you should sacrifice the present for the future!
There is youth, health, fire in the present; the future is smoke
and deception!
As soon as you are twenty, begin to live.'

I then read the second one, a poem by Raymond Carver, which I also determined to think about more. I was not sure if I was beloved, but I was sure that I wanted to be.

Late Fragment

And did you get what
you wanted from this life, even so?
I did.
And what did you want?
To call myself beloved, to feel myself
beloved on the earth.

'Hortense was very much beloved by us, and everyone that knew her. We always believed her to be beautiful and special, and this is how she will remain in our memories. Thank you so much for coming to celebrate her life. For those who wish to accompany us, we will now move into the churchyard, and then we welcome everyone back to my house in Antugnac for refreshments.'

The bearers came forward and carried Hortense out of the church and into the graveyard. We all followed and stood in the bright sunshine, a cool breeze blowing our hair into disarray as she was buried alongside Charles, her brother, and Christiane, his wife and our aunt. I thought about what she had said when we had last visited her.

'Ma part est terminée. C'est fait!' Then in English: 'My part is finished. It is done!'

She had known what was going to happen, but was fearless. As far as I was concerned, her part would never be finished whilst we lived. And after that? Who knew?

We stood at the entrance to the graveyard and greeted everyone as they left. Except for a few of the villagers, all said they were coming down to the house. The last person through the gate was the bishop. He held out his hand, embraced me and said, 'See you shortly.' I assumed this meant he was coming to the house. He certainly wasn't welcome, but I could hardly have told him he couldn't come.

'Keep your eyes on him, Caro. Everything's in the safe, but he's not to be trusted, as we know. Make sure you're not on your own with him anywhere.'

'I was going to say the same to you. What is he thinking of? Time for a bit of plain speaking, if you ask me.'

CHAPTER SIXTY-NINE

Back in Antugnac, people were parking up and were soon in the house. We uncovered the food, poured drinks, and I lit the fire. There were several elderly people there, and if they were anything like Hortense, they would welcome the warmth greatly. Anyway, it was very comforting after a difficult and emotional morning and we mingled, making sure that we spoke to everyone.

Arnaud and Mathilde had brought a box of vegetables, eggs, and a large cake for the table. He said he had been worried since we seemed to be shut in the house a lot of the time. I made various excuses, but as a wise countryman, I could see he wasn't fooled. He went to give me one of his thumps of affection, but I was alert and it ended with a less painful slap on the back. He offered help, 'anytime Benoît, for anything,' and I thanked him from the heart.

Caro was now engaged in talking to the smart, elderly lady and her son, who had accompanied her and the two gentlemen to the funeral. They were ex-colleagues of Hortense, almost as old as she was, and Caro seemed enthralled by the stories she was being told. I would have liked to sit down with them, but politeness meant that this was not possible. The Italian hadn't come, and wasn't in the graveyard either, so I assumed he had made a hasty exit.

The bishop was sat on the sofa talking animatedly to the mayor, who had been a good friend to Hortense over the past few years. Inspector Niort held a large glass of my best cognac over ice and was 'working the room.' I watched him move slowly over to Caro's group and sit down to join in their conversation. No doubt he was hoping to glean information. Good luck to him. I had caught him watching me a couple of times, and it had unnerved me. He was no fool and would no doubt pounce when he thought it was advantageous to do so.

Pascal the priest had demolished two plates of food, and I encouraged him to take more. When he left, I intended to send him home with a large bag of goodies, enough to last him for a day or two. He was a very likeable man, and had many interests including wine, literature, and geology, in which he held a degree, taken before he had decided to join the priesthood. The mountains and diverse rock formations were some of the attractions of this area for him, but he admitted to finding his life too isolated and lonely, and thought a move elsewhere would soon be on the cards.

Eventually, everyone began to leave, and it was nearly six when the only person left was the bishop. We were exhausted and collapsed onto the sofa, fresh drinks in hand. I looked over to him, just as he was putting his hand into the inside pocket of his jacket. For a second

I thought he was about to pull out a gun, and moved quickly to grab Caro's arm, but what he brought out was a small flat package, wrapped in brown paper, and tied with string.

Then he spoke, quietly, and with a single tear making its way down his left cheek.

* * *

'Please forgive me, both of you. I've behaved like an idiot and am no more than a common thief. I'm so ashamed of myself... so very ashamed.'

He handed the package to me and I undid the string. I knew what it was, of course; the copy journal, and the removal of the paper revealed exactly this.

'Please let me explain,' he went on. 'I'm not making any excuses for what I did, but I hope if you understand a little more about who I am and what I've come from, then you might feel more able to forgive me. As you know, Benoît, I come from a large Irish family. There were eight children, a drunken, layabout father and a beaten, crushed mother. It wasn't good. We were half starved, and stole and scavenged to bring home a bit of food. We had a dreadful reputation for being a pack of thieving, lying cheaters and that was exactly what we were.

'Things went from bad to worse after mother died. I was just nine. My two brothers had already gone to join the army, which left me and my five sisters. There were no social services in those days... parents did what

395

they liked with their children, even if it eventually killed them. The following year, one of my sisters died from drowning in the sea. She was trying to catch fish and a big wave bowled her over. They found her washed up on the beach the following day.

'Eventually, the priest arranged for us to go to the local children's home, run by nuns. They were hard women, and it was no bed of roses, but at least we were fed, kept clean, and sent to school, and were grateful for that. Father finally drank himself to death the following year. The two youngest were adopted, and the older three were put into service until they married. You might remember that the eldest died a couple of years ago, but I still have the four, all happy and well, which is wonderful.' He continued.

'The priest took me under his wing, and with his guidance I decided to join the priesthood. It could have been a lot worse, and it's a decision I've never regretted, but even then, I never felt good enough. No matter how hard I worked or what I achieved, inside I was still the lying, thieving vagabond... as you see.'

He paused for a moment, and took out a large striped handkerchief to wipe his face. My heart went out to him, and I saw Caro slip her hand over his and hold it tight.

'To finish the tale; many years ago, because of my position, and people that I became involved with in Rome, I heard about some parchments that had come from Rennes-le-Château that totally dispelled the crucifixion of Jesus. They had been found by your Bérenger Saunière. He kept the ones he found, and hid them, but the Vatican still has the copies. That's why they didn't kill him. He made it clear that they would become public knowledge if anything happened to him. We knew that two of the original parchments had duplicates and had been hidden somewhere in Rome for many hundreds of years.

'Your parents had been pulled into Rome on the pretence of finding them, but that wasn't true. They had served their purpose, knew far too much, and were killed – the car crash was no accident. I had nothing to do with it, I'm not a murderer, I hope you believe that. Recently we heard that the parchments had been found. I had a crazy idea that if I found them, or discovered where they were, that this might bring me some advancement. I've been a bishop for years, and began to think that this was a far as I would ever go. If you know the right people just about anything can be found out, and I discovered that you had copies of them in your possession.' I nodded, acknowledging what he had said.

'Then the journal turned up. Its existence had been known about for some time, but it became lost... until you found it. You see, if it all became public knowledge, there would have been nothing in it for me. It links Rennes-le-Château, the parchments, and your village in England, doesn't it, Ben? I haven't worked out quite how though, nor why, and I no longer want to.

'I'd had a rough night; bad dreams about when I was a child, and it suddenly came to me that I was behaving like a complete idiot. The reason I hadn't advanced any further in the church was because I didn't have it in me.

No parchments or anything else would change that, and it's quite something that I've got this far. I've resigned, and leave at the end of the summer. I'm going back to Ireland to live near one of my sisters. I think I told you she had a cottage by the sea.'

He shifted his position, and sat forward, wiping his face again, and letting go of Caro's hand.

'So, there you have it. I understand if you want no more to do with me, but I hope you will find your way to forgive my foolishness.' He looked at us both in turn.

'Do you think you can?'

We both spoke at the same time. 'Of course.'

Caro continued. 'We all do stupid things… and I don't mind saying that you caused us a lot of upset and worry, but in the overall scheme, it's not the worst that we've been through over the past week. Let's top up our drinks. Are you driving? Have you booked anywhere to stay?'

'I have a hire car, and no I haven't booked anywhere yet. Is there a local B&B?'

'You must stay with us, August. There's a spare room the size of football pitch at the top of the house.'

'Well, if you're sure. I must be away first thing because I'm meeting a friend in Narbonne late morning. It's a shame I couldn't have come here in better circumstances, although I did get to have a quick look around Rennes-le-Château. What a delightful place it is!'

'I'm so sorry about your aunt. You're still in danger, though, you know that? Not from bumbling fools like me, but lunatics like Adrian Harcourt. I'm told he's part of a ruthless gang of now excommunicated Vatican officials. In fact, ruthless is putting it mildly. They would stop at nothing to get their hands on the parchments or anything else that can be turned into power or cash, preferably both. They were the ones who killed your parents, and intended to kill your aunt, but she beat them to it, I gather. I've still got a few contacts at the Vatican from the old days, so if there's anything I can possibly do to help, do ask. Mostly they're good people, but everyone has their own agenda, I suppose. The truth is usually the least popular one!'

'I need to ask you something, Bishop. Did you manoeuvre me into the area to keep an eye on me because I might potentially be useful?'

'I knew you would ask that, so here's the answer. When the job came up, I did think of you because it would suit both you and the Church, but I would be lying if I said it didn't cross my mind that you might have information that could be useful, because of your parents' past involvement. Once again, I'm so sorry; I'm a weak and stupid man. But, Benoît, please believe me when I tell you how much I value your friendship. It means so much to me.'

Once again, tears were rolling down his face; his hands shaking whilst trying to wipe them away.

'Forget it. After everything that's happened over the past few weeks it's insignificant. Let's move on.'

The three of us chatted until the early hours. His frankness about his humble beginnings and childhood trauma had deeply touched us both, and despite issues with my own parents, my childhood had been perfect in comparison. We waved him off the following morning, promising to keep in touch.

CHAPTER SEVENTY

'Listen, Ben, I've been thinking. We've done what we've had to do so far to keep safe, and it's worked, but we can't hide here for ever. I know I said the players would all show their hands eventually, and that's proved to be true, but I think it's now time to change the game. We need to become the hunters, not the hunted. We should contact Niort and see if he has found out any more. The bishop said he would help if he could, so it might be a good idea to ask him if any of his contacts know where Harcourt is. I suspect that once we start snooping around again, he and his henchmen won't be far behind. That's when we backtrack and start to follow them. I know we won't have guns, but we're also not being driven by greed, which makes us smarter. The Italian will soon hear of what we're doing and may show himself too. What do you think?'

She was right – it was time to change the game and up the tempo, but as a strategy it carried its risks. They would have guns, and we wouldn't. It's hard to argue with a gun, and being shot was a rather conclusive ending.

'I agree with you, but my main concern is being either seriously injured or killed. They wouldn't hesitate to shoot us to get what they want. We need to play it smart so that they still wouldn't get what they wanted, even if they did kill us. More than that, we need to make it the very worst thing that they could do. You're right about Franco, and I agree that he won't be far behind. If I could just talk to him, I'm sure I could work something out. I'll give the bishop a ring and see if he knows any more. You call Niort – you might antagonise him less than I seem to.'

The bishop answered his mobile within a couple of rings. He had stopped in Esperaza to buy water and had been lured into the café by the smell of strong black coffee. He listened carefully.

'Leave it with me, Ben, and I'll get back to you as soon as I can. Do be careful; Harcourt's a lunatic from what I hear. I'm off to Narbonne now to meet my friend who's a priest there. I'll leave my phone on all the time, and can drive straight back if you need me.'

He rang off, and I listened whilst Caro spoke to Inspector Niort. She had switched the phone to loudspeaker.

'I was wondering if you had found out anymore, inspector. I mean, my aunt is dead, and we seem to be targets too. Surely you must know something?'

'Professor de Morny – you know far more than you are telling me, that is quite clear. It seems to me that you brought trouble with you when you came from England. If I knew what that was, I might be able to help. As it is, I only have half the picture, and unusually, when I enquire further I am finding doors slammed shut in my face. At a guess, I would say that you and your brother – yes, professor, I found that much out – have something that someone else wants.'

I didn't like the tone of his voice at all. Not only was he angry, but he sounded menacing and threatening. I looked at her and shook my head. She nodded.

'Inspector, if I knew what was going on, I wouldn't be phoning you, would I? You sound very angry, and I'm sorry that I've upset you. For the record, we have only just found out about not being cousins. My aunt told us just before she died. It's been quite a shock, particularly for Benoît, and has certainly not been deliberately withheld from you.'

'Maybe, but whatever is going on also involves your Aunt. With her history, that's not surprising, but why wait until she is nearing death to raid her house or try to kill her? It makes no sense at all, and she hadn't worked for years. Something has been stirred up and it involves you all. My family has lived in this region for more than a thousand years and, like you, I'm aware of its history. This isn't the first time that people have been killed because of what they know, including my own relatives, nor will it be the last. But this is different… even the people who usually help me are refusing to speak through fear.'

'Let's hope something turns up soon. We look forward to hearing from you with any news you may have. Good day, inspector.' She put down the phone.

'Well handled. I've begun to feel very mistrustful of his motives. Just instinct, but really, who's rattled his cage?'

403

'We have, Ben. He's a man who's used to getting his own way, but I also think there's more to him than meets the eye. Whilst you and the bishop were snoring your heads off last night, I ran a few checks on him online. His behaviour at Hortense's wake yesterday made me suspicious. I recognised his name the first time we met him, Niort, or Aniort. They were lords around here a long time ago. In fact, one of his ancestors, Guilhaume Othonis, was lord of Rennes-le Château way back in the 1100s. His two sons both became Templars.'

'I'm beginning to think that the saying "all roads lead to Rome" isn't altogether correct. It should be "all roads lead to Rennes-le-Château." Seriously. I think it was, and still is, far more important than either of us has ever realised. Holding the secret about Jesus and his mortality has given it so much power over the years, but there's more to it than that. I'm struggling to put it into words, but it feels like it's the central point of everything. I know that sounds ridiculous, but lately all my old disciplines are slowly being thrown out of the window. I'm covered in goosebumps just talking about it. Certain people are special, so why not a place?' She raised her hand in Hortense style, and continued.

'We acknowledge the greatness of Gandhi, or Mandela, or Darwin, or Martin Luther King, all remarkable because of what they knew, or had discovered, or stood for. They were ridiculed for their discoveries or beliefs, even killed for them, and yet they left legacies behind that have never been forgotten, because truth will find its way out in the end. It always does and I believe it's about to again. The time wasn't right when Saunière made his discoveries, but he did do everything he could to speak out.'

* * *

'I've a possible truth I'd like to share with you.'

'Cough up, then, but I warn you, Ben, nothing will surprise me… not now.'

'We shall see. I wasn't snoring my head off all night, as you so kindly stated. I woke really early, and came down here to look up a few things.'

'Let me guess: the price of Parma ham?'

'Very funny, Caro. Listen – this is serious. It's just a theory, but I think we've got a few things wrong in our research. Well, one thing mainly, but the most important thing of all.'

She sat up straight, looking directly at me.

'I had been running the last letter that Hortense wrote through my head, and her warnings about treasure maps and the Ark. Then I started to think about the old Baptist church under her house, and people only remembering the name St Peter's, and the church at Arques being renamed. I got her letter out, look here.' I pointed to where she has reiterated the name *John the Baptist* in a sentence on its own.

'I did notice that when we read it first.'

'Me too, but this morning when I was going over things, something else came to me. The Cathars and Templars both revered John above Jesus. They were intelligent men, and if they revered John, there must have been a reason. A quote from the Gospel of Thomas came to mind:

Know what is in front of your face,
and what is hidden from you will be disclosed to you.
For there is nothing hidden that will not be revealed.

'It really struck a chord, and I thought about the clues left by Saunière, and the side chapel at Brenac, and then started to look up more artwork from the medieval period and just after.

'Have you seen how many paintings there are with Mary Magdalene, John the Baptist, and Mary, Jesus and John's mother, holding a baby? They're portrayed as being the Virgin Mary and Jesus, but that's ridiculous, even with artistic licence, because John and Mary Magdalene are shown as adults. Most biblical references state that John and Jesus were about the same age, even if they had different mothers, which I don't believe they did.

'To name just a few, there's Procaccini, Previtali, Cesari, Cima da Conegliano... I could go on, there are so many. And lots of them place a hand or some cloth in a strategic position, so that you can't see if the baby is a boy or a girl.'

As I spoke, Caro started to tap away on her laptop.

'I see what you mean. I've never really searched for them, but you're right. I had no idea there were so many of John and Mary together as adults, let alone with a baby. Here's the one by Previtali.' She pushed her laptop back so that we could both see the painting displayed on the screen.

At first glance, it was a fairly typical religious scene, showing the supposed 'Virgin' Mary with a baby, her hand placed to hide any clue as to whether it was a boy or girl. John the Baptist and Mary Magdalene stood to her left. Looking at them more closely, John could be seen clearly pointing the usual single finger, and Mary too, as well as forming a triangle with her thumb and forefinger.

'Well, Ben, we know what the symbolism of a triangle is, and in this context, I would definitely say it was man, woman, and their offspring.'

'Yes, but whose offspring?'

CHAPTER SEVENTY-ONE

'What are you saying? That the baby belongs to John the Baptist and Mary Magdalene? And John and Jesus's mother is holding their baby?'

'That's exactly what I'm saying... or another version, which is that the person holding the baby is also Magdalene. This painting, and so many others, are simply more allegorical, pictorial narratives. The Brenac chapel with Joseph, Mary holding a baby, Germaine the stepchild, and Jesus taken down from the cross and put below them on the floor? It's incredibly disrespectful, and so very odd in a Christian church; it must hold some meaning, as a lowering of status. Well, maybe the step-parent is Jesus. Maybe he's placed where he is to say several things: one, that he didn't die on the cross; two, that his status has been downgraded; and three, that he was a step-parent, and in that sense below John. Maybe the baby that's being held is Sara?'

'I hardly know what to say.'

'That doesn't happen very often! Look, we know that the laws of that time stated that a man only had to marry his deceased brothers widow if she had no children, but he could have married her if she was pregnant, in which case the baby would be John's anyway. If the Sara

408

we assume to be the child of Jesus and Mary was John the Baptist's instead, where does that leave everything? Maybe Mary and Jesus went on to have other children, although there wouldn't have been many if you look at the time scales involved. I'm inclined to think there were no further offspring. Maybe she tricked Jesus into marrying her by pretending that she wasn't pregnant, and then claimed the baby to be his after they had consummated their marriage.'

Caro became visibly paler. 'I've just had a shiver down my spine. Looking at that a little more kindly, perhaps being a single parent in those days would have been a real stigma, or perhaps Jesus knew about her being pregnant and wanted to marry her anyway?'

'All possible, but I've wondered if that was where she got her bad reputation from, formally declared by Pope Gregory in 591 AD in an ongoing attempt to tidy up a few loose ends. It was only in 1969 that Pope Paul VI made a half-hearted announcement to say the Church had got it all wrong. Of course, even then he didn't actually state what the real position was. Now, look at the painting of John, Magdalene, and the supposed Virgin with a baby.' She tapped away, within seconds displaying the painting on screen.

'OK. John and Magdalene are at the back, both looking stern and cross. Oddly, the woman holding the baby, once again, giving nothing away about its sex, looks exactly like the Magdalene at the back, blonde hair, straight nose. John raises one finger again. He's saying, "I was the first son, the first husband; it's my first child."

Perhaps they are shown looking so indignant because of the injustice in their lives being altered in such a way. Another allegorical story. Like I said, there are lots of them, but a quick look at one by Luini makes the point again.' A few clicks and it was on screen.

'This one shows just Martha and Mary. Martha is looking stern, her two forefingers raised in front of Mary's face, and the other hand in her lap, pointing with the forefinger only.'

'She's saying, "you are the second wife,"' said Caro. 'It's like she's trying to pull rank, isn't it? And her left forefinger points to Mary, the other three fingers raised. Using your theory, and finger symbolism, she's acknowledging Mary's baby, and the triad of the relationship between them all. I must say, Magdalene looks amazingly smug, and I suppose Martha would have got a pretty raw deal overall, having to share her husband. And here's another thought to add to the mix. The sealed jar that she carries with her all the time... perhaps everyone's got that wrong too, or been deliberately misled. It's not a pot of healing balm... it's symbolism for a secret that she is carrying with her everywhere, quite literally, sealed.'

'Maybe. I hadn't thought that far, but I am clear in my own mind that the Marys of Bethany and Magdala are the same person, and Lazarus was just a convenient miracle added in. It's interesting that Saunière built memorials to both, with his Magdala Tower and Bethany Villa, which adds a little weight to the theory.'

'I'll second that. I'm just uploading the painting by Procaccini.'

'Hang on…' She sat back in her chair, letting out a long breath. 'Ben, look at it.'

'I have.'

'Magdalene with John and Jesus, all three looking highly sexual. It's the seventeenth-century version of porn! And the title, *Mary Magdalene, John the Baptist and an Angel*? Some angel… he's the spitting image of John… the twins!

'Overall, though, your theory would explain an awful lot: the Cathars, Templars, Mary so often with a skull symbolising John, and the living twig cross for Jesus, the leaves symbolic of him being alive, not dead. It might also explain the forming of the Knights of St John the Baptist, aka Hospitaller and Knights of Malta. They started out as Italian Benedictine monks, eventually becoming a military order taking part in the crusades.'

'They were certainly in this area in the Middle Ages, and in Gloucestershire too; I did a bit of research when I was last in Oxford. It might explain Roncalli choosing to add to the **22** Pope Johns, or perhaps he was trying to get rid of the number itself and assist with the cover up.

'We also know there were Jewish settlers right here in Croux, Antugnac, because of the Mikveh ritual cleansing pool discovered there. It dates to the third century, so that could be less than two hundred years after John and Jesus. I wonder what became of them and why they left Croux? Perhaps they just got assimilated into Constantine's Christianity? I bet they would have a few tales to tell. Oh, for a time machine!'

'I'll echo that, Ben.'

CHAPTER SEVENTY-TWO

'The JMS symbols in Rennes-le-Château, and other churches nearby could just as likely be John, Mary, and Sara as Jesus, Mary and Sara, although there's no reason why they can't be symbolic of both men. Have you got a photo on your computer of the symbol in Rennes-le-Château?'

'Yes, hang on a minute... here it is.'

'The inverted J branches off into two Js, one going to the left and the other to the right, which also becomes an M for Mary. And it's just as I thought... if you look carefully, you can see a B laid on its side. Have you got one from Brenac too?'

'Yes, they're in the same folder.'

'Can you enlarge it, please? There you go... it's slightly different from Saunière's, but there's a J and B joined together, an S going through the middle, and an M to one side. John the Baptist, or both. The church is dedicated to Saint Julien and Basilisse, so one might first think the J and B stands for them, but why not for John the Baptist as well? And maybe their story is another allegorical tale of Jesus and Mary. Apparently, they were forced to marry, but then both did their own thing, she, starting up a convent and he, gathering a large group of monks. Between them they supposedly turned their home into an enormous hospital, and he became a martyr after being murdered by the Romans.'

'You're right. How come I missed that?'

'It's not just you. Everyone has missed it, including me up until now. Germaine is in just about every church around here, as is John the Baptist. Remember the John statue here in Antugnac? Its base was smashed and repaired, as well as the right arm. Once again, someone got there before us, and had the clout to do whatever they wanted. Even the Fleury mount at Rennes-le-Château? Perhaps it was Saunière's way of saying that Jesus was a stepfather, the flowers being yet another clue from Germaine, who was a stepdaughter?

'And the side chapel at Brenac? Perhaps the statues are of John the Baptist, holding a black branch to signify his death, Magdalene holding baby Sara, Germaine the step daughter, and Jesus – down from the cross and below them – in second place, both as the second twin to be born and the stepfather. Even in that position, his hand very clearly shows two raised fingers. In fact, similar symbolism is shown in lots of the churches around here. Once you know what to look for, it's everywhere.

'I also need to point out that in certain occult societies the two fingers raised in this way are symbolic of the false messiah, and is almost always shown in modern statues and pictures of Baphomet, who the Templars were accused of worshipping. Make of that what you will.'

'Well, you've stolen my thunder, that's for sure. Be thankful I'm not a murderous lunatic like Harcourt, or I would be chasing you up the stairs with your own rifle! We've been searching since we were children, and yet we're still only beginning to see what Saunière and his colleagues left.'

'I almost didn't say... I knew you'd get there in the end...'

'I'm glad you did.'

'It's just a theory, Caro, and it needs a hell of a lot more research, which I'll leave to you. I've got other things I want to do, like going to Lithuania, for a start. But there's more. I can hardly believe it myself, but there is. Like your discoveries, it was right in front of us all the time.'

'Tell me, Ben... tell me, I can't bear the suspense.'

* * *

'OK. We've both held the opinion that Jesus wasn't crucified and came to France, and as far as I'm concerned that's still true. I also believe that he died in England, before Joseph, his brother-in-law and companion. What I don't believe is that he died from natural causes. He was killed... not on the cross, but was killed nonetheless, and by the Romans too.'

'I think I'm going to have a heart attack in a minute... quick, tell me more.'

'Well, it's clearest in Brenac, but once you know, you can see the clues everywhere.'

'Ben, if you don't just get on with it and tell me, I'll give you the biggest thump you've ever had!'

'Be quiet, and I'll tell you. In Brenac church, along with the others, is a statue of St Cecelia. The truth of her story is much argued, but many believe that her existence is historical fact. The first early Roman/Christian church dedicated to her was in the fourth century, in the Trastevere district of Rome supposedly on the site of her house. Her feast day is the **22**nd November, which should interest you. That's a **22** and a pair of 'II' for the twins if you include November. She's the patron saint of music and apparently sang to God during her marriage to the pagan Valerian. She refused his advances, and eventually he, and his brother, Tibertius, went about saving martyrs from death by the Romans. They became martyrs themselves, after being slain under the emperor Marcus Aurelius in the second century, although the actual emperor involved is argued about.'

'Well, it was an awfully long time ago,' said Caro.

'True enough. The Romans then tried to behead Cecelia, only to find they couldn't cut her head off, despite three blows with a sword, and she eventually died three days after. Note the **3**s and their symbolism. The Roman meaning of the name Cecelia is *blind*. In *The Second Nun's Tale*, written by Chaucer about St Cecelia, he put forward other meanings, including "the way for the blind" and "the lily of heaven," both of which are rather appropriate for what is, in this context, another allegorical tale told by Courtade, even more so when you remember that Jesus and John's father, Joseph, is so often portrayed with a lily.

'Given the dates, I might even suggest that the story

of Cecelia is a Romanised rendition of an actual account of Mary Magdalene, John the Baptist, and Jesus. It wasn't that long after their existence, after all. Mary wasn't beheaded, of course, but it was a good way to get rid of her, especially by making her a martyr after Constantine had done his deed of conversion at Nicaea. There are a few fantastic paintings of the three of them together, including one by Botticini, with a small female child in the corner. He also painted one of the supposed Virgin and child, but she's wearing a bright red dress, which is much more likely to be Mary Magdalene. I know one can only read so much into this type of thing, but as part of an overall trail, it's reasonably convincing.'

'You're a dark horse, Ben – maybe downright sneaky. If there's anything else you want to shock me with, spit it out now.'

* * *

'There's just one small thing left. It's still at Brenac; the cartouche on the wall of the Ark.'

'I know it, I've got a photo here.'

'Good. You see, Moses apparently said that under no circumstances were the staves that the Ark was carried by supposed to be removed… not ever, in fact, no one was ever to touch it at all, or the power of the Ark would kill them. The staves probably acted as some sort of seal to the chest, but anyway, look at the picture, Caro… the staves are off and are shown in a cross behind the Ark. What do you make of it?'

'It's obviously deliberate, since Courtade would undoubtedly have known about the staves. It must be another clue, but what? Considering what Hortense said in her letter, it's doubtful that the Ark has been found, but the map might have been, I suppose. She strongly warned us off, though. I've no doubt that she knew more than she let on, about both the Ark and the map, but if she said it would bring nothing but misery she was probably right. I must admit, though, despite the warnings I'm beginning to find the whole idea of the Ark exciting.'

'I don't. She was as wise as they come, and we would be idiots not to listen to her. Forget all about maps and treasure.'

'OK, Ben. You're right of course.'

'I know I am. It's probably not worth mentioning, but rather than risk another accusation of being secretive there's another tiny detail I noted at Brenac.'

CHAPTER SEVENTY-THREE

'There's more?'

'I started to go through my photos. I've nowhere near as many as you, but I remembered one that interested me at the time, and then I forgot all about it. Still in Brenac, it's the base of the statue of Joan of Arc. Her name is quite obviously not painted on properly, and is over to one side. I thought little of it, but it wasn't until I went over the photos that I could see that the base had possibly been reused for Joan. Perhaps they smashed her original one looking for something? Anyway, in the photo you can clearly see the word *meus* meaning mine, a letter B, and two children's heads. Look, I've got it here.' I pushed my laptop over to her.

'How bizarre. Even if they did reuse the base, why not paint Joan's name correctly? It's like it's been deliberately left as some sort of clue. The plot thickens. It reminds me of the painters from the Middle Ages, leaving their messages whenever they could, just like Saunière. I wonder how they knew?'

'Maybe they didn't know for sure, but like us, had other clues that had been passed down and theories that they could incorporate into their paintings? Or maybe they copied older ones? It certainly gives more credence to a group of Gnostics of some kind, and why not? Like

Giotto, and others who weren't artists, they all knew what had happened to the Cathars and Templars and maybe were secret supporters of them and their beliefs, or their powerful patrons were? Quite unlike our parents, I might add, who spent their lives suppressing the truth, and getting paid for it!'

Caro looked at me, her face showing concern and her eyes full of tears.

'I know, Ben, but let's not judge them, not now anyway. We know so little about their work and we've got quite enough to be getting on with without any more upset.'

I nodded. 'I'm struggling to be as forgiving as you, but I definitely agree that we have enough to be going on with!'

* * *

'There are a few more observations I've made. One of the most recognisable Templar symbols is of two men on one horse. Is that deliberate symbolism of the twins, Jesus and John? Then I remembered going into the Templar church at Serres, on the road to Arques. Have you seen the medieval wall paintings that have been uncovered?'

'Yes,' replied Caro. 'They're amazing and very early; twelfth or thirteenth century, I think.'

'Then you'll have seen the two huge crosses on the ceiling. And the wall paintings of two men, one holding a globe-like object with one finger raised, and the other some documents, with two fingers very obviously placed at its front. Even that far back, they were trying to pass the message on about Jesus and John, the twins. Possibly of no relevance at all, but the name Serres is spelt the same both forward and backwards.'

'I'd noticed that. It's odd.'

'I think so, but symbolically it's the same in two parts, like twins. Oh, I almost forgot. Back at Brenac again, it seems to keep its service book permanently open on the 22nd September. I looked it up, and it's the beginning of the Autumn equinox, and is sometimes associated with John the Baptist. Some consider it to be a satanic feast day. That's another **22** for your list, anyway. Given that Brenac has quite a few Masonic symbols painted on the walls and ceiling, it might be worth mentioning that the Scottish Rite Masonic order, also known as Rose Croix, is sometimes thought of as having Satanic beliefs, although I've no idea if that's true or not. And do you remember when I said to note the 3s in Cecelia's story?'

'Yes?'

'Well, the Scottish Rite is the 33rd degree. I have little doubt that Courtade used the story to reveal his connection to them, as well as the general **3** symbolism, and the allegorical tale. Some believe that the 33rd degree masons are the keepers of the holy bloodline of Jesus, or of Satan. Take your pick. And the ladders he uses with other masonic symbols around the walls? Well, they are most commonly used for the 32nd degree York Masonic order, or the Order of the Knights Templar. It's complex stuff and needs to be researched properly, but a tiny snippet to add weight to it back at Rennes-le-Château, are the thirty-three postcards that Saunière had made for sale. Also, when you were talking about Asmodeus, you mentioned that he was the

32nd demon in the spell book, The Lesser Key of Solomon? I don't doubt that this is another clue from Saunière about Templar involvement using the number 32 to identify the 32nd degree Masonic Order of the Knights Templar.'

Caro looked concerned. 'Well spotted, Ben. I'll second all of that, but the Satanic possibilities? What a scary idea. I don't like the sound of it at all.'

'My belief, right now anyway, is that it isn't satanic in the way we think of it. Certainly, Baphomet, who the Templars were supposed to revere, is now thought of as satanic, but was only brought into those circles much more recently. And the pictures that are everywhere of a horned, devil-like creature, were only put together in the nineteenth century. I favour the view that they did indeed idolise a skull, quite likely that of John the Baptist, found in one of their raids along with various other things, that convinced them enough to revere him in this way.'

'It makes sense, doesn't it?'

I nodded. 'The name Baphomet is interesting, and was first recorded in the late eleventh century. I don't hold with the suggestion that it's a version of Muhammad. Assuming that the language used is Latin, my view is that the *Bap* at the beginning quite literally refers to Baptist, or Baptiste; the *hom* in the middle refers to homine, which means man, and the *met* at the end, if looked at backwards and reusing the *m,* is *tem* for Templar or templum, meaning temple or church. I played around with it for ages, and using Latin abbreviations it could also translate to something like "father of the temple." Using my version as well, that places John the Baptist as the father and quite literally, the head of the temple or church, so it's most likely a combination of the both with joint meaning. I especially like the "man" bit. They knew he was a man, not a divine being, and that was important to them.'

'I think you're right. That's amazing. Another code broken?'

'Maybe, Caro. And here's another thought, perhaps all the twos are symbolic of the twins, as well as other things?'

'And all the II symbols in Peter's church, is that the twins too? Poor Peter, what a waste...'

'Isn't it just? And even more smokescreens and mirrors – it's admirable really. And is this it, or is there more to discover?'

'Let's come back into the present, sum up, and decide our next move.'

'Right. Harcourt wants the journal, because it connects Rennes-le-Château and Antugnac to the village in England. He wants the Roman parchments because they are integral to the story, and for their potential worth in both money and power. Franco has the originals, but we have copies. Presumably Franco has his well-hidden, but they're obviously after him, as well. He may also want information about the codes in Saunière's church, hence his visit to Hortense. He can't possibly know about the cellar room or the parchments that were there, nor about the gold discs and cube. The only treasure map we know of for sure is the one that was left in the cellar, and surely Charles, Hortense, and our parents took all that gold years ago. Maybe he knows that there is a map, but assumes it was one that Saunière found?'

'Let's look at the worst-case scenario. Peter's dead, so he isn't a threat to us anymore. Harcourt's not going to kill us without speaking to us first. If he managed to get one of us, say me, for instance, then he could blackmail you into handing over what we know or he'll threaten to kill me. I found some old court and press details about him on the internet. He was very violent when he was married and put his wife in hospital several times. He sounds like a misogynist. He served time in prison for one of the assaults, although he was living in another part of the country then. He'll have enemies too, and a weak spot. Everyone has; ours is each other. Here's another thought. What about trying Bill from your village for more information? He seems to know everything that's going on. You do as a teacher… I found that myself. Why don't you give him a ring?'

I thought for a moment. 'That's not a bad idea. I'll do it now.'

* * *

Caro went into the kitchen to make coffee, and I looked up Bill's number and put on the speakerphone. He answered after a few rings and seemed delighted to hear my voice, which made me feel guilty, since I was only calling to pump him for information.

'Hello Bill, how are you?'

'Padre, what a surprise. I'm very well. A few twinges of pain, but getting about with more ease every day. I've been by your cottage several times. I've even stuck my nose against the window, and everything looks fine. Is there anything you want doing? I don't mind at all, just say the word.'

'To be honest, I wanted to ask you something. I can't fully explain why, so if you feel you would rather not answer, I understand, but I was wondering what you know about Adrian Harcourt?'

'Ah, Harcourt... a nasty piece of work. I never understood why the church let him get involved. I just assumed they didn't know about him. Bit of a psychopath, I'd say; can charm the birds from the trees, but it doesn't do to cross him. He's got a nasty temper, and has been in court several times for violence, I believe, and was banged up once, some years back. I never believed all that stuff about an accident either. It strikes me that he ran up against someone who didn't like him, and that wouldn't be hard. Rumour says he's involved in various shady dealings. And those icons he paints? I heard that they weren't entirely kosher either, and he uses them as a front for something else. He's got a couple of children. Did you know that? I taught them very briefly, and they were terrified of him. I believe there's a court order preventing him from seeing them now. All local gossip, which is amazingly effective, as you know.'

'I thought you'd be the best person to ask. Caro said teachers hear a lot of things. Once again, I'm sorry I can't explain myself right now, but does he have any weaknesses that you know of? Fears? I know that's a strange question to ask.'

'Don't worry... I don't mind. The only thing I can say, is that I once saw one of the mums lay into him by the school gates. He'd been yelling at one of his children

424

about something. He totally caved in, apologised, and crawled off like a worm, whilst all the other parents cheered. He's like any bully, psychopath or not. They prey on the weak and vulnerable. Look, Benoît, I hope it's OK to call you that… I sense you're in a bit of trouble. That break-in wasn't the work of the usual brainless criminal – they were after something. Do let me help. I know I've had this hip thing, but I'm no wimp. I was in the TA for years.'

'Thank you so much, Bill. I may be coming back in the next day or so, and you'd be the first person I would call if I needed help. Do let me know if you think of anything else.' We rang off.

'You were right, Caro. The worm, as Bill called him, has most definitely got a weakness: women. He may detest them, but he's also scared of them. That's certainly something to remember. Perhaps you should become a dominatrix. You know… slap him about a bit.'

She laughed. 'Yes, I'd certainly like to do that. Hit him with big stick, more like. I always thought I missed my vocation.'

'Perhaps we should just wear masks and try to frighten him to death. What about booing him as he walks around the corner, like we used to do to each other, and give him a heart attack. Much more our style, and you were especially good at it.' We were soon both convulsed with laughter at the absurdity of my suggestion and the images that it raised. Hysteria or not, after a time of so much stress and unhappiness it was a huge relief to give in to it. We had just begun to calm down when the phone rang.

425

CHAPTER SEVENTY-FOUR

'Benoît, it's Bishop August. I've managed to find out a bit more about Harcourt. He was in France... well, Rennes-le-Château to be precise. It was he that your aunt shot. Jesus! That was one wonderful woman. He's back in England now, though. Too many police crawling around for him to stay there, so he got a private jet home, and is now back in his lair. Look, I shall be home tomorrow and I'll phone you as soon as I get there. Or you phone me if you decide to make a move. If I always know where you are, I can charge in if needs be. I know I'm a decrepit old fool, but I can swing a cricket bat as well as the rest of them. Safety in numbers, Benoît, and watch your back at all times. There's none so mad as a wounded animal.'

I promised to do just that. Once again, I noticed how strong his Irish accent became when he was out of his bishop role. It seemed much more authentic, and I liked him all the better for it.

'OK, Caro, so we go back to England. Most animals can be enticed from their lairs with food, but somehow I don't think a bowl of pasta piselli left by the door would snare him. We've got the bishop back on side, though, and Franco will certainly know we've made a move. If only we could speak to him.'

'What about a nice strong fish stew? No, seriously, we have something much more enticing than food; the journal and the copies of the parchments for starters, and we need to look at the documents that Merry found. It's probably too much to ask, but they may well be the ones that Hortense mentioned. Or they might give us a clue as to where else to look. We need to have a quick check up on my house and Hortense's cottage, make sure that both are properly secured, and speak to Niort to tell him we're leaving. You can say that you have work to attend to, and I'm coming with you for a break after the death of our aunt. He can't prevent us from going, can he?'

'I don't think so. I'll call him now and book our flights. I'll ask Arnaud for a lift to the airport, or we can always get the train from town. I'm glad I've got a car here, though. We didn't need the survival stuff I put in the boot in the end, which is something, I suppose. I'm not as hardy as I used to be, and I didn't really fancy sleeping on a damp cave floor.'

'Don't speak too soon. We haven't left yet!'

I went online and booked our flights for the following afternoon. Arnaud declared himself to be at our service for the drive up, and I put some money in an envelope for the petrol and his time. I left a message for Niort, leaving my telephone number and address in England, although no doubt he could get these easily enough for himself. Then I called the bishop, who announced that he was on the same flight back and insisted on his driver taking us home from the airport, which would save us a lot of time and effort. I protested a little through politeness, but soon gave in and thanked him.

427

It was nearly one when we got into the car, my rifle on the back seat covered with a coat. As I drove up the steep road, I noticed a white car pull out from a lay-by. From his position and with binoculars, he would have had an excellent view of the house. Clearly, we were still under surveillance, but by whom?

'We've got a tail, Caro.'

'Oh no, not again. It's all becoming so tedious.'

I looked in the mirror, and the driver raised his hand a little in acknowledgement. I could see his face clearly, and recognised him straight away as Black Coat from England.

'It's OK, it's Black Coat minus the black coat, but in a black shirt instead, and glasses. What a relief.'

I thought for a moment.

'Dearest sister of mine, because of our personal bodyguard, I am going to treat you to lunch at the Jardin de Marie. I haven't eaten there for ages, and the food's great. We deserve a treat.' The Jardin de Marie was an outdoor restaurant opposite Villa Bethany, the house that Saunière had built, but never lived in.

'Are you sure the moths in your wallet can survive the cost? We wouldn't want to traumatise the poor things, Benoît. In fact, I'm surprised that your trouser pocket isn't torn with the weight of them all. They must have become a national collection by now. Perhaps I should pay?'

It was good to be teased again, and so soon after our laughing fit yesterday. Was it too premature to hope that things might return to normal in the very near future? I was desperate for the freedom that 'normality' would bring. It was hard to believe that so much had happened over the past couple of weeks. I suspected that the future held many more changes for me, but I could face this wholeheartedly if I knew that we were both safe and not being terrorised by a gang of murderous thugs.

* * *

We checked Hortense's cottage and walked quickly to the restaurant. It was busy, but there was an empty table set under the trees, which we quickly claimed. The owner took our order and whilst we waited we looked around.

'I'd almost forgotten what it was like to be free. Thank goodness for Black Coat.'

I could see his car from here, and ours in the car park. He was nowhere to be seen, but was hopefully lurking about somewhere.

'I've had an idea. Have you got a piece of paper in that sack you carry around with you? It's a wonder you don't have a curvature of the spine with its enormous weight.'

'It is a little heavy, granted, but which one of us has the paper that is currently so badly needed?'

I conceded this point as the paper and a pen were passed over. On it I wrote:

F, we are going back to England tomorrow. AD on our side.
AH is there. Can you help? Please contact. BB.

I showed it to her. 'We'll stick it under his wipers and wait until he picks it up. I can't believe that Franco intends to stay in hiding forever, and I suspect that like us, he fully intends to turn the tables sometime soon. He'll be armed, I'm guessing, so at least he'll be a match for Harcourt, but personally I'd like to finish him off by something other than a bullet.'

'What with the bishop's cricket bat, Bill's walking stick, my lead-filled handbag and your most likely weapon, which would be a bag of food from the nearest deli in one hand and a glass of vintage prosecco in the other, I would say that we had a distinct advantage.'

We both started to laugh again, but before it descended any further, she spoke, a much sterner look on her face.

'If we want to frighten him off for good we need to be much smarter than he is. We certainly don't want to be involved in a murder. There must be another way.'

At this point our food arrived. We had both ordered cassoulet, and were silent for the next ten minutes until we had wiped our plates clean with the last bits of bread.

'That was delicious… I could eat here every day. In fact, I might just do that, and no washing up afterwards! Shall we have a quick coffee and get going?'

I slipped the note under the wiper blades of Black Coat's car and we drove to the exit to wait and see if he picked it up when he got back. That was exactly what happened, and we watched for a second whilst he read it, put it in his pocket, and started the engine. Stopping at Caro's house, she went inside to get a few things and I checked all the windows. With the alarm reset we were

430

soon on our way to Antugnac, our white tail closely behind us.

* * *

Back in the house, we tidied up, packed cases for tomorrow, and put together a box of unused food to give to Mathilde and Arnaud. It was early evening before we both sat down at the table with our laptops and a glass of wine apiece. I skimmed through the unread emails, deleting them as I went or writing quick replies to those that required it. There was nothing from Merry, and I was about to exit when a new message came through. There was no heading, and when I clicked on it, there was just one line.

I hope there's room for two more in the graveyard. Start digging.

I showed it to Caro. 'There's no address to reply to, and really, it's more disturbing than frightening, and so very juvenile; I've no doubt that it's from Harcourt. He's sounds seriously unhinged, and is behaving like a second-rate TV gangster, never mind a Templar. It's pathetic, and his ancestors would be thoroughly ashamed of him.'

'He really is pathetic, in every sense of the word, but we need to use that to our advantage, although I'm not quite sure how at this point.'

For the first time in days, I switched on the TV, which we watched with calm oblivion for a few hours before going to bed.

431

CHAPTER SEVENTY-FIVE

Arnaud was at the door at nine-thirty the following morning, and within an hour, we had arrived at Carcassonne Airport. The bishop was already there and waved as we walked through to the departure lounge. With a coffee apiece, we sat and discussed general plans, and the bishop told us about Narbonne. He had lived there for a few years in the eighties, and was particularly enamoured with the beautiful cathedral, and the Languedoc in general.

On the plane, our seats were several rows apart, so we didn't speak much whilst in the air, but several hours later we found ourselves in the back of his large, comfortable car. The whole journey seemed remarkably quick and easy, and although we knew there were difficult times ahead, it felt good to be facing our problems rather than hiding from them.

'It's very important that you let me know where you are at every moment throughout the day. A simple text will do, even one every hour, then if trouble hits I'll know where you were heading.'

'Yes, that's a good idea.'

'I think he'll try to separate you, and then use blackmail. That's what you need to be most wary of.

He wants the journal and the copies of the parchments, in the hope that one or the other will lead him to the originals. I don't think the copies are much use to him because he would never be able to prove they weren't fakes, but the journal might give him more information. He knows of your parents' friend Franco, of course, and may try to involve him in the blackmail – you know the type of thing. "Give me the originals or I'll kill them."'

'That's just what we thought. It's what we need to be most careful about.'

'Definitely. I'm guessing that he's given up on finding anything at Rennes-le-Château. I'm sure that whatever was there is gone, unless your Bérenger Saunière was particularly cautious and clever. I do know that the Vatican have copies of the Roman parchments, but I'm not so sure if they have copies of the other things he found. It's likely that they have, but if so, it's been kept top secret. You may well both know more than me, in fact, I'm sure you do, but I feel a lot better for being out of it. I have no desire to be involved at all now, apart from helping to keep you both safe and to bring Harcourt to his knees. What happens after that is up to you both.'

'Fair enough.'

'I'll be in Ireland in a couple of months, with my camera, books, and a decent wine cellar. Please say you'll come and visit. The cottage is too small for overnight guests, but there's an excellent hotel just five minutes away.'

'We would love to come, August. Ben's spent some time in Ireland, but I've never been at all.'

'I shall look forward to it, but I'm getting ahead of myself. We need to deal with Harcourt first. I'm going to put my thinking cap on tonight, and let's speak again in the morning. Remember, a text from one or the other of you every hour until bed. Ask Declan to stop at a shop on the way home to get milk and the like.'

* * *

An hour later, Declan dropped the bishop off in Oxford, staying outside until he saw him enter the house. Later, he kindly stopped at a small supermarket and eventually we pulled up outside the cottage. It felt like months had gone by since I had left, although it had only been just over a week. We thanked him, and refusing a tip, he waited outside until we had let ourselves in before driving away.

'Here we are, Ben… it's so cold compared to France.' She shivered and rubbed her bare arms.

I picked up the mail from the floor and went to put the shopping away.

'Go and unpack, and I'll put the kettle on and light the fire. You forget how chilly it still is in the evenings here, even in early summer. I'd better text the bishop too.' A few hours later we both jumped when we heard a loud rapping on the door.

'Who's there?'

'It's me, Bill. I saw the lights on.'

I let him in. He looked well, and although he had a stick, he didn't appear to be limping at all. I introduced him to Caro, as my newly discovered sister, not cousin, and I heard them strike up an engaging conversation as I made more tea.

'Welcome back. By the way, I saw Merry earlier. Apparently, Peter left a note with his will saying that he didn't want to be buried at the parish church under any circumstances, and wanted a simple service at the crematorium. How bizarre is that? Family only, no flowers, which I also thought odd considering his love of gardening. Anyway, she seems to be coping well, but Peter's death is still cloaked in mystery. The official explanation is that he had a heart attack, but I don't believe a word of it.'

'I'll call her later.'

'She'll like that, I'm sure. I've taken to walking all over the place because of trying to get my hip back into full working order, so I've become the village busybody. It's astonishing what you see when you pace the streets. Anyway, something odd happened today, and if you hadn't been back I was going to email you about it.

'I was walking around the allotments, despairing at the state of mine, and as I left I thought I would go into the church and have a look around. I was up at the front, looking at the carved stone crosses in the wall, when I heard the door go. The lights were off, and it was quite dark at the back, but I could see two men bending over the font. They had tools and were trying to peel back the lead lining. Then one of them walked up to the old

435

piscina and started prodding the wall and the wooden panelling nearby with a screwdriver. The other one went up to the chancel and started poking about in Temple Corner, you know, where the other piscina is? The head with the locked mouth? I jumped out from the shadows at that point, and yelled at them. The one in the chancel nearly knocked me over as he ran by, but I got a good look at him.'

'Did you recognise him?'

'No, I've never seen him before, but he had a scar through his left eyebrow where the hair hadn't grown back, which would make him easy to recognise again. I didn't get a good look at the other one until I dashed to the door, and watched them go through the churchyard to their car. He was hobbling quite badly, in fact, he made me feel like an Olympic runner; but then he turned to look at me and I saw his face. Harcourt... Adrian Harcourt. That look would have turned cream sour, and I fear my card has been marked. In fact, I'm sure of it. He won't forget me in a hurry.'

'Did you call the police?'

'I thought about it, but Harcourt and his gang would just say they were looking around, like I was, and deny everything, so I didn't think there would be much point. I went straight to the vicarage and got a key to lock the place up. I thought it best to keep it locked, at least until there's a new vicar, and Merry agreed. She's going to speak to the warden, and I'm keeping a key at my place. The poor woman has enough to contend with.'

'Look, Bill, you were right when you said that I

was in trouble. I don't want to give you all the details because it places you in danger, but suffice to say I have come across some papers that Harcourt is determined to get his hands on. That he would kill for them is not in doubt. Even the very fact that you saw him poking about in the church puts you at some risk. You will need to be very careful indeed.'

'You're right about that. As I told you, he's a nasty piece of work. I may well have to install a spike on the end of my walking stick. Good job I took that metalworking class a couple of years ago. Seriously, though, I'm guessing that it's connected to the church, and the weird rumours and oddities. I knew there would be some truth in the old tales, of course; there always is. You don't have to tell me more, so don't worry. But what are you going to do? Could the police help? Sorry, that's a stupid question. If they could you wouldn't be in this position now.'

Caro nodded. 'We haven't quite worked that out yet, Bill. We've been thinking that with men like him, it doesn't do to look weak, so we may end up confronting him, but there are some concerns over firearms. We won't have any, of course, but he might. We need to scare him off, enough to keep him away for good, so that we're not in hiding for the rest of our lives.'

'I've got a hunting rifle. I used to do a lot of shooting a few years back, and was in the TA for years. I grew up on a farm, and my brother runs it now with his son, not far from here. I never fancied farming myself... far too gruelling for me, up at five every morning. I preferred a nice orderly academic life surrounded by my books. So, let's get this clear. You need to scare him off permanently, without injuring him or yourselves, without police involvement, and without losing control of the papers.'

I thought for a second. 'Yes, that's about it, Bill. Very well put. Any ideas? I'm starving again. Anyone fancy some soup? It's not homemade, but it's fresh and I've got a fresh loaf too.'

'You'll soon learn, Bill, that with Benoît, his stomach comes first. He may speak perfect English, but he's French all the way through.'

'You can talk! Who was it that used to pinch my sweets when we were children? I tell you, Bill, for months I couldn't understand why no matter how frugal I was with them, there never seemed to be as many in the tin as I thought there should be. And then I caught her at it; trotters right in the trough!' Both Caro and I began to laugh.

'Sibling rivalry, eh? I can see I might need my headmaster's sternness before long.'

Soon, the three of us were laughing together, and I could see Caro looking at him with small sideways glances. I left them to it, whilst I heated the soup, opened a bottle of wine, and updated the bishop. Bill was good company, and we waved him off an hour later, with him promising to give our 'little problem' some thought.

I was soon ensconced on the sofa bed, the fire still warming the room. The events of the past few weeks drifted through my head, as did my realisation of being lucky enough to have good friends around. Old ones like Arnaud and the re-admitted bishop, and new ones like Pascal the priest, and Bill.

CHAPTER SEVENTY-SIX

I woke early and before Caro came down had already spoken to the bishop, who intended to call me later with some information he said he was waiting for. We sat at the table to drink our coffee.

'You seemed to get on well with Bill last night. He's a really nice chap, isn't he?'

'Yes, he is, and I know what you're hinting at, Benoît, but back off. We've got other things to attend to, in case you've forgotten. We still need a plan.'

'I know. Has anyone ever told you how bossy you are?'

Yes, you! Frequently! Right now, you should be glad of it!'

'Oh, I am, I am.'

'Huh. I gave our situation quite a bit of thought last night before I went to sleep. I think we need to go over to Harcourt's house, catch him in his den, and threaten him. We need to stand strong and firm, and show no fear whatsoever. He may have thugs and guns, but realistically, here in England, it isn't quite that simple. Killing us all can't possibly be his aim, because he'd never get away with it. We need to speak to Merry and look at the documents she found in Peter's desk. I'll call her later. I want to tell her how sorry I am, and offer support too. The documents will most likely be the ones that Hortense told us about, but there may be a few surprises in store yet!'

'Please, no more surprises… Harcourt will want the original parchments, because that gives him the most power, but we'll have to trust that Franco can take care of himself. I don't doubt that Harcourt knows that Franco will want to protect us because of his friendship with our parents, and that gives him some advantage, but I think Franco will already have that covered.'

'Agreed.'

'At no point must we be separated, nor anyone who might be with us, because that's his main strength, since none of us values what we know, or have, as much as we value each other. He will see that as a weakness.'

'Remember the Templar cube? *Love conquers all*. I wish we had the cube here – I want to hold it.' Caro was silent and looked thoughtful for a moment, gazing into the distance, her eyes filled with tears. I watched as she slowly gathered herself, and sat up straight in her chair, just like Hortense might have done.

'I suggest we watch his house for a day or two and see what his movements are. He's injured, so I don't imagine he'll be going very far. Good old Hortense. Then, once we can establish that he's in there and on his own, we strike. We corner him and tell him that we have sent letters to important people, to say that if anything happens to us, he's the one to go looking for. We say that we have evidence of his involvement, that the French police are after him in connection with Hortense's death, and the English ones will be too if we make just one phone call. His bullet wound will be a real giveaway to illegal involvement, even if he was treated privately somewhere.'

'That's true, and Niort may well be on his case for all we know. We can tell him that all his movements are being watched, and have been for some time; that we have connections with the Vatican and the Secret Service, which is almost true; and that the decision has already been made to face up to any documents that might be made public, accusing the possessors as being blackmailers and frauds. We can also say that the journal has been burned, as have the copy parchments, and anything else he may be after is nothing to do with us, and that even the slightest attempt to harass us will end with him being banged up again. He won't like that.'

'Remember what Bill said when a mother stood up to him at the school gates? He crumbled, and he won't want everyone knowing about his criminal record, or being thrown out of the SAS for psychological instability. Our final threat is that he is in grave danger of being got rid of, just like Peter, and that it might be in his best interests if he clears off for good. There you go, Benoît. What do you think?'

'It sounds reasonable, but I would like to add a few things if I may. The man's insane – we mustn't forget that, and he may do something that a person who had a normal thought process wouldn't do. Secondly, I want to ask the bishop to come with us. He'll probably insist

442

on it, and he still holds some influence and has good contacts at the Vatican. We must let Franco know; I'm sure he'll be in touch over the next day or so. If he could provide some discreet back-up support, then I'd be a lot happier. What about Bill?'

'Well, we've involved him now. We can talk to him about the plan and see what he says. I'm going to call Merry, and I suggest you speak to the bishop and Bill. We can carry out a few reconnaissance missions to assess Harcourt's house; the best way in, and even if he's there at all.'

'I've been there half a dozen times, so I can help with basic layout. Let's make our phone calls and take it from there.'

CHAPTER SEVENTY-SEVEN

Caro went into the sitting room and I stayed in the kitchen with my mobile. The bishop answered almost immediately and I explained our plans.

'I was just about to call you, Benoît. Harcourt's around alright. I'm told his wound is infected and he's staying close to home. I want to come with you; the more of us that storm the place the better. I know a few of his ex-Vatican contacts, and could cause quite a stir if I chose to. As you know, the church doesn't want to promote the image of control, dominance, and connections to criminality any more. I'm not saying they've achieved that, but I truly think that's the way it's going, and I hope they achieve it. What about Franco?'

'I'm hoping he'll contact me today, and if he does, I'll ask for back-up. I'll let you know as soon as I hear anything.' I told him about Bill and his timely meeting with Harcourt in the church, explaining that he would most likely be with us when we finally faced our demon.

'I wanted to talk to you about my work. You know I don't want the permanent post of priest? Bishop, I'm sorry to ask, but I need to take a sabbatical. I know how things are, but so much has happened, and I need to take time out to consider my position and where I go from here. My beliefs haven't changed, and I'm sure they never will, but there are issues I haven't dealt with, and things I need to find out about my parents. I need time for that. I've only had one proper sabbatical in my entire career in the priesthood, and that was twenty years ago. Would you consider it, please?'

He answered without any pause. 'Benoît, consider it granted. You've been through an awful lot, and I fully understand your desire to take stock and reflect before you move on. I shall be in Ireland by the end of the summer myself – nothing stays the same for ever! Let us both grasp the time we've been given. "Life is what is happening whilst we're busy making other plans." That's what John Lennon said, wasn't it?'

'Thank you. I really appreciate it. Yes, that was a quote of his, and a very appropriate one right now.'

'Indeed. OK, so unless I hear otherwise, I'll set aside tomorrow for our mission. Would you both join me for lunch at The Swan, in Bibury? Declan will pick you up at one, so no need to drive, and do bring Bill. I met him once at a memorial service. He's a good man, and it sounds like he's being very supportive and we could all do with that. Then we can go back to your cottage and take it from there.'

I agreed to this arrangement and rang off. My next call was to Bill. As expected, he insisted on coming to Harcourt's with us, and I passed on the lunch invitation, which was gratefully accepted. 'I know how to handle bullies like Harcourt, Ben. I'll take a few drives by his house too, and report back. I'll speak to you later.'

* * *

In the sitting room, Caro was still talking to Merry. I turned to go back into the kitchen to give her some privacy, but she waved her hand and ended the call, confirming that we would see her in the morning.

'I hope that was OK… she sounded so low. Can we find some flowers from somewhere today for her? I said we'd go for coffee at ten.'

Synchronising our conversations, we agreed to pop into town to buy flowers and drive by Harcourt's house to refresh my memory of the entrance, outside lighting, paths, and where we might park without being seen.

There was no one in sight when we got into the car, and the village seemed almost deserted. Parking right outside the flower shop, Caro went inside, whilst I stood on watch, looking up and down the street until she came back out, her arms full of flowers.

'Black Coat's on duty, I see. I shall really miss him when he's gone.'

'Where? I didn't see him.'

'Right there, by the jewellery shop.'

She was right, and he raised an eyebrow at me as I caught his eye. I wound down the window, and made a gesture of a phone to my ear. Once again, a slight raise of an eyebrow. I didn't doubt that he knew what I meant, and we drove off in the direction of Adrian's house. Within ten minutes we were passing it, and I immediately saw that there were two cars on his drive. There was a secluded lay-by just before the house, which would be an ideal place to park. There were no street lights out here, and it would be dark if we timed it correctly.

There was only one door at the top of a stone-slabbed path, with an outside light that may or may not be on. There were no windows on that side of the house, which was good since he wouldn't be able to see us approach. A blob of chewed gum would be in my mouth, ready to place over the spyhole that I knew was there. If he called out to see who it was, I would call back, 'It's Benoît, I have something for you.' We turned around and passed by again, and I ran my thoughts by Caro.

'The gum is ingenious, Ben. I don't know how you manage to think up such brilliant tactical strategies.'

I looked at her to see if she was teasing, and we both burst out laughing. 'Seriously, it's a good idea, but just sounds so ridiculous. You're a priest and I'm a history professor. What the hell are we doing?'

I assumed the question was rhetorical, and concentrated on getting back to the cottage as fast as possible. When we drew up outside I immediately saw a large, black BMW parked facing us on the opposite side. The windows were darkened and it was difficult to see who was inside.

'Look, Ben, it's Black Coat plus one. They're doubling up on our protection – let's get inside quick.'

'How can you see that? You've got the eyesight of a fox! Either that or I'm going to have to get my eyes tested.'

447

CHAPTER SEVENTY-EIGHT

The phone was ringing as we stepped inside.

'Benoît, it's Franco. I'm walking up your path right now. Please can you let me in?'

I quickly unbolted the door to find Franco in front of me. He was short, no more than five feet seven, and was deeply tanned, with neat black hair and dark brown eyes. We gazed at each other for a moment and then he threw his arms around me, in true Italian style, enveloping me in the familiar smell of pine forests and cedar, whilst firmly kissing both of my cheeks.

Somewhat taken aback, I was, for a moment, rendered speechless. Despite being short, he was powerfully built and held a huge presence. The warmth and humility in his face was unmistakable, and I led him through into the sitting room and offered him a seat. Caro came out, and I introduced them.

'Will you have a drink, Franco? I feel that we should at least celebrate our meeting at last. I must admit, I feel rather overwhelmed.'

'Yes, it's a moment of celebration amidst the trouble. Anything you have, Benoît.'

I went to fetch the champagne that had been in the fridge for some time and popped it into the freezer for a few minutes whilst getting out the glasses, preparing the ice bucket, and putting a few olives in a dish. I had been looking for an excuse to open this bottle for ages, and I fully intended to drink it exactly as I liked it; freezing cold.

Franco and Caro were talking away, and she seemed to be answering questions about her career, and what she hoped to do now she was retired. I watched them as I gently popped the cork and poured the champagne. I had the most curious sensation of knowing this man well, and yet I had never met him.

'This is delicious, Benoît. Your mother always said you had superb taste. Please may I talk for a while? I have so much to say.'

I nodded. His accented English was quite mesmerising, and I recognised him immediately as one of those rare people who had immense charisma, and an inexplicable spellbinding presence. I wanted nothing more at that moment than to listen to what he had to say. Caro was silent; staring at him, and looked like she was in a trance.

'As you know, I was a great friend and colleague of your parents. They were like my family, and when they were killed, I was devastated. Benoît, I have always thought of you as a godson. I was just twenty when I started to work with your parents. All my family were killed in the war; I was going to join the priesthood, but another path was chosen for me, and here I am; seventy-five, and meeting you for the first time. I often sent you things: books, toys, a patchwork quilt that I had made for you in Sicily?'

'I still have it on my bed in France. Thank you so much, Franco, I treasure it.'

'When the current situation is resolved, I'm retiring and going home to Sicily. I managed to buy back my old family home, and over the past two years it has undergone restoration. I know it's said that you cannot ever truly go back home, but this isn't the case for me. It's the only place where I can possibly live, and I think you understand this, Benoît?

'I must tell you that my entire estate, which is considerable, is left to you. It gives me great pleasure to know that it will all be yours one day, although I have no intention of dying just yet! I hope you will both visit me there and consider it to be your home too, since you are my only family now. I think you know that gangster Vatican officials killed your parents? I've heard that the Vatican has cut them off altogether now, but Harcourt belongs to their group and is a very dangerous man, mostly because he is a psychopath, which makes him unpredictable. When I heard that Hortense had shot him, I laughed for an hour. However, I regret that she didn't manage to kill him, since it would have saved us all a lot of trouble.'

I put down my glass. 'Franco, it's wonderful to meet you.' Caro echoed this. 'And I know I can speak for us both when I say we would love to visit you in Sicily. As for being your main beneficiary, all I can do is thank you. Once again, I'm overwhelmed. As you know, we have no family left at all now, so it's an honour to have found a new member.'

I went on to tell him about our plan for the following evening, and the people involved. He thought for a moment.

'I agree for the most part, but you must understand the unpredictability of the situation. Harcourt may well back down and give up on the parchments, but there are others that might not. I'll make sure my people are watching to help if there are difficulties. I can't have either of you hurt. I promised Celestine and Henrikas that I would look out for you both if anything happened to them, and I intend doing this. I should never have sent you the parchments, and I sincerely apologise for that.'

'Thank you. I involved Caro, which I also regret.'

'When you were in Rome, Benoît, I had my men follow you all the time. I think you were aware that you were being followed? I also tried to talk to Harcourt, but he wouldn't co-operate in any way. Aldo will be waiting for you tomorrow at nine in the evening. He can take you all to the house and come in with you. It was he who saved you from the vicar, Peter, in Rennes-le-Château. I know that you have other discoveries that you have made there, as well as in England, but it is for you to decide what to do with these things – both of you. There are many ways to tell the truth. Please remember this.'

* * *

We drank the rest of the champagne, and Franco gave us his phone numbers and address in Sicily.

'I'll phone you in the next day or so, but if you need anything at all, please call me.'

We watched him go down the path to the car, and back in the cottage, we sat down for a few moments, saying nothing. Caro broke the silence.

'That was surreal! So... Benoît le paysan becomes even more loaded with money! Perhaps you can now afford some new underwear? What you have is more holes than fabric. What if you were run over and had to go to hospital? Think of how embarrassed you would be, wearing pants full of holes. Perhaps we should go on a spending spree to Harrods? What do you think?'

'Trust you to bring things down to base level so quickly. If you remember, I have been run over in the past, and I can assure you the state of my underwear was of no concern to anyone. However, you're right, it does need replacing and I will attend to it, but not Harrods, please. You know I hate London.'

We both laughed. The money was irrelevant, but I was intrigued with Franco's offer of a holiday in Sicily, and we agreed to arrange this as soon as things were more settled. It was now early evening, and we were both tired and hungry. We had bought a couple of large, fresh pizzas yesterday, and salad, so I left Caro to deal with them and sorted out a few emails, bills, and letters that needed attention. The night had turned cold and blustery, and I lit the fire, which was soon roaring away. Just as we were about to eat, there was banging on the door, and I let Bill in, hair blown about and smelling of fresh, cold air.

'Sorry to bother you, but I was driving by, and

thought it was just as easy to pop in as to phone.'

Caro came through from the kitchen. 'Come in, Bill. We were just about to eat, but do join us. It's only pizza but there's loads. As usual we bought too much.'

'Are you sure? I don't want to be a nuisance.'

I spoke. 'There's no chance of that, Bill, so please eat with us, and we can share information.'

We went through into the kitchen and sat down. Caro had opened a bottle of the red Lacryma Christi, which was perfect with the pizza, and we updated each other on the latest developments. Our discussion moved on to our lunch invitation from the bishop, which included Bill.

'It was kind of him to invite me. We have met once or twice, and I always thought he was a decent chap. I've been thinking of joining a few clubs and things and even going on some singles' trips. I've enough to do, and some friends and family, but I hadn't realised how much of that came with the job. Anyway, I'm determined not to become a curmudgeonly old git!'

'There's no chance of that, Bill,' said Caro.

'I'm not so sure. I've seen quite a few colleagues go downhill rapidly after they retired. The Swan has a great restaurant. I was there just a few weeks ago, with an old friend from university, who lives in Spain now. Anyway, I've driven past Harcourt's place a couple of times. There was just his car on the drive and the front door has no view from inside the house, so we should be able to sneak up the path without being seen. There is a spyhole, though.'

'The famous Inspector Benoît Clouseau has a good idea for that. He'll be keeping a piece of gum moist in his mouth ready to stick over it,' said Caro, smiling broadly.

Bill held his salad-laden fork a few inches from his mouth and stared at us both. He then roared with laughter, dropping the fork, which clattered onto his plate. This, of course, set us both off which was never difficult.

'Well, I must say, the plan's ingenious, Benoît,' which set us all off again.

'Seriously, though, what if Harcourt pulls a gun on us? I've no idea if he even has one, but he might. Like I said, I do have a hunting rifle, fully licenced.'

'You're right, Bill, he might, but there's no need for the rifle. All I can say is that if that happens then we'll be looked after... sorry to be mysterious.'

He looked at me questioningly for a moment, and then nodded. He left a short while later and we waved him off into the dark night. It had been a good evening, and the more I knew of him, the more I liked him. I didn't need to ask to see that Caro felt the same.

In my sleeping bag, later that night, I thought about tomorrow. I knew it would be upsetting for us all when we saw Merry. Her husband's death, and our connection to it, had made our newfound friendship a complex one, and I had no idea how it would pan out.

Oddly, perhaps, I had given little thought to the papers that she had found in Peter's desk. Thinking about it now, I had the feeling that what she held was likely to be of extreme importance. Hortense had said she believed that all the parchments that Saunière had found were replicated, and were hidden in the village church. What if Merry had them in in her possession at this very moment, quietly waiting, but ready to reveal their secrets and potentially change our lives for ever?

CHAPTER SEVENTY-NINE

Caro and I had decided to drive to the vicarage the following morning. It seemed ridiculous since it was a five-minute walk, but it was raining, and until this evening was over, I didn't want to take any risks.

Merry answered the door with a wide smile on her face and her usual generous welcome, but the strain of the past week showed in her eyes, and by the dark circles under them. My heart went out to the woman as I held her close. Caro put her arms around her too, and we stood like that for a few moments, finally pulling apart and handing over the huge bunch of flowers that was standing on the doorstep.

In the kitchen, coffee was already waiting on the table, along with a walnut cake which looked freshly made, and a large, tatty brown package, tied up with a thin red ribbon.

'These flowers are beautiful, thank you so much. I love all lilies but the orange ones are my favourite. Do sit down – I made a cake early this morning. I couldn't sleep, and it seemed pointless to just lie there.'

She looked at us, perfectly composed and yet with tears slipping silently down her cheeks.

'I hardly know what to say. Things have changed

so much in the past few weeks, and I'm still in shock. The police have told me a bit more. I think I told you that Peter belonged to some odd group who believe themselves to be modern crusaders? The chief inspector said that he thought they were also responsible for the murder of the archaeologist who wrote the report I gave you. They were involved in some sort of conspiracy to prevent any type of modernisation of the Christian faith. They've all been arrested, apparently.' She paused for a moment.

'Look, both of you, I know there's more to it than I've been told. I'm not entirely stupid, even though I've spent the past twenty years baking cakes. I think you both know more than you're letting on, and one day I hope you'll tell me. Right now, though, I don't want to know any more; I'm sick of religion and all that goes with it.'

'Well…' I tried to respond, but she carried on talking.

'Can I tell you something else? I don't believe in God and I never have. I've gone along with the vicar's wife thing and done my duty, but I don't have to pretend any more, nor will I. Peter was a very different man when I first met him, and I have my three beautiful sons, so I can't regret our marriage, but they're growing up and in a couple of months will all be at university. I know they'll still be at home a lot, but I'm going to start looking after myself now. It won't be easy, but not having to live a lie is a huge relief.'

She sat down, poured the coffee, and cut us a large slice of cake each.

'I'm so glad that neither of you was injured – I would have found that very hard to bear. I consider you both to be good friends even though our friendship is quite a new thing. I hope you feel the same?' We both assured her of this, and I continued.

'I can't tell you how sorry we are for how things have turned out. Neither of us had ever heard about the cult that Peter belonged to, please be assured of that. If I may, I'll tell you just a little so that you understand our part?'

She nodded, her tears now gone, and she looked at both of us in turn, her hands held tightly together on the tabletop.

* * *

'A few important documents came into circulation, and I unwittingly became involved in my role as a translator. They've caused quite a stir elsewhere too, but we're hopeful that the whole episode will be safely diffused very soon. When you're ready to know more, do please ask. Meanwhile, if you need anything, anything at all, please call. What's going to happen with the vicarage? Will you have somewhere to live? Do you need any money?'

'Actually, I do have somewhere to go. The diocese has said not to rush, but I know they want me gone as soon as possible. We were lucky to have stayed here so long, as most of these large, old houses were sold years ago, and I've no doubt that this will go on the market the second I walk out the door.'

I acknowledged this. Most vicars now lived in modest, modern houses; the village vicarage must be amongst the very last to be sold off.

'Both of my parents are dead, but they left me a small house in Morlaix, Brittany, which was where they retired to. It's right on the estuary, and has fabulous views. We used to go there when the boys were small, but in past years Peter never wanted to go anywhere, so I let the place out to a painter. He was there for eight years but gave his notice a few months back, so it's empty now. I think it'll need a bit of work, but I may well end up there eventually. For now, though, I'm going to rent a house in town, big enough for the four of us. I don't have to worry about university fees as my parents left the boys an education trust fund, and I'm going to get a job. So, you see, I'm not so badly off, and it could be a lot worse.'

'Oh, I'm so glad,' said Caro. 'But do let us know if we can help. I can't say that our DIY skills are brilliant, but we can wield a paintbrush the same as the next person. I've been to Morlaix several times. It's so ancient and beautiful, and if you need any money, just to help until you start earning please, please do ask. Neither Benoît nor I are exactly hard up… quite the opposite.'

I concurred this point.

'I'm so grateful, and you would be the first people that I would come to if I needed anything. My eldest son is going back to Oxford later today, but the younger two are going to stay around for a while. They're both getting jobs locally until we're all settled, and they start university in the autumn. It will all work out just fine, you'll see. They've gone shopping with my friend, who's staying for a few more days, and then I'm going to start packing up. I don't have an exact date, but I'm still hopeful that the funeral will be towards the end of next week – family only.'

'If we can help with anything, please ask,' Caro said again.

'Thank you, although I can't think of anything right now, Oh, and I almost forgot, here are the documents I found in Peter's desk. Some of them look very old, but I haven't read them. I don't want to, and would be grateful if you could take them. I know that some of what has gone on is connected to our church, I'd worked that much out, but, as I said, right now I don't want anything to do with any of it. Please, have them. I want them gone from here.'

She pushed the package towards us, and I saw she had started to cry again, soon to be joined by Caro.

We got up to leave promising to call her tomorrow, and she stood in the doorway and waved until we were out of sight.

CHAPTER EIGHTY

Back in the cottage, I placed the brown package on the table. We both looked at it, and then each other.

'Later, Ben; let's look at it later, when we get back from lunch. You must bring it with you, though, in your manbag. We mustn't let it out of our sight, nor your laptop. We shouldn't have left that here when we went out.'

I put both in my bag ready, and Caro went upstairs whilst I made a pot of tea. I couldn't get the image of Merry crying out of my head. I intended to do all I could to help her to resettle, and I knew that Caro would help me. After shouting up the stairs to her twice, she finally came down, and the transformation was quite startling.

She had changed into a smart black suit with a silky blue blouse that intensified the blue of her eyes. Around her shoulders was a fine pashmina shawl that Hortense had bought her from a trip to India, some years back. She had carefully applied make up and smelt of a delicate perfume. I rarely saw her dressed up like this.

'Wow, you look fantastic.'

'Thank you. You don't. Get upstairs and smarten up.'

I did as I was told, although my smartening up was

far subtler, and consisted of brushing my hair and teeth and changing into a new shirt and a dark blazer that I hardly ever wore. As I descended the stairs, there was a bang at the door, and I let Bill in just as Declan pulled up outside in the bishop's car. Bill also looked extremely smart and, as I walked behind them both, I saw what a fine-looking couple they made.

In that moment, I was aware of a shift inside me, a fracture of thin glass, maybe even a premonition of the change that was to come. I had been lucky enough to have Caro to myself for all our fifty-five years, and realised that this was no longer going to be so. I would try to embrace the change, because I genuinely believed that if her life were to be enhanced then mine would be too. However, if I were to be true to the emotion that was pulsing around my body, I knew I would howl with the pain of one who was truly bereft.

CHAPTER EIGHTY-ONE

We pulled up outside The Swan and got out of the car. The village was, as usual, crowded with coaches and tourists. Inside the inn, though, it was a haven of peace and calm. I had forgotten how beautiful the building was. The bishop was already waiting, and we were soon drinking wine and choosing food from a delectable menu.

He was utterly charming, and I watched as various waiters scurried around to do his bidding. We went into the lounge with our coffee, and for the first time since we had arrived, we discussed the evening to come.

'We met Franco, and he's arranging to pick us up and provide some security.' I explained. The bishop listened carefully.

'Very well. I'm sure Franco knows what he's doing, so we'll go with that. I don't think it will help to over rehearse what we're going to say, because it will depend on Harcourt's responses, but between us, we'll corner him like the sewer rat he is. He's in, because I've been having the place watched.'

I shivered, and in that moment smelt the roasting chestnuts of my childhood. I felt no comfort, though, only foreboding. True, perhaps, to form, if Caro's opinion was anything to go by, I had little concern for my own safety, apart from not wanting to die. I even felt some not altogether unpleasant anticipation at the thought of facing up to Harcourt. She had seen this side of me, and now raised in my own mind, I realised that it was true.

My concern was for Caro's safety. I thought of Franco's offer of a holiday in Sicily, and if we got through this in one piece, I would arrange it immediately. It felt like going back to childhood, with no cares, worries, or responsibilities.

The bishop interrupted my thoughts. 'Are you OK, Ben? You look miles away.'

'I was miles away… Sicily to be precise. Franco has asked us to go over for a holiday, and I was just thinking how terrific that would be.'

'You're worried about tonight. Look, all of you, you don't have to go through with this. We'll find another way around it.'

'No, I think we must go through with it. I can't live like this any longer, and Harcourt needs to be dealt with.'

The others agreed, and thanking the bishop for the wonderful meal, we arranged to see him at the cottage later. Declan was waiting outside, and we arrived home at around four. The bishop had been very generous. It wasn't often that I was taken to a fine restaurant in a chauffeur-driven car, and I intended to find a way to thank him. Bill went off to change, and Caro and I both did the same. Neither of us felt inclined to open the package from Peter's desk, although we did discuss what to do with it whilst we were out this evening.

'If it all goes wrong, the last thing we need is to let them get into his hands. Where can we hide them? There must be somewhere where a thief wouldn't look.'

I considered this for a moment. 'Well, the curtains are out, considering the last lot were shredded and I haven't bought any more, but I have thought of a place. I was thinking about it on the way home from lunch. In the courtyard, there's a lean-to, with the bin and a few gardening things in it. I bought a new bag of compost a few weeks back to plant some pots up, but I haven't yet got around to it. I'm going to open the compost bag and put my laptop and the parcel in there. It should be bone dry, but even if it rains, it's only for a few hours. You left your laptop in the safe in France, so nothing else needs hiding. We'll read them all when we get back tonight, and they can go to the bank vault tomorrow.'

'So, Clouseau strikes again. It sounds as wacky as the chewing gum trick, but I suppose it will do, just for this evening. Why don't you make some tea whilst I call Merry? Oh, I nearly forgot… I wanted to ask you something. When we were at The Swan, just before we went into the lounge for coffee, did you smell roasting chestnuts? I did, you see, and you went all strange and I wondered if you had smelt it too?'

'Yes, I did, and I felt foreboding, but I suppose that's only natural. I doubt this evening will be easy, and I do worry that someone will get hurt. Truthfully, I don't think Adrian will pull a gun on us. Unless he shot us all, there would be little point, and even he can't be so crazy

465

as to do that and risk life imprisonment. You'll be the only woman, though, and that makes you a target.'

'Possibly, but it also gives me a position of strength, considering what Bill said. I can be dominant and bossy, as you well know.'

'You're the bossiest and most dominant woman I know, but considering I'm a priest, it doesn't count for much.' She reached over and caught me a punch on the shoulder. I leapt back. 'You see? You're violent too. I'm a victim of domestic abuse… how awful!'

'You'd better watch out, then. There's plenty more where that came from.' She picked up the phone and was soon engaged in a lengthy conversation.

* * *

The phone rang several times with parishioners needing assistance, and other problems, like the never-ending need for repairs and maintenance of old church buildings. I knew I had given little time of late to my temporary flock, and I engaged as fully as I could. Caro made a few sandwiches at around seven, and we sat at the table together, discussing the evening ahead.

'I keep thinking about our parents and Hortense,' she said. 'Given what we now know, they must have faced situations like this on a regular basis. It's bizarre that even with our different careers, we're now doing the same thing: keeping secrets, courting danger with shady criminals, guns, even murders. Sadly, we've no children, but I do see how difficult it might be to tell

466

them something like this, especially if it was a regular occurrence.'

'I'm not sure I have the empathy that you do. You're very generous, and I admire you for it, Caro, really I do, but they should have thought about their children more, and the impact it might have on them.'

'Maybe, or maybe not. I'm not sure if a person can live a life solely for their children. Who wants a martyr for a parent? Certainly not me. There are plenty of those in the Church, and as far as I'm concerned, they can stay there. I think you need to reassess a few things.'

She got up and went upstairs, leaving me with the typically Caro-like frankness echoing through my head. Did I need to reassess a few things? I wasn't sure. Even if she was right, would I be able to let the past go, or alter my version of the events that shaped our lives? And where would it leave me if I did?

CHAPTER EIGHTY-TWO

I got changed and went outside to hide my laptop and the package given to us by Merry. Bill knocked on the door shortly after that and we discussed tactics. I expressed my concern about keeping Caro safe, and we agreed to keep her between us at all times. If things took a turn for the worse, we would both move in front of her. We could do no more.

She came down the stairs and greeted Bill.

'How's Merry?' he asked.

'Sounding a bit better. I'm going to call her every day. I don't mind if she wants to come back to France with me for a few weeks. I'm going to suggest it, anyway.'

There was more banging on the door, and I let the bishop in. As usual he looked immaculate, and like he had just stepped off a catwalk: black trousers, black jacket, and a beautiful white linen shirt that even I would have liked to own.

I decided at that moment that I would let Caro take me on a shopping spree. It would make her happy, and I really did need to get a few things. I would even let her choose where, so long as it wasn't London. I wanted to tell her now, and did so, whilst the bishop was engaged in conversation with Bill.

'I can't wait, Ben. We'll make a day of it, and it'll be fun, you'll see,' and she reached up to kiss my cheek.

My mobile phone began to ring, and I answered it to hear who I assumed to be Aldo, telling me he was waiting outside.

CHAPTER EIGHTY-THREE

'Here we go, guys… the car's here. Please remember, safety first. Now, let's finish Harcourt off, the vile snake.' Oddly, and to my surprise, the bishop put his arm across my shoulder.

'Don't worry, Ben. I believe Franco's men are already outside. We'll be fine.'

A different car to the one Franco had arrived in yesterday was waiting outside. It was large enough for all of us, and Aldo opened the doors to let us in. There was another man behind the wheel, and Aldo and I sat on the wide front seat, with the others in the back. He spoke in his highly accented English.

'If I say get down, you must get down on the floor. If I say run, go to the car – she will be waiting for you. Do not wait for me. There will be other cars for me.'

We acknowledged what he had said and fell silent as we sped through the countryside. My previous apprehension now gone, I felt alert, angry, and ready to tackle whatever came my way. Looking back to the others I nodded my head and they all nodded back.

Was this how it had been for my parents and Hortense – danger, fear, and excitement? I could quite see how addictive it must be to live in this way, with just sharp wits and instinct to keep one safe. Instinct... I remembered my mother's advice from long ago.

My instinct tonight said that we were all in huge danger, but that instinct wasn't enough to make me stop the car and take us all back home. So be it, then.

I popped the chewing gum into my mouth to block Harcourt's door spyhole and smiled, remembering Caro and Bill's reaction.

CHAPTER EIGHTY-FOUR

The car pulled into the lay-by just before Harcourt's house, totally hidden by trees and shrubs. There were no street lights and I could see nothing; no men in trees or anything else to suggest that there was any type of back-up there.

We all got out and walked in silence; the house now in full view. A few pools of light from the windows shone over the bushes at the front, but at the side, we remained unseen. The light over the door was off, and after one more nod to each other, we walked up the path. All humour now gone, I plugged the spyhole with the gum and pressed the doorbell. The light came on immediately, and after a few seconds, I heard movements from behind the door and Adrian shouting.

'Who is it?'

My heart was thumping, but I held my voice steady and shouted back.

'It's Benoît. I've got something for you.'

Aldo had moved to my side, his hands in his pockets, his face impassive. Then came the sound of a chain being undone and the lock turning. The door opened and there he was, smaller than I remembered, thinner and pale.

The look of shock on Adrian's face as we all pushed

by, was, for me, one of the highlights of the night. Aldo grabbed him by the throat, shoved him through the hall into the sitting room, and then threw him onto the sofa. He pulled out a small pistol, aimed it at him and stood back.

'What the bloody hell's going on? How dare you barge in here? I'll call the police.' Hearing this, we all laughed.

'Go ahead, Harcourt. Why don't you?' I snatched his phone from the side and threw it at him. He didn't move. 'Well, go on… call.

'The number's 999 in case you'd forgotten. Perhaps we should call them for you. Caro, would you like to call for him? As you can see, the poor man's hurt his leg. What a shame… oh yes, I remember now. Our aunt shot him when he broke into her house to rob and kill her.

'Pity she didn't kill you, Harcourt,' I continued. 'But then, we wouldn't all be having such a nice time now, would we? How about pouring us all a drink? Where are your manners? Oh yes, I forgot again, the leg.' I walked over to the collection of bottles on a side table, poured out five glasses of his best cognac, and handed them round, deliberately not giving him one.

'I don't suppose you can drink with an infected bullet wound.' Adrian looked up at me, surprise on his face. 'Oh yes, I hear everything – you vile bastard.'

I had stepped into another role. Not an amiable Clouseau, not Benoît, the French priest, but someone entirely different. I was a cold, compressed spring, ready to uncoil at any moment. The feeling of power was tangible and adrenaline surged through me. I listened to myself, as if from outside, and was shocked… but not shocked enough to want to stop.

Caro then stepped forward. 'You've been under surveillance for weeks, Harcourt. Did you know that? The French and British police. Just waiting for their dinner to go down before pouncing. They've got blood samples, you see, so you don't stand a chance. I believe the French justice system is particularly harsh with crimes against the frail and elderly, but then you've been in prison before, so you're probably used to it. Beating up women, I heard. Nice! What a charming man you are.'

His already-pale face was now drained of all colour, and for a moment, I wondered if he was going to pass out. Then he spoke with more venom that I had ever heard any man utter.

'Go to hell, you filthy whore. You women are all the same… whores. The best place for the lot of you is six feet under, like your aunt. There's nothing I would have liked more than to feel my hands around her scrawny neck, but she died before I had the chance.' He then moved his head backwards and spat, Caro quickly jumping out of the way. His eyes rolled upwards, and at that moment, I saw the insanity everyone had spoken of. There was a movement from behind me and Bill moved forward. He kicked at Harcourt's leg as hard as he could, and the room was filled with screams of pain. We watched and waited for a moment, and then Caro stepped forward again and spoke, her voice strong and steady.

'You don't scare me, you pathetic little worm. I know all about you. Frightened of women, in fact scared stiff! Didn't mummy love you enough? That's hardly surprising, is it? Just one look at you would fill anyone with disgust. You're ugly all the way through, so there's nothing there to love, but I imagine you know that already; you must have been given some therapy in prison. A typical misogynist, I would say; injured by mother and then transfers all his hatred onto other women. We don't need Freud to tell us that, do we, Adrian dear?'

She moved even nearer, and Bill and I moved with her. Adrian cowered back into the sofa, covering his face with his hands and whimpering softly. None of us spoke for a moment and then I heard the bishop's melodic voice.

'The journal's gone, Harcourt... burned, as are any copies. I watched them go up in flames myself this afternoon. As for the parchments, the originals are now in the Vatican vaults which is the best place for them, I'm sure you'll agree. Oh, they know all about you – they've been watching you too, you see. A very famous man you are, film recordings; everything. Oh yes, very famous indeed. Enough there for a movie, I should say, but then you wouldn't want that, being such a private man and all.' His Irish accent was as strong as I had ever heard it, and for the first time ever, I saw him for who he truly was: a strong and courageous man who, despite his weaknesses, was full of spirit and fire... traits that I felt I lacked, but in that moment, desperately wanted.

'I've also heard that there's a contract out on you.' Adrian uncovered his face and looked up at the bishop. 'One wrong move and that's it... curtains... finito... the end. But then, I imagine a strong Christian man like yourself is not afraid of death, especially having lived such a blameless life. Not afraid of going to hell are you, Harcourt? Nice and warm, I hear, although the pitchforks are a trifle sharp.'

The bishop laughed at his own joke, made to move away, then leant in and struck him with a sharp backhand across the face.

'Hear me, you piece of pond scum. One wrong move, just one, and you'll be in prison for the rest of your life, or dead and in a gutter somewhere. Do you hear me? Say you hear me – I can't hear your voice – louder, Harcourt, we all want to hear you… louder.' He aimed a kick at Harcourt's leg and screams filled the room.

'I hear you – yes, I hear you. I understand. Now go… go and leave me alone. You won't hear from me again, I promise. Please just go… please.'

Adrian was now cowered in the corner of the sofa. There was a blood stain showing through his grey trousers, and he looked so small that for a moment, I felt for the damaged child he truly was. Then I remembered Hortense, and I moved closer, to stand right in front of him.

'Just in case you change your mind, Harcourt, remember all that we've said. One squeak from you and the game's up. You've got so many people after you, I don't see how you can leave the house ever again. Or perhaps you should leave it and never come back? Au revoir, Adrian. Think yourself lucky that it's just us that have paid you a nice sociable visit, this evening. In fact, you should be very grateful indeed. Thanks for the drink!'

CHAPTER EIGHTY-FIVE

We filed out, one after the other. Aldo was last, and he stopped by the curled figure on the sofa, and held a gun to Adrian's head. He whimpered softly, begging Aldo to not kill him. Saying nothing, Aldo followed us out into the dark garden and we moved quickly down the path.

'L'instinct est tout, Benoît.' I heard my mother's voice echo loudly in my head. 'Instinct is everything.'

'GET DOWN EVERYONE, GET DOWN!' I shouted. 'GET DOWN!' I pushed Caro to the ground and Bill followed. Aldo also started to shout.

'GET DOWN ALL OF YOU. GET DOWN!'

The bishop looked at me and then moved, in what seemed like slow motion, to stand directly in front of me. He turned his back to me and then a shot rang out – just one, echoing into the dark night... then silence. The bishop fell backwards and I fell under him. Aldo started to shoot at a car as it sped by, black and almost invisible without head lights... and then was gone.

Bill got up first, pulled out his mobile and dialled 999. 'Ambulance! There's been an accident! A gun shot! Hurry – he may die – hurry!' I heard him give directions, and then he and Aldo slowly and gently moved the bishop from on top of me, and laid him on the ground.

Caro had started to sob, repeating over and over…

'Benoît, Benoît, Benoît.'

'I'm fine – I'm fine. The bishop's been shot, not me… he took the bullet for me. I saw him do it. Quick, he's bleeding badly.'

Caro pulled off her scarf, and pressed it to his side.

'Hold it down hard. I need to check if Harcourt called anyone. I'll finish him off myself if he did.'

Aldo and I ran back into the house, but Harcourt was still where we'd left him, with the phone on the other side of the sofa. I was sure that he hadn't moved, nor made any calls, and when he realised we were back in the house he started to whine.

'No, leave me alone, I won't ever bother you again, I'll move away. I don't care about the journal or the parchments. Just leave me alone. I promise I'll move away.'

'Shut up, Harcourt, and listen. The bishop's just been shot. If it was your men that did it, you're dead, but for now, gather yourself.' I slapped his face, and he sat up, startled.

'The police will be here any minute. Get up and go and put on clean trousers. We were here for a Church meeting, that's all. None of us knows anything about who might have fired a gun. Do you hear me?'

He dragged himself off the sofa. 'Yes, I hear you… a meeting – a Church meeting. It wasn't me, Benoît – I swear it wasn't. I didn't move.' He walked slowly, limping into the hall, and we went back outside.

Caro and Bill were on their knees, Bill now holding

his sweater over the bishop's wound, with Caro's coat tucked under his head.

'Hang on, Bishop,' she said, 'hang on. You'll be fine. We're all here, and we love you… just hang on.'

I could hear the sirens getting closer. Was this how it was all to end? The bishop dead? And for what? A few stupid parchments and a journal? Jesus? Religion? Power and money? I couldn't give a damn for any of them! Caro was right, as were the Templars who had made the cube and written on the cellar walls in my house. For a human being, love was everything; there was nothing else, and without it we had nothing and were nothing. Without it, we entirely ceased to exist. History was repeating itself, like it always had, and I was powerless to stop it.

CHAPTER EIGHTY-SIX

Aldo quickly came over to me as I knelt on the floor to hold the bishop's cold hand.

'I have to go. It won't help you if I am here. Deny everything, Benoît, and all will be fine. Your car will be here any minute, parked around the corner, and you can say you drove here yourselves. Franco will be in touch soon… please understand.'

He ran down to the car and it sped off, silent and dark, like the assassin's car had done. Of course, he had to go. He had no part in a local church group and wouldn't be able to explain who he was to the police.

'Everyone, we're here on Church business, discussing the needs of the parish, renovation costs, and a new priest. Do you understand? The bishop was shot by someone in a car speeding by as we were leaving. Caro, don't mention France and Hortense. Start crying if you feel too pressured, and they'll back off for a few minutes whilst you gather your thoughts. They won't make any connections instantly, but if they do state the basic facts and no more. Say you don't understand any of it. Harcourt's been briefed. Don't mess up – not now.'

The ambulance arrived, and the paramedics ran up the path. More sirens could be heard, no doubt the police. I looked up and saw Harcourt walking down the path, in blood-free trousers, and doing all he could to not limp.

He spoke, in a voice quite unlike his own. 'How awful – how awful, why would anyone want to shoot the bishop – such a good man? How can this have happened?'

The paramedics weren't listening, and had already put a drip in the bishop's arm, put an oxygen mask on his face, and cut open his beautiful white shirt, now stained red with blood, to apply thick wadding onto the wound. One of them was on his radio, giving instructions to the emergency unit at the hospital where they were headed.

I looked up at Harcourt and mouthed to him 'don't overdo it,' and he nodded. The bishop was now on a stretcher and was being wheeled towards the ambulance.

'I'm going with him. Don't try to stop me – he can't go on his own.' Caro's voice was now strong and clear.

'I'll go too,' said Bill. 'You stay here, Benoît, and we'll call you from the hospital.' The police pulled up just as the ambulance was about to drive away. They spoke briefly to Caro and Bill before they jumped in the back with the paramedic, and I watched until they were gone, with loud sirens, and lights blazing.

Adrian and I went into the house with the officers, and as was usual in traumatic circumstances, tea was made, and we began to answer the barrage of questions that were repeatedly put to us. Two hours later, and I was finally allowed to leave, with clear instructions for both of us to not leave the country without notifying them first. I needed to get home, take off my blood-stained clothes, and shower before going to the hospital.

As Aldo had said, my car was waiting for me in the lay-by, a shiny new key in the ignition, although most definitely not mine. I had no idea how they had managed it, and frankly, I didn't care. I drove home as fast as I could and went straight to the main telephone. The message light was flashing and I hit the play button. It was Caro.

'Benoît, the bishop's gone into theatre. It's not looking good. The bullet went straight through him. We're staying here. I tried to call you on your mobile but it seemed dead. I'll call again as soon as I know something… I love you.'

CHAPTER EIGHTY-SEVEN

I peeled off my jacket and reached inside the pocket to get my phone out. It looked odd, and when I studied it closer I could see that the whole thing was bent and twisted. Wedged at its centre, was a long bullet. The bullet that was meant for me… I knew that. The assassin wasn't after the bishop. He had known that, which was why he had stepped in front of me to take the bullet instead. If he didn't survive, I would never know why, nor ever be able to thank him. Pulling off the rest of my clothes, I threw them in a plastic bin liner.

I stood under a hot shower for some minutes, washing the blood off and letting the water stream over my head and face. There was a bruise coming up on my lower ribs, where the bullet had hit the phone. Strangely, at the time I had felt nothing, although perhaps that was because the bishop had fallen backwards on top of me, and I had felt that instead?

I found myself going over the events of the evening as the water cascaded down. Harcourt no longer posed any threat, I was sure of that, so who was the person that wanted me dead? Was it the same one had that tried to push me under a train and run me down in his car? If so, who was it? Why was someone so desperate to kill me?

As I dried myself, the phone rang.

'No more news, Ben; he's still in theatre, so don't rush. Have something to eat and rest for a bit. When you get here, we'll come back and clean up.'

I had only just put the phone down when it rang again. This time it was Franco.

'Are you alright? And Caro? Aldo told me what happened. I know you will want to get to the hospital, but I had to speak with you. I'll call you again tomorrow.'

'Franco, the bullet was meant for me. The bishop seemed to know and moved in front of me. It went straight through him and is now wedged in my mobile phone. Who wants me dead so badly, and why?'

'We will meet soon and talk. For now, you will be safe, I'm sure of that. Please, call me tomorrow, and let me know if you get a new mobile number.' He hung up.

More secrets… a seemingly never-ending chain of them. I quickly dressed, then went downstairs and out into the yard. The package of documents and my laptop were still there, and I brushed off the compost as I went back into the cottage. I put the laptop to one side, pulled the ribbon from the tattered envelope, and tipped out the contents. Whatever was in there was now going to reveal itself. I couldn't and wouldn't wait, nor put it off any longer. Enough blood had been shed and now it needed to stop!

CHAPTER EIGHTY-EIGHT

I stared at the dusty bundle on the table in front of me. The largest packet was wrapped in several layers of worn linen cloth and thick paper. One glance, and I knew exactly what they were; Franco's Roman parchments. Not so old – definitely not Roman, but almost identical copies. If I had to date them, I would guess at somewhere around the early to mid-eleventh century.

There was another batch, this time wrapped in what looked like thin cow hide. It was almost translucent with age, the edges sealed with red wax, and was similar to the parchments that Hortense had given us, taken from the cellar of my house in France. I went to the kitchen to get the small bag of tools that I used for these jobs. I had opened many sealed parchments, and always felt a huge thrill at being the first to see something that had been written many hundreds of years before, but at this moment, I felt none of that. The events of the night had left me feeling shaken and nauseous.

I took my camera from the cupboard, since my phone was now unusable, and took shots of the Roman copies and the unopened cowhide envelope. Using my sharp, razor knife, I slowly began to slice through the wax across the top, stopping every thirty seconds or so to take more photos.

After a few minutes, it was fully opened and I carefully pulled out several thick, velum parchments. They were written in a different hand, but as far as I could tell without further investigation, were from a similar period. The first was a simple genealogy, folded into three and written in Latin, still clear despite its age and easily decipherable. I was particularly careful as I unfolded it, desperate to do no damage. As usual, the smell of dust, age, and history came to life; filtering through my nostrils as I took a deep breath to quell the rising nausea.

It was exactly as Hortense had said, and I followed the names from the bottom up, covering some five hundred years of the first millennium AD. Then I noticed that it had been cut. The genealogy started with Sara, and anything that had been written before that, had been neatly sliced off, and not very long ago given the cleanness of the cut and parchment edge. Perhaps Peter had done it? If so, where was the cut-off piece now? I looked in the envelope again, but it was empty. Jumping from the chair, I ran to the bathroom, where I vomited repeatedly. Eventually, the nausea subsided, and after washing my face and fetching a glass of water, I went back to the table.

So, here it was, the evidence that everyone had been searching for, but with the most important bit missing. And it was a copy, albeit a very ancient one. Where was the original? Did it even still exist? Had it been hidden in the piscina pedestal at Antugnac, and was now buried in the Vatican vaults, or somewhere else? I knew that if Caro were here she would be wild with excitement or fury as she examined the document, but I felt nothing. Right

486

now, I couldn't give a damn about Sara, her ancestors, or anything connected to the whole sordid story.

* * *

I refolded the parchment and picked up another. This was of the same age and style and written in Latin. It was a simple declaration, once again exactly as Hortense said. It described the arrival of Jesus, Mary Magdalene, Martha, Sara, and Joseph of Arimathea, by boat to the then Roman Gaul, in the south of France. It told the tale of their settlement in the Rhedae area, of Mary's work as an alchemist and healer, and the departure of Jesus and Joseph to England a couple of years later, which was where they had both died, Jesus first, then Joseph.

* * *

I picked up the last parchment, which was dry and dusty, and in a much poorer condition than the others. At a guess, though, it was less old, and probably nearer to the fourteenth century in date.

Some of the words were very faded, and I composed myself, as I always did for the documents that were more difficult to read. As I worked my way through, I recognised the story as that depicted on my cellar walls in France. It described the journey of two Knights Templar from Rhedae, bringing with them the remains of a body to Corinium Dobunnorum, the old Latin name for Cirencester.

A few words here and there were almost completely

missing, but what was left was enough to understand that the contents of the wooden coffin that they described were the remains of Mary Magdalene, and their destination was the village in which I was now living. Their desire was to 'reunite her with her husband, Jesus, who has been waiting there for more than a millennium.

Hortense had known, of course, as no doubt had my parents. Both Caro and I had also made the links, although we hadn't yet voiced this to each other. My mind recalled the mysterious medieval tomb of the couple in the local graveyard with the turned-down blanket or shroud, perhaps signifying both childbirth and an unveiling of the truth. The Roman sarcophagus found nearby and also placed in the graveyard – had its movers in much more recent times known that this was where it belonged?

How many people knew the truth but stayed silent? Dozens? Hundreds? Thousands? Quite likely more than that. Was I also going to remain silent? Could it really be that the mystery that had surrounded a handful of people for so long was now solved?

Or was this just another cleverly orchestrated but fraudulent smokescreen, to truths that would always refuse to be fully revealed?

I suddenly remembered what Hortense had said in one of her letters.

One can always hope that they were stupid enough to be unable to decipher the narrative of truth. A narrative of lies and greed is always preferable, n'est-ce pas?

CHAPTER EIGHTY-NINE

The phone rang again.

'The bishop is out of theatre and on life support, but it's touch and go. Bill and I are going to sit with him for another hour or two and then come back.'

'But surely, if he made it through the surgery he stands a chance? I'll be leaving shortly. My mobile doesn't work because the bullet that hit the bishop is wedged inside it. Let's not talk about it now, though, I can't face it.' There was a pause for a moment.

'You've opened it up... the package from Peter's desk? I knew you would. They're both in the churchyard, aren't they? It's on your cellar walls. But Benoît, I feel nothing. No excitement, no awe... nothing. I just want the bishop to be OK.'

'I know, that's how it is with me too. Anyway, even if they were once there, after all this time, there won't be anything left but dust. I can't help thinking that somewhere along the line we've missed the point entirely.'

'You may well be right. We've been discussing similar things.'

'I've just got to tidy up and pack a few clothes, and I'll be there. Then I'm not going to leave him; not until he either recovers or dies. Perhaps when you're back and have had a rest, you could get me another mobile phone? I'll see you soon.' I went back to the table, quickly taking more photos and then carefully putting the parchments back into their cowhide envelope. There were just two envelopes remaining, one much larger and older than the other.

Inside the smaller one, were two letters, each in its own envelope. I thought, and hoped, that one of them might be from Bigou, and I felt the usual shiver of awe and excitement. I was glad. It meant that the shock was receding and I could function more appropriately to my current circumstances. I would certainly need this to help the bishop, and indeed myself, over the coming days and weeks, whatever they brought.

* * *

My hands shook as I carefully opened the first envelope. As I had hoped, it was a letter written by Abbé Antoine Bigou, and I was sure that it was an original. Written in French, once again, it was exactly as Hortense had said. As I read it through, I felt the stirring inside me of connection to another human being in a time of deep distress and heightened emotion. Clearly, he carried the burden of what he had discovered or been told very heavily. At the bottom of the letter were four lines. They were heartbreaking to read, and my eyes filled with tears: tears for Bigou, for the bishop, and for myself.

God has gone from me and my life is to be lived without meaning or purpose. I will now exit the place that is at the centre of the universe. I have played my part and now it is over. It is done, and cannot be undone. However, I will return. We all return.

Antoine Bigou. 22 March 1793

It echoed some of the things that Hortense had said, and Caro too, when she declared that all roads led to Rennes-le-Château, and I felt deeply moved.

* * *

Pushing the second smaller envelope to one side, I reached for the much larger, older one, made of thick faded velum and covered with dirt and stains. Without further study, it looked to be contemporary in age to Franco's Roman parchments. It had already been opened and holding my breath, I carefully pulled it out. Narrow lines of dry, grey, dust lay in the creases, and I brushed this away and sat back to take a good view. Once again, the musty smell that I used to love wafted up, and I swallowed several times to quell the rising nausea.

There was little doubt that it was a map, faded and torn in places, and as stained and dirty as the envelope. It was, however, far less old, and not contemporary to its ancient envelope at all. At a wild guess, I would place it somewhere in the eleventh or twelfth century.

Despite its age, the lines and shapes on the map were quite clear, in a dark, blood red, and defined in places with black, possibly having been redrawn in much more

491

recent times. There were small areas of script all over it, although not in any language that I recognised.

With no time to study to further, I carefully folded it up and slid it back in its envelope. It wouldn't go in fully, and pulling it out again I turned the envelope upside down, and out fluttered a small piece of paper, about ten centimetres wide and five deep.

Yellowed, but not old, it had a date – 08/07/43 – and a stamped insignia of an eagle over a swastika, a common Nazi symbol. In its top right corner were three numbers written in faded red ink: **666**. Of course I recognised it. The number of the beast from the Book of Revelations in the New Testament. In Greek manuscripts it was titled 'The Apocalypse of John.' It might certainly be applied to the Nazis, but I knew that it was far more complex than being solely a symbol of the devil, and had many mysterious meanings. I turned it over. On the back, written in the same red ink, were three initials.

H D M.

The handwriting was unmistakable… Hortense de Morny. Was this the Ark map she had written about in her letter? And was this her way of warning us, or anyone who might find it, of the potential danger linked to the map? Why hadn't she just destroyed it if she felt so strongly as to mark it in this way? I remembered the warning to us in her final letter. I had no belief at all in the map being either jinxed or unlucky, nor in fact, of the Ark itself being either of these things. I agreed with Hortense that the danger it brought would be one of greed and power. Nonetheless, her warning of misery and destruction filled me with a foreboding that raised the hairs on the back of my neck.

I had no doubt that she had hidden it; perhaps here in the church, or maybe someone, possibly Peter, had found it elsewhere and brought it here? I doubted that I would ever know for sure.

I had no desire to look at it again, and had no intention of doing so in the future. If Caro knew I had it, then at the very least she would want to see it. Even if she had no intention of going searching, which I doubted, I had put her in enough danger already, and did not intend to do that for a second time. I was not going to show it to her. My mind was made up.

* * *

I opened the last small envelope to reveal another letter. It was one that I had not expected to find, nor hoped would exist. Caro would treasure it like no other, but there was no time now to examine it further, as I had to go. I still had the present and hopefully a future, and like all those who had gone before me, I too would play my hand; I could do no more.

I took more photos and then ran upstairs to fetch a change of clothes. I carefully packed up the parchments and letters, got my laptop and camera, and put the lot into my bag. As soon as I could, I would take it to the bank vault, its fate to be decided when I had given it the thought it deserved. I had money and a credit card for drinks and the payphone at the hospital; all I wanted now was to be with the bishop.

* * *

My strength and resolve had returned with the reading of the last letter. If the writer could continue with courage and face the world when everything had crumbled around him, then so could I.

At the end of the day, it was present connections that mattered. The lure of the past was immensely strong but served little purpose, apart from being an aid to avoidance of what was going on in the moment, rather like a drug might do. If there were any truths at all to be found amongst the letters and parchments, then this was the one that spoke out to me, loud and clear, and I fully intended to listen.

CHAPTER NINETY

An hour later, I walked through the corridors of the large county hospital to find Caro and Bill waiting for me outside the bishop's room. They looked exhausted – still in clothes that were splattered with dried blood.

'He's still alive,' Caro said. 'But be warned; there are wires, tubes, and machines everywhere, and he looks awful. We saw the consultant just before you got here, and he said we mustn't raise our hopes. He lost a huge amount of blood, and the bullet has damaged his liver quite badly.'

Bill continued. 'We'll clean up, Ben, have a quick rest, and then I'll go out and get you a new phone. Do eat and drink something, won't you? You have to look after yourself if you want to be here for the bishop.'

I nodded, and hugged them both. I watched as they walked down the corridor, hand in hand, like they had known each other for ever. Once again, I felt the fracture inside me twist, and a solid black mass of grief attempted to escape from my mouth in the form of a sob, directly from my heart.

'Benoît... je suis avec toi.' My mother's voice. 'I am with you.' I looked around, but as I already knew, I was alone in the brightly lit corridor.

'About time too,' I replied.

* * *

I turned and opened the door of the bishop's room. The lights were subdued and a young, female doctor was standing in front of the various monitors. She beckoned me in.

'Father Benoît?' I nodded. 'No change I'm afraid. It's early days. His family have been called but it'll be a while before they get here. Stay for as long as you like, and do talk to him if you want to. Sometimes it helps. Any problems, I'll be at the desk in the corridor. The police have been around, but I've sent them packing.'

She left, closing the door quietly behind her. I looked around me. The bishop lay on the bed, looking exactly as Caro had described. His eyes were closed and he was almost as white as the sheets that covered him. Wires were attached from every direction, tiny lights and numbers pulsed on the various screens, and drips silently slipped their contents into his still body.

I sat down on the chair by the side of the bed, my bag still slung across my front, where it would remain unless forcibly removed from me.

EPILOGUE

For we are but of yesterday, and know nothing,
because our days upon earth are a shadow:
(Job 8:9)

'Bishop? It's me, Benoît... I'm here. There's no need to worry about anything. We all love you, and I'm not going anywhere until you're well. You are not alone.' I reached out to gently hold his hand in mine.

And so, my vigil had begun. I recalled other vigils that I had lived through, particularly when I was very young, and my parents had once again disappeared into the dark night, gone away to some place unknown to me, with their return uncertain.

Unable to sleep or rest for a moment, I was like a sentinel on duty, knowing this: that whilst I watched and waited all would be well.

I would wait this night out too, and all the others that might follow, for if I could maintain my position of guard, then both the bishop and I would be safe.

22 September 1891

Life seldom turns out to be that which we expected. History has unfolded itself before me, taunting, teasing, and destroying all that I believed to be true and hoped to build my life upon. I have been robbed of it all, and now I am forced to build another life, like other men have done, except for me my life is now, and always will be, one of lies, deception, and pretence. How does a man live his life without faith? Can he build another faith from the shards of broken glass that remain? Will I survive for long enough to know? I fear that I shall not; that I shall be removed, and will disappear into the oblivion of death before I am ready to greet it with open arms.

I shall entrust this letter to the future, and like those who have gone before me, I will play my dealt hand with all the mastery that I possess. I will pass on what I know to be true, in any way that I can. The instinct for survival is strong.

Judge me not, for you in turn will be judged... it is the way of things.

Abbé Bérenger Saunière

A NOTE FROM B.B. BALTHIS

This book is the result of several years of intense and exhaustive research. The facts discovered during this time have been woven into a narrative that includes fictional characters. Any resemblance to real persons is entirely coincidental. Fiction has also been used to fill the gaps that history refused to explain.

It has been my aim to add to the information already in the current arena, to inspire others to keep searching, and to encourage those who hold more facts to step forward. Many more books need to be written. Despite my best intentions, I realise that I have barely scratched the surface of what there is to reveal. There was simply not enough time nor space within these pages.

The search for truth and its exposure is of paramount importance. As time passes, it is slowly and deliberately being either entirely removed, or more subtly eroded away. Without doubt, it is disappearing. Opposing forces present themselves continually and I suspect that this will always be so.

Take heart, be brave, and never be intimidated by anyone – ever.

To follow…

The Lithuanian

REFERENCE

Carver, R., *A new path to the waterfall,* Atlantic Monthly Press, 1989.

Chekhov, A., *Complete Works of Anton Chekhov,* Delphi Classics, 2016.

Gaskell, E., *Mary Barton,* Penguin Classics, 2003.

Graves, R., *The Complete Poems,* Penguin Classics, 2003.

Olsen, T., *Tell me a riddle,* Bison Books, 2013.

Shakespeare, W., *Macbeth,* Wordsworth Classics, 1992